EVERYMAN,

I WILL GO WITH THEE,

AND BE THY GUIDE,

IN THY MOST NEED

TO GO BY THY SIDE

EVERYMAN'S POCKET CLASSICS

PARTY STORIES

EDITED BY ELLA CARR

EVERYMAN'S POCKET CLASSICS
Alfred A. Knopf New York London

THIS IS A BORZOI BOOK
PUBLISHED BY ALFRED A. KNOPF

This selection by Ella Carr first published in Everyman's Library, 2025

A list of acknowledgments to copyright owners appears at the back of this volume.

Published in the United States by Alfred A. Knopf, a division of Penguin Random House LLC, 1745 Broadway, New York, NY 10019. Published in the United Kingdom by Everyman's Library, 50 Albemarle Street, London W1S 4BD and distributed by Penguin Random House UK, One Embassy Gardens, 8 Viaduct Gardens, London SW11 7BW.

everymanslibrary.com   penguinrandomhouse.com
www.penguin.co.uk/about/publishing-houses/everyman

ISBN 979-8-217-00760-8 (US)
978-1-84159-638-9 (UK)

A CIP catalogue reference for this book is available from the British Library

Typography by Peter B. Willberg

Typeset in the UK by Input Data Services Ltd, Bridgwater, Somerset

Printed and bound in Germany by GGP Media GmbH, Pössneck

The authorized representative in the EU for product safety and compliance is Penguin Random House Ireland, Morrison Chambers, 32 Nassau Street, Dublin D02 YH68, Ireland, https://eu-contact.penguin.ie

Contents

LAST HURRAHS

PARTYING TO EXCESS

DISHONOURED GUESTS

OLD FRIENDS AND REMEMBRANCES

PREFACE

As Jhumpa Lahiri, author of the final story in this anthology, put it in a *New Yorker* interview, parties act as 'parentheses' in our lives, akin to vacations and other journeys that punctuate the humdrum of ordinary existence. They contain their own internal plots, defined by a beginning, a middle and an end, which make them ideal vehicles for short stories but also for set pieces in novels – often the defining scenes or turning points of the story. But beyond their structural convenience, why do parties make such a rich backdrop for navigating human experience? Perhaps because, beneath their veneer of frivolity, parties are rarely just spaces for pleasure-making. Instead, guests and hosts alike are governed by far more serious objectives – whom to impress, whom to seduce, whom to disdain – that cut to the heart of what it means to be an individual navigating a society. If life is a stage, then parties are the ultimate performance.

Parties are also where we take our first steps into adulthood, a scene for 'firsts': first crushes, first kisses, first heartaches and humiliations. The word 'debut' may connote a very gendered tradition, a girl's 'coming out' into society, but it speaks to a far more universal experience that every reader can relate to. For a young person, parties become repositories for their hopes and fears, where the stakes can seem monumentally high. In some of the stories of this anthology, these dreams are realized, as in the scene of Natasha's first ball in Tolstoy's *War and Peace*, where she dazzles the guests with her guileless charm and dances with the man who will become her first love. Often, however, debuts in literature reflect pivotal moments of disillusionment, where the scales fall from the protagonist's eyes, as in 'Come into the Drawing Room, Doris' by Edna O'Brien, whose 'mountainy' girl brims with excitement at the prospect of her first party, only to realize she's been invited as a waitress, and to be ogled and harassed by the male attendees. Parties are inductions into life, its pleasures but also, more poignantly, its cruelties.

For many of the revellers in these stories, parties are not simply portals to experience but a means of escape – a brief suspension from the ceaseless march of time and the inevitability of death. However, like a Dutch vanitas painting, amidst the voluptuous glamour of these scenes there is often to be found an inconvenient memento mori, a reminder that this escape is only temporary, whether this is the literal appearance of Death himself in Poe's famous story 'The Masque of the Red Death', or the speech of a dying poet in Tom Wolfe's *The Bonfire of the Vanities*, referencing Poe's very same story, which causes a moment of social discord among the guests of the Bavardages' dinner party and foreshadows 'the ruin of the dissolute' in 1980s New York.

Modernist writers in particular were drawn to the unusual temporality of parties, using them as complex stages for their explorations into consciousness. In *The Great Gatsby* and *The Sun Also Rises*, Fitzgerald and Hemingway depict the careless behaviour of the 'lost generation' of the inter-war period, partying to forget the trauma of war and unable to meaningfully move forward.

But it is perhaps James Joyce and Virginia Woolf, in 'The Dead' and *Mrs Dalloway*, who best capture the strange alchemy of parties, and the endless contradictions of human behaviour by which they are governed: the small moments of joy and unity, of friends being brought together by common values and shared memories, feelings of excitement and anticipation and freedom and elation cut through with shards of awkwardness and envy and embarrassment, moments of isolation and alienation, of authenticity and performance and self-consciousness and foolhardiness, and the unceasing quest for human connection that ultimately reflects the patina of our existence, and which makes literary parties such a joy to delve into.

Ella Carr

DEBUTS AND YOUNG HEARTS

LEO TOLSTOY

NATASHA'S FIRST BALL

From *War and Peace*

(1868)

Translated by Louise and Aylmer Maude

CHAPTER 15

NATASHA HAD NOT had a moment free since early morning and had not once had time to think of what lay before her.

In the damp chill air and crowded closeness of the swaying carriage, she for the first time vividly imagined what was in store for her there at the ball, in those brightly lighted rooms – with music, flowers, dances, the Emperor, and all the brilliant young people of Petersburg. The prospect was so splendid that she hardly believed it would come true, so out of keeping was it with the chill darkness and closeness of the carriage. She understood all that awaited her only when, after stepping over the red baize at the entrance, she entered the hall, took off her fur cloak and, beside Sonya and in front of her mother, mounted the brightly illuminated stairs between the flowers. Only then did she remember how she must behave at a ball, and tried to assume the majestic air she considered indispensable for a girl on such an occasion. But, fortunately for her, she felt her eyes growing misty, she saw nothing clearly, her pulse beat a hundred to the minute and the blood throbbed at her heart. She could not assume that pose, which would have made her ridiculous, and she moved on almost fainting from excitement and trying with all her might to conceal it. And this was the very attitude that became her best. Before and behind them other visitors were entering, also talking in low tones and wearing ball-dresses. The mirrors on the landing reflected ladies in white, pale-blue, and pink dresses, with diamonds and pearls on their bare necks and arms.

Natasha looked in the mirrors and could not distinguish her reflection from the others. All was blent into one brilliant procession. On entering the ball-room the regular hum of voices, footsteps, and greetings deafened Natasha, and the light and glitter dazzled her still more. The host and hostess, who had already been standing at the door for half an hour repeating the same words to the various arrivals, '*Charmé de vous voir*,' greeted the Rostovs and Peronskaya in the same manner.

The two girls in their white dresses, each with a rose in her black hair, both curtsied in the same way, but the hostess's eye involuntarily rested longer on the slim Natasha. She looked at her and gave her alone a special smile, in addition to her usual smile as hostess. Looking at her she may have recalled the golden, irrevocable days of her own girlhood and her own first ball. The host also followed Natasha with his eyes and asked the count which was his daughter.

'Charming!' said he, kissing the tips of his fingers.

In the ball-room guests stood crowding at the entrance doors awaiting the Emperor. The countess took up a position in one of the front rows of that crowd. Natasha heard and felt that several people were asking about her and looking at her. She realized that those noticing her liked her, and this observation helped to calm her.

'There are some like ourselves and some worse,' she thought.

Peronskaya was pointing out to the countess the most important people at the ball.

'That is the Dutch ambassador, do you see? That grey-haired man,' she said, indicating an old man with a profusion of silver-grey curly hair, who was surrounded by ladies laughing at something he said.

'Ah, here she is, the Queen of Petersburg, Countess Bezukhova,' said Peronskaya, indicating Hélène who had just entered. 'How lovely! She is quite equal to Marya Antonovna. See how the men, young and old, pay court to her. Beautiful and clever . . . they say Prince — is quite mad about her. But see, those two, though not good-looking, are even more run after.'

She pointed to a lady who was crossing the room followed by a very plain daughter.

'She is a splendid match, a millionairess,' said Peronskaya. 'And look, here come her suitors.'

'That is Bezukhova's brother, Anatole Kuragin,' she said, indicating a handsome officer of the Horse Guards who passed by them with head erect, looking at something over the heads of the ladies. 'He's handsome, isn't he? I hear they will marry him to that rich girl. But your cousin, Drubetskoy, is also very attentive to her. They say she has millions. Oh yes, that's the French ambassador himself!' she replied to the countess's inquiry about Caulaincourt. 'Looks as if he were a king! All the same, the French are charming, very charming. No one more charming in society. Ah, here she is! Yes, she is still the most beautiful of them all, our Marya Antonovna! And how simply she is dressed! Lovely! And that stout one in spectacles is the universal Freemason,' she went on, indicating Pierre. 'Put him beside his wife and he looks a regular buffoon!'

Pierre, swaying his stout body, advanced making way through the crowd and nodding to right and left as casually and good-naturedly as if he were passing through a crowd at a fair. He pushed through, evidently looking for someone.

Natasha looked joyfully at the familiar face of Pierre, 'the buffoon', as Peronskaya had called him, and knew he was looking for them, and for her in particular. He had promised to be at the ball and introduce partners to her.

But before he reached them Pierre stopped beside a very handsome, dark man of middle height, and in a white uniform, who stood by a window talking to a tall man wearing stars and a ribbon. Natasha at once recognized the shorter and younger man in the white uniform: it was Bolkonsky, who seemed to her to have grown much younger, happier, and better-looking.

'There's someone else we know – Bolkonsky, do you see, mamma?' said Natasha, pointing out Prince Andrew. 'You remember, he stayed a night with us at Otradnoe.'

'Oh, you know him?' said Peronskaya. 'I can't bear him. *Il fait à présent la pluie et le beau temps*. He's too proud for anything. Takes after his father. And he's hand in glove with Speransky, writing some projects or other. Just look how he treats the ladies! There's one talking to him, and he has turned away,' she said, pointing at him. 'I'd give it him if he treated me as he does those ladies.'

CHAPTER 16

SUDDENLY EVERYBODY STIRRED, began talking, and pressed forward and then back, and between the two rows, which separated, the Emperor entered to the sounds of music that had immediately struck up. Behind him walked his host and hostess. He walked in rapidly, bowing to right and left as if anxious to get the first moments of the reception over. The band played the polonaise in vogue at that time on account of the words that had been set to it, beginning: 'Alexander,

Elisaveta, all our hearts you ravish quite . . .' The Emperor passed on to the drawing-room, the crowd made a rush for the doors, and several persons with excited faces hurried there and back again. Then the crowd hastily retired from the drawing-room door, at which the Emperor reappeared talking to the hostess. A young man, looking distraught, pounced down on the ladies, asking them to move aside. Some ladies, with faces betraying complete forgetfulness of all the rules of decorum, pushed forward to the detriment of their toilettes. The men began to choose partners and take their places for the polonaise.

Everyone moved back, and the Emperor came smiling out of the drawing-room leading his hostess by the hand but not keeping time to the music. The host followed with Marya Antonovna Naryshkina; then came ambassadors, ministers, and various generals, whom Peronskaya diligently named. More than half the ladies already had partners and were taking up, or preparing to take up, their positions for the polonaise. Natasha felt that she would be left with her mother and Sonya among a minority of women who crowded near the wall, not having been invited to dance. She stood with her slender arms hanging down, her scarcely defined bosom rising and falling regularly, and with bated breath and glittering, frightened eyes gazed straight before her, evidently prepared for the height of joy or misery. She was not concerned about the Emperor, or any of those great people whom Peronskaya was pointing out – she had but one thought: 'Is it possible no one will ask me, that I shall not be among the first to dance? Is it possible that not one of all these men will notice me? They do not even seem to see me, or if they do, they look as if they were saying, "Ah, she's not the one I'm after, so it's not worth looking at her!" No, it's impossible,' she thought. 'They must know how I long to dance, how splendidly I dance, and how they would enjoy dancing with me.'

The strains of the polonaise, which had continued for a considerable time, had begun to sound like a sad reminiscence in Natasha's ears. She wanted to cry. Peronskaya had left them. The count was at the other end of the room. She and the countess and Sonya were standing by themselves as in the depths of a forest, amid that crowd of strangers, with no one interested in them and not wanted by anyone. Prince Andrew with a lady passed by, evidently not recognizing them. The handsome Anatole was smilingly talking to a partner on his arm, and looked at Natasha as one looks at a wall. Boris passed them twice and each time turned away. Berg and his wife, who were not dancing, came up to them.

This family gathering seemed humiliating to Natasha – as if there were nowhere else for the family to talk but here at the ball. She did not listen to or look at Vera, who was telling her something about her own green dress.

At last the Emperor stopped beside his last partner (he had danced with three) and the music ceased. A worried aide-de-camp ran up to the Rostovs requesting them to stand farther back, though as it was they were already close to the wall, and from the gallery resounded the distinct, precise, enticingly rhythmical strains of a valse. The Emperor looked smilingly down the room. A minute passed but no one had yet begun dancing. An aide-de-camp, the Master of Ceremonies, went up to Countess Bezukhova and asked her to dance. She smilingly raised her hand and laid it on his shoulder without looking at him. The aide-de-camp, an adept in his art, grasping his partner firmly round her waist, with confident deliberation started smoothly, gliding first round the edge of the circle, then at the corner of the room he caught Hélène's left hand and turned her, the only sound audible, apart from the ever-quickening music, being the rhythmic click of the spurs on his rapid, agile feet, while at every third beat his partner's velvet dress spread out and seemed to flash as she whirled round. Natasha gazed at them and was ready to cry because it was not she who was dancing that first turn of the valse.

Prince Andrew, in the white uniform of a cavalry colonel, wearing stockings and dancing-shoes, stood looking animated and bright in the front row of the circle not far from the Rostovs. Baron Firhoff was talking to him about the first sitting of the Council of State to be held next day. Prince Andrew, as one closely connected with Speransky and participating in the work of the legislative commission, could give reliable information about that sitting, concerning which various rumours were current. But not listening to what Firhoff was saying, he was gazing now at the sovereign, and now at the men intending to dance who had not yet gathered courage to enter the circle.

Prince Andrew was watching these men abashed by the Emperor's presence, and the women who were breathlessly longing to be asked to dance.

Pierre came up to him and caught him by the arm.

'You always dance. I have a protégée, the young Rostova, here. Ask her,' he said.

'Where is she?' asked Bolkonsky. 'Excuse me!' he added, turning to the baron, 'we will finish this conversation elsewhere – at a ball one must dance.' He stepped forward in the direction Pierre indicated. The despairing, dejected expression of Natasha's face caught his eye. He recognized her, guessed her feelings, saw that it was her début, remembered her conversation at the window, and with an expression of pleasure on his face approached Countess Rostova.

'Allow me to introduce you to my daughter,' said the countess, with heightened colour.

'I have the pleasure of being already acquainted, if the Countess remembers me,' said Prince Andrew with a low and courteous bow quite belying Peronskaya's remarks about his rudeness, and approaching Natasha he held out his arm to grasp her waist before he had completed his invitation. He asked her to valse. That tremulous expression on Natasha's face, prepared either for despair or rapture, suddenly brightened into a happy, grateful, childlike smile.

'I have long been waiting for you,' that frightened happy little girl seemed to say by the smile that replaced the threatened tears, as she raised her hand to Prince Andrew's shoulder. They were the second couple to enter the circle. Prince Andrew was one of the best dancers of his day and Natasha danced exquisitely. Her little feet in their white satin dancing-shoes did their work swiftly, lightly, and independently of herself, while her face beamed with ecstatic happiness. Her slender bare arms and neck were not beautiful – compared to Hélène's her shoulders looked thin and her bosom undeveloped. But Hélène seemed, as it were, hardened by a varnish left by the thousands of looks that had scanned her person, while Natasha was like a girl exposed for the first time, who would have felt very much ashamed had she not been assured that this was absolutely necessary.

Prince Andrew liked dancing, and wishing to escape as quickly as possible from the political and clever talk which everyone addressed to him, wishing to break up the circle of restraint he disliked, caused by the Emperor's presence, he danced, and had chosen Natasha because Pierre pointed her out to him and because she was the first pretty girl who caught his eye; but scarcely had he embraced that slender supple figure, and felt her stirring so close to him and smiling so near him, than the wine of her charm rose to his head, and he felt himself revived and rejuvenated when after leaving her he stood breathing deeply and watching the other dancers.

KATE CHOPIN

HER FIRST PARTY

(1905)

THE PARTY DRESS, a white organdy with touches of delicate pink, was finished, and hung beneath the chandelier in Millie's room.

She had never been to an entertainment of any importance, and was not quite old enough to go to one now. But this was not wholly a grown-up affair – one of the arguments which she and her brother Bob had brought to bear upon their mother. Bob's class was giving it over at College Hall, only a few blocks away. There were to be charades, tableaus and recitations, in all of which Millie was to take a leading rôle.

All her acquaintances were going; everybody that was anybody, between sixteen and twenty, was going. But surely none looked forward to it with such rapture, such blissful anticipation, such expectancy as did Millie. All night she anticipated the event in dreams, and all day she posed or declaimed or danced through the halls and apartments as if possessed by the very spirit of Terpsichore.

If anything were to happen! Millie sickened at the thought. But what could happen, except rain, perhaps, and the weather prophet was taking care of that. To be sure, her Aunt Mildred, a couple of hundred miles away, was quite sick, and her mother was wearing a saddened face betimes.

Again, the party dress might catch fire and burn up, and there would be no time to make another. She herself might take a tumble in one of those fantastic flights through the house, and sprain an ankle. The thought sobered her for twenty seconds or less.

At breakfast the morning of the party Millie found it difficult to keep up a pretense of interest in anything so prosaic as toast and mutton-chops.

She plied Bob with questions, she worried him with her misgivings. She quitted her seat to embrace her mother violently, then she was off to the kitchen, and dragging Kitty, the maid, up two flights to view the creation in pink and white beneath the chandelier.

A while later the restless Millie stood out upon the front steps, gazing up into the misty October sky in search of weather indications upon which she might base some prognostications of her own. It was then that the postman came along, and with a polite greeting handed her the morning mail – quite a batch of it.

She slowly turned into the house, glancing over the circulars and letters, and in a manner assorting them. There was a letter to her mother from her Aunt Jane, – she knew the stiff, formal handwriting, – mailed from the distant town in which her Aunt Mildred lay sick.

A dread that for the moment made her feel faint took possession of Millie. She crept into the quiet parlor and sat there undisturbed, staring at the outside of her Aunt Jane's letter. Her fingers seemed to feel for the annoyance which that sealed envelope might cover; her eyes seemed to penetrate and unveil the threat against her longed-for and looked-for pleasure.

What difference would a day make? She turned and turned the letter about. What difference *could* a day make? None whatever, as Millie counted days. Yet she could feel her heart thump with guilty excitement as she slipped the letter into her pocket.

She then went on up-stairs and laid the mail in the usual place upon the sitting-room table, glad that her mother was not there at the moment to unmask her shamefaced consciousness.

It was a hateful occurrence, that threw a damper upon her joy. During the school hours the letter concealed in her pocket seemed like a live thing, a reptile, a slimy thing, when her hand accidentally encountered it. She almost made up her mind to deliver it to her mother when she returned at three o'clock.

Oh, but the merry time ahead! What chatter! Like the twittering sparrows among the russet leaves as the girls walked home beneath the trees. What breathless chatter of gowns, of hair ornaments, of slippers and fluttering ribbons! But Millie knew there was nothing that would compare with the pink-and-white cloud floating beneath the chandelier in her room. All her eagerness returned, and nothing marred it, not even the sight of her mother's face, perplexed with an uneasy sadness.

Bob was distinctly proud of his pretty sister when she stood revealed for household inspection that night, but he would have considered it an unpardonable weakness to say so.

'You'll do, Millie. Rub some of the paint off your cheeks.' Oh, what a joke! Kitty, the maid, howled at the humor of it.

'You'll be afther tellin' her to take the spharkle out of her shinin' eyes next, Misther Bob. Go way wid ye!'

Millie, in an exalted state, turned like a show-window automaton while the gentle mother enveloped her in a fleecy white cape, brought to light for the occasion from the relic trunk.

There have been thousands of parties just exactly like that one, but no one could have made Millie believe so.

What applause at her recitation! What side-splitting laughter over the charades! What a hush of appreciation over the beautiful tableaus! And then the attentions of the college boys, the compliments, the mountains of ice-creams, the islands of sponge-cake, the running river of lemonade!

Millie's excitement held her all the way home. Clinging to Bob's arm, her little, nervous steps kept a dancing pace to his unthinking stride. It followed her to her very pillow.

But there, before she closed her eyes, a lull came upon her senses; the joy all melted out of her soul, and the vision of a letter held sway in her dreams all through the night.

There was nothing haphazard in the fact that Millie stationed herself upon the front steps the following morning. She was pale. Something had, as Bob would have said, rubbed the paint off her cheeks, and that same something had taken the sparkle out of her eyes, and left in its stead a dull anxiety.

She was waiting for the postman. When he handed her the scanty mail she augmented it with the letter in her pocket and carried it directly to her mother, who sat at the sitting-room table, bending over some sewing.

Millie did not withdraw, but stood there, watching at a little distance. Somehow she was not startled when the letter trembled in her mother's hand, when the tears gathered and fell upon the fluttering sheets.

'What is it, mother?' asked Millie, in a dry voice that did not sound to her like her own. She darted forward, and with an encircling arm drew her mother's head against her throbbing heart. 'What is it, mother, dear? What makes you cry?'

'Your Aunt Mildred cannot recover. The doctors have given her up. I am going – I *must* go to her!' rising with agitation and clasping Millie closely.

'You never had a sister, my sweet child – you cannot

know' – between broken sobs – 'a favorite sister! We were everything to each other until we married. Jane was not the same; she was older and stern. I must go. Send Kitty,' relinquishing the trembling girl. 'I must get ready at once. God grant I find her alive.'

From the time the train left the station, bearing her mother away, Millie became the prey of a feverish restlessness. It was Saturday, and there was no school. She walked alone far out into the suburbs, walked rapidly, as if her own motion might hasten the flying wheels of the engine. All her thoughts were concentrated in the reiteration:

'She will be there in so and so many hours, and it will be all right.'

She had seen her Aunt Mildred but at rare intervals, and her sorrow was not active; it was but the reflection of her mother's.

All her thoughts were for her mother. In the house, going from one room to another, she watched the clocks, almost counting the slow seconds. At luncheon Bob urged her to eat, but she could not. She only poured the tea with cold hands, and her eyes, brooding, cast down upon the white cloth.

In the afternoon a telegram came, directed to her mother. Bob opened it, and they read it together:

Mildred died at one o'clock to-day. – Jane.

Bob could not understand the wild paroxysm of grief that seized upon his sister, that made of her for hours a pitiable object of his solicitude. He has not understood it to this day. For it was not to Bob her confession was made, in abject contrition, a veritable suffering penitent, imploring the forgiveness which was not withheld.

* * *

Millie, quite grown up by this time, has been to many a party since then; but none was ever again like that one.

'Do you remember her the night of the party at College Hall, when she recited?' said an amiable chaperon, lifting her lorgnette, one evening not long ago. 'How she has changed! What dignity! What quiet poise! But it seems to me she has lost something.'

'Do you think so?' from a second amiable chaperon, with clearer eyes that needed no lorgnette. 'It seems to me she has gained something.'

KATHERINE MANSFIELD

THE GARDEN PARTY

(1921)

AND AFTER ALL the weather was ideal. They could not have had a more perfect day for a garden party if they had ordered it. Windless, warm, the sky without a cloud. Only the blue was veiled with a haze of light gold, as it is sometimes in early summer. The gardener had been up since dawn, mowing the lawns and sweeping them, until the grass and the dark flat rosettes where the daisy plants had been seemed to shine. As for the roses, you could not help feeling they understood that roses are the only flowers that impress people at garden parties; the only flowers that everybody is certain of knowing. Hundreds, yes, literally hundreds, had come out in a single night; the green bushes bowed down as though they had been visited by archangels.

Breakfast was not yet over before the men came to put up the marquee.

'Where do you want the marquee put, mother?'

'My dear child, it's no use asking me. I'm determined to leave everything to you children this year. Forget I am your mother. Treat me as an honoured guest.'

But Meg could not possibly go and supervise the men. She had washed her hair before breakfast, and she sat drinking her coffee in a green turban, with a dark wet curl stamped on each cheek. Jose, the butterfly, always came down in a silk pettitcoat and a kimono jacket.

'You'll have to go, Laura; you're the artistic one.'

Away Laura flew, still holding her piece of bread-and-butter. It's so delicious to have an excuse for eating out of doors, and besides, she loved having to arrange things; she always felt she could do it so much better than anybody else.

Four men in their shirt-sleeves stood grouped together on the garden path. They carried staves covered with rolls of canvas, and they had big tool-bags slung on their backs. They looked impressive. Laura wished now that she was not holding that piece of bread-and-butter, but there was nowhere to put it, and she couldn't possibly throw it away. She blushed and tried to look severe and even a little bit short-sighted as she came up to them.

'Good morning,' she said, copying her mother's voice. But that sounded so fearfully affected that she was ashamed, and stammered like a little girl, 'Oh – er – have you come – is it about the marquee?'

'That's right, miss,' said the tallest of the men, a lanky, freckled fellow, and he shifted his tool-bag, knocked back his straw hat and smiled down at her. 'That's about it.'

His smile was so easy, so friendly, that Laura recovered. What nice eyes he had, small, but such a dark blue! And now she looked at the others, they were smiling too. 'Cheer up, we won't bite,' their smile seemed to say. How very nice workmen were! And what a beautiful morning! She mustn't mention the morning; she must be business-like. The marquee.

'Well, what about the lily-lawn? Would that do?'

And she pointed to the lily-lawn with the hand that didn't hold the bread-and-butter. They turned, they stared in the direction. A little fat chap thrust out his under-lip, and the tall fellow frowned.

'I don't fancy it,' said he. 'Not conspicuous enough. You see, with a thing like a marquee,' and he turned to Laura in his easy way, 'you want to put it somewhere where it'll give you a bang slap in the eye, if you follow me.'

Laura's upbringing made her wonder for a moment whether it was quite respectful of a workman to talk to her of bangs slap in the eye. But she did quite follow him.

'A corner of the tennis-court,' she suggested. 'But the band's going to be in one corner.'

'H'm, going to have a band, are you?' said another of the workmen. He was pale. He had a haggard look as his dark eyes scanned the tennis-court. What was he thinking?

'Only a very small band,' said Laura gently. Perhaps he wouldn't mind so much if the band was quite small. But the tall fellow interrupted.

'Look here, miss, that's the place. Against those trees. Over there. That'll do fine.'

Against the karakas. Then the karaka-trees would be hidden. And they were so lovely, with their broad, gleaming leaves, and their clusters of yellow fruit. They were like trees you imagined growing on a desert island, proud, solitary, lifting their leaves and fruits to the sun in a kind of silent splendour. Must they be hidden by a marquee?

They must. Already the men had shouldered their staves and were making for the place. Only the tall fellow was left. He bent down, pinched a sprig of lavender, put his thumb and forefinger to his nose and snuffed up the smell. When Laura saw that gesture she forgot all about the karakas in her wonder at him caring for things like that – caring for the smell of lavender. How many men that she knew would have done such a thing. Oh, how extraordinarily nice workmen were, she thought. Why couldn't she have workmen for her friends rather than the silly boys she danced with and who came to Sunday night supper? She would get on much better with men like these.

It's all the fault, she decided, as the tall fellow drew something on the back of an envelope, something that was to be looped up or left to hang, of these absurd class distinctions. Well, for her part, she didn't feel them. Not a bit, not an atom . . . And now there came the chock-chock of wooden hammers. Someone whistled, someone sang out, 'Are you right there, matey?' 'Matey!' The friendliness of it, the – the— Just to prove how happy she was, just to show the tall fellow how at home she felt, and how she despised stupid conventions, Laura took a big bite of her bread-and-butter as she stared at the little drawing. She felt just like a work-girl.

'Laura, Laura, where are you? Telephone, Laura!' a voice cried from the house.

'Coming!' Away she skimmed, over the lawn, up the path, up the steps, across the veranda, and into the porch. In the hall her father and Laurie were brushing their hats ready to go to the office.

'I say, Laura,' said Laurie very fast, 'you might just give a squiz at my coat before this afternoon. See if it wants pressing.'

'I will,' said she. Suddenly she couldn't stop herself. She ran at Laurie and gave him a small, quick squeeze. 'Oh, I do love parties, don't you?' gasped Laura.

'Ra-ther,' said Laurie's warm, boyish voice, and he squeezed his sister too, and gave her a gentle push. 'Dash off to the telephone, old girl.'

The telephone. 'Yes, yes; oh yes. Kitty? Good morning, dear. Come to lunch? Do, dear. Delighted of course. It will only be a very scratch meal – just the sandwich crusts and broken meringue-shells and what's left over. Yes, isn't it a perfect morning? Your white? Oh, I certainly should. One moment – hold the line. Mother's calling.' And Laura sat back. 'What, mother? Can't hear.'

Mrs Sheridan's voice floated down the stairs. 'Tell her to wear that sweet hat she had on last Sunday.'

'Mother says you're to wear that sweet hat you had on last Sunday. Good. One o'clock. Bye-bye.'

Laura put back the receiver, flung her arms over her head, took a deep breath, stretched and let them fall. 'Huh,' she sighed, and the moment after the sigh she sat up quickly. She was still, listening. All the doors in the house seemed to be open. The house was alive with soft, quick steps and running voices. The green baize door that led to the kitchen regions swung open and shut with a muffled thud. And now there came a long, chuckling absurd sound. It was the heavy piano being moved on its stiff castors. But the air! If you stopped to notice, was the air always like this? Little faint winds were playing chase in at the tops of the windows, out at the doors. And there were two tiny spots of sun, one on the inkpot, one on a silver photograph frame, playing too. Darling little spots. Especially the one on the inkpot lid. It was quite warm. A warm little silver star. She could have kissed it.

The front door bell pealed, and there sounded the rustle of Sadie's print skirt on the stairs. A man's voice murmured; Sadie answered, careless, 'I'm sure I don't know. Wait, I'll ask Mrs Sheridan.'

'What is it, Sadie?' Laura came into the hall.

'It's the florist, Miss Laura.'

It was, indeed. There, just inside the door, stood a wide, shallow tray full of pots of pink lilies. No other kind. Nothing but lilies – canna lilies, big pink flowers, wide open, radiant, almost frighteningly alive on bright crimson stems.

'O-oh, Sadie!' said Laura, and the sound was like a little moan. She crouched down as if to warm herself at that blaze of lilies; she felt they were in her fingers, on her lips, growing in her breast.

'It's some mistake,' she said faintly. 'Nobody ever ordered so many. Sadie, go and find mother.'

But at that moment Mrs Sheridan joined them.

'It's quite right,' she said calmly. 'Yes, I ordered them. Aren't they lovely?' She pressed Laura's arm. 'I was passing the shop yesterday, and I saw them in the window. And I suddenly thought for once in my life I shall have enough canna lilies. The garden party will be a good excuse.'

'But I thought you said you didn't mean to interfere,' said Laura. Sadie had gone. The florist's man was still outside at his van. She put her arm round her mother's neck and gently, very gently, she bit her mother's ear.

'My darling child, you wouldn't like a logical mother, would you? Don't do that. Here's the man.'

He carried more lilies still, another whole tray.

'Bank them up, just inside the door, on both sides of the porch, please,' said Mrs Sheridan. 'Don't you agree, Laura?'

'Oh, I *do*, mother.'

In the drawing-room Meg, Jose and good little Hans had at last succeeded in moving the piano.

'Now, if we put this chesterfield against the wall and move everything out of the room except the chairs, don't you think?'

'Quite.'

'Hans, move these tables into the smoking-room, and bring a sweeper to take these marks off the carpet and – one moment, Hans—' Jose loved giving orders to the servants, and they loved obeying her. She always made them feel they were taking part in some drama. 'Tell mother and Miss Laura to come here at once.'

'Very good, Miss Jose.'

She turned to Meg. 'I want to hear what the piano sounds like, just in case I'm asked to sing this afternoon. Let's try over "This life is Weary".'

Pom! Ta-ta-ta *Tee*-ta! The piano burst out so passionately that Jose's face changed. She clasped her hands. She looked mournfully and enigmatically at her mother and Laura as they came in.

> This Life is *Wee*-ary,
> A Tear – a Sigh.
> A Love that *Chan*-ges,
>   This Life is *Wee*-ary,
> A Tear – a Sigh.
> A Love that *Chan*-ges,
> And then . . . Goodbye!

But at the word 'Goodbye', and although the piano sounded more desperate than ever, her face broke into a brilliant, dreadfully unsympathetic smile.

'Aren't I in good voice, mummy?' she beamed.

> This Life is *Wee*-ary,
> Hope comes to Die.
> A Dream – a *Wa*-kening.

But now Sadie interrupted them. 'What is it, Sadie?'

'If you please, m'm, cook says have you got the flags for the sandwiches?'

'The flags for the sandwiches, Sadie?' echoed Mrs Sheridan dreamily. And the children knew by her face that she hadn't got them. 'Let me see.' And she said to Sadie firmly, 'Tell cook I'll let her have them in ten minutes.'

Sadie went.

'Now, Laura,' said her mother quickly, 'come with me

into the smoking-room. I've got the names somewhere on the back of an envelope. You'll have to write them out for me. Meg, go upstairs this minute and take that wet thing off your head. Jose, run and finish dressing this instant. Do you hear me, children, or shall I have to tell your father when he comes home tonight? And – and, Jose, pacify cook if you do go into the kitchen, will you? I'm terrified of her this morning.'

The envelope was found at last behind the dining-room clock, though how it had got there Mrs Sheridan could not imagine.

'One of you children must have stolen it out of my bag, because I remember vividly – cream-cheese and lemon-curd. Have you done that?'

'Yes.'

'Egg and—' Mrs Sheridan held the envelope away from her. 'It looks like mice. It can't be mice, can it?'

'Olive, pet,' said Laura, looking over her shoulder.

'Yes, of course, olive. What a horrible combination it sounds. Egg and olive.'

They were finished at last, and Laura took them off to the kitchen. She found Jose there pacifying the cook, who did not look at all terrifying.

'I have never seen such exquisite sandwiches,' said Jose's rapturous voice. 'How many kinds did you say there were, cook? Fifteen?'

'Fifteen, Miss Jose.'

'Well, cook, I congratulate you.'

Cook swept up crusts with the long sandwich knife and smiled broadly.

'Godber's has come,' announced Sadie, issuing out of the pantry. She had seen the man pass the window.

That meant the cream puffs had come. Godber's were

famous for their cream puffs. Nobody ever thought of making them at home.

'Bring them in and put them on the table, my girl,' ordered cook.

Sadie brought them in and went back to the door. Of course Laura and Jose were far too grown-up to really care about such things. All the same, they couldn't help agreeing that the puffs looked very attractive. Very. Cook began arranging them, shaking off the extra icing sugar.

'Don't they carry one back to all one's parties?' said Laura.

'I suppose they do,' said practical Jose, who never liked to be carried back. 'They look beautifully light and feathery, I must say.'

'Have one each, my dears,' said cook in her comfortable voice. 'Yer ma won't know.'

Oh, impossible. Fancy cream puffs so soon after breakfast. The very idea made one shudder. All the same, two minutes later Jose and Laura were licking their fingers with that absorbed inward look that only comes from whipped cream.

'Let's go into the garden, out by the back way,' suggested Laura. 'I want to see how the men are getting on with the marquee. They're such awfully nice men.'

But the back door was blocked by cook, Sadie, Godber's man and Hans.

Something had happened.

'Tuk-tuk-tuk,' clucked cook like an agitated hen. Sadie had her hand clapped to her cheek as though she had toothache. Hans's face was screwed up in the effort to understand. Only Godber's man seemed to be enjoying himself; it was his story.

'What's the matter? What's happened?'

'There's been a horrible accident,' said cook. 'A man's been killed.'

'A man killed! Where? How? When?'

But Godber's man wasn't going to have his story snatched from under his nose.

'Know those little cottages just below here, miss?' Know them? Of course, she knew them. 'Well, there's a young chap living there, name of Scott, a carter. His horse shied at a traction-engine, corner of Hawke Street this morning, and he was thrown out on the back of his head. Killed.'

'Dead!' Laura stared at Godber's man.

'Dead when they picked him up,' said Godber's man with relish. 'They were taking the body home as I come up here.' And he said to the cook, 'He's left a wife and five little ones.'

'Jose, come here.' Laura caught hold of her sister's sleeve and dragged her through the kitchen to the other side of the green baize door. There she paused and leaned against it. 'Jose!' she said, horrified, 'however are we going to stop everything?'

'Stop everything, Laura!' cried Jose in astonishment. 'What do you mean?'

'Stop the garden party, of course.' Why did Jose pretend?

But Jose was still more amazed. 'Stop the garden party? My dear Laura, don't be so absurd. Of course we can't do anything of the kind. Nobody expects us to. Don't be so extravagant.'

'But we can't possibly have a garden party with a man dead just outside the front gate.'

That really was extravagant, for the little cottages were in a lane to themselves at the very bottom of a steep rise that led up to the house. A broad road ran between. True, they were far too near. They were the greatest possible eyesore, and they had no right to be in that neighbourhood at all. They were little mean dwellings painted a chocolate brown. In the garden patches there was nothing but cabbage stalks, sick hens and tomato cans. The very smoke coming out of their chimneys was poverty-stricken. Little rags and shreds of smoke, so unlike the great silvery plumes that uncurled from the Sheridans' chimneys. Washerwomen lived in the lane and sweeps and a cobbler, and a man whose house-front was studded all over with minute bird-cages. Children swarmed. When the Sheridans were little they were forbidden to set foot there because of the revolting language and of what they might catch. But since they were grown up, Laura and Laurie on their prowls sometimes walked through. It was disgusting and sordid. They came out with a shudder. But still one must go everywhere; one must see everything. So through they went.

'And just think of what the band would sound like to that poor woman,' said Laura.

'Oh, Laura!' Jose began to be seriously annoyed. 'If you're going to stop a band playing every time someone has an accident, you'll lead a very strenuous life. I'm every bit as sorry about it as you. I feel just as sympathetic.' Her eyes hardened. She looked at her sister just as she used to when they were little and fighting together. 'You won't bring a drunken workman back to life by being sentimental,' she said softly.

'Drunk! Who said he was drunk?' Laura turned furiously on Jose. She said just as they had used to say on those occasions, 'I'm going straight up to tell mother.'

'Do, dear,' cooed Jose.

'Mother, can I come into your room?' Laura turned the big glass door-knob.

'Of course, child. Why, what's the matter? What's given you such a colour?' And Mrs Sheridan turned round from her dressing-table. She was trying on a new hat.

'Mother, a man's been killed,' began Laura.

'Not in the garden?' interrupted her mother.

'No, no!'

'Oh, what a fright you gave me!' Mrs Sheridan sighed with relief, and took off the big hat and held it on her knees.

'But listen, mother,' said Laura. Breathless, half-choking, she told the dreadful story. 'Of course, we can't have our party, can we?' she pleaded. 'The band and everybody arriving. They'd hear us, mother; they're our neighbours!'

To Laura's astonishment her mother behaved just like Jose; it was harder to bear because she seemed amused, she refused to take Laura seriously.

'But, dear child, use your common sense. It's only by accident we've heard of it. If someone had died there normally – and I can't understand how they keep alive in those poky little holes – we should still be having our party, shouldn't we?'

Laura had to say 'yes' to that, but she felt it was all wrong. She sat down on her mother's sofa and pinched the cushion frill.

'Mother, isn't it terribly heartless of us?' she asked.

'Darling!' Mrs Sheridan got up and came over to her, carrying the hat. Before Laura could stop her she had popped it on. 'My child!' said her mother, 'the hat is yours. It's made for you. It's much too young for me. I have never seen you look such a picture. Look at yourself!' And she held up her hand-mirror.

'But, mother,' Laura began again. She couldn't look at herself; she turned aside.

This time Mrs Sheridan lost patience just as Jose had done.

'You are being very absurd, Laura,' she said coldly. 'People like that don't expect sacrifices from us. And it's not very sympathetic to spoil everybody's enjoyment as you're doing now.'

'I don't understand,' said Laura, and she walked quickly out of the room into her own bedroom. There, quite by chance, the first thing she saw was this charming girl in the mirror, in her black hat trimmed with gold daisies, and a long black velvet ribbon. Never had she imagined she could look like that. Is mother right? she thought. And now she hoped her mother was right. Am I being extravagant? Perhaps it was extravagant. Just for a moment she had another glimpse of that poor woman and those little children, and the body being carried into the house. But it all seemed blurred, unreal, like a picture in the newspaper. I'll remember it again after the party's over, she decided. And somehow that seemed quite the best plan . . .

Lunch was over by half past one. By half past two they were all ready for the fray. The green-coated band had arrived and was established in a corner of the tennis-court.

'My dear!' trilled Kitty Maitland, 'aren't they too like frogs for words? You ought to have arranged them round the pond with the conductor in the middle on a leaf.'

Laurie arrived and hailed them on his way to dress. At the sight of him Laura remembered the accident again. She wanted to tell him. If Laurie agreed with the others, then it was bound to be all right. And she followed him into the hall.

'Laurie!'

'Hallo!' he was half-way upstairs, but when he turned round and saw Laura he suddenly puffed out his cheeks and goggled his eyes at her. 'My word, Laura! You do look stunning,' said Laurie. 'What an absolutely topping hat!'

Laura said faintly 'Is it?' and smiled up at Laurie, and didn't tell him after all.

Soon after that people began coming in streams. The band struck up; the hired waiters ran from the house to the marquee. Wherever you looked there were couples strolling, bending to the flowers, greeting, moving on over the lawn. They were like bright birds that had alighted in the Sheridans' garden for this one afternoon, on their way to – where? Ah, what happiness it is to be with people who all are happy, to press hands, press cheeks, smile into eyes.

'Darling Laura, how well you look!'

'What a becoming hat, child!'

'Laura, you look quite Spanish. I've never seen you look so striking.'

And Laura, glowing, answered softly, 'Have you had tea? Won't you have an ice? The passion-fruit ices really are rather special.' She ran to her father and begged him. 'Daddy darling, can't the band have something to drink?'

And the perfect afternoon slowly ripened, slowly faded, slowly its petals closed.

'Never a more delightful garden-party . . .' 'The greatest success . . .' 'Quite the most . . .'

Laura helped her mother with the goodbyes. They stood side by side in the porch till it was all over.

'All over, all over, thank heaven,' said Mrs Sheridan. 'Round up the others, Laura. Let's go and have some fresh coffee. I'm exhausted. Yes, it's been very successful. But oh, these parties, these parties! Why will you children insist on giving parties!' And they all of them sat down in the deserted marquee.

'Have a sandwich, daddy dear. I wrote the flag.'

'Thanks.' Mr Sheridan took a bite and the sandwich was gone. He took another. 'I suppose you didn't hear of a beastly accident that happened today?' he said.

'My dear,' said Mrs Sheridan, holding up her hand, 'we did. It nearly ruined the party. Laura insisted we should put it off.'

'Oh, mother!' Laura didn't want to be teased about it.

'It was a horrible affair all the same,' said Mr Sheridan. 'The chap was married too. Lived just below in the lane, and leaves a wife and half a dozen kiddies, so they say.'

An awkward little silence fell. Mrs Sheridan fidgeted with her cup. Really, it was very tactless of father . . .

Suddenly she looked up. There on the table were all those sandwiches, cakes, puffs, all un-eaten, all going to be wasted. She had one of her brilliant ideas.

'I know,' she said. 'Let's make up a basket. Let's send that poor creature some of this perfectly good food. At any rate, it will be the greatest treat for the children. Don't you agree? And she's sure to have neighbours calling in and so on. What a point to have it all ready prepared. Laura!' She jumped up. 'Get me the big basket out of the stairs cupboard.'

'But, mother, do you really think it's a good idea?' said Laura.

Again, how curious, she seemed to be different from them all. To take scraps from their party. Would the poor woman really like that?

'Of course! What's the matter with you today? An hour or two ago you were insisting on us being sympathetic, and now—'

Oh well! Laura ran for the basket. It was filled, it was heaped by her mother.

'Take it yourself, darling,' said she. 'Run down just as you are. No, wait, take the arum lilies too. People of that class are so impressed by arum lilies.'

'The stems will ruin her lace frock,' said practical Jose.

So they would. Just in time. 'Only the basket, then. And, Laura!' – her mother followed her out of the marquee – 'don't on any account—'

'What mother?'

No, better not put such ideas into the child's head! 'Nothing! Run along.'

It was just growing dusky as Laura shut their garden gates. A big dog ran by like a shadow. The road gleamed white, and down below in the hollow the little cottages were in deep shade. How quiet it seemed after the afternoon. Here she was going down the hill to somewhere where a man lay dead, and she couldn't realize it. Why couldn't she? She stopped a minute. And it seemed to her that kisses, voices, tinkling spoons, laughter, the smell of crushed grass were somehow inside her. She had no room for anything else. How strange! She looked up at the pale sky, and all she thought was, 'Yes, it was the most successful.'

Now the broad road was crossed. The lane began, smoky and dark. Women in shawls and men's tweed caps hurried by. Men hung over the palings; the children played in the doorways. A low hum came from the mean little cottages. In some of them there was a flicker of light, and a shadow, crab-like, moved across the window. Laura bent her head and hurried on. She wished now she had put on a coat. How her frock shone! And the big hat with the velvet streamer – if only it was another hat! Were the people looking at her? They must be. It was a mistake to have come; she knew all along it was a mistake. Should she go back even now?

No, too late. This was the house. It must be. A dark knot of people stood outside. Beside the gate an old, old woman with a crutch sat in a chair, watching. She had her feet on a newspaper. The voices stopped as Laura drew near. The group parted. It was as though she was expected, as though they had known she was coming here.

Laura was terribly nervous. Tossing the velvet ribbon over her shoulder, she said to a woman standing by, 'Is this Mrs

Scott's house?' and the woman, smiling queerly, said, 'It is, my lass.'

Oh, to be from this! She actually said, 'Help me, God,' as she walked up the tiny path and knocked. To be away from those staring eyes, or be covered up in anything, one of those women's shawls even. I'll just leave the basket and go, she decided. I shan't even wait for it to be emptied.

Then the door opened. A little woman in black showed in the gloom.

Laura said, 'Are you Mrs Scott?' But to her horror the woman answered, 'Walk in, please, miss,' and she was shut in the passage.

'No,' said Laura, 'I don't want to come in. I only want to leave this basket. Mother sent—'

The little woman in the gloomy passage seemed not to have heard her. 'Step this way, please, miss,' she said in an oily voice, and Laura followed her.

She found herself in a wretched little low kitchen, lighted by a smoky lamp. There was a woman sitting before the fire.

'Em,' said the little creature who had let her in. 'Em! It's a young lady.' She turned to Laura. She said meaningly, 'I'm her sister, miss. You'll excuse 'er, won't you?'

'Oh, but of course!' said Laura. 'Please, please don't disturb her. I – I only want to leave—'

But at that moment the woman at the fire turned round. Her face, puffed up, red, with swollen eyes and swollen lips, looked terrible. She seemed as though she couldn't understand why Laura was there. What did it mean? Why was this stranger standing in the kitchen with a basket? What was it all about! And the poor face puckered up again.

'All right, my dear,' said the other. 'I'll thenk the young lady.'

And again she began, 'You'll excuse her, miss, I'm sure,' and her face, swollen too, tried an oily smile.

Laura only wanted to get out, to get away. She was back in the passage. The door opened. She walked straight through into the bedroom where the dead man was lying.

'You'd like a look at 'im, wouldn't you?' said Em's sister, and she brushed past Laura over to the bed. 'Don't be afraid, my lass,' – and now her voice sounded fond and sly, and fondly she drew down the sheet – ''e looks a picture. There's nothing to show. Come along, my dear.'

Laura came.

There lay a young man, fast asleep – sleeping so soundly, so deeply, that he was far, far away from them both. Oh, so remote, so peaceful. He was dreaming. Never wake him up again. His head was sunk in the pillow, his eyes were closed; they were blind under the closed eyelids. He was given up to his dream. What did garden parties and baskets and lace frocks matter to him? He was far from all those things. He was wonderful, beautiful. While they were laughing and while the band was playing, this marvel had come to the lane. Happy . . . happy . . . All is well, said that sleeping face. This is just as it should be. I am content.

But all the same you had to cry, and she couldn't go out of the room without saying something to him. Laura gave a loud childish sob.

'Forgive my hat,' she said.

And this time she didn't wait for Em's sister. She found her way out of the door, down the path, past all those dark people. At the corner of the lane she met Laurie.

He stepped out of the shadow. 'Is that you, Laura?'

'Yes.'

'Mother was getting anxious. Was it all right?'

'Yes, quite. Oh, Laurie!' She took his arm, she pressed up against him.

'I say, you're not crying, are you?' asked her brother.

Laura shook her head. She was.

Laurie put his arm round her shoulder. 'Don't cry,' he said in his warm, loving voice. 'Was it awful?'

'No,' sobbed Laura. 'It was simply marvellous. But Laurie—' She stopped, she looked at her brother. 'Isn't life,' she stammered, 'isn't life—' But what life was she couldn't explain. No matter. He quite understood.

'*Isn't* it, darling?' said Laurie.

EDNA O'BRIEN

COME INTO THE DRAWING ROOM, DORIS

(1962)

MARY HOPED THAT the rotted front tyre of her bicycle would not burst. As it was, the tube had a slow puncture, and twice she had to stop and use the pump – a tiring business, because the pump had no connection and had to be jammed on over the corner of a handkerchief. For as long as she could remember, she had been pumping bicycles, carting peat for the fire, cleaning outhouses – doing a man's job. Her father and her two older brothers worked for the forestry, so she and her mother had to do all the odd jobs; there were young children to care for, and fowl and pigs and churning. Theirs was a mountainy farm in Ireland, and life was hard.

But this cold evening in early autumn she was free. She rode along the mountain road, between the bare thorn hedges, thinking pleasantly about the party. Although she was seventeen, this was her first party. The invitation had come only that morning from Mrs Rodgers, of the Commercial Hotel. The postman brought word that Mrs Rodgers wanted her down that evening, without fail. She was to stay overnight. At first, her mother did not wish Mary to go; there was too much to be done – gruel to be made, and one of the twins had earache and was likely to cry in the night. (Mary slept with the year-old twins, and sometimes she was afraid that she might lie on them or smother them, the bed was so small.) She begged her mother to be let go. 'What use would it be?' her mother said. To her mother, all outings were useless, unsettling; they gave you a taste of something you couldn't have. But finally her mother gave in, mainly because Mrs Rodgers, as owner of the Commercial Hotel, was an important woman, and also she had a brother who was a bishop in Australia. 'You can go so long as you're back in time for the milking in the morning. And mind you don't lose your head and do anything flighty,' her mother warned. Then Mary plaited her dark hair, and later, when she combed it, it fell in crinkly waves over her shoulders. She was allowed to wear the black lace dress that had come from America years ago and belonged to no one in particular. Her mother gave her a bottle of cream to take to Mrs Rodgers, sprinkled her with holy water, conveyed her to the top of the lane, and warned her again never to touch alcohol.

Mary felt happy as she rode along slowly, avoiding the loose stones and potholes, which were thinly iced over. The frosted fields glistened white in the weak sunshine. If it went on like this for days, the cattle would have to be brought into the shed and given hay. The road turned and curled and rose; she turned and curled with it, climbing little hills and descending again towards the next hill. At the descent of the Big Hill, she got off the bicycle – the brakes were unreliable – and looked back, out of habit, at her own house. It was the only house there on the side of the mountain – small and whitewashed, with a few scraggy trees around it, and a patch at the back that you could hardly call a garden; there was a rhubarb bed, and shrubs over which they emptied tea leaves, and a stretch of grass where they kept a chicken run in the summer, moving it from one patch to the next every other day.

She looked away, walked on, and settled down to think of John Roland. Two years before, he had come to their district, riding a motorcycle, scattering dust on her hair and the milk cloths she had put out to dry, and stopped to ask the way. He was staying in the Commercial Hotel down in the village and had come up to see the mountain lake, which was famous for its colours. It changed colour with the changing sky – it would be blue and ice green and vicious black, all within an hour. At sunset, it was often a strange burgundy – not like a lake at all but like wine. ' 'Tis down there,' she said to the stranger, pointing to the lake below with a small island in the middle of it. He had taken a wrong turning. 'What a remarkable landscape,' he said, looking round. Hills and narrow cornfields descended steeply towards the water. The colour of the hills was sharpened by the fine, hard blue of limestone boulders, and the small cornfields were bleaching already, in midsummer; the ditches were ragged, the garden overgrown with foxglove and smells and thistles, the milk sour five hours after it had been put in the tanker. She had no interest in views herself, so she just looked up at the high blue sky and saw that a hawk had halted in the air above them. It was like a pause in her life – the hawk above them, perfectly still. But just then her mother came out to see who the stranger was. He took off his helmet and said hello to her mother very courteously. He introduced himself as John Roland, an English painter who lived in Italy. Mary did not remember exactly how it happened, but after a while he walked into their kitchen with them and sat down to tea.

Two years since, but she had never given up hoping that she would see him again – perhaps this evening. The postman had said that someone special in the Commercial Hotel expected her. She felt happiness such as she had not known for years, so that she spoke to her bicycle, and it seemed to her that her happiness somehow glowed in the pearliness of the cold evening sky, in the white fields turning blue in the dusk, in the cottage windows she passed. Her father and mother were rich and happy; the twin had no earache, and the kitchen fire did not smoke. Now and then, she smiled at the thought of how she would appear to him – taller and with breasts now, and a black lace dress, the sleeves of which ruffed out into wide frills as they fell over her wrists. She forgot about the rotted tyre, mounted, and cycled quickly down the hill.

The five street lights were on when she pedalled into the village. There had been a cattle fair that day, and the main street was covered with dung. The townspeople had their windows protected against the animals with wooden half shutters and makeshift arrangements of planks and barrels. Some were out scrubbing their own pieces of footpath with bucket and brush. There were cattle wandering around mooing, the way cattle do when they're in a strange street, and drunken farmers with sticks trying to identify their own.

When she came to the shop-window of the Commercial Hotel, Mary heard loud conversation, and men singing. The window was frosted glass, so she could not identify any of them; she could just see their heads moving about inside. It was a shabby hotel. The yellow-washed walls needed a coat of paint – they hadn't been done since the time de Valera came to the village during the election campaign five years before. De Valera had gone upstairs, and sat in the parlour, and written his name with a penny pen in an autograph book, and sympathized with Mrs Rodgers on the recent death of her husband.

Mary thought of resting her bicycle against the porter barrels under the shop-window and then climbing the three stone steps that led to the hall door, but suddenly the latch of the shop door clicked, and in terror she ran up the alley by the side of the shop, afraid it might be someone who knew her father and would say he had seen her going in through the public bar. She wheeled her bicycle into a shed and approached the back door. It was open, but, being a mountainy girl, she did not enter without knocking.

Two town girls rushed to answer her knock. One was Doris O'Beirne, the daughter of the harness maker. She was the only Doris in the whole village, and she was distinguished for that, as well as for the fact that one of her eyes was blue and the other a dark brown. She was learning shorthand and typing at the local technical school, and she meant to be a secretary to some famous man or other in the government up in Dublin. 'God, I thought it was someone important,' she said when she saw Mary standing there, blushing, pretty, and with a bottle of cream in her hand. Another girl! Girls were two a penny in that neighbourhood. People said that it had something to do with the lime water that so many girls were born – girls like Mary, with pink skins, long, wavy hair, and neat figures.

'Come in or stay out,' said Eithne Duggan, the second girl. It was supposed to be a joke, but neither of them liked the look of Mary. They hated sly ones from the mountain.

Mary came in. She put the cream on the dresser and took off her coat. The girls nudged each other when they saw her dress. In the kitchen was a distinct smell of cow dung and fried onions. 'Where's Mrs Rodgers?' Mary asked.

'Serving,' Doris said, in a saucy voice; as if any fool ought to know.

Two old men sat at the table, eating. 'I can't chew; I have no teeth,' one of the men said to Doris. ' 'Tis like leather,' he said, holding the plate of burned steak towards her. He had pale-blue eyes and he blinked childishly.

Was it true, Mary wondered, that eyes got paler with age, like bluebells in a jar?

' 'Tis good for you, chewing is,' Eithne Duggan said,

teasing him. She and Doris began to giggle. Eithne Duggan laughed so much that she had to put a dishcloth over her mouth.

Mary went through to the shop.

Mrs Rodgers came from the counter for a moment to speak to her. 'Mary, I'm glad you came. That pair in there are no use at all – always giggling. Now, first thing we have to do is to get the parlour upstairs straightened out. Everything has to come out of it except the piano. We're going to have dancing and everything tonight.'

Mary realized that she was being given work to do, and she blushed with shock and disappointment.

'Pitch everything into the back bedroom, the whole shootin' lot,' Mrs Rodgers was saying as Mary thought of her good lace dress, and of how her mother wouldn't even let her wear it to Mass on Sundays. 'And we have to stuff a goose, too, and get it started,' Mrs Rodgers said, and went on to explain that the party was in honour of Mr Brogan, the local Customs and Excise Officer, who was retiring because his wife had won some money in the Sweep. Two thousand pounds. His wife lived thirty miles away, at the far side of Limerick, and he lodged in the Commercial Hotel from Monday to Friday, going home for the weekends.

'There's someone here expecting me,' Mary said, trembling with the pleasure of being about to hear his name pronounced. She wondered which room was his, and if he was likely to be in at that moment. Already, in imagination, she had climbed the rickety stairs, and knocked on the door, and heard him move around inside.

'Expecting you!' Mrs Rodgers said, and looked puzzled. 'Oh, that lad from the slate quarry was inquiring about you – he said he saw you at a dance once. He's as odd as two left shoes.'

'What lad?' Mary said, and she felt the joy leaking out of her heart.

'Oh, what's his name?' Mrs Rodgers said, and then to the men with empty glasses who were shouting for her, 'Oh, all right, I'm coming.'

Upstairs, Doris and Eithne helped Mary move the heavy pieces of furniture. They dragged the sideboard across the landing, and one of the casters tore the linoleum. She was expiring, because she had the heaviest end, the other two being at the same side. She felt that it was on purpose; they ate sweets without offering her one, and she caught them making faces at her dress. The dress worried her, too, in case anything should happen to it; if one of the lace threads caught in a splinter of wood or on a porter barrel, she would have no business going home in the morning. They carried out a varnished bamboo whatnot, a small table, knickknacks, and a chamber pot with no handle, which held some withered hydrangeas. They looked like rusted dish mops and smelled awful.

' "How much is that doggie in the window, the one with the waggely tail?" ' Doris O'Beirne sang to a white china dog, and swore that there wasn't ten pounds' worth of furniture in the whole shebeen.

'Are you leaving your curlers in, Dot, till it starts?' Eithne Duggan asked.

'Oh, def,' Doris O'Beirne said. She wore an assortment of curlers – white pipe cleaners, metal clips, and pink plastic rollers.

Eithne had just taken hers out, and her hair, dyed blond, stood out, all frizzed and alarmed. She reminded Mary of a moulting hen about to attempt flight. She was, God bless her, an unfortunate girl with a squint, jumbled teeth, and crooked lips – like something put together hurriedly. And her skin was bad. How surprising with all that rain and fresh air that she hadn't a nicer complexion, but that was the luck of the draw.

'Take these,' Doris O'Beirne said, handing Mary bunches of yellowed bills stuck on skewers.

Do this! Do that! They ordered her around like a maid. She dusted the piano, top and sides, and the yellow and black keys; then the baseboards and the wainscoting. The dust, thick on everything, had settled into a hard film because of the damp in the room. A party! She'd have been as well off at home. At least it was clean dirt, attending to calves and pigs and the like.

Doris and Eithne amused themselves, hitting notes on the piano at random and wandering from one mirror to the next. There were two mirrors in the parlour, and one side of the folding fire screen was a blotchy mirror, too. The other two sides were of water lilies painted on black cloth, but, like everything else in the room, the screen was old and dismal.

'What's that?' Doris and Eithne asked each other as they heard a hullabaloo downstairs. They rushed out, and Mary followed. Over the banisters they saw that a young bullock had got in the hall door and was slithering over the tiled floor, trying to find his way out again.

'Don't excite him, don't excite him, I tell ye,' the toothless old man was saying to the young boys trying to drive the black bullock out, when Mrs Rodgers came into the hall and dropped a glass of porter. The beast backed out the way he'd come, shaking his head from side to side.

Eithne and Doris clasped each other in laughter, and then Doris drew back so that none of the boys would see her in her curling pins and call her names.

Mary had gone back to the room, downcast. Wearily, she

pushed the chairs against the wall and swept the linoleum floor where they were to dance.

'She's bawling in there,' Eithne Duggan told her friend Doris. They had locked themselves into the bathroom with a bottle of cider.

'God, she's a right-looking eejit in the dress,' Doris said. 'And the length of it!'

'It's her mother's,' Eithne said. She had admired the dress before that, when Doris was out of the room, and had asked Mary where she bought it.

'What's she crying about?' Doris wondered aloud.

'She thought some lad would be here. Do you remember that lad stayed here the summer before last and had a motorcycle?'

'He was a Jew,' Doris said, as if that explained everything. 'God, she'd shake him in that dress – he'd think she was a scarecrow.' She tightened a curling pin that had come loose and said, 'Her hair isn't natural, either; you can see it's curled.'

'I hate that kind of black hair. It's like a gypsy's,' Eithne said, drinking the last of the cider. They hid the bottle under the scarred bath.

'Have a cachou,' Doris said. 'Take the smell off your breath.' She hawed on the bathroom mirror and wondered if she would get off with that fellow O'Toole, from the slate quarry, who was coming to the party.

In the front room, Mary polished glasses. Once more the tears ran down her cheeks, so she did not put on the light. She foresaw how the party would be; they would all stand around and consume the goose, which was now simmering in the turf range. The men would be drunk, the girls silly. Having eaten, they would dance, and sing, and tell ghost stories, and in the morning she would have to get up early and be home in time to milk. She moved towards the dark pane of window with a glass in her hand and looked out at the dirtied streets, remembering how once she had danced with John on the upper road to no music at all – just their hearts beating, and the sound of happiness.

He had come into their house for tea that summer's day, and on her father's suggestion he lodged with them for four days, helping with the hay and oiling farm machinery. Mary made his bed in the daytime and carried up a ewer of water from the rain barrel every evening, so that he could wash himself. She washed the checked shirt he wore, and that day his bare back got red from too much sun. She put milk on it to soothe it. It was his last day with them. After supper, he proposed giving each of the grown-up children a ride on the motorcycle. Her turn came last; she felt that he had planned it that way, but it may have been that her brothers were more persistent about being first. She would never forget that ride. She had warmed from head to foot in wonder and joy. He praised her as a good balancer, and at odd moments he took one hand off the handlebar and gave her clasped hands a comforting pat. The sun went down, and the gorse flowers blazed yellow. They did not talk for miles; she had his stomach enfolded in the delicate and frantic grasp of a girl in love, and no matter how far they rode they seemed always to be riding into a golden haze. He saw the lake at its most glorious. They got off at the bridge five miles away and sat on the limestone wall, which was cushioned by moss and lichen. She took a tick out of his neck and kissed the spot where the tick had drawn one pinprick of blood; it was then they had danced to the sound of larks and running water. The hay cut in the fields was lying green and ungathered, and the air was pure with the smell of it. They danced.

'Sweet Mary,' he said, looking earnestly into her eyes. Her eyes were a greenish brown. He confessed that he could not love her, because he already loved his wife and children. 'And anyhow,' he said, 'you are too young and innocent.'

Next day, as he was leaving, he asked if he might send her something in the post, and it came eleven days later: a black-and-white drawing of her – very like her, except that the girl in the drawing was prettier.

'A fat lot of good that is,' her mother, who had been expecting a gold bracelet or a brooch, said. 'That wouldn't take you far.'

They hung it on a nail in the kitchen for a while, and then one day it fell down and someone (probably her mother) used it to sweep dust onto. Ever since, it was used for that purpose. Mary had wanted to treasure it, to put it away in a trunk forever, but she was ashamed to. They were hard people, and it was only when someone died that they could give in to sentiment or crying.

'Sweet Mary,' he had said. He never wrote. Two summers passed, devil's-pokers flowered for two seasons, thistle seed blew white in the harsh mountain wind, and the trees in the forestry plantation were a foot higher. She had a feeling that he would come back sometime, and a gnawing fear that he might not.

' "Oh, it ain't goin' to rain no more, no more, it ain't goin' to rain no more. How in hell can the old folks tell it ain't goin' to rain no more." ' So sang Brogan, whose party it was, in the upstairs room of the Commercial Hotel. Unbuttoning his brown waistcoat, he sat back and said what a fine spread it was.

They had carried the goose up on a platter, and it lay in the centre of the mahogany table with potato stuffing swelling out of it. There were sausages also, and polished glasses standing rim downwards, and plates and forks for everyone. 'A fork supper' was how Mrs Rodgers described it. She had read about it in the paper. It was all the rage now in posh houses in Dublin, this fork supper where you stood up for your food and ate with a fork only. Mary had brought knives in case anyone got into difficulties.

''Tis America at home,' Hickey said, putting turf on the smoking fire.

The pub door was bolted downstairs, the shutters across, as the eight guests upstairs watched Mrs Rodgers carve the goose and then tear the loose pieces away with her fingers. Every so often, she wiped her fingers on a tea towel. 'Here you are, Mary; give this to Mr Brogan, as he's the guest of honour.' Mr Brogan got a lot of breast and some crispy skin as well. 'Don't forget the sausages, Mary,' Mrs Rodgers said.

Mary had to do everything – pass the food around, serve the stuffing, ask people whether they wanted paper plates or china ones. Mrs Rodgers had bought paper plates, thinking they were very sophisticated.

'I could eat a young child,' Hickey said.

Mary was surprised that people in towns were so coarse and outspoken, and when he squeezed her finger she did not smile at all. She wished that she were at home now. She knew what they were doing at home – the school-going boys at their lessons, her mother baking a cake of whole-meal bread because there was never enough time during the day to bake, her father rolling cigarettes and talking to himself. John had taught him how to roll cigarettes, and every night since, he rolled four and smoked four. He was a good man, her father, but dour and thrifty. In another hour, they'd be saying the Rosary in her house and going up to bed – the rhythm of their lives never changed; the fresh bread was always cool by morning.

'Ten o'clock,' Doris said, listening to the chimes of the landing clock.

The party had begun late – the men were late getting back from the dogs in Limerick. They had killed a pig on the way, in their anxiety to get back quickly. The pig had been wandering on the road, and the car coming round the corner ran over it instantly.

'Never heard such roarin' in all me born days,' Hickey said, reaching for a wing of goose, the choicest bit.

'We should have brought it with us,' Michael O'Toole said. O'Toole worked in the slate quarry and knew nothing about pigs or farming; he was tall and thin and bony. He had bright-blue eyes and a face like a greyhound's; his hair was so blond that it looked dyed, but in fact it was bleached by the weather. No one had offered him any food. 'A nice way to treat a man,' he said.

'God bless us, Mary, didn't you give Mr O'Toole anything to eat yet?' Mrs Rodgers said as she thumped Mary on the back to hurry her up.

Mary brought him a large helping on a paper plate, and he thanked her and said that they would dance later. To him she looked far prettier than those good-for-nothing townsgirls; she was tall and thin like himself, and she had long black hair that some people might think streelish, but not him – he liked long hair and decent, simple-minded girls. Maybe later on he'd get her to go into one of the other rooms and they could cuddle down, nice and snug. She had funny eyes, too – green at first sight, but brown when you looked into them, like a bloody boghole. 'Have a wish,' he said to her as he held the wishbone up.

She wished that she would go to America on an aeroplane,

and on second thought she wished that she would win a lot of money and could buy her mother and father a big house down near the main road.

'Is that your brother the bishop?' Eithne Duggan, who knew well that it was, asked Mrs Rodgers concerning the potato-faced clerk over the fireplace.

Unknown to herself, Mary had traced the letter 'J' on the dust of the picture glass earlier on, and now they all seemed to be looking at it, knowing how it came to be there.

'That's him, poor Charlie,' Mrs Rodgers said proudly, and was about to elaborate, but Brogan began to sing.

'Let the man sing, can't you?' O'Toole said, hushing two of the girls, who were having a joke about the armchair they shared; the springs were hanging down underneath, and the girls said that at any minute the whole thing would collapse.

Mary shivered in her lace dress – and, another thing, the sleeves were dipping into everything. The room smelled cold and damp, even though Hickey had got up a good fire. There hadn't been a fire in that room since the day de Valera signed the autograph book.

When Brogan finished, O'Toole asked if any of the ladies would care to sing.

There were five ladies in all – Mrs Rodgers, Mary, Doris, Eithne, and Crystal O'Meara, the local hairdresser, who had a new red rinse in her hair and who insisted that the food was a little heavy for her. The goose was greasy and undercooked; she did not like its raw, pink colour. She liked dainty things – little bits of cold chicken, with beetroot and sweet pickles. Her real name was Carmel, but when she started up as a hairdresser she changed to Crystal and dyed her brown hair red.

'I bet you can sing,' O'Toole said to Mary.

'Where she comes from they can hardly talk,' Doris said.

Mary felt the blood rushing to her cheeks. She would not tell them, but her father's name had been in the paper once, because he had seen a pine marten in the forestry plantation; and they ate with a knife and fork at home, and had a plastic cloth on the kitchen table, and a tin of coffee in case strangers called. She would not tell them anything. She just hung her head and said that she couldn't sing.

O'Toole put 'Far Away in Australia' on the horn gramophone, in honour of the bishop over the fireplace, who presided in Sydney. The sound issued forth with rasps and scratchings, and Brogan said he could do better than that himself.

'Christ, lads, we forgot the soup!' Mrs Rodgers said suddenly, as she threw down her fork and went towards the door. There had been soup scheduled to begin with.

'I'll help you,' Doris O'Beirne said, stirring herself for the first time that night, and they both went down to get the pot of giblet soup that had been simmering all day.

'Now we need two pounds from each of the gents,' said O'Toole, taking the opportunity while Mrs Rodgers was away to mention the delicate matter of money. The men had agreed to pay two pounds each to cover the cost of the drink; the ladies did not have to pay anything, but were invited to lend a pleasant and decorative atmosphere to the party, and, of course, to help with the food.

O'Toole went round with his cap held out, and Brogan said that as it was *his* party he ought to give a fiver. 'But I suppose ye wouldn't hear of that,' Brogan said, and handed up two pound notes.

Hickey paid up, too, and O'Toole himself, and Long John Salmon, who was the most silent guest of all. O'Toole gave the money to Mrs Rodgers when she returned and told her to clock it up against the damages.

'Sure, that's too kind altogether,' she said as she put it behind the stuffed owl on the mantelpiece, under the bishop's watchful eye. She served the soup in cups, and Mary was asked to pass them around. The grease floated like specks of molten gold on the surface of each cup.

'See you later, alligator,' Hickey said as she gave him his. Then he asked her for a piece of bread, because he wasn't used to soup without bread. 'Tell us, Brogan,' said Hickey. 'What'll you do, now that you're a rich man?'

'Oh, go on, tell us,' said Doris O'Beirne.

'Well,' Brogan said, thinking for a minute, 'we're going to make some changes at home.' None of them had ever visited Brogan's home, because it was situated in Adare, thirty miles away. None of them had ever seen his wife, either, who, it seems, lived there and kept bees.

'What sort of changes?' someone said.

'We're going to do up the drawing room, and we're going to have some flower beds,' Brogan told them.

'And what else?' Crystal asked, thinking of all the lovely clothes she could buy with that money – lovely clothes and jewellery.

'Well,' said Brogan, thinking again, 'we might even go to Lourdes. I'm not sure yet; it all depends.'

'I'd give my two eyes to go to Lourdes,' Mrs Rodgers said.

'And you'd get 'em back when you arrived there,' Hickey said, but no one paid any attention to him.

O'Toole poured out four half tumblers of whiskey and then stood back to examine the glasses to see that each one had the same amount. There was always great anxiety among the men about being fair with drink. Then O'Toole stood bottles of stout in little groups of six and told each man which group was his. The ladies had gin and orange.

'Orange for me,' Mary said, but O'Toole told her not to

be such a fool, and when her back was turned he put some gin in her orange.

They drank a toast to Brogan.

'To Lourdes,' Mrs Rodgers said.

'To Brogan,' O'Toole said.

'To myself,' Hickey said.

'Mud in your eye,' said Doris O'Beirne, who was already unsteady from tippling cider.

'Well, we're not sure about Lourdes,' Brogan said, 'but we'll get the drawing room done up anyhow, and the flower beds put in.'

'We've a drawing room here,' Mrs Rodgers said, 'and no one ever sets foot in it.'

'Come into the drawing room, Doris,' said O'Toole to Mary, who was serving jelly from a big enamel basin. They'd had no nice bowl to put it in. It was red jelly with whipped egg white in it, but it hadn't set properly. She served it in saucers and thought what a rough-and-ready party it was. There wasn't a proper cloth on the table, either, just a plastic one, and no napkins, and that big basin with the jelly in it. Maybe people washed in that basin, downstairs.

'Well, someone tell us a bloomin' joke,' said Hickey, who was getting fed up with talk about drawing rooms and flower beds.

'I'll tell you a joke,' said Long John Salmon, who had been silent up till then.

'Good,' said Brogan, as he sipped from his whiskey glass and his stout glass alternately.

'Is it a funny joke?' Hickey asked of Long John Salmon.

'It's about my brother,' said Long John Salmon. 'My brother Patrick.'

'Oh, no, don't tell us that old rambling thing again,' Hickey said at once, and O'Toole nodded his own protest.

'Oh, let him tell it,' said Mrs Rodgers, who'd never heard the story anyhow.

Long John Salmon began, 'I had this brother Patrick and he died; the heart wasn't too good.'

'Holy Christ, not this again,' said Brogan, recollecting which story it was.

But Long John Salmon went on, undeterred by the sighs from the three men. 'One day I was standing in the shed, about a month after he was buried, and I saw him coming out of the wall, walking across the yard.'

'Oh, what would you do, if you saw a thing like that,' Doris said to Eithne.

'Let him tell it,' Mrs Rodgers said. 'Go on, Long John.'

'Well, it was walking towards me, and I said to myself, "What do I do now?" 'Twas raining heavy, so I said to my brother Patrick, "Stand in out of the wet or you'll get drenched." '

'And then?' said one of the girls anxiously.

'He vanished,' said Long John Salmon.

'Ah, God, let us have a bit of music,' said Hickey, who had heard that story nine or ten times. They put a record on, and O'Toole asked Mary to dance. He did a lot of fancy steps and capering, and now and then he let out a mad 'Yippee!' Brogan and Mrs Rodgers were dancing, too, and Crystal said that she'd dance if anyone asked her.

'Come on, knees up, Mother Brown,' O'Toole said to Mary as he jumped around the room, kicking the legs of chairs as he moved. She felt funny; her head was swaying round and round, and in the pit of her stomach there was a nice ticklish feeling that made her want to lie back and stretch her legs – a new feeling that frightened her. Perhaps he had put gin in her orange when she wasn't looking.

'Come into the drawing room, Doris,' he said, dancing

her right out of the room and into the cold passage, where he kissed her clumsily.

Inside, Crystal O'Meara had begun to cry. That was how drink affected her; either she cried or talked in a foreign accent and said, 'Why am I talking in a foreign accent?' This time she cried. 'Hickey, there is no joy in life,' she said as she sat at the table with her head laid in her arms and her blouse slipping up out of her skirt band. She had taken off her left shoe because it pinched.

'What joy?' said Hickey, who had all the drink he needed, and a pound note he had slipped from behind the owl when no one was looking.

Doris and Eithne sat on either side of Long John Salmon, asking if they could go out to his place next year when the sugarplums were ripe. Long John Salmon lived by himself, way up the country, and he had a big orchard. He was odd and silent; he took a swim every day, winter and summer, in the river, at the back of his stone house.

'Two old married people,' Brogan said as he put his arm round Mrs Rodgers and urged her to sit down because he was out of breath from dancing. He said he'd go away with happy memories of them all, and, sitting down, he drew her onto his lap. She was a heavy woman, with straggledy brown hair that had once been a bright nut colour.

'There is no joy in life,' Crystal sobbed as the gramophone made crackling noises and Mary ran in from the landing, away from O'Toole.

'I mean business,' O'Toole said, and winked.

O'Toole was the first to get quarrelsome. 'Now ladies, now gentlemen, a little laughing sketch – are we ready? he asked.

'Fire ahead,' Hickey told him.

'Well, there was these three lads, Paddy th' Irishman,

Paddy th' Englishman, and Paddy the Scotsman, and they were badly in need of—'

'Now, no smut,' Mrs Rodgers snapped, before he had uttered a wrong word at all.

'What smut?' said O'Toole, getting offended. 'Smut!'

'Think of the girls,' Mrs Rodgers said.

'Girls!' O'Toole sneered as he picked up the bottle of cream, which they'd forgotten to use with the jelly and poured it into the carcase of the goose.

'Christ sake, man,' Hickey said, taking the bottle of cream out of O'Toole's hand.

Mrs Rodgers said that it was high time everyone went to bed, as the party seemed to be over.

The guests would spend the night in the Commercial. It was too late for them to go home, and also Mrs Rodgers did not want them to be observed staggering out of the house at that hour. The police watched her like hawks, she said, and she didn't want any trouble – until Christmas was over at least. The sleeping arrangements had been decided earlier on. There were three bedrooms. Brogan would have the room he always slept in, the other three men were to pitch in together in the second big bedroom, and the girls were to share the back room with Mrs Rodgers herself.

'Come on, everyone – blanket street,' Mrs Rodgers said, as she put a guard in front of the dying fire and took the money from behind the owl.

'Sugar you,' O'Toole said, pouring stout now into the carcase of the goose.

Long John Salmon wished that he had never come. He thought of daylight and of his swim in the mountain river at the back of his grey stone house. 'Ablution,' he said aloud, taking pleasure in the word and in the thought of cold water touching him. He could do without people; people were dirty. He remembered catkins on a tree outside his window, catkins in February, as white as snow.

'Crystal, stir yourself,' Hickey said, as he put on her shoe and patted the calves of her legs.

Brogan kissed the four girls and saw them across the landing to the bedroom. Mary was glad to escape without O'Toole noticing; he was very obstreperous, and Hickey was trying to control him.

In the bedroom, she sighed – she had forgotten all about the furniture being pitched in there. Wearily, they began to unload the things. The room was so crammed that they could hardly move in it. Mary suddenly felt alert and frightened, because O'Toole could be heard yelling and singing out on the landing. There had been gin in her orangeade, she knew now, because she breathed closely onto the palm of her hand and smelled her own breath. She had broken her confirmation pledge, broken her promise; it would bring her bad luck always.

Mrs Rodgers came in and said that five of them would be too crushed in the bed, so that she herself would sleep on the sofa in the parlour for one night. 'Two of you at the top and two at the bottom,' she said, and she warned them not to break any of the ornaments, and not to stay talking all night. ' 'Night and God bless,' she said as she shut the door behind her.

'Nice thing,' said Doris O'Beirne, 'bunging us all in here. I wonder where she's off to.'

'Will you loan me curlers?' Crystal asked. To Crystal, hair was the most important thing on earth. She would never get married, because you couldn't wear curlers in bed. Eithne Duggan said she wouldn't put curlers in now if she got five million for doing it; she was jaded. She threw herself down on the quilt and spread her arms out. She was a noisy, sweaty girl, but Mary liked her better than the other two.

'Ah, me old honeybunch,' O'Toole said, pushing their door in. The girls exclaimed and asked him to go out at once, as they were preparing for bed.

'Come into the drawing room, Doris,' he said to Mary, and curled his forefinger at her. He was drunk and couldn't focus her properly, but he knew that she was standing there somewhere.

'Go to bed; you're drunk,' Doris O'Beirne said, and he stood very upright for an instant and asked her to speak for herself.

'Go to bed, Michael; you're tired,' Mary said to him. She tried to sound calm, because he looked so wild.

'Come into the drawing room, I tell you,' he said as he caught her wrist and dragged her towards the door.

She let out a cry, and Eithne Duggan said she'd brain him if he didn't leave the girl alone. 'Give me that flowerpot, Doris,' Eithne Duggan called, and then Mary began to cry for fear there might be a scene. She hated scenes. Once, she had heard her father and a neighbour having a row about boundary rights and she'd never forgotten it; they had been both a bit drunk, after a fair.

'Are you cracked, or are you mad?' O'Toole said when he perceived that she was crying.

'I'll give you two seconds,' Eithne warned, as she held the flowerpot high, ready to throw it at O'Toole's greyhound face.

'You're a nice bunch of hard-faced aul crows,' he said. 'Wouldn't give a man a squeeze,' and he went out cursing each one of them.

They shut the door very quickly and dragged the sideboard in front of the door, so that he could not break in when they were asleep. They got into bed in their underwear,

Mary and Eithne at one end, with Crystal's feet between their faces. 'You have lovely hair,' Eithne whispered to Mary. It was the nicest thing she could think of to say. They each said their prayers, and shook hands under the covers, and settled down to sleep.

'Hey,' Doris O'Beirne said a few seconds later, 'I never went to the lav.'

'You can't go now,' Eithne said. 'The sideboard's in front of the door.'

'I'll die if I don't go,' Doris O'Beirne said.

'And me, too, after all that orange we drank,' Crystal said.

Mary was shocked. At home, you never spoke of such a thing.

They heard feet on the landing, and then the sound of choking and coughing, and later O'Toole cursing and swearing and hitting the wall with his fist. Mary curled down under the clothes, thankful for the company of the girls.

'I was at a party. Now I know what parties are like,' Mary said to herself as she tried to force herself asleep. She heard a sound as of water running, but it did not seem to be raining outside. Later, she dozed, but at daybreak she heard the hall door bang, and she sat up in bed abruptly. She had to be home early to milk, so she got up, took her shoes and her lace dress, and let herself out by dragging the sideboard forward and opening the door slightly.

There were newspapers spread on the landing floor and in the lavatory, and a heavy smell pervaded. Downstairs, porter had flowed out of the bar into the hall. Someone – probably O'Toole – had turned on the taps of the five porter barrels, and the stone-floored bar and sunken passage outside were a lake of black porter. Mrs Rodgers would kill somebody. Mary put on her high-heeled shoes and picked her steps carefully across the room to the door. She left without even making a cup of tea.

She wheeled her bicycle down the alley and into the street. The front tyre was dead flat. She pumped for ten minutes, but it remained flat.

The frost lay like a spell upon the street, upon the sleeping windows and the slate roofs of the crumbling houses. It had magically made the dunged street white and clean. She did not feel tired but was relieved to be out and stunned by lack of sleep and the beauty of the morning. She walked briskly, sometimes looking back to see the track that her bicycle and her feet made on the white road.

Mrs Rodgers wakened at eight and stumbled out in her big nightgown from Brogan's warm bed. She smelled disaster instantly and hurried downstairs to find the lake of porter in the bar and the ground hall. Then she ran to call the others. 'Porter all over the place, every drop of drink in the house is on the floor – Mary Mother of God, help me in my tribulation! Get up, get up!' She rapped on their door and called the girls by name. The girls rubbed their sleepy eyes, yawned, and sat up.

'She's gone,' Eithne said, looking at the place on the pillow where Mary's head had been.

'Oh, a sneaky country one,' Doris said, as she got into her taffeta dress and went down to see the flood. 'If I have to clean that in my good clothes, I'll die,' she said. But Mrs Rodgers had already brought brushes and pails and got to work. They opened the bar door and began to bail the porter into the street. Dogs came to lap it up, and Hickey, who had come down, stood and said what a crying shame it was to waste all that drink. Outside, it washed away an area of frost and revealed the dung of yesterday's fair day. O'Toole, the culprit, had fled; Long John Salmon was gone for his swim; and upstairs, in bed, Brogan snuggled down for a last-minute heat and deliberated on the joys that he would miss when he left the Commercial for good.

'And where's my lady with the lace dress?' Hickey asked, recalling very little of Mary's face but distinctly remembering the sleeves of her black dress, which dipped into every damn thing.

'Sneaked off, before we were up,' Doris said.

They all agreed that Mary was no bloody use and should never have been asked.

'And 'twas she set O'Toole mad, egging him on and then disappointing him,' Doris said, and Mrs Rodgers swore that O'Toole, or Mary's father, or someone, would pay dear for the wasted drink.

'I suppose she's home by now,' Hickey said as he rooted in his pocket for a butt. He had a new packet, but if he produced that they'd all be puffing at his expense.

Mary was half a mile from home, sitting on a ditch. If only I had a sweetheart, something to hold on to, she thought as she cracked some ice with her high heel and pitied the poor birds who could get no food, as the ground was frozen hard.

Walking again, she wondered if she would ever go to another party and what she would tell her mother and her brothers about it, and if all parties were as bad. She came over the top of the hill and suddenly saw her own house, like a little white box at the end of the world, waiting to receive her.

ALAN HOLLINGHURST

TOBY FEDDEN'S 21ST

From *The Line of Beauty*

(2004)

HE LOOKED IN at the door of Toby's bedroom. A group of his friends had come up here when the music stopped at two, and they seemed lazily to assess him. 'Come in and close the door, for god's sake,' said Toby, beckoning from the vast bed where he was propped up among sprawling friends. He had been given the King's Room, where Edward VII had slept – the swags of blue silk above the bedhead were gathered into a vaguely comic gilded crown. On the opposite wall hung a comfortable Renoir nude. Nick picked his way between groups sitting on the floor in front of an enormous sofa where fat Lord Shepton was lying with his tie undone and his head on the thigh of an attractive drunk girl. The curtains were parted and a window open to carry the reek of marijuana far away from the nose of the Home Secretary. Somehow they had re-created the mood of a college room late at night, girls' stockinged feet stretched out across boyfriends' knees, smoke in the air, two or three voices dominating. Nick felt the charm as well as the threat of the group. Gareth Lane was holding forth about Hitler and Goebbels, and his lecturing drone and yapping laughs at his own puns brought back something dreary from the Oxford days. He was said to be the 'ablest historian of his year', but he had failed to get a first, and seemed now to be acting out some endless redemptive viva. The talk went on, but there felt to Nick's tingling drunk ears to be a residual silence in the room, on which his own movements and words were an intrusion . . . and yet left no trace. Several of his other pals were here, but the two months since term had distanced them more than he could explain. Some simple but strong and long-prepared change had occurred, they had taken up their real lives, and left him alone in his. He came back and perched on the edge of the bed and Toby leaned forward and passed him the joint.

'Thanks . . .' Nick smiled at him, and at last some old sweetness of reassurance glowed between them, what he'd been waiting for all night.

'God, darling, you smell like a tart's parlour,' Toby said. Nick carried on gazing at him, paralysed for the moment by the need to hold in the smoke, a tickle in his throat, blushing with shame and pleasure. He was holding in the unprecedented 'darling' and it was making him as warm and giddy as the pot. Then he let out the smoke and saw the baldly hetero claims of the rest of the remark. He said,

'And how would you know?' – wondering primly if Toby really had been to a tart's parlour. It was an image of him lurching up a narrow staircase.

Toby winked. 'Having a good time?'

'Yes, fantastic.' Nick looked around appreciatively, glossing over his inner vision of the night as a long stumbling journey, half chase, half flight, like one of his country-house dreams, his staircase dreams. 'What's happened to Sophie, by the way?'

'She had to go back to London. Yeah. She's got an audition on Monday.'

'Ah . . . right . . .' This was good news to Nick, and Toby himself, drunk, stoned, eyes glistening, seemed happy about it – he liked the adult note of responsibility in sending her home, and he liked being free of her too. He raised his voice and said,

'Oh, do shut up about fucking Goebbels!' But after a brief incredulous whirr Gareth's shock-proof mechanism rattled on.

Toby was king tonight, on his great big bed, and his friends for once were his subjects. He was acting the role with high spirits, in a childishly approximate way. Nick found it very touching and exciting. As the pot took its delayed effect, squeezing and freeing like some psychic massage, he reached back and took Toby's hand, and they lolled there like that for thirty or forty seconds of heaven. It was as if the room had been steeped in a mood of amorous hilarity as sweetly unignorable as 'Je Promets'. He recalled what Polly had said in the garden long before, and thought that maybe, at last, for once, Toby would actually be his.

There was a surrounding murmur of stoned gossip, heads nodding over rolling papers, the figures blurred but glowing in the lamplight. 'But did the Führer license the Final Solution?' Gareth asked himself; and it was clear that the arguments on this famous question were about to be passed in detailed review.

There was a giggling protest from Sam Zeman, curly-headed genius who'd gone straight into Kesslers on twenty thousand a year. 'You're in a house full of Jews here, can you shut up about the fucking Final Solution, it's a party . . .' – and he reached for his drink with the frown and snuffle of a subtle person obliged to be brusque.

'I can go on to Stalin . . .' said Gareth facetiously.

After a minute's reflection Roddy Shepton said robustly, 'Well, I'm not bloody Jewish.'

'Tobias is,' said his girlfriend, 'aren't you, darling?'

'For god's sake, Claire . . .' said Roddy.

Claire gazed at Toby with eyes of deepening conviction.

'Wasn't someone saying the Home Sectary's Jewish too . . .?' she said.

'Calm down, Claire!' said Roddy furiously. It was his own conviction that his large placid girlfriend, who had never been known to raise her voice, was dangerously excitable. Perhaps it was his way of implying he had tamed a sexual volcano; which in turn perhaps helped him to explain why he was going out with a strictly middle-class girl, the daughter of his father's estate manager.

Claire looked round in pursuit of her new idea. 'You're Jewish, aren't you, Nat?'

'I am, darling,' said Nat, 'or half Jewish, anyway.'

'And the other half's a bloody Welshman,' said Roddy. He turned his head on her knee and squinted up at her. 'God, you're drunk,' he said.

This was the kind of insult that passed for wit at the Martyrs' Club, and was in fact one of the things most often said there. Toby had once taken Nick to the club's poky panelled dining room, where Christ Church toffs and Union hacks conformed deafeningly to type and boozed and plotted and howled unacceptable remarks at each other and at the harried staff. It was another world, defiantly impervious, in which it was a shock to find that Toby had a place.

'You are so fucking drunk, Shepton,' Toby said. He had pulled off his socks and rolled them into a ball and he threw them very hard and accurately at the fat peer's head.

'Fucking Christ, Fedden,' Roddy muttered, but left it at that.

Nick was explaining about the sea in Conrad's novels being a metaphor for both escape from the self and discovery of the self – a point which took on more and more revelatory force as he repeated it. He laughed at the beauty of it. He wasn't a strong smoker, and a second frowning toke, taken in the belief that the first one had had no effect, could leave him swimming and gabbling for hours. Nat Hanmer was sitting on the floor beside him, and his warm thigh was pressed against his own. There was something charmingly faggy about Nat tonight. He nodded and smiled into Nick's eyes as he was talking. Nick thought the pressure of the dope on his temples was as if his skull was being gently squeezed by Nat's big hands. Sam Zeman was nodding and smiling too and corrected, as if it really didn't matter, a plot detail in *Victory* that Nick had got wrong. Nick loved Sam because he was an economist but he'd read everything and played the viola and took a flattering interest in people less sublimely omniscient than himself.

He wanted to lie back and listen and perhaps have a long deep snog with Nat Hanmer, whose lips were not so full and soft as Leo's, but who was (Nick hadn't seen it before) almost beautiful, as well of course as being a marquess. The two of them in their shirtsleeves. Nat said he was having a go at writing a novel himself. He'd bought a computer, which he said was 'a really sexy machine'. In the warm explanatory light of the pot Nick saw what he meant. 'I'd love to read it,' he said. Across the room Gareth had switched wars and was describing the Battle of Jutland to a paralysed circle of young women. His big velvet bow tie was all donnish conceit. He was going to go on like this for forty-five years.

Nick heard himself saying how he missed his boyfriend, and then his heart speeded up. Sam smiled – he was purely and maturely straight, but he was cool with everything. Nat said broad-mindedly, 'Oh, you've got a . . . you've got a bloke?' and Nick said, 'Yeah . . .' and already he'd told them all about answering the advertisement, and their meeting and having sex in the garden and the funny episode with Geoffrey from two doors down. And how they were now going out together on a regular basis. Pot was a kind of truth drug for him – with a twist. He had an urge to tell, and show himself to them as a functioning sexual being, but as he did so he seemed to hear how odd and unseen his life was, and added easy touches to it, that made it more shapely and normal.

'I didn't know about all this,' said Toby, who was going round in his bare feet with a bottle of brandy. He was grinning, slightly scandalized, even hurt perhaps that Nick hadn't told him he was having an affair.

'Oh, yes . . .' said Nick, 'sorry . . . He's this really attractive black guy, called Leo.'

'You should have brought him tonight,' Toby said. 'Why didn't you say?'

'I know,' said Nick; but he could only imagine Leo here in his falling-down jeans and his sister's shirt, and the jarring of his irony against the loaded assumptions of the Oxford lot.

'May one ask why?' said Lord Shepton, who had lately been snoring but had now been tickled awake and had a blearily vengeful look. Nobody knew what he was talking about. 'We've already got bloody . . . Woggoo here,' and he struggled upright, with a grimace of pretended guilt, to see if Charlie Mwegu, the Worcester loose-head prop and the only black person at the party, was in the room. 'I mean, fucking hell,' he said. Shepton was a licensed buffoon, an indulged self-parody, and Nick merely raised his eyebrows and sighed; for a moment the old dreariness and wariness surfaced again through the newer romance of the pot.

Claire was looking tenderly at Nick, and said, 'I think black men can be so attractive . . . they have sweet little ears, don't they . . . sometimes . . . I don't know . . . It must be nice—'

'*Calm down, Claire!*' barked Roddy Shepton, as if his very

worst fears had been confirmed. He struggled towards his glass on the floor.

'No, I'm quite jealous actually,' said Claire, and gave Lord Shepton a playful poke in the stomach.

'Oh, you cow!' said Lord Shepton; his attention refocusing, slowly but greedily, on Wani Ouradi, who had just come into the room. 'Ah, Ouradi, there you are. I hope you're going to give me some of that white powder, you bloody Arab.'

'Oh, really!' said Claire, appealing hopelessly to the others.

But Wani ignored Shepton and stepped through the group towards the bed and Toby. He had changed into a green velvet smoking jacket. Nick had a moment of selfless but intensely curious immersion in his beauty. The forceful chin with its slight saving roundness, the deep-set eyes with their confounding softness, the cheekbones and the long nose, the little ears and springy curls, the cruel charming curve of his lips, made everything else in the house seem stale, over-artful, or beside the point. Nick longed to abandon handsome Nat and climb back on to the King's bed. He rolled his eyes in apology for Shepton, but Wani gave no answering sign of special recognition. And the group soon started talking about something else. Wani lay back on his elbow beside Toby for a minute, and took in the room through the filters of his lashes. Toby had picked up one of the girls' pink chiffon scarves, and was winding it into a turban with drunk perseverance. Wani said nothing about the turban, as if they were almost too familiar with each other to comment, as if they were figures of some other time and culture. Nick heard him say, 'Si tu veux . . .' before getting up and going into the bathroom. Toby sat a while longer, laughing artificially at the conversation, and then went off with a yawn and a stumble after him. Nick sat sunk in himself, jealous of both of them, shocked almost to the point of panic by what they were doing. When they came back, he watched them like a child curious for evidence of its parents' vices. He could see their tiny effort to muffle their excitement, the little mock solemnity that made them seem oddly less happy and smashed than the rest of the party. They had a gleam of secret knowledge about them.

A joint came round again, and Nick took a serious pull on it. Then he got up and went to the open window, to look out at the damp still night. The great beeches beyond the lawn showed in grey silhouette against the first vague paling of the sky. It was a beautiful effect, so much bigger than the party: the world turning, the bright practical phrases of the first birds. Though there were hours still, surely, before sunrise . . . He stiffened, grabbed at his wrist, and held his watch steady in front of him. It was 4.07. He turned and looked at the others in the room, in their stupor and animation, and his main heavy thought was just how little any of them cared – they could never begin to imagine a date with a waiter, or the disaster of missing one. He made the first steps towards the door, and slowed and stopped as the pot took his sense of direction away. Where, after all, was he going? Everything seemed to have petered into a silence, as if by agreement. Nick felt conspicuous standing there, smiling cautiously, like someone not on to a joke; but when he looked at the others they seemed equally stilled and bemused. It must be some amazingly strong stuff. Nick thought his way towards moving his left leg forward, he could coax his thought down through the knee to the foot, but it died there with no chance of becoming an action. It was slightly trying if he had to stand here for a long time. He looked more boldly round the others, not easy to name at the moment, some of them. Slow blinks, little twitches of smiles. 'Yah . . .' said Nat

Hanmer, very measuredly, nodding his head, agreeing with some statement that only he had heard. 'I suppose . . .' said Nick; but stopped and looked around, because that was part of a conversation about Gerald and the BBC. No one had noticed, though. 'But you're thinking, wasn't that Bismarck's whole point?' Gareth said.

Nick wasn't sure how it started. Sam Zeman was laughing so much he lay back on the floor, but then choked and had to sit up. One of the girls pointed at him mockingly, but it wasn't mockery, she was laughing uncontrollably herself. Nat was red in the face, pinching the tears out of his eyes and pulling down the corners of his mouth to try to stop it. Nick could only stop giggling by glaring at the floor, and as soon as he looked up he was giggling again convulsively, it was like hiccups, it was hiccups, all mixed up together with the whooping, inexplicable funniness of the brandy bottle, the Renoir lady, the gilded plaster crown above the bed, all of them with their ideas and bow ties and plans and objections.

TESSA HADLEY

VINCENT'S PARTY

(2024)

THE PARTY WAS in full swing. Evelyn could hear the sexy blare of the trad jazz almost as soon as she got off the bus at St Mary Redcliffe and began walking over to the Steam Packet, the pub that Vincent – who was a friend of Evelyn's older sister, Moira – had commandeered for the evening. He'd decided that they all needed a party to cheer them up, because the winter had been so bitter, and because now, in February, the incessant rain had turned the snow to slush. It was raining again this evening; the bus's wiper had beat its numb rhythm all the way into town, the pavements were dark, and the gutters ran with water. Frozen filthy formless lumps, the remainders of the snow, persisted at the street corners and in the deep recesses between buildings, loomed sinisterly in the gaping bomb sites. Crossing the road, Evelyn had to put up her umbrella – actually, her mother's worn old green umbrella with the broken rib and the duck's-head handle, which she'd borrowed without asking on her way out, because she'd lost her own somewhere. Probably she'd get in trouble for this tomorrow, but she didn't care; she was too full of agitated happiness. Anything could happen between now and tomorrow.

Evelyn couldn't believe her luck, that she was going to an actual party – and not just any dull, ordinary party but this wild one with her sister's friends, in a half-derelict old pub with a terrible reputation, hanging over the black water in the city docks. If her parents had known where the party was, they'd never have let her out, but she'd lied to them fluently and easily, saying that Moira had promised to look after her, and that they were meeting in the Victoria Rooms. She was proud of herself. Who knew that you could be a Sunday-school teacher one minute, asking the children to crayon in pictures of Jesus with a lost lamb tucked under his arm, and then lie to your parents with such perfectly calibrated, innocent sweetness?

The rain didn't matter; Evelyn was impervious to it. Picking her way between the streams of water rippling across the roads, not wanting to spoil her fashionable, unsuitable black ballet flats, she enjoyed the contrast between this desolate outer universe and the heat of the life burning inside her. When she'd had to change buses at the Centre, she'd gone into a cubicle in the Ladies' to take off her Wellington boots, and also the decent wool dress she'd put on over her party clothes, so that her parents couldn't see what she was wearing: skintight black slacks zipped up along the inside of her calves, black polo-neck jumper, wide red leather belt with a black buckle. Evelyn was very thin, with a long neck – a swan neck, she thought – a flat stomach, and jutting hip bones. She hoped that she looked spectacular, her hair scraped back from her face like a dancer's and breasts thrust upward in a new brassiere; she longed for and feared the moment when she would shed her thick winter coat and reveal herself. To tell the truth, she feared everything; part of her wanted to get right back on the 28 bus and go home. Peering at her reflection in the square of tin that served as a mirror above the sink in the Ladies' toilet, she had clipped huge false pearls to her ears – those were her mother's, too – and painted her mouth stickily with red lipstick. The boots and the dress were bundled now into a shopping bag, which she'd have to jettison somewhere, along with her coat and the umbrella, for collection later.

The Steam Packet's austere silhouette, three storeys tall, was stark against the gaps that bombs had left in the skyline: the rows of windows on the upper floors were dark or boarded up, but a yellowish light shone enticingly from the ground floor. A clamour of raised voices drew Evelyn towards it, her body beginning to move already to the music. Moira hadn't promised to look after her – in fact, Moira didn't even know that she was coming to the party, and probably wouldn't want her there, but Evelyn was desperate to be part of her sister's crowd. The girls were born two years apart; Moira had always complained about her kid sister tagging along after her friends. Evelyn had usually tagged along anyway, when they were turned out of the house to fend for themselves for the day, Moira jolting their baby brother along in the pram and intent on some mission with her gang, rolling up leaves in cigarette papers to smoke them, or climbing onto the roof of the glasshouse in the park, or spying on their neighbour who'd lost his mind and walked around nude in the garden.

It was Vincent who'd invited Evelyn to the party, last week when she'd bumped into him in Queens Road on her way to a lecture; he told her he'd persuaded the landlord of the Packet to let him take the place over for an evening. Vincent knew everyone: not just the arty people, although he was an art student like Moira, but also taxi-drivers and bookies and chip-shop owners, pub landlords and veteran soldiers who'd lost limbs in the first war; he talked to these characters for hours and learned their stories, catching them in clever charcoal drawings in his sketchbook. He paid court to a toothless old woman who ran a secondhand clothes shop, where garments were heaped in a rotting dark mulch against the window; you could see the moths and the fleas jumping out, Moira said, from between the layers of clothes. This old woman would save certain items for Vincent, so that he came to classes dressed in an airman's leather jacket or an evening cloak lined in red satin; Moira refused to sit near him then, because of the fleas and because the old clothes stank of naphthalene from the mothballs. Vincent was tall, with eager, moist brown eyes, a booming voice, and a lot of curly chestnut-brown hair. He wore a wide-brimmed soft black felt hat like Augustus John and played in a jug band.

'Vincent's very good-looking,' Evelyn had said experimentally to Moira once, as Moira was cutting out a skirt pinned with a paper pattern on the dining-room table, crunching her scissors confidently through the fabric, which parted cleanly in their wake. She was studying fashion at college and could do tailoring like a professional.

'Ye-es.'

'What do you mean, "ye-es"?'

'Shush, Evelyn, let me concentrate. I don't know. He's got all the ingredients but somehow he isn't attractive. Not to me, at any rate.'

Moira's discriminations were subtle and absolute.

Evelyn dropped her voice, so that their mother couldn't hear from the kitchen. 'Is he queer?'

'God, no. Don't be an idiot.'

'Well, I don't know. I've never known anyone who was queer.'

'You've known loads of them, only you never noticed it. Half of the awful old spinsters who taught at our school, for instance. But not Vince. Vince tries to get off with everyone. He'll probably try with you. You'd better watch out. Unless you do find him attractive, of course.'

'No, I don't think I do,' Evelyn said. How could she find him attractive, after Moira had said he wasn't? 'I know what you mean. He's sort of woolly, somehow.'

Moira laughed, in spite of herself. 'Woolly?'

'Yes, like a fuzzy old favourite toy or something. A Teddy bear with big glassy eyes.'

'Well, he's not my favourite toy.'

'Nor mine, either,' Evelyn said.

The Steam Packet was already full, with the band squeezed into a corner, blasting out music, and everyone shouting to be heard over it. The place was dimly lit by bare electric bulbs, dangling from loops of wire festooned along the old beams of the ceiling. Vincent explained delightedly that the pub hadn't been connected to mains electricity since the war; it was just piggybacking off someone else's supply. A few couples were dancing already, in a tight space where the tables had been pushed back; there was sawdust on the stone-flagged floor, the rough-hewn benches and tables and three-legged stools were scarred and gouged, and the plaster walls – stained a dark mahogany by tobacco smoke – were crowded with advertising for brands of beer and rum and pipe tobacco which hadn't existed for decades, alongside paintings of ships set on choppy blue seas. A chunk of tree smouldered sulkily to ash in a dirty open hearth at the far end of the room. The young people by this time were generating their own heat.

Vincent was officiating behind the bar, where a few sticky bottles were assembled in front of the ornate mirror glass; he was ladling out cider from an open tin bucket, and the pub landlord – wizened and tiny as a jockey, with blue eyes like clear chips of ice – was sitting on a barstool in front of it, overseeing things sceptically. He didn't drink the cider himself, apparently; he preferred neat gin – Hollands, he called it. Vincent said that he was pickled in it. Some of the rough-looking men standing at the bar were most likely his regular customers: it was a dockers' pub, Vincent had said, where prostitutes came looking for customers. Evelyn had never seen prostitutes, but she'd read about them in novels. It was a big thing among the art students to want to mingle across the boundaries of class that their parents were so intent upon policing: their mothers putting doilies on cake plates, objecting to milk or ketchup bottles on the table, ironing handkerchiefs and socks and dusters as if respectability depended upon it. Many of the students hadn't come far from the working class themselves; Vincent's dad was a plumber in Ashley Down. Moira and Evelyn's maternal grandfather had been a coal miner – and yet their father was petitioning to join the Masons. After the war, he'd got a job with the Port of Bristol Authority, and they'd moved down to Avonmouth from the north east of England, leaving their history behind, along with a whole tribe of aunts and uncles and cousins on their mother's side.

'Oh, it's you,' Moira remarked without enthusiasm when Evelyn had stowed her coat, and the bag with her boots and dress and umbrella, under a table in a corner, which was a makeshift cloakroom. Moira absorbed her sister's outfit in one scouring, appraising glance. 'Looks nice,' she said, grudging but fair. Evelyn thought now, however, that her Left Bank-themed black clothes had perhaps been the wrong choice for the Packet. Moira was wearing her striped full skirt and a cream blouse; someone had told her once that you should aim to make the other women in the room look overdressed. That was the difference between Moira and her, Evelyn thought. She would go for something striking and zany, which might work and might not, while Moira would never be so foolish as to take that risk. Evelyn veered between two extremes; either she spent hours dressing herself up extravagantly, or she slopped around at home in her oldest skirt and cardigan and slippers. Her scruffy self was her reading self. To give herself properly to a book she had to be crumpled and snug, oblivious of her appearance, scrunched up in an armchair with her shoes off and her legs tucked under her. When she was really reading, she forgot who she was. Yet when she went out to lectures or classes – she was in her first year at the university, studying French – she worked anxiously in front of the mirror to make herself look more like a student and an intellectual: beret tilted to one side, silk scarf fastened insouciantly around her throat. 'Insouciant,' she murmured with a French accent, gazing adoringly at herself, finishing off her outfit with a couple of books under her arm.

The two sisters weren't completely unalike in their appearance. There was a family stamp on both of them, and on their younger brother: they were all strong-featured, full-lipped, dark-browed, with a long doleful nose the girls hated, although it actually made their faces more interesting. The nose came from their father, who was handsome and stern: it was all right on a man, a war hero, first lieutenant on an aircraft carrier that had escorted merchant convoys across the Atlantic. Both sisters were good-looking, although Moira insisted that she wasn't, that she just knew how to make the best of herself.

'I look more like him,' Moira said. 'You're the lucky one.'

Their mother had pretty, soft Irish looks, although she'd let herself go and grown shapeless, because she was unhappy in the south and in her marriage. Moira was always telling her off for slouching, or eating too much starch. Moira was critical of her own defects, too, staring them down, calculating and resigned. 'I hate these lumps of fat under my arms, for instance. These I do have from Mam.'

Whenever she and Evelyn went out together, though, it was Moira the men were drawn to, with her self-possession and sophisticated allure; beside her, Evelyn felt girlish and gauche, no matter how hard she tried. 'You shouldn't talk too much,' Moira advised unhelpfully. 'Don't talk right in their faces.'

At Vincent's party, Moira had the dreamily smiling, assured look she wore in public, her attention only brushing gauzily against the present moment. And she'd managed to get a table in just the right position – not so near the band that conversation was difficult but commanding a good view. She was sitting with Josephine LaPalma and two men Evelyn had never seen before. Josephine modelled at the art college and was one of Vincent's characters, glamorous and dangerous, with a broad Bristol accent. It was a coup for him that he'd persuaded her to come. She was said to have gypsy blood, and her black hair reached down to her waist when she undid it; it was in a thick plait tonight, wound around her head. Everything about Josephine fitted in with the students' romantic idea of a bohemian life. She was even having an affair with a married man, a talented painter who taught at the college.

The two men looked keenly at Evelyn as she joined the table, and stood up to be introduced, as if they belonged somewhere more formal; the older one bent over the hand she held out, to kiss it. They fussed about getting her a chair until she said she could just squeeze onto the bench with Moira – 'Oho! Slumming it!' they cried. Their names were Paul and something she didn't quite catch, like Sandy or Simon, and they weren't quite right for Vincent's party: too conventional, something artificial and sneering barely concealed under the sugary surface. They behaved with that mixture of assurance and awkwardness which was a sign of being privileged and posh. Even Evelyn could see that their clothes were good – expensive, made with fine cloth – and the one who'd kissed her hand smelled of some subtle cologne. In the crowd jostling around them, the women wore peasant skirts and striped sailors' tops, and none of the men, apart from these two, were wearing ties. Evelyn couldn't help sneaking glances at the younger one, Paul, who didn't talk as much as his friend, and looked as if he might be quite drunk already. His movements and his speech were slow and syrupy, and he smiled privately, communing with himself, brilliantined treacle-coloured hair flopping across his forehead, blinking eyes and dimpled chin making him seem sleepy and childlike. His perfect features were like an angel's in a picture: upper lip very full, the curve of his cheek like a peach. He might be corrupt, Evelyn thought, remembering some of the poetry she knew.

Paul insisted on buying Evelyn a drink and she said she'd have a gin-and-orange. She hadn't really learned to like the taste of alcohol yet; she only liked its effects. The men thought she was very wise. 'The cider's undrinkable. We think that creatures have drowned in it.'

'Oh, they encourage creatures to drown in it,' Moira assured them solemnly. 'Everything adds to the flavour.'

She and Josephine were drinking the cider laced with blackcurrant, to make it palatable – most of the students did that.

'Well, Evelyn,' the older man asked, 'are you an art student, too?'

She told them that she wasn't, that she was studying French.

'French? La belle dame sans merci! Gosh, what brainy girls you all are. I'm perfectly terrified.'

Josephine reassured him languorously that he needn't worry; she was an absolute idiot. 'You don't look like an idiot to me,' he said. 'I expect you know which side your bread's buttered on.'

'She isn't an idiot,' Evelyn said. 'The artists all want to paint her.'

'I'll bet they do. I suppose they pay you to model, do they?' he asked Josephine.

'Nobody works for free.'

'Clothes on or off?'

He wasn't looking at Josephine as he asked this, but grinning at Paul.

Josephine was indifferent. 'Mostly off.'

'I wouldn't let any daughter of mine earn money that way.'

She laughed at him. 'Your daughter might be too ugly. Maybe they wouldn't want to paint her.'

This man had springy pale hair and rubbery, froggy features; his manicured hands – gathering the empty glasses or reaching to light their cigarettes, a gold signet ring on one stubby finger – made Evelyn think of that trick where you move coloured pots around so fast that no one can guess where the bean is hidden. Under cover of his attention to her and Moira, Evelyn saw, he was more fascinated by Josephine. He spoke to her differently – jeering and presumptuous and yet afraid of her. He said that he and Paul didn't know anyone at the party. They'd never met Vincent before; they'd bumped into him on the street outside and he'd persuaded them to come in. 'So you have to take pity on us and look after us,' he said, in a tone of wheedling, teasing flirtation.

Evelyn decided that these two men didn't care about art or literature, and she wished that Vincent hadn't invited them; yet Moira was energized and spiky, as if she were enjoying their sparring. Mostly she was talking to the older one, but, of course, her attention was really on the beautiful boy, Paul, who rested his chin on his fist and stared into his drink. The older man's name was Sinden, it turned out, which was his surname. He didn't like his Christian name, he explained, and wouldn't tell them what it was, however much they begged him. 'I can't believe the things women get interested in,' he protested. 'Now, you see, a man wouldn't care less about my Christian name, once I said I wasn't using it. What does it matter, something my mother chose at a time when I didn't have any say in it? I wouldn't trust her to name a dog of mine.'

'But imagine if there weren't any women in the world,' Evelyn said.

Sinden pretended he was anguished by that idea, grabbing her hand and pressing it against his shirtfront to make her feel his heart beating fast; the material of his white shirt was clammy from his body heat, slippery against the vest he wore underneath. He groaned suggestively. 'No women! Alas, alack! What would we do without them? But I'll let you in on a little secret, Evelyn: it isn't your curiosity we adore you for.'

'But, no, seriously, imagine it,' Evelyn persisted, trying to have a proper conversation. 'No one would find anything out if there were no women asking questions. All the secrets would just rot away unnoticed. There would just be a sort of empty framework left. Like one of those wire things they build up plaster on. An armature.'

'I love a bit of gossip,' Josephine said. 'Keeps the world going round.'

Sinden winked at her. 'It isn't gossip keeps it going round.'

'You think it's money, then? Or sex?'

'That's a poser for you, Sinden,' Paul said, lifting his head from his drink. 'Money or sex, old chap?'

'Depends what time of day,' Sinden said. 'Depends how many drinks I've had.'

'You need the money first,' Paul said. 'To buy the drinks that make you think that you don't care about the money.'

Sinden beckoned them closer, speaking in a hoarse whisper; Evelyn moved her knees away from his under the table. 'My friend here has got plenty of it, too,' he said. 'Money coming out of Paul's ears, doesn't need to do a day's work in his life. Let's just say that once upon a time his family were in the tobacco industry, and, when they sold, they invested the proceeds wisely.'

Listening to this description of his wealth, Paul looked bashful and complacent, almost coy. Sinden told them that Paul had been giving him a tour of the war damage in Bristol; he'd never visited before. 'Little did we know we were going to bump into you girls! So Paul's been showing me around and I'm convinced there are opportunities here. For the right sort of people. A fresh start for the city. Building for the future.'

'Do you know about building, then?' Moira asked. 'Is that what you do?'

'I'm not a builder.' He laughed. 'Do I look like a builder? But I do have very good contacts, with the right sort of men who have the right sort of friends. Contacts are the important thing.'

'Sounds like profiteering to me,' Josephine said. 'I hate profiteering.'

'And what's wrong with making a nice clean profit, out of something everybody wants? That way we win all round.'

'They should just cut out the middleman. Then everything in this city would be a damn sight cheaper. Building by the people, for the people.'

'She's a Red!' Sinden exclaimed delightedly, staring at her with his goggle eyes. 'I've never met a real live Red before! Seen a few dead ones.'

'Take a good look,' Josephine said. 'Looking is free.'

She settled herself as if she were posing, presenting her head in its dramatic profile, magnificent as a ship's figurehead. Sinden couldn't believe, he said, staring at her, why three such lovely girls hadn't been snapped up. How come they weren't wearing engagement rings? Weren't there any red-blooded men around here?

'Moira is engaged,' Evelyn blurted out, as if she were defending their honour, or Moira's at least. 'Sort of engaged. Her boyfriend's gone as a policeman to Malaya.'

'Cass isn't my boyfriend.'

'Christ, the poor sap,' Sinden said.

Evelyn protested, astonished. 'Why a poor sap?'

'I doubt if you'll see him again.'

'But we will see him!'

'Don't suppose he speaks a word of Chinese. I know that game. Put him in charge of a squad of men he can't talk to, armed with weapons he doesn't know how to use, in a terrain he doesn't understand. They'll supply him with some soft-skinned Austin or Land Rover. Done for at the first road ambush, driving between the plantations he's supposed to be protecting.'

'But how do you know all that?'

He tapped the side of his nose. 'I know what I know.'

'And why are you gloating? It sounds as if you're glad that he might die.'

Sinden's horrible knowingness was hard and irrefutable as a rock, Evelyn thought. You couldn't push back against it unless you understood about guns and vehicles and politics, all those brutally real things. Moira stared at him dry-eyed, challenging him to find the least sign that she cared. 'Cass wasn't my boyfriend. I told him not to go. I knew it was stupid. We never were engaged. He kept on about this cash bonus they were offering, at the end of one year.'

'Good luck with that,' he scoffed. 'Getting through to the end of a year.'

'Risking his neck,' Paul said, stirring to wakefulness and slurring his words, 'when he could have been spending the evening here with you.'

'You see? Paul likes you,' Sinden said triumphantly. 'I knew that he'd like you. He's pretty choosy, our friend Paul, but he likes you, Moira. Now, why don't you two lovebirds get dancing, while I buy us more drinks?'

Josephine said then that she was leaving, going on to another party. Evelyn didn't want anything; she hadn't finished her first gin-and-orange. The band was playing a bluesy number, and as Paul stood up from the table he pretended to be parping along on an imaginary slide trombone, as if the music were a comedy laid on for his benefit; Sinden joined in on an imaginary snare drum, screwing up his face to feel the beat. Evelyn was buffeted by a gust of rage at their obliviousness. Didn't they know that this music was serious, it came out of human suffering, it wasn't a game? The student crowd were all jazz enthusiasts, worshipping Louis Armstrong and Buddy Bolden and King Oliver, whose lives and art set a high-water mark for everything tragic and joyous. The musicians in the band were all just white Bristolians, but seemed to borrow something of that glamour.

'First the good news, Mr Edmonds, you're going to get closure.'

Evelyn thought that Moira might refuse to dance, if she was upset by how Sinden had spoken about Cass. But she moved suavely enough into Paul's arms, with a remote, vague look as if she hardly saw him. Paul wasn't tall, but he wasn't slight like a boy: he was muscled and substantial, more authoritative now that he was on his feet. When they'd squeezed their way among the couples on the dance floor, he let his head droop onto Moira's shoulder and his body rested heavily against hers, as if he really were drunk. He danced well, though, responding to the music's sluggish melancholy. Evelyn had the surprising thought that bodies were sometimes wiser than the people inside them. She'd have liked to impress somebody with this idea, but couldn't explain it to Sinden, who would misunderstand her deliberately. When she saw Paul rouse and lift his head to say something in Moira's ear, pulling her closer with his slow smile and sleepy eyes, Evelyn was stricken with envious desire, in spite of everything. Whatever he said ignited some response in Moira, so that she smiled back secretively, pretending to reproach him, pushing him off a little, not giving anything away. Evelyn had a horror then of Sinden asking her to dance out of sheer obligation, taking second best. She didn't want to dance with him anyway; she didn't like him. So when he got up to go to the bar she made her escape with Josephine, said she was popping outside for a bit of air.

'Don't fall in the water,' Sinden said. 'It's dark out there.'

Emerging so abruptly from the noise and heat of the pub into the night's blackness and wetness and quiet, Evelyn wondered for a moment if she was drunk, but that didn't seem likely after one gin. 'Don't men just like to talk?' Josephine said. 'They love the sound of their own voices.' Then she hurried away, her big coat flapping, her head down in her gypsy scarf, heels clacking on the pavement, as she weaved her way among the shadowy, slouching men, not afraid of walking by herself through the docklands. It wasn't quite dark: there were street lamps on the road and lights on some of the wharves and in the timber yards. Light seeped from the pub windows onto its forecourt, where the cobbles gleamed wetly although it had stopped raining; beyond this forecourt a wall dropped abruptly to the water, ten feet below, in a narrow channel that cut through from the Floating Harbour into the Basin. On summer nights, couples would sit on the wall, swinging their legs, drinking the lethal Kingston Black cider, but in winter the idea of that enclosed invisible water was furtive and chilly. When something splashed in the blackness, Evelyn thought of rats. A call from one of the ships in the Basin, in no language she recognized, bounced eerily along the surface of the water.

Probably there wasn't really any other party, she thought; probably Josephine was hurrying to meet her lover, the married artist. Then she felt sick with loneliness. She longed for a lover of her own and was ashamed of her inexperience, her poor judgement. Things had been hopeless when she was still a schoolgirl, but she'd thought that something would happen now that she'd started at the university – where surely she would thrive, because she was clever. She'd imagined herself surrounded by admirers, and had even been afraid that she'd settle too easily, for someone who wasn't good enough. Evelyn could have loved Moira's Cass, for instance, Robert Cassidy, although she didn't know him well; she'd met him only a few times, when Moira had allowed her to come to the pub with her crowd. Moira kept her emotional life strictly apart from her family, and their parents weren't to be told that she and Cass were engaged – and, anyhow, now apparently they weren't. Yet he'd seemed enthralling to Evelyn: bullish, talented, popular, a burly, freckled, red-headed rugby player, his blue eyes watchful and wary. He was a joker and a tease, with a gift for drawing caricatures of his friends. Since Cass had gone off to Malaya, Evelyn had loyally taken a great interest in the Emergency, looking out for snippets about it in the newspapers. It was called an Emergency, their father said, because if they called it a war then the plantation owners wouldn't be covered by their insurance.

It was too cold outside without her coat; Evelyn had only come out, anyway, to get away from where she was stuck in that corner with Moira and Sinden and Paul. She needed another drink to give her the courage to throw herself back into the party, where she barely knew anyone, and no one was interested in her. A character in a novel, in her situation, would break in on conversations and introduce herself, then turn out to be charming and brilliant; people would be amazed by her ideas and her sex appeal, her stylish gamine haircut. Just as Evelyn was imagining this, she heard someone come out from the pub entrance behind her and say hello. It was Donald, from her French class at the university. When Vincent invited her to the party, Evelyn had been on her way to meet Donald in Carwardines for coffee – they were going to go over some ideas about Racine's *Phèdre*. She'd passed the invitation on, wanting to impress Donald with her bold sociability, mingling with the rough life in the docks, but hadn't imagined that he'd dare to come. He was wearing the same unsuitable striped blazer that he wore to classes.

'Are you having a good time?' he said.

'Isn't this just an amazing place? Very "Fleurs du Mal".'

'Is that the name of the cider?'

'Oh, dear, did you drink it? I should have warned you – you need to put blackcurrant in, to take the taste away. Was it very awful?'

'Definitely the worst thing I've ever drunk. You look stunning, by the way. I'd drink the cider bucket dry, it goes without saying, for the chance of spending an evening with you. The sort of ordeal knights undergo in the old stories.'

'I never heard of one drinking a bucket of cider.'

'They always give girls the expurgated version.'

Evelyn liked Donald, but – it was just her luck – he wouldn't do for a boyfriend. He looked about sixteen, to start with: overeager and stumbling and pallid, with sticking-out ears and a tense, lumpy jaw. He'd been a boarder at Queen Elizabeth's Hospital, where the boys' uniform hadn't changed in centuries – a sort of long dress buttoning up the front, with yellow stockings and black shoes. Evelyn had seen these boys tormented in the street by children from the local schools, and, once she knew that Donald had worn the yellow stockings, couldn't help imagining him in them. When Moira first met him, she'd said that he was really sweet, pity he was so N.P.A., which meant Non-Physically Attractive. Donald took off his blazer when Evelyn shivered and put it around her shoulders. 'You should come here in the summer,' she said, encouragingly. 'In the summer you can sit out on the dock.'

'I should think people fall in, though. After a pint or two of Fleurs du Mal.'

'Are you drunk, Don? I don't think I've ever seen you when you're drunk. I wonder what you're like.'

'I'm adorable, apparently.'

'Do you feel drunk now?'

He frowned, as if testing himself inwardly. 'Drunk enough to fall in the water, not drunk enough to risk going anywhere near it. It's an odd kind of drunkenness, different to beer, lighter and more extreme, as if someone had just sliced off the top of my mind, like taking the top off an egg. Yet ask me to supply the past historic first-person plural of the verb saisir, and I bet I could still do it.'

'Nous saisîmes, of course, you oaf.'

He sighed and complained that she was too quick for him.

Evelyn shuddered inside the blazer's warmth and Donald

put an arm tentatively around her shoulders. 'Don, if we went back inside,' she said, 'would you buy me a drink? Because I need a boost. I'm not really enjoying myself much at this party. I'm not talking to anybody, or not anybody I actually like – I mean, apart from you, of course. I'm always disappointed at parties. I long to be, you know, a succès fou, but I never am.'

'You're a succès fou with me,' he said.

'Yes,' she said with a flare of irritation. 'But that's not enough, is it?'

'I suppose not.'

Donald bought Evelyn a gin-and-orange with double gin in it, and after that the party went much better. She wasn't exactly a succès fou, but she submerged herself effectively in the flamboyant, quarrelsome, ecstatic, flirting mass, drifting between different groups as if she were always on her way somewhere else. More drinks were bought for her from time to time, by one man or another; she danced with a couple of these men. In lieu of a lover, she decided to be in love with the glorious, sinuous, shameless music, and with the whole jazz band collectively, from the droopy-faced ironic pianist wreathed in his cigar smoke to the grinning drummer perched so tautly and eagerly upright on his stool; she even included the brooding trumpet player, whip-thin, the quiff of his thick black hair oiled like a pelt, who glared at her when she said something loudly, by mistake, over his solo in 'West End Blues'. She danced with Donald only once: predictably, he was a hopeless dancer, with no sense of rhythm. 'Are you actually counting?' she asked, accusingly.

'I thought that was what you were supposed to do.'

'Only when you're learning. Afterwards, you've got to just feel it, in your limbs.'

'I apologize for my unfeeling limbs,' he said.

'And the counting's supposed to relate to the beat of the music. It's not just something random ticking over inside your own head.'

'Sorry.'

Evelyn didn't lose sight of her sister, in her circulation around the party. Moira hadn't stuck with those two men, thank goodness; she'd shaken them off and danced with different people. She'd been at the heart of the knots of fun and laughter that Evelyn had most wanted to break into. Had someone replaced Robert Cassidy in Moira's affections? Evelyn kept a lookout, but couldn't see anything obvious. Towards the end of the evening, when Evelyn was thinking she needed to leave, to catch the last bus home to Avonmouth, she made her way to where Moira was standing, talking again, as it happened, to Sinden and Paul, who had their coats on and their hats in their hands. Evelyn didn't know whether Moira was coming home with her or not; often she stayed over in town with friends.

'We're making efforts to abduct you and your sister,' Sinden said jocularly to Evelyn. 'Paul wants to give you girls a lift somewhere, anywhere. The night outside is not only dismal – it's also young. I know a little place we can get a drink after hours, something that doesn't taste of dead animals. Surely nobody wants to go to bed yet?'

'No matter how dog-tired I am, I can't sleep,' Paul volunteered unexpectedly with a drunk's solipsism, more or less talking to himself. 'Soon as the old head hits the pillow, bang! Whole caboodle starts up again, the merry-go-round.'

Evelyn said she didn't want a lift, though it was very kind. She'd rather get the bus.

'No monkeying around,' Sinden assured her. 'Evelyn, I swear. If you want to go straight home, we'll take you straight home. But there's a business proposition I'd like to discuss with your sister.'

She looked at Moira anxiously. 'What kind of business proposition?'

'A good friend of mine is in lingerie,' Sinden said. 'Very exclusive and expensive. He has a salon and a small workshop in London, and I'm aware he's wanting to expand into dress design. All I'm saying is that I'd like to take a look at Moira's portfolio – not tonight, of course, but some other time. If I thought her work was good, then I could introduce her to my friend. At least let me give you my card, Moira, with my telephone number.'

Moira said it was an interesting idea and she would think about it; she took the card and put it in her purse. Sinden insisted again that in the meantime they should come for a spin in the Bentley. 'I'm happy to take the wheel, if you're afraid Paul's had a few too many.'

Evelyn was about to repeat that she'd rather not, when Moira seized her by the arm and jerked her away. 'Wait for us here,' she said to Sinden. 'We'll get our coats, then we need to pop upstairs and powder our noses.'

'But I don't want to, Moira,' Evelyn protested sotto voce, as her sister pulled her towards the bar. 'I hate those men.'

'Just follow me,' Moira hissed, not letting go of her grip. They found their coats and Evelyn's bag; when Evelyn saw Donald watching her, solitary, across the room, she was smitten with compunction. Perhaps before she left she'd dance with him once more, even though he was hopeless. The sisters hesitated, coats over their arms, at the foot of a dark staircase; they'd seen girls disappearing up here in the course of the evening, presumably in search of the toilet – impossible to tell, when those girls came down again, if they'd been successful. The men just went to pee whenever they needed, in the harbour outside. 'Is there a Ladies' upstairs?' they asked Vincent, who looked doubtful and said that not many ladies drank in the Packet as a rule.

Evelyn was hesitant. 'We could wait until we get home.'

'I can't wait.'

Now that they'd imagined relieving themselves, they were both desperate to go. It was very dark on the stairs. Evelyn discovered a light switch and tried it, but nothing came on; they felt their way, hanging on to a greasy handrail. Moira found a book of matches in her bag and by their wavering feeble light – they were only little paper ones, the kind they give you in hotels – she and Evelyn climbed the winding wood-panelled staircase and peered into rooms, one after another, of an extraordinary ancientness and awfulness. Some had their windows boarded up; in others, they could make out, by a dim light creeping through filthy windowpanes, looming forms that might have been rolled-up drugget, broken chairs, crates full of bottles, coiled rope, heaps of white china crockery, a birdcage, a painted sign lying on its side. The staves of a barrel, whose hoops had burst, fanned in a toothy grin. Each time a match went out, the dank smell of the place – tarry and rotten – settled on them like the whole foul weight of the past. 'I suppose this would be Vincent's idea of heaven,' Moira said disparagingly. The top floor was emptier, but still none of these rooms was any kind of bathroom or toilet; in one of them, where iron bedsprings were propped against one wall and the torn old wallpaper was printed with flower baskets, Moira exclaimed, 'Oh, I'm just going to go right here.'

Evelyn squealed. 'You can't! Moira!'

'I can! No one will ever know. The place stinks anyway. Hold my coat, will you, and strike another match for me? I don't want to get pee on my dress.'

They were probably both drunker than they realized. Moira hoicked up her skirt and petticoat, pulled down her knickers, spread her legs, and peed against the wall with a satisfying splashing. 'God, that's good,' she said, laughing. And when she finished she struck the last match for Evelyn, who had more difficulty, tugging her tight slacks down.

'What if anyone comes? What about rats?'

'Well, hurry up, then.'

Evelyn screamed while she peed, imagining the rats. When the match went out, as she struggled to pull up her slacks, Moira told her that Cass was dead.

'What?'

'His mother wrote to me last week, at the art college. He was ambushed. I suppose he was shot, just like the man said. It was all my fault. Which is what his mother more or less thinks, too.'

Evelyn stood frozen with her slacks halfway up her thighs. 'Oh, Moira. Oh, no.'

'I feel so awful. He said he'd sign up if I wouldn't go with him to Paris.'

'That doesn't make it your fault.'

'I told him that I didn't love him. That I loved someone else.'

Moira sobbed just once, or at least Evelyn thought it was a sob: an ugly barking noise, roughly torn out of her, almost like exasperation. When Evelyn tried to console her, Moira pushed her away, wiping her eyes brusquely with the back of her hand. Evelyn sobbed, too, in sympathy with her sister; she couldn't truly grieve for Robert Cassidy, she realized, because she'd hardly known him. His death was too improbable – he had seemed so solidly alive, with his loud laugh, the explosion of his freckles. As the girls grew used to the dark, each could make out the other's shape; the darkness anyhow seemed thinner up here at the top of the building. There must have been a broken windowpane, because the wind whistled and a draught blew around their shoulders.

'So who is the someone else?'

'I can't tell you. Because it isn't really anything. Not yet.'

'Who, though? You have to tell!'

Moira couldn't suppress her shudder of voluptuousness. 'The trumpet player.'

Evelyn felt like a fool. Of course it was: with his forbidding frown and his high notes. She saw, in a flash of revelation, that Moira had been performing that entire evening, dancing and flirting with Paul and all those other men, for the eyes of the trumpet player only. 'And does he know? I mean, what you feel about him?'

'He sort of knows. He knows, yes. Though he's still with someone else right now.'

In her sister's expression – vivid even in the dimness, and so familiar from their childhood – Evelyn saw recklessness, fear, concealment, power. Moira had made such efforts to transform herself, when they moved down to Bristol, into this controlled, poised young woman. Yet some essence of the fierce, bold child persisted in her, and had been diverted into new channels, sexual and personal.

'And now,' Moira declared, 'we have to get away from those hideous men.'

'I thought you liked them!'

'I hate them. I could kill them.'

At one end of the landing on this upper floor, light came weakly through a half-glassed metal-framed door, which led onto a fire escape. Moira tried the door handle, tugging it abruptly so that the door opened and boisterous wet night rushed in. 'I thought so,' she exclaimed in triumph, her voice whipping away from her in the blast.

'No, Moy, I can't. I'm not going down there. Not in a thousand years.'

'You can!'

'Why don't we just go downstairs normally and insist on getting the bus home?'

'Because you can never get away from that kind of man. They'll inveigle us into something or other and then it'll be too late.'

Evelyn was sure that she could have got away from them. But Moira had buttoned up her coat already and stepped out onto the rickety, rusty platform. Evelyn screamed again: was the fire escape swaying away from the stuccoed side of the building? 'It's fine,' Moira reassured her. 'Just a little bit shaky. I'll go first.'

This was more or less what she'd said all those years ago, when they'd walked on the metal struts across the glasshouse roof in the park, up in the north. That hadn't ended well: Moira had put her foot through the glass and needed twelve stitches – they'd got into serious trouble. At least this fire escape was a proper stairway, with a banister to hold on to, and not just one of those ladders attached to a wall. Moira ran down swiftly and lightly, with a jangle of her heels on the iron, to the bottom, which was still about six feet off the ground, in an open yard at the side of the pub. Then she jumped like a cat, landing gracefully in a crouch on all fours, pale coat billowing around her in the wet.

'See! It's easy.'

Evelyn stood on the narrow platform at the top, sick and dizzy and exalted, while the wind flew at her and threw rain at her. Lights on the ships in the Basin and on the wharves were reflected in the black water; beyond the harbour she could make out the great masses of the city against the night sky, its ghostly terraces climbing the hills. How could she take in that Cass was dead, while she was still alive and young? All the kingdoms of the world, and the glory of them, were in that giddy moment spread beneath her. Evelyn made her way down the fire escape more cautiously than Moira, then hesitated at the bottom.

'Throw me your bag,' Moira said. 'What's in it?'

'A dress I wore so that they couldn't see me. And Mam's umbrella.'

'She'll be annoyed. It's her whist drive tonight.'

'Oh, Moira, are you full of grief?'

'Just jump,' Moira said impatiently. 'Trust me.'

And Evelyn jumped and she was all right. She was jubilant, landing in a crunch of gravel beside her sister, though the jolt shocked all thought out of her body for a moment, and her palms stung from the sharpness of the stones, down there in that filthy salty bitter underworld of dark.

LAST HURRAHS

EDGAR ALLAN POE

THE MASQUE OF THE RED DEATH

(1842)

THE 'RED DEATH' had long devastated the country. No pestilence had ever been so fatal, or so hideous. Blood was its Avatar and its seal – the redness and the horror of blood. There were sharp pains, and sudden dizziness, and then profuse bleeding at the pores, with dissolution. The scarlet stains upon the body and especially upon the face of the victim, were the pest ban which shut him out from the aid and from the sympathy of his fellow-men. And the whole seizure, progress, and termination of the disease, were the incidents of half an hour.

But the Prince Prospero was happy and dauntless and sagacious. When his dominions were half depopulated, he summoned to his presence a thousand hale and light-hearted friends from among the knights and dames of his court, and with these retired to the deep seclusion of one of his castellated abbeys. This was an extensive and magnificent structure, the creation of the prince's own eccentric yet august taste. A strong and lofty wall girdled it in. This wall had gates of iron. The courtiers, having entered, brought furnaces and massy hammers and welded the bolts. They resolved to leave means neither of ingress nor egress to the sudden impulses of despair or of frenzy from within. The abbey was amply provisioned. With such precautions the courtiers might bid defiance to contagion. The external world could take care of itself. In the meantime it was folly to grieve, or to think. The prince had provided all the appliances of pleasure. There were buffoons, there were improvisatori, there were ballet-dancers, there were musicians, there was Beauty, there was wine. All these and security were within. Without was the 'Red Death.'

It was toward the close of the fifth or sixth month of his seclusion, and while the pestilence raged most furiously abroad, that the Prince Prospero entertained his thousand friends at a masked ball of the most unusual magnificence.

It was a voluptuous scene, that masquerade. But first let me tell of the rooms in which it was held. There were seven – an imperial suite. In many palaces, however, such suites form a long and straight vista, while the folding doors slide back nearly to the walls on either hand, so that the view of the whole extent is scarcely impeded. Here the case was very different; as might have been expected from the duke's love of the *bizarre*. The apartments were so irregularly disposed that the vision embraced but little more than one at a time. There was a sharp turn at every twenty or thirty yards, and at each turn a novel effect. To the right and left, in the middle of each wall, a tall and narrow Gothic window looked out upon a closed corridor which pursued the windings of the suite. These windows were of stained glass whose color varied in accordance with the prevailing hue of the decorations of the chamber into which it opened. That at the eastern extremity was hung, for example, in blue – and vividly blue were its windows. The second chamber was purple in its ornaments and tapestries, and here the panes were purple. The third was green throughout, and so were the casements. The fourth was furnished and lighted with orange – the fifth with white – the sixth with violet. The seventh apartment was closely shrouded in black velvet tapestries that hung all over the ceiling and down the walls, falling in heavy folds upon a carpet of the same material and hue. But in this chamber only, the color of the windows failed to correspond with the decorations. The panes here were scarlet – a deep blood color. Now in no one of the seven apartments was there any lamp or candelabrum, amid the profusion of golden ornaments that lay scattered to and fro or depended from the roof. There was no light of any kind emanating from lamp or candle within the suite of chambers. But in the corridors that followed the suite, there stood, opposite to each window, a heavy tripod, bearing a brazier of fire, that projected its rays through the tinted glass and so glaringly illumined the room. And thus were produced a multitude of gaudy and fantastic appearances. But in the western or black chamber the effect of the fire-light that streamed upon the dark hangings through the blood-tinted panes was ghastly in the extreme, and produced so wild a look upon the countenances of those who entered, that there were few of the company bold enough to set foot within its precincts at all.

It was in this apartment, also, that there stood against the western wall, a gigantic clock of ebony. Its pendulum swung to and fro with a dull, heavy, monotonous clang; and when the minute-hand made the circuit of the face, and the hour was to be stricken, there came from the brazen lungs of the clock a sound which was clear and loud and deep and exceedingly musical, but of so peculiar a note and emphasis that, at each lapse of an hour, the musicians of the orchestra were constrained to pause, momentarily, in their performance, to hearken to the sound; and thus the waltzers perforce ceased their evolutions; and there was a brief disconcert of the whole gay company; and, while the chimes of the clock yet rang, it was observed that the giddiest grew pale, and the more aged and sedate passed their hands over their brows as if in confused revery or meditation. But when the echoes had fully ceased, a light laughter at once pervaded the assembly; the musicians looked at each other and smiled as if at their own nervousness and folly, and made whispering vows, each to the other, that the next chiming of the clock should produce in them no similar emotion; and then, after the lapse of sixty minutes (which embrace three thousand and six hundred seconds of the Time that flies), there came yet another chiming of the clock, and then were the same disconcert and tremulousness and meditation as before.

But, in spite of these things, it was a gay and magnificent revel. The tastes of the duke were peculiar. He had a fine eye for colors and effects. He disregarded the *decora* of mere fashion. His plans were bold and fiery, and his conceptions glowed with barbaric lustre. There are some who would have thought him mad. His followers felt that he was not. It was necessary to hear and see and touch him to be *sure* that he was not.

He had directed, in great part, the movable embellishments of the seven chambers, upon occasion of this great *fête*; and it was his own guiding taste which had given character to the masqueraders. Be sure they were grotesque. There were much glare and glitter and piquancy and phantasm – much of what has been since seen in 'Hernani.' There were arabesque figures with unsuited limbs and appointments. There were delirious fancies such as the madman fashions. There were much of the beautiful, much of the wanton, much of the *bizarre*, something of the terrible, and not a little of that which might have excited disgust. To and fro in the seven chambers there stalked, in fact, a multitude of dreams. And these – the dreams – writhed in and about, taking hue from the rooms, and causing the wild music of the orchestra to seem as the echo of their steps. And, anon, there strikes the ebony clock which stands in the hall of the velvet.

And then, for a moment, all is still, and all is silent, save the voice of the clock. The dreams are stiff-frozen as they stand. But the echoes of the chime die away – they have endured but an instant – and a light, half-subdued laughter floats after them as they depart. And now again the music swells, and the dreams live, and writhe to and fro more merrily than ever, taking hue from the many-tinted windows through which stream the rays from the tripods. But to the chamber which lies most westwardly of the seven there are now none of the maskers who venture; for the night is waning away; and there flows a ruddier light through the blood-colored panes; and the blackness of the sable drapery appals; and to him whose foot falls upon the sable carpet, there comes from the near clock of ebony a muffled peal more solemnly emphatic than any which reaches *their* ears who indulge in the more remote gaieties of the other apartments.

But these other apartments were densely crowded, and in them beat feverishly the heart of life. And the revel went whirlingly on, until at length there commenced the sounding of midnight upon the clock. And then the music ceased, as I have told; and the evolutions of the waltzers were quieted; and there was an uneasy cessation of all things as before. But now there were twelve strokes to be sounded by the bell of the clock; and thus it happened, perhaps that more of thought crept, with more of time, into the meditations of the thoughtful among those who revelled. And thus too, it happened, perhaps, that before the last echoes of the last chime had utterly sunk into silence, there were many individuals in the crowd who had found leisure to become aware of the presence of a masked figure which had arrested the attention of no single individual before. And the rumor of this new presence having spread itself whisperingly around, there arose at length from the whole company a buzz, or murmur, expressive of disapprobation and surprise – then, finally, of terror, of horror, and of disgust.

In an assembly of phantasms such as I have painted, it may well be supposed that no ordinary appearance could have excited such sensation. In truth the masquerade license of the night was nearly unlimited; but the figure in question had out-Heroded Herod, and gone beyond the bounds of even the prince's indefinite decorum. There are chords in the hearts of the most reckless which cannot be touched without emotion. Even with the utterly lost, to whom life and death are equally jests, there are matters of which no jest can be made. The whole company, indeed, seemed now deeply to feel that in the costume and bearing of the stranger neither wit nor propriety existed. The figure was tall and gaunt, and shrouded from head to foot in the habiliments of the grave. The mask which concealed the visage was made so nearly to resemble the countenance of a stiffened corpse that the closest scrutiny must have had difficulty in detecting the cheat. And yet all this might have been endured, if not approved, by the mad revellers around. But the mummer had gone so far as to assume the type of the Red Death. His vesture was dabbled in *blood* – and his broad brow, with all the features of the face, was besprinkled with the scarlet horror.

When the eyes of Prince Prospero fell upon this spectral image (which, with a slow and solemn movement, as if more fully to sustain its *rôle*, stalked to and fro among the waltzers) he was seen to be convulsed, in the first moment with a strong shudder either of terror or distaste; but, in the next, his brow reddened with rage.

'Who dares' – he demanded hoarsely of the courtiers who stood near him – 'who dares insult us with this blasphemous mockery? Seize him and unmask him – that we may know whom we have to hang, at sunrise, from the battlements!'

It was in the eastern or blue chamber in which stood the Prince Prospero as he uttered these words. They rang throughout the seven rooms loudly and clearly, for the prince was a bold and robust man, and the music had become hushed at the waving of his hand.

It was in the blue room where stood the prince, with a group of pale courtiers by his side. At first, as he spoke, there was a slight rushing movement of this group in the direction of the intruder, who, at the moment was also near at hand, and now, with deliberate and stately step, made closer approach to the speaker. But from a certain nameless awe with which the mad assumptions of the mummer had inspired the whole party, there were found none who put forth hand to seize him; so that, unimpeded, he passed within a yard of the prince's person; and, while the vast assembly, as if with one impulse, shrank from the centres of the rooms to the walls, he made his way uninterruptedly, but with the same solemn and measured step which had distinguished him from the first, through the blue chamber to the purple – through the purple to the green – through the green to the orange – through this again to the white – and even thence to the violet, ere a decided movement had been made to arrest him. It was then, however, that the Prince Prospero, maddening with rage and the shame of his own momentary cowardice, rushed hurriedly through the six chambers, while none followed him on account of a deadly terror that had seized upon all. He bore aloft a drawn dagger, and had approached, in rapid impetuosity, to within three or four feet of the retreating figure, when the latter, having attained the extremity of the velvet apartment, turned suddenly and confronted his pursuer. There was a sharp cry – and the dagger dropped gleaming upon the sable carpet, upon which, instantly afterward, fell prostrate in death the Prince Prospero. Then, summoning the wild courage of despair, a throng of the revellers at once threw themselves into the black apartment, and, seizing the mummer, whose tall figure stood erect and motionless within the shadow of the ebony clock, gasped in unutterable horror at finding the grave cerements and corpse-like mask, which they handled with so violent a rudeness, untenanted by any tangible form.

And now was acknowledged the presence of the Red Death. He had come like a thief in the night. And one by one dropped the revellers in the blood-bedewed halls of their revel, and died each in the despairing posture of his fall. And the life of the ebony clock went out with that of the last of the gay. And the flames of the tripods expired. And Darkness and Decay and the Red Death held illimitable dominion over all.

GUY DE MAUPASSANT

THE NECKLACE

(1884)

Translated by Marjorie Laurie

(*La Parure*)

SHE WAS ONE of those pretty and charming girls who, by some freak of destiny, are born into families that have always held subordinate appointments. Possessing neither dowry nor expectations, she had no hope of meeting some man of wealth and distinction, who would understand her, fall in love with her, and wed her. So she consented to marry a small clerk in the Ministry of Public Instruction.

She dressed plainly, because she could not afford to be elegant, but she felt as unhappy as if she had married beneath her. Women are dependent on neither caste nor ancestry. With them, beauty, grace, and charm take the place of birth and breeding. In their case, natural delicacy, instinctive refinement, and adaptability constitute their claims to aristocracy and raise girls of the lower classes to an equality with the greatest of great ladies. She was eternally restive under the conviction that she had been born to enjoy every refinement and luxury. Depressed by her humble surroundings, the sordid walls of her dwelling, its worn furniture and shabby fabrics were a torment to her. Details which another woman of her class would scarcely have noticed, tortured her and filled her with resentment. The sight of her little Breton maid-of-all-work roused in her forlorn repinings and frantic yearnings. She pictured to herself silent antechambers, upholstered with oriental tapestry, lighted by great bronze standard lamps, where two tall footmen in knee-breeches slumbered in huge arm-chairs, overcome by the oppressive heat from the stove. She dreamed of spacious drawing-rooms with hangings of antique silk, and beautiful tables laden with priceless ornaments; of fragrant and coquettish boudoirs, exquisitely adapted for afternoon chats with intimate friends, men of note and distinction, whose attentions are coveted by every woman.

She would sit down to dinner at the round table, its cloth already three days old, while her husband, seated opposite to her, removed the lid from the soup-tureen and exclaimed, '*Pot-au-feu!* How splendid! My favourite soup!' But her own thoughts were dallying with the idea of exquisite dinners and shining silver, in rooms whose tapestried walls were gay with antique figures and grotesque birds in fairy forests. She would dream of delicious dishes served on wonderful plate, of soft, whispered nothings, which evoke a sphinx-like smile, while one trifles with the pink flesh of a trout or the wing of a plump pullet.

She had no pretty gowns, no jewels, nothing – and yet she cared for nothing else. She felt that it was for such things as these that she had been born. What joy it would have given her to attract, to charm, to be envied by women, courted by men! She had a wealthy friend, who had been at school at the same convent, but after a time she refused to go and see her, because she suffered so acutely after each visit. She spent whole days in tears of grief, regret, despair, and misery.

One evening her husband returned home in triumph with a large envelope in his hand.

'Here is something for you,' he cried.

Hastily she tore open the envelope and drew out a printed card with the following inscription:

'The Minister of Public Instruction and Madame Georges Ramponneau have the honour to request the company of Monsieur and Madame Loisel at an At Home at the Education Office on Monday, 18th January.'

Instead of being delighted as her husband had hoped, she flung the invitation irritably on the table, exclaiming:

'What good is that to me?'

'Why, my dear, I thought you would be pleased. You never go anywhere, and this is a really splendid chance for you. I had no end of trouble in getting it. Everybody is trying to get an invitation. It's very select, and only a few invitations are issued to the clerks. You will see all the officials there.'

She looked at him in exasperation, and exclaimed petulantly:

'What do you expect me to wear at a reception like that?'

He had not considered the matter, but he replied hesitatingly:

'Why, that dress you always wear to the theatre seems to me very nice indeed . . .'

He broke off. To his horror and consternation he saw that his wife was in tears. Two large drops were rolling slowly down her cheeks.

'What on earth is the matter?' he gasped.

With a violent effort she controlled her emotion, and drying her wet cheeks said in a calm voice:

'Nothing. Only I haven't a frock, and so I can't go to the reception. Give your invitation to some friend in your office, whose wife is better dressed than I am.'

He was greatly distressed.

'Let us talk it over, Mathilde. How much do you think a proper frock would cost, something quite simple that would come in useful for other occasions afterwards?'

She considered the matter for a few moments, busy with

her calculations, and wondering how large a sum she might venture to name without shocking the little clerk's instincts of economy and provoking a prompt refusal.

'I hardly know,' she said at last, doubtfully, 'but I think I could manage with four hundred francs.'

He turned a little pale. She had named the exact sum that he had saved for buying a gun and treating himself to some Sunday shooting parties the following summer with some friends, who were going to shoot larks in the plain of Nanterre.

But he replied:

'Very well, I'll give you four hundred francs. But mind you buy a really handsome gown.'

The day of the party drew near. But although her gown was finished Madame Loisel seemed depressed and dissatisfied.

'What is the matter?' asked her husband one evening. 'You haven't been at all yourself the last three days.'

She answered: 'It vexes me to think that I haven't any jewellery to wear, not even a brooch. I shall feel like a perfect pauper. I would almost rather not go to the party.'

'You can wear some fresh flowers. They are very fashionable this year. For ten francs you can get two or three splendid roses.'

She was not convinced.

'No, there is nothing more humiliating than to have an air of poverty among a crowd of rich women.'

'How silly you are!' exclaimed her husband. 'Why don't you ask your friend, Madame Forestier, to lend you some jewellery. You know her quite well enough for that.'

She uttered a cry of joy.

'Yes, of course, it never occurred to me.'

The next day she paid her friend a visit and explained her predicament.

Madame Forestier went to her wardrobe, took out a large jewel case and placed it open before her friend.

'Help yourself, my dear,' she said.

Madame Loisel saw some bracelets, a pearl necklace, a Venetian cross exquisitely worked in gold and jewels. She tried on these ornaments in front of the mirror and hesitated, reluctant to take them off and give them back.

'Have you nothing else?' she kept asking.

'Oh, yes, look for yourself. I don't know what you would prefer.'

At length, she discovered a black satin case containing a superb diamond necklace, and her heart began to beat with frantic desire. With trembling hands she took it out, fastened it over her high-necked gown, and stood gazing at herself in rapture.

Then, in an agony of doubt, she said:

'Will you lend me this? I shouldn't want anything else.'

'Yes, certainly.'

She threw her arms round her friend's neck, kissed her effusively, and then fled with her treasure.

It was the night of the reception. Madame Loisel's triumph was complete. All smiles and graciousness, in her exquisite gown, she was the prettiest woman in the room. Her head was in a whirl of joy. All the men stared at her and inquired her name and begged for an introduction; all the junior staff asked her for waltzes. She even attracted the attention of the minister himself.

Carried away by her enjoyment, glorying in her beauty and her success, she threw herself ecstatically into the dance.

She moved as in a beatific dream, wherein were mingled all the homage and admiration she had evoked, all the desires she had kindled, all that complete and perfect triumph, so dear to a woman's heart.

It was close on four before she could tear herself away. Ever since midnight her husband had been dozing in a little, deserted drawing-room together with three other men whose wives were enjoying themselves immensely.

He threw her outdoor wraps round her shoulders, unpretentious, every-day garments, whose shabbiness contrasted strangely with the elegance of her ball dress. Conscious of the incongruity, she was eager to be gone, in order to escape the notice of the other women in their luxurious furs. Loisel tried to restrain her.

'Wait here while I fetch a cab. You will catch cold outside.'

But she would not listen to him and hurried down the staircase. They went out into the street, but there was no cab to be seen. They continued their search, vainly hailing drivers whom they caught sight of in the distance. Shivering with cold and in desperation they made their way towards the Seine. At last, on the quay, they found one of those old vehicles which are only seen in Paris after nightfall, as if ashamed to display their shabbiness by daylight.

The cab took them to their door in the Rue des Martyrs and they gloomily climbed the stairs to their dwelling. All was over for her. As for him, he was thinking that he would have to be in the office by ten o'clock.

She took off her wraps in front of the mirror, for the sake of one last glance at herself in all her glory. But suddenly she uttered a cry. The diamonds were no longer round her neck.

'What is the matter?' asked her husband, who was already half undressed.

She turned to him in horror. 'I . . . I've . . . lost Madame Forestier's necklace.'

He started in dismay. 'What? Lost the necklace? Impossible!'

They searched the pleats of the gown, the folds of the cloak, and all the pockets, but in vain.

'You are sure you had it on when you came away from the ball?'

'Yes, I remember feeling it in the lobby at the Education Office.'

'But if you had lost it in the street we should have heard it drop. It must be in the cab.'

'Yes. I expect it is. Did you take the number?'

'No. Did you?'

'No.'

They gazed at each other, utterly appalled. In the end Loisel put on his clothes again.

'I will go over the ground that we covered on foot and see if I cannot find it.'

He left the house. Lacking the strength to go to bed, unable to think, she collapsed into a chair and remained there in her evening gown, without a fire.

About seven o'clock her husband returned. He had not found the diamonds.

He applied to the police, advertised a reward in the newspapers, made inquiries of all the hackney cab offices; he visited every place that seemed to hold out a vestige of hope.

His wife waited all day long in the same distracted condition, overwhelmed by this appalling calamity.

Loisel returned home in the evening, pale and hollow-cheeked. His efforts had been in vain.

'You must write to your friend,' he said, 'and tell her that you have broken the catch of the necklace and that you are having it mended. That will give us time to think things over.'

She wrote a letter to his dictation.

After a week had elapsed, they gave up all hope. Loisel, who looked five years older, said:

'We must take steps to replace the diamonds.'

On the following day they took the empty case to the jeweller whose name was inside the lid. He consulted his books.

'The necklace was not bought here, madam; I can only have supplied the case.'

They went from jeweller to jeweller, in an endeavour to find a necklace exactly like the one they had lost, comparing their recollections. Both of them were ill with grief and despair.

At last in a shop in the Palais-Royal they found a diamond necklace, which seemed to them exactly like the other. Its price was forty thousand francs. The jeweller agreed to sell it to them for thirty-six. They begged him not to dispose of it for three days, and they stipulated for the right to sell it back for thirty-four thousand francs, if the original necklace was found before the end of February.

Loisel had eighteen thousand francs left to him by his father. The balance of the sum he proposed to borrow. He raised loans in all quarters, a thousand francs from one man, five hundred from another, five louis here, three louis there. He gave promissory notes, agreed to exorbitant terms, had dealings with usurers, and with all the money-lending hordes. He compromised his whole future, and had to risk his signature, hardly knowing if he would be able to honour it. Overwhelmed by the prospect of future suffering, the black misery which was about to come upon him, the physical privations and moral torments, he went to fetch the new necklace, and laid his thirty-six thousand francs down on the jeweller's counter.

When Madame Loisel brought back the necklace, Madame Forestier said reproachfully:

'You ought to have returned it sooner; I might have wanted to wear it.'

To Madame Loisel's relief she did not open the case. Supposing she had noticed the exchange, what would she have thought? What would she have said? Perhaps she would have taken her for a thief.

Madame Loisel now became acquainted with the horrors of extreme poverty. She made up her mind to it, and played her part heroically. This appalling debt had to be paid, and pay it she would. The maid was dismissed; the flat was given up, and they moved to a garret. She undertook all the rough household work and the odious duties of the kitchen. She washed up after meals and ruined her pink finger-nails scrubbing greasy dishes and saucepans. She washed the linen, the shirts, and the dusters, and hung them out on the line to dry. Every morning she carried down the sweepings to the street, and brought up the water, pausing for breath at each landing. Dressed like a working woman, she went with her basket on her arm to the greengrocer, the grocer, and the butcher, bargaining, wrangling, and fighting for every farthing.

Each month some of the promissory notes had to be redeemed, and others renewed, in order to gain time.

Her husband spent his evenings working at some tradesman's accounts, and at night he would often copy papers at five sous a page.

This existence went on for ten years.

At the end of that time they had paid off everything to the last penny, including the usurious rates and the accumulations of interest.

Madame Loisel now looked an old woman. She had become the typical poor man's wife, rough, coarse, hard-bitten. Her hair was neglected, her skirts hung awry, and her hands were red. Her voice was no longer gentle, and she washed down the floors vigorously. But now and then, when her husband was at the office, she would sit by the window and her thoughts would wander back to that far-away evening, the evening of her beauty and her triumph.

What would have been the end of it if she had not lost the necklace? Who could say? Who could say? How strange, how variable are the chances of life! How small a thing can serve to save or ruin you!

One Sunday she went for a stroll in the Champs-Élysées, for the sake of relaxation after the week's work, and she caught sight of a lady with a child. She recognized Madame Forestier, who looked as young, as pretty, and as attractive as ever. Madame Loisel felt a thrill of emotion. Should she speak to her? Why not? Now that the debt was paid, why should she not tell her the whole story? She went up to her.

'Good morning, Jeanne.'

Her friend did not recognize her and was surprised at being addressed so familiarly by this homely person.

'I am afraid I do not know you – you must have made a mistake,' she said hesitatingly.

'No. I am Mathilde Loisel.'

Her friend uttered a cry.

'Oh, my poor, dear Mathilde, how you have changed!'

'Yes, I have been through a very hard time since I saw you last, no end of trouble, and all through you.'

'Through me? What do you mean?'

'You remember the diamond necklace you lent me to wear at the reception at the Education Office?'

'Yes. Well?'

'Well, I lost it.'

'I don't understand; you brought it back to me.'

'What I brought you back was another one, exactly like it. And for the last ten years we have been paying for it. You will understand that it was not an easy matter for people like us, who hadn't a penny. However, it's all over now. I can't tell you what a relief it is.'

Madame Forestier stopped dead.

'You mean to say that you bought a diamond necklace to replace mine?'

'Yes. And you never noticed it? They were certainly very much alike.'

She smiled with ingenuous pride and satisfaction.

Madame Forestier seized both her hands in great distress.

'Oh, my poor, dear Mathilde! Why, mine was only imitation. At the most it was worth five hundred francs!'

EVELYN WAUGH

BELLA FLEACE GAVE A PARTY

(1934)

BALLINGAR IS FOUR and a half hours from Dublin if you catch the early train from Broadstone Station and five and a quarter if you wait until the afternoon. It is the market town of a large and comparatively well-populated district. There is a pretty Protestant Church in 1820 Gothic on one side of the square and a vast, unfinished Catholic cathedral opposite it, conceived in that irresponsible medley of architectural orders that is so dear to the hearts of transmontane pietists. Celtic lettering of a sort is beginning to take the place of the Latin alphabet on the shop fronts that complete the square. These all deal in identical goods in varying degrees of dilapidation; Mulligan's Store, Flannigan's Store, Riley's Store, each sells thick black boots, hanging in bundles, soapy colonial cheese, hardware and haberdashery, oil and saddlery, and each is licensed to sell ale and porter for consumption on or off the premises. The shell of the barracks stands with empty window frames and blackened interior as a monument to emancipation. Someone has written *The Pope is a Traitor* in tar on the green pillar box. A typical Irish town.

Fleacetown is fifteen miles from Ballingar, on a direct uneven road through typical Irish country; vague purple hills in the far distance and towards them, on one side of the road, fitfully visible among drifting patches of white mist, unbroken miles of bog, dotted with occasional stacks of cut peat. On the other side the ground slopes up to the north, divided irregularly into spare fields by banks and stone walls over which the Ballingar hounds have some of their most eventful hunting. Moss lies on everything; in a rough green rug on the walls and banks, soft green velvet on the timber – blurring the transitions so that there is no knowing where the ground ends and trunk and masonry begin. All the way from Ballingar there is a succession of whitewashed cabins and a dozen or so fair-size farmhouses; but there is no gentleman's house, for all this was Fleace property in the days before the Land Commission. The demesne land is all that belongs to Fleacetown now, and this is let for pasture to neighbouring farmers. Only a few beds are cultivated in the walled kitchen garden; the rest has run to rot, thorned bushes barren of edible fruit spreading everywhere among weedy flowers reverting rankly to type. The hot-houses have been draughty skeletons for ten years. The great gates set in their Georgian arch are permanently padlocked, the lodges are derelict, and the line of the main drive is only just discernible through the meadows. Access to the house is half a mile further up through a farm gate, along a track befouled by cattle.

But the house itself, at the date with which we are dealing, was in a condition of comparatively good repair; compared, that is to say, with Ballingar House or Castle Boycott or Knode Hall. It did not, of course, set up to rival Gordontown, where the American Lady Gordon had installed electric light, central heating and a lift, or Mock House or Newhill, which were leased to sporting Englishmen, or Castle Mockstock, since Lord Mockstock married beneath him. These four houses with their neatly raked gravel, bathrooms and dynamos, were the wonder and ridicule of the country. But Fleacetown, in fair competition with the essentially Irish houses of the Free State, was unusually habitable.

Its roof was intact; and it is the roof which makes the

difference between the second and third grade of Irish country houses. Once that goes you have moss in the bedrooms, ferns on the stairs and cows in the library, and in a very few years you have to move into the dairy or one of the lodges. But so long as he has, literally, a roof over his head, an Irishman's house is still his castle. There were weak bits in Fleacetown, but general opinion held that the leads were good for another twenty years and would certainly survive the present owner.

Miss Annabel Rochfort-Doyle-Fleace, to give her the full name under which she appeared in books of reference, though she was known to the entire countryside as Bella Fleace, was the last of her family. There had been Fleces and Fleysers living about Ballingar since the days of Strongbow, and farm buildings marked the spot where they had inhabited a stockaded fort two centuries before the immigration of the Boycotts or Gordons or Mockstocks. A family tree emblazed by a nineteenth-century genealogist, showing how the original stock had merged with the equally ancient Rochforts and the respectable though more recent Doyles, hung in the billiard-room. The present home had been built on extravagant lines in the middle of the eighteenth century, when the family, though enervated, was still wealthy and influential. It would be tedious to trace its gradual decline from fortune; enough to say that it was due to no heroic debauchery. The Fleaces just got unobtrusively poorer in the way that families do who make no effort to help themselves. In the last generations, too, there had been marked traces of eccentricity. Bella Fleace's mother – an O'Hara of Newhill – had from the day of her marriage until her death suffered from the delusion that she was a negress. Her brother, from whom she had inherited, devoted himself to oil painting; his mind ran on the simple subject of assassination and before his death he had executed pictures of practically every such incident in history from Julius Caesar to General Wilson. He was at work on a painting, his own murder, at the time of the troubles, when he was, in fact, ambushed and done to death with a shot-gun on his own drive.

It was under one of her brother's paintings – Abraham Lincoln in his box at the theatre – that Miss Fleace was sitting one colourless morning in November when the idea came to her to give a Christmas party. It would be unnecessary to describe her appearance closely, and somewhat confusing, because it seemed in contradiction to much of her character. She was over eighty, very untidy and very red; streaky grey hair was twisted behind her head into a horsy bun, wisps hung round her cheeks; her nose was prominent and blue veined; her eyes pale blue, blank and mad; she had a lively smile and spoke with a marked Irish intonation. She walked with the aid of a stick, having been lamed many years back when her horse rolled her among loose stones late in a long day with the Ballingar Hounds; a tipsy sporting doctor had completed the mischief, and she had not been able to ride again. She would appear on foot when hounds drew the Fleacetown coverts and loudly criticize the conduct of the huntsman, but every year fewer of her old friends turned out; strange faces appeared.

They knew Bella, though she did not know them. She had become a by-word in the neighbourhood, a much-valued joke.

'A rotten day,' they would report. 'We found our fox, but lost again almost at once. But we saw Bella. Wonder how long the old girl will last. She must be nearly ninety. My father remembers when she used to hunt – went like smoke, too.'

Indeed, Bella herself was becoming increasingly occupied

with the prospect of death. In the winter before the one we are talking of, she had been extremely ill. She emerged in April, rosy cheeked as ever, but slower in her movements and mind. She gave instructions that better attention must be paid to her father's and brother's graves, and in June took the unprecedented step of inviting her heir to visit her. She had always refused to see this young man up till now. He was an Englishman, a very distant cousin, named Banks. He lived in South Kensington and occupied himself in the Museum. He arrived in August and wrote long and very amusing letters to all his friends describing his visit, and later translated his experiences into a short story for the *Spectator*. Bella disliked him from the moment he arrived. He had horn-rimmed spectacles and a B.B.C. voice. He spent most of his time photographing the Fleacetown chimney-pieces and the moulding of the doors. One day he came to Bella bearing a pile of calf-bound volumes from the library.

'I say, did you know you had these?' he asked.

'I did,' Bella lied.

'All first editions. They must be extremely valuable.'

'You put them back where you found them.'

Later, when he wrote to thank her for his visit – enclosing prints of some of his photographs – he mentioned the books again. This set Bella thinking. Why should that young puppy go poking round the house putting a price on everything? She wasn't dead yet, Bella thought. And the more she thought of it, the more repugnant it became to think of Archie Banks carrying off her books to South Kensington and removing the chimney-pieces and, as he threatened, writing an essay about the house for the *Architectural Review*. She had often heard that the books were valuable. Well, there were plenty of books in the library and she did not see why Archie Banks should profit by them. So she wrote a letter to a Dublin bookseller. He came to look through the library, and after a while he offered her twelve hundred pounds for the lot, or a thousand for the six books which had attracted Archie Banks's attention. Bella was not sure that she had the right to sell things out of the house; a wholesale clearance would be noticed. So she kept the sermons and military history which made up most of the collection, the Dublin bookseller went off with the first editions, which eventually fetched rather less than he had given, and Bella was left with winter coming on and a thousand pounds in hand.

It was then that it occurred to her to give a party. There were always several parties given round Ballingar at Christmas time, but of late years Bella had not been invited to any, partly because many of her neighbours had never spoken to her, partly because they did not think she would want to come, and partly because they would not have known what to do with her if she had. As a matter of fact she loved parties. She liked sitting down to supper in a noisy room, she liked dance music and gossip about which of the girls was pretty and who was in love with them, and she liked drink and having things brought to her by men in pink evening coats. And though she tried to console herself with contemptuous reflections about the ancestry of the hostesses, it annoyed her very much whenever she heard of a party being given in the neighbourhood to which she was not asked.

And so it came about that, sitting with the *Irish Times* under the picture of Abraham Lincoln and gazing across the bare trees of the park to the hills beyond, Bella took it into her head to give a party. She rose immediately and hobbled across the room to the bell-rope. Presently her butler came into the morning-room; he wore the green baize apron in which he cleaned the silver and in his hand he carried the plate brush to emphasize the irregularity of the summons.

'Was it yourself ringing?' he asked.

'It was, who else?'

'And I at the silver!'

'Riley,' said Bella with some solemnity, 'I propose to give a ball at Christmas.'

'Indeed!' said her butler. 'And for what would you want to be dancing at your age?' But as Bella adumbrated her idea, a sympathetic light began to glitter in Riley's eye.

'There's not been such a ball in the country for twenty-five years. It will cost a fortune.'

'It will cost a thousand pounds,' said Bella proudly.

The preparations were necessarily stupendous. Seven new servants were recruited in the village and set to work dusting and cleaning and polishing, clearing out furniture and pulling up carpets. Their industry served only to reveal fresh requirements; plaster mouldings, long rotten, crumbled under the feather brooms, worm-eaten mahogany floorboards came up with the tin tacks; bare brick was disclosed behind the cabinets in the great drawing-room. A second wave of the invasion brought painters, paperhangers and plumbers, and in a moment of enthusiasm Bella had the cornice and the capitals of the pillars in the hall regilded; windows were reglazed, banisters fitted into gaping sockets, and the stair carpet shifted so that the worn strips were less noticeable.

In all these works Bella was indefatigable. She trotted from drawing-room to hall, down the long gallery, up the staircase, admonishing the hireling servants, lending a hand with the lighter objects of furniture, sliding, when the time came, up and down the mahogany floor of the drawing-room to work in the French chalk. She unloaded chests of silver in the attics, found long-forgotten services of china, went down with Riley into the cellars to count the few remaining and now flat and acid bottles of champagne. And in the evenings when the manual labourers had retired exhausted to their gross recreations, Bella sat up far into the night turning the pages of cookery books, comparing the estimates of rival caterers, inditing long and detailed letters to the agents for dance bands and, most important of all, drawing up her list of guests and addressing the high double piles of engraved cards that stood in her escritoire.

Distance counts for little in Ireland. People will readily drive three hours to pay an afternoon call, and for a dance of such importance no journey was too great. Bella had her list painfully compiled from works of reference, Riley's more up-to-date social knowledge and her own suddenly animated memory. Cheerfully, in a steady childish handwriting, she transferred the names to the cards and addressed the envelopes. It was the work of several late sittings. Many of those whose names were transcribed were dead or bedridden; some whom she just remembered seeing as small children were reaching retiring age in remote corners of the globe; many of the houses she wrote down were blackened shells, burned during the troubles and never rebuilt; some had 'no one living in them, only farmers'. But at last, none too early, the last envelope was addressed. A final lap with the stamps and then later than usual she rose from the desk. Her limbs were stiff, her eyes dazzled, her tongue cloyed with the gum of the Free State post office; she felt a little dizzy, but she locked her desk that evening with the knowledge that the most serious part of the work of the party was over. There had been several notable and deliberate omissions from that list.

'What's all this I hear about Bella giving a party?' said Lady Gordon to Lady Mockstock. 'I haven't had a card.'

'Neither have I yet. I hope the old thing hasn't forgotten me. I certainly intend to go. I've never been inside the house. I believe she's got some lovely things.'

With true English reserve the lady whose husband had leased Mock Hall never betrayed the knowledge that any party was in the air at all at Fleacetown.

As the last days approached Bella concentrated more upon her own appearance. She had bought few clothes of recent years, and the Dublin dressmaker with whom she used to deal had shut up shop. For a delirious instant she played with the idea of a journey to London and even Paris, and considerations of time alone obliged her to abandon it. In the end she discovered a shop to suit her, and purchased a very magnificent gown of crimson satin; to this she added long white gloves and satin shoes. There was no tiara, alas! among her jewels, but she unearthed large numbers of bright, nondescript Victorian rings, some chains and lockets, pearl brooches, turquoise earrings, and a collar of garnets. She ordered a coiffeur down from Dublin to dress her hair.

On the day of the ball she woke early, slightly feverish with nervous excitement, and wriggled in bed till she was called, restlessly rehearsing in her mind every detail of the arrangements. Before noon she had been to supervise the setting of hundreds of candles in the sconces round the ball-room and supper-room, and in the three great chandeliers of cut Waterford glass; she had seen the supper tables laid out with silver and glass and stood the massive wine coolers by the buffet; she had helped bank the staircase and hall with chrysanthemums. She had no luncheon that day, though Riley urged her with samples of the delicacies already arrived from the caterer's. She felt a little faint; lay down for a short time, but soon rallied to sew with her own hands the crested buttons on to the liveries of the hired servants.

The invitations were timed for eight o'clock. She wondered whether that were too early – she had heard tales of parties that began very late – but as the afternoon dragged on unendurably, and rich twilight enveloped the house, Bella became glad that she had set a short term on this exhausting wait.

At six she went up to dress. The hairdresser was there with a bag full of tongs and combs. He brushed and coiled her hair and whiffed it up and generally manipulated it until it became orderly and formal and apparently far more copious. She put on all her jewellery and, standing before the cheval glass in her room, could not forbear a gasp of surprise. Then she limped downstairs.

The house looked magnificent in the candle-light. The band was there, the twelve hired footmen, Riley in knee breeches and black silk stockings.

It struck eight. Bella waited. Nobody came.

She sat down on a gilt chair at the head of the stairs, looked steadily before her with her blank, blue eyes. In the hall, in the cloakroom, in the supper-room, the hired footmen looked at one another with knowing winks. 'What does the old girl expect? No one'll have finished dinner before ten.'

The linkmen on the steps stamped and chafed their hands.

At half-past twelve Bella rose from her chair. Her face gave no indication of what she was thinking.

'Riley, I think I will have some supper. I am not feeling altogether well.'

She hobbled slowly to the dining-room.

'Give me a stuffed quail and a glass of wine. Tell the band to start playing.'

The *Blue Danube* waltz flooded the house. Bella smiled approval and swayed her head a little to the rhythm.

'Riley, I am really quite hungry. I've had nothing all day. Give me another quail and some more champagne.'

Alone among the candles and the hired footmen, Riley served his mistress with an immense supper. She enjoyed every mouthful.

Presently she rose. 'I am afraid there must be some mistake. No one seems to be coming to the ball. It is very disappointing after all our trouble. You may tell the band to go home.'

But just as she was leaving the dining-room there was a stir in the hall. Guests were arriving. With wild resolution Bella swung herself up the stairs. She must get to the top before the guests were announced. One hand on the banister, one on her stick, pounding heart, two steps at a time. At last she reached the landing and turned to face the company. There was a mist before her eyes and a singing in her ears. She breathed with effort, but dimly she saw four figures advancing and saw Riley meet them and heard him announce:

'Lord and Lady Mockstock, Sir Samuel and Lady Gordon.'

Suddenly the daze in which she had been moving cleared. Here on the stairs were the two women she had not invited – Lady Mockstock the draper's daughter, Lady Gordon the American.

She drew herself up and fixed them with her blank, blue eyes.

'I had not expected this honour,' she said. 'Please forgive me if I am unable to entertain you.'

The Mockstocks and the Gordons stood aghast; saw the mad blue eyes of their hostess, her crimson dress; the ballroom beyond, looking immense in its emptiness; heard the dance music echoing through the empty house. The air was charged with the scent of chrysanthemums. And then the drama and unreality of the scene were dispelled. Miss Fleace suddenly sat down, and holding out her hands to her butler, said, 'I don't quite know what's happening.'

He and two of the hired footmen carried the old lady to a sofa. She spoke only once more. Her mind was still on the same subject. 'They came uninvited, those two . . . and nobody else.'

A day later she died.

Mr Banks arrived for the funeral and spent a week sorting out her effects. Among them he found in her escritoire, stamped, addressed, but unposted, the invitations to the ball.

DELMORE SCHWARTZ

NEW YEAR'S EVE

(1948)

To Edna Phillips

THE EVENING OF the profound holiday drew much strength and unhappiness from such depths as the afternoon, the week, the year of unhappiness, and the lives that long had been lived. This secular holiday is full of pain because it is both an ending and a beginning. In this way, it participates in some of the strangeness and difficulty of both birth and death.

On this memorable evening and at this New Year's party, the idiom which prevailed might perhaps be said to be that of unpleasant cleverness. The party had not been the object of careful thought, nor had it been inspired by the emotion of celebration. Hence some of the guests hoped vaguely until the afternoon darkened that they might be asked to come to some other party. This hope communicated itself like uproarious laughter as some of the guests spoke to each other during the winter afternoon. Each in his tone of voice unknowingly communicated the sense that this party was not the party which, in the depths, the psyche desired like first prize.

Grant Landis was the only human being who did not have this feeling about the party. He labored all afternoon in the office of Centaur Editions, a small publishing house of which he was one of the owners, and when anyone called him upon the telephone or visited him, he invited each one to come to the party too. He was a human being who possessed an infinite interest in other human beings and an inexhaustible energy, an energy so great that it triumphed over reality when it was dismal by moving forward to fresh arenas of frenzied activity.

Early in the afternoon, Shenandoah Fish, a youthful author of promise, entered the office and Grant immediately invited him to the party. Shenandoah had come to the office because he had little else that he wanted to do, because he wanted to converse with Grant Landis, and because he hoped to hear more praise of his small book, which Centaur Editions had published in October.

Eager to hear more about his small book, the invitation to the party came as a major pleasure. However, he tried to conceal his delight, saying that he had promised to spend the evening with two of his friends, Nicholas O'Neil and Wilhelmina Gold.

'Bring them too,' said Grant, as Arthur Harris, the other owner of the press, entered the office, returning from lunch. Since nine o'clock in the morning Arthur had heard more and more strangers invited to the party. Hearing of this fresh addition, he had difficulty in concealing the annoyance which rose to his face. However, he greeted Shenandoah with a warmth which broke through his annoyance, asking the youthful author what he was writing now? Another dialogue?

The mixed and complicated character of this question, as it struck Shenandoah, can be understood only by mentioning the nature of the youthful author's first work. It was a satirical dialogue between Freud and Marx in which Freud comes to agree that capitalism is organized anal eroticism when Marx agrees in return that the oedipus complex is an oppression rooted in the ownership of the means of reproduction. In asking Shenandoah if he was writing a new dialogue, Arthur did not intend to make an ironic remark.

But it was ironic. And the irony, though inspired by Arthur's annoyance at the new additions to the New Year's party, had an objective foundation in the fact that the youthful author's first work might well be an accident and not the proof of a lasting gift. Although Shenandoah recognized the irony, and sought to disregard it, he misunderstood its true cause. He thought that Arthur supposed him capable of composing nothing but satirical dialogues, a misunderstanding inspired in him by the deep fear that it might be true.

Nonetheless Shenandoah said nothing in reply and decided to return to the rooming house where he lived. When he had closed the glassed door of the office, Arthur criticized Grant for his indiscriminate invitations. Since both of them were intellectuals, both resorted to theories about the nature of a party and about each other's characters. A party at which too many of the guests are strangers is likely to fall flat, Arthur argued.

'There is enough alienation in modern life,' he said roundly, 'without installing it in the living room.'

'Everyone is interesting,' Grant replied and it was true that he found everyone interesting.

'Everyone is interesting to you,' said Arthur harshly, 'because you talk all the time—'

'Spontaneity,' said Grant, recognizing with laughter this description of his character, 'strangers bring spontaneity to a party.'

The argument continued thus, full of abstractions, but motivated nonetheless by a conflict which was founded upon two different feelings about life. And as they argued and as they irritated each other, elsewhere in other boxes of the great city old conflicts were renewed and new ones quickly engendered. Grant's wife, Martha Landis, quietly quarreled with her mother-in-law upon the telephone.

Frances Harris, Arthur's wife, became more and more angry because Arthur had not come home on time.

'He is holding a theoretical conversation somewhere,' she said to herself.

Meantime Shenandoah was visited by his friend Nicholas O'Neil, who was unhappy and who suffered from a cold, the outcome perhaps of the fact that this was his birthday, or the outcome of his depression that he was twenty-five years of age and not yet famous. Nicholas and Shenandoah had become annoyed with each other, arguing about the merits of a poem. Nicholas in his annoyance and depression declared sullenly that he did not want to go to Grant's party. He said this repeatedly, although the prospect of being at home with his family during the New Year evening was unbearable.

And meanwhile Grant Landis returned from the office to his apartment and found his wife Martha pale with annoyance because of her mother-in-law's remarks, remarks which were made unknowingly to a successful rival who had scored an overwhelming victory. Hearing Martha's version of these remarks, Grant became very angry with his mother, an anger in which the thirty-six years of his life were revived. Thinking of these remarks, Grant became more and more angry until his anger was such that he might have still been unmarried.

During the sooty afternoon, a light rain began to fall. The weather was not cold and shining, as it should have been for the winter holiday. The weather was boring and gray. Nevertheless in the streets of the first capital of the world, the capital of the accessibility to experience, there was some gaiety, leftover gaiety from the Christmas holiday. Christmas trees shone with a toytown brilliance in apartment house windows, as evening slipped down. Few human beings looked at the trees, however, and fewer were aware of them, for they had been present for more than a week.

And at the same time Wilhelmina Gold argued with her parents as she prepared to go downtown to meet Shenandoah. The argument concerned the fact that Wilhelmina was going to meet Shenandoah downtown, instead of his obeying the manners of the middle class and coming to call for her. This kind of behavior had been the cause of many disputes between the parents and the daughter. The parents were not sure that Shenandoah was more than a mere friend of Wilhelmina. He did not behave like a suitor or prospective son-in-law. But then he did not behave like any one they had viewed in almost fifty years of life. This made them suspect every possibility. Apart, however, from any concern with marriage, they found Shenandoah's behavior inexplicable. For example, his self-consciousness was so extreme that he stumbled whenever he thought that anyone was looking at him when he crossed the room.

'Some day he will fall flat on his face,' said Mrs Gold, enjoying the idea and yet fearing this young man.

He was incapable of saying, How do you do? with the least aplomb, although on the other hand once he began to speak it was difficult to interrupt him. He never dressed well although he seemed to them to be smart and to know many things, when he spoke, he spoke with such passion and contempt and with so many speech defects that it was difficult to imagine that he would ever be successful and well-to-do. Worst of all, from the point of view of the Golds, he was not the kind of young man who, when married to Wilhelmina, would come with her for dinner every Friday night after taking an apartment not far from the Golds.

The argument in progress between parents and daughter went back to the old and estranged past. The parents had objected grievously from the beginning because Shenandoah did not always come to call for Wilhelmina, but she met him on a street-corner or if it was cold in a cafeteria. It was useless to explain as Wilhelmina had tried to explain to her parents, poor souls who had known youth at the turn of the century, that a girl was not of necessity a loose woman merely because she waited for a young man on a street-corner. Yet such is the capacity of the human heart to accustom itself to infamy, they had come to accept the fact that Shenandoah did not always come to call for her because there were times when, in an effort to ease her difficulties, he did call for her.

Mr Gold blamed his daughter's acceptance of this peculiar young man, if acceptance it was, upon the university she had attended for four years, and where she had met Shenandoah. He forgot that before going to the university Wilhelmina had rejected with violence and contempt the *mores* and ethos of her parents. Mr Gold felt that she might have altered and become sensible if she had only met the right young man.

Wilhelmina's sensibility was that of an only child who for twenty-four years has been adored, tended, and nagged by her parents. As Mrs Gold helped her pretty daughter to dress, she made remarks which shifted between ruthless criticism and infatuated admiration. She observed once again that her daughter had the legs of a Ziegfield Follies girl and a face as refined as those she studied on the Sunday society pages. But, given such native gifts, why, at the age of twenty-four, a late age for an unmarried girl, did she have to go out only with this strange author in unpressed pants? Mrs Gold was unable to penetrate this unpleasant act. Her disappointment with her husband, who was not rich and hence to her mind a failure, united with her hope and her disappointment in her daughter, and all these feelings, which had their beginning in the first week of her marriage, arose to the point of compulsion. She made remarks which she knew would enrage her daughter because they had enraged her many times before.

'Why,' she asked her daughter as she helped her to adjust her dress, 'did you discourage Herman like that? After all, he wanted to marry you so much.'

The fantastic character of this question will be understood from the fact that Herman had been married for four years now and was the father of three children, all girls. But more than that, Herman was a dentist, extremely prosperous. During his suit, he had argued long and stubbornly with Wilhelmina about her disdain for *Collier's*, which he read with passion from week to week, impatient for the appearance of each new number because of the unbearable excitement which the serial inevitably inspired in him. And he had pointed out to Wilhelmina that if she married him, she would have no dental bills, and when Wilhelmina had said, 'What a vulgar argument to make to a girl,' he had observed that what she regarded as vulgarity now would seem merely good sense to her when she had begun to cope with 'the facts of life,' a phrase which made Wilhelmina wince as if it were a dental drill.

Wilhelmina's detestation of Herman had a general and representative character to such an extent that the mention of his name was enough to annoy her. When her mother, forced by a compulsion she did not in the least understand, once more regretted Wilhelmina's rejection of Herman, Wilhelmina donned her coat quickly and left the house, declaring that once she was married she would have nothing whatever to do with her parents. Consequently, Wilhelmina's ride downtown in the subway was one in which she was sickened by her sense of guilt, while Mrs Gold spent New Year's Eve in tears, tears interrupted only to renew her quintessential criticism of her husband, who quietly damned the day that he had decided to send his daughter to the university.

And at this time, Shenandoah and Nicholas travelled crosstown in a street-car, standing up in the press and brushing against human beings they would never see again. They continued their argument which on the surface concerned the question, should Nicholas go to a party where he would for the most part be a stranger? This was a type of the academic argument, since the street-car slowly went crosstown, bearing the young men to the argument's conclusion. Yet the dispute had come to the point where each young man, oppressed, cited and bore in mind only the other's faults of character, and Shenandoah was becoming aware that the other passengers were listening in amazement to their virtually ontological discussion of character when the street-car arrived at their destination, and they dismounted. Immediately they saw Wilhelmina on the street-corner, angry at her mother, Shenandoah, and chiefly herself. But her anger vanished as he arrived and there was no longer any reason to be impatient.

Nicholas, Wilhelmina and Shenandoah entered the remodeled tenement in which Grant lived just as the drizzle of rain turned into a downpour.

'Hello,' Grant cried loudly to them from the top of the stair after the antiphonal buzzes and the shoving of the door. He shouted down the stairwell at them from sheer love of the act of greeting. But this was complicated by another habit, just as frequent, that of crying down a question in a troubled or virtually mystified voice.

'Shenandoah?' he cried down the stairwell, as if some pressing problem had been uttered. And when the question was answered by Shenandoah in an unclear voice, unclear because he was always uneasy in formal matters, Grant then shouted back a greeting, a greeting in which his voice sometimes broke or grew hoarse, while his visitors ascended, unseeing, and unseen, and unable to shout back at him because they did not enjoy his temperament or his pathological excess of energy.

As soon as the visitors arrived at the head of the fourth floor, they found that Grant, Martha, and another couple, Oliver Jones and his wife, Delia, were in their coats and about to depart. Grant explained that Arthur had called and asked them all to come to his house because he could not come uptown to Grant's.

'Arthur thinks he has a cold,' said Grant in a tone which plainly implied that this was one more manifestation of hypochondria. To Nicholas and Wilhelmina, Grant said, 'I am overjoyed that you decided to come,' a remark inexplicable and so much in excess of any real need of the moment, that Nicholas and Wilhelmina were left tonguetied, and Nicholas became anxious with the fear that somehow Shenandoah had communicated his doubt about coming to Grant.

As they left the house, and looked for a taxi, Grant resumed his argument with Oliver Jones, trying at the same time to signal a taxi and to enlist Shenandoah in the argument. In the background, pale, thin and nervous, stood Delia Jones, wishing that one of them would speak to her. She was sure that no one was aware of her presence. Nicholas suffered from precisely the same feelings.

'That is the only possible explanation,' he said to himself, still preoccupied with Grant's greeting and Shenandoah's betrayal of him. Since no one paid any attention to him, he decided to become active, useful and prominent. He went out into the middle of the street to hail a taxi, and finally stopped one, but at the same time his feet became soaked as he stepped into a black puddle near the sewer. Consequently Nicholas lost interest in everything but his wet feet and his cold. As they seated themselves in the taxi, Delia Jones became very self-conscious about the pressure of the bodies of the other human beings, and she wished again that she had stayed at home.

When these guests arrived at the apartment house where Arthur Harris lived, Nicholas was disturbed so much by the possibility of pneumonia that immediately upon being introduced to Frances Harris he asked her if he might please have a pail of hot water in which to bathe his feet. Frances was thunderstruck by this request, but since it seemed to have been made with the utmost seriousness, she gave him a pail for hot water, making no comment, for she was one of perfect tact.

The party had not become a unique kind of being as yet. One reason for this was that not everyone had arrived. Yet it was already clear that the great psychological *place* of the party was the sense of having-nowhere-better-to-go.

In general, the guests already present suffered in one or another way from the emotions which had distorted the newcomers. Some felt that they were not wanted before they arrived, and when they arrived they saw that this view was incorrect, since no one seemed to care very much who was present. Thus, corrected by incontestable perception, some of them felt that they would not have been invited if this had been an important party, the kind of a party they had supposed it to be when they felt the emotion of flattery upon being invited.

Soon after their arrival, a long and important conversation began between Shenandoah and Oliver Jones.

Oliver was an interesting and unfortunate human being.

Shenandoah liked him very much and was ashamed of liking him, for the only reason for liking him was personal charm. Oliver wrote fiction in which his desire to be a circulating library success was at war with his desire to be a serious author. He had a true talent for fiction, but he was unaware or unsure of this fact, and this made him dishonest in a variety of ways. This dishonesty might not have mattered very much, had he remained able to be honest with himself and honest in the activity of authorship. But his sense of guilt pressed him to the point where for relief it was necessary for him to deny to himself that anyone was honest and that honesty had any real existence. Consequently, his native gift for understanding other human beings was often annulled by his need to deny that other human beings were unlike himself; and thus he suspected everyone of everything because he suspected and convicted himself of many wrongs. He had recently shocked his already overworked conscience by writing a review of stupendous praise for a work by an extremely influential and foolish literary critic who had befriended him and who might befriend him many times again. This review went so far in false praise that the critic himself was embarrassed as well as pleased. But before writing the review Oliver had read passages of the book to many of his friends to show them how foolish the book was. He had done this because he suffered, like so many other human beings, from a desperate desire to be honest some of the time. He bore in mind these occasions of deprecation and consequently apologized too often for the extreme praise he had given the book, forgetting that no one cared very much whether he was honest. And all this behavior would have been unnecessary to Oliver, had he only known that he was really a gifted author! Unsure of his gifts, Oliver was ashamed of his wife Delia, and they had what Oliver assumed to be an understanding that each was free to become involved in amorous interludes. Delia did not understand this understanding, she suffered very much because her husband had not made love to her for years, and she tried very hard but without success to become involved in what Oliver termed amorous interludes, concerning which he had stipulated only that she be discreet and keep them a private and personal matter.

As Shenandoah conversed with Oliver, Delia surveyed the living room, wondering against intelligent doubt if tonight might not be the beginning of an amorous interlude.

Shenandoah and Oliver were discussing Gide's *Journal* which both had lately read. Shenandoah did not know French very well and he may have been mistaken in his comments, which concerned Gide's jealousy of Proust. This jealousy did not show itself directly, but it seemed to Shenandoah to express itself in Gide's sentences about Proust's grammatical errors and his irrational resentment that Proust had chosen to conceal or invert the homosexuality of the protagonist in *A la Recherche du Temps Perdu*.

'. . . How foolish jealousy is, among authors,' said Shenandoah, after he had spoken of Gide, 'Proust, Eliot, Rilke, Mann and Valéry all produced great works and received the recognition they deserved. Literature is not like space and business. One great work does not displace another great work . . .'

This view irritated Oliver. Had he been in better health and had he drunk less, he might have concealed his irritation. He was irritated both because he thought that what Shenandoah said was untrue and also because he wished with all his heart that he were able to believe that it was true.

'Don't be naive,' said Oliver, 'it's obvious that authors

compete for fame. Not only that, Proust wrote the work which Gide should have written and he took from Gide his hold upon the rising generations of intellectuals . . .'

'I don't mean to deny the *hallucination* of competition,' said Shenandoah, intoxicated by the benevolence of his idea, 'and I certainly don't deny the existence of jealous feelings. But consider how, after twenty years, both Gide and Proust are studied as great authors. They do not get in each other's way and the rising generation reads the works of both with the same attention and admiration.'

Oliver said nothing for the moment. He was trying to restrain his irritation. We are probably both wrong, said Shenandoah to himself, for this had often been true. Oliver passed to the possibility that Shenandoah was denying the actuality of competition because he feared the feelings of his rivals. Next, Oliver felt that what Shenandoah had said was an attack, however unknowing, upon his own acute sense of rivalry. He had to decide that Shenandoah was right and he had been foolish for years, or that he was right and Shenandoah was ignorant and innocent. The latter view immediately triumphed and his irritation took hold of him and he felt compelled to wound Shenandoah.

'How old are you?' said Oliver with a beautiful hardness upon his face.

'Twenty-four years of age,' said Shenandoah. He knew very well that the question was an affront, but he did not want to quarrel with Oliver.

'You are just an infant,' said Oliver, determined to hurt Shenandoah's feelings, 'you have just not lived long enough.' Thus, with this sentence, he declared that Shenandoah did not know what he was saying and he won the argument.

'How old are you?' said Shenandoah with awkward

constraint. His determination not to be angry had quickly broken down.

'You know how old I am, thirty-four,' said Oliver in fury, 'I've told you a dozen times.'

'Well for that matter,' said Shenandoah, 'you know how old I am, but I was too polite to mention the fact.' He knew that this remark was self-righteous an instant too late to halt himself.

'O never mind,' said Oliver, for his mind had shifted to the much more serious irritation he felt because he was thirty-four years of age, a thought which became most urgent and most productive of feelings of anxiety and despair on a birthday or on New Year's Eve.

Shenandoah moved away as Oliver looked at the carpet and then at nothing at all. Oliver felt a pang of guilt as Shenandoah departed and consequently he sought to remember all that was wrong with Shenandoah.

Shenandoah expects everyone to be as interested in him as he is interested in himself, Oliver thought, as he sought self-extenuation; he has decided that competition does not exist because it makes him uncomfortable, which is one form of egotism, and because he thinks very well of himself, which is the worst form of egotism.

Shenandoah had departed ostensibly to freshen his drink, but actually to hide his despair at his inability not to get into arguments with other human beings, especially those he liked.

He was overcome by a convenient self-pity as he reached for cold ice to put in his highball glass. His self-pity was convenient because it made it unnecessary for him to engage in further thought.

All I ever wanted, he said to himself brokenly, was to have friends and to go to parties. Shenandoah had for long cherished the belief that if he were an interesting and gifted author, everyone would like him and want to be with him and enjoy conversation with him.

He criticized the self-pity which wept in him, he criticized it and repudiated it from the top of his mind, for all the good it did.

In other cages of the room, other human beings were trying without success to get along with each other.

Nicholas O'Neil sat on the bathtub rim, his feet in a pail of hot water, full of self-pity and self-absorption, wondering what disease would take him to an early grave.

Arthur Harris remarked to Wilhelmina Gold that much might be said of the truth of the remark that drinking was an inexpensive form of mysticism. Wilhelmina replied that it was far from inexpensive. The party bored her because she did not like to drink.

Martha Landis looked across the living room at Delia Jones and regarded her gown, which was intended to suggest to many minds the delightful possibility of taking it off. Martha knew of the domestic agreement of the Joneses, since Oliver was unable to hold his tongue about matters interesting to him, and she saw both the intimacy and the pathos of the gown. Delia, who was beginning her second drink, was still unhappy and uneasy, for no one had spoken to her very much, a silence which often occurred at parties. Because of her uneasiness, Delia tried to down her drink quickly. She began to feel miserable because she had not married the man who had courted her for two years before she encountered Oliver. She had refused him because, when they went out to dinner, he filled his pockets with granulated sugar, a habit contracted during a poverty-beslummed and unsweetened childhood. During the courtship he was earning a great deal of money and there was no reason for any hoarding of sugar: it was merely a tic which continued from childhood, and absentmindedly, yet compelled by the whole being. He had other such habits, although they were less public. Thinking about these habits, Delia felt that she had regarded them as being too important, for she forgot, after these years, how expressive and significant they were. And after all, why should anyone have to pay for another human being's childhood? One has to pay for one's own, and one is in debt as it is because of the continuous expense. The pain of these thoughts was so keen that Delia went to get another drink, and drank it down quickly in the hope of false serenity and false joy.

Delia was attractive and intelligent. She was unable to understand why no amorous interludes occurred, for certainly Oliver was not in the least at a loss, and she heard everywhere of extra-marital episodes of other human beings. She did not understand that it was not a question of a defect in her, but of the difficulty of direct communication in modern life, the difficulty of making clear her willingness. At times she entertained this explanation, but the passing recognition was ineffectual and melted away because more powerful by far was her fear that she was not attractive. By attributing her poverty in love to an unattractiveness which did not exist, she arrived at a picture of her plight which was coherent and which required no activity on her part, but merely sorrow. This view permitted her an uneasy acquiescence in continuous unhappiness.

And now the party had become an entity and an event like a snowfall in a metropolitan city. Everyone had had enough to drink, just enough to make them amiable. Everyone shone. The charms of each human being sparkled like theatre marquees. The conversation seemed, in the warm subjectivity of choice spirits, to be as brilliant as Mozart. In some ways, the exchanges resembled a ballroom dance. In other ways, they were like the moment when the silent and everwondrous snow has overcome the great city and made a new thing of it, full of innocence, freshness, and unexpected marvels of whiteness.

The stories which were told were not lacking in malice, but the malice was gentle, it was apologized for, and it was introduced only because, as everyone knows, it is very difficult to be funny without attacking some other human being for whom one has, as a whole, some admiration and affection.

Frances Harris told the story of the Polish schoolgirl who, when asked what her religion was, replied that she was an antagonist.

'We are all antagonists,' said Shenandoah to himself in easy despair, looking across the room at Oliver.

Wilhelmina looked at Shenandoah, saw his unhappiness, supposed that he had had an unfortunate conversation, and knowing Shenandoah, thought he must have said something utterly without tact.

'He always tells other human beings what he regards as the bitter truth about each one of them and then he is astonished that they get angry.'

In another room, Grant Landis was making telephone calls without pause in an effort to secure signatures to a petition which protested against a suppression of civil liberties in the activity of labor leaders. His purpose was noble, but on the other hand he spoke in the same way, with the same intonations, giggles, and implications of intimacy to each of the different human beings, and this suggested that perhaps each of them existed for him only in a limited sense as a unique individuality.

Delia Jones was now free of the inhibitions which had

tormented her so much. She had had four strong highballs. She began to look about at the men of the party whom she did not know and wonder what it would be like to have them make love to her. It is different with everyone, one of her female friends had told her. It is the same with everyone, Oliver had reported. Delia did not look at the men she already knew, deluded by the view that they had already decided against her, since she was not attractive enough.

Nicholas O'Neil remained outside of the zone of false or specious well-being. He still sat upon the bathroom rim and left only when someone else wanted to enter. This became more and more frequent as the drinking continued. Since Nicholas had had nothing to drink, he was alienated from the party in every sense. Finally he decided that it was useless to remain in the bathroom any longer, for he was discommoded so often by the tide of events. Hence he donned his wet socks and shoes again, returned to the living room, and looked with a critical eye at the happy people.

Wilhelmina regarded Shenandoah as he sat relaxed and thus free from the distortions of self-consciousness. He seemed almost attractive now, but not at other times, for he was so self-conscious that he was unable to sing with thousands when the Star-Spangled Banner was played at Madison Square Garden. Wilhelmina told the story of the labyrinthine bureaucracy of the Emergency Relief Bureau where she was employed. St Francis himself, she explained, would be regarded as difficult by the Bureau, if he were on relief, because he gave food away to the birds.

Hearing Wilhelmina and suffering from echolalia and a banal association of ideas, Nicholas exclaimed:

'Jesus, Mary, and Joseph!' for the idea of St Francis as unable to get relief in the Irish Catholic city of New York struck him as being as inconceivable as the Immaculate Conception.

Oliver Jones, disturbed more and more because he had hurt Shenandoah's feelings, tried to renew conversation with him. But Shenandoah was lost in the thought of how happy he might be, were he but able to believe in the divinity of Jesus Christ.

'God in a girl's womb! it is inconceivable,' he said sadly and half-aloud.

Oliver, being unable to gain Shenandoah's attention, looked to see what Delia was doing. She was sitting next to Horatio Lapin, a limited person who came to parties only to drink. But Delia was not acquainted with this fact. At other and less decorous parties Horatio Lapin had often been accosted by young women of some beauty. He had looked at the young lady, scrutinized his drink, and then invariably decided to have another drink. It was less trouble.

Oliver knew that Delia might soon begin to behave amorously and conspicuously. He decided to do nothing, however.

'Let her have a good time,' he said to himself warmly.

His eyes fell on the bookshelves and he saw a copy of *Axel's Castle* by Edmund Wilson. He drew down the book, brushed through the pages, and his eye and heart were caught by the following passage, which he arose and recited as if it were blank verse:

> 'It is at the death of Bergotte that Proust's narrator, in what is perhaps the noblest passage of the book, affirms the reality of those obligations, culminating in the obligation of the writer to do his work as it ought to be done, which seem to derive from "some other world," "based on goodness, scrupulousness, sacrifice," so little sanction

can we recognize them as having in the uncertain and selfish world of humanity – those "laws which we have obeyed because we have carried their precepts within us without knowing who inscribed them there – those laws to which we are brought by every profound exercise of the intelligence, and which are invisible – and are they really? – to fools".'

Oliver dropped his exalted tone of voice. He was in all truth devoted very much to the sentiments he had quoted, but he did not think that many others felt like that. Hence, after some hesitation, he made a remark which was intended to diminish or discount his allegiance to Proust's words:

'These noble sentiments,' he said in a tone of unpleasant cleverness, 'would be more becoming, if Proust had not been homosexual, dishonest, insincere, a snob, a literary politician, and a pet Jew.'

Although some had been oppressed by the rapture with which Oliver recited the passage, all were offended by his facile cynicism and attack on Proust.

'He is the last one to cast the first stone,' said Arthur to himself, 'especially after writing that review.'

'His overworked conscience,' said Shenandoah to himself, 'has just enjoyed some relief by spitting itself in the face.'

In the other room, Grant Landis continued to devote himself to the making of phone calls which might help the lot of the jailed labor leaders.

In general, Oliver's cynicism was the end of the period of good feeling, which might have ended anyway because of the progress of the drinking.

Then the telephone pierced everyone's ears. Grant had ceased his calls for a moment in order to look up a number in the directory. As Arthur went to answer the phone, everyone forgot about Oliver's remark, though the sourness of the emotion remained like dregs.

Leon Berg was on the telephone. He was detested or disliked by everyone at the party because his chief activity was to explain to all authors that they were without talent. From what Arthur was saying in reply, it was clear that Leon wanted to come to the party, and had sufficiently downed his resentment at not being asked to the party to humiliate himself by asking if he might come.

At the party a discussion of Leon's character began, and in this discussion, the truth was used as a form of falsehood, since bias, like a squint, selected only his unpleasant and evil traits.

Meanwhile Leon left the room in which he lived and stopped to exchange a word with Claude Kagan, a minor poet who admired and feared him, impressed by the fact that he wrote nothing at all and condemned everyone, including Shakespeare. Leon told Claude where he was going and when Claude asked without much hope if he might come too, Leon replied that such an addition would be quite impossible. He then remarked quickly that all modern poets were worthless because they did not have the effect upon History of John L. Lewis and Bing Crosby, and concluded by saying that there would be no new world war because so many human beings expected a war and so many human beings had never been right about anything.

At the party the conversation continued to be a discussion of Leon, and Oliver revived the rumor that Leon's second name had been Bergson, shortened by him because he was unable to endure the rivalry between his own ambition and Bergson's fame. In fairness to Leon, some of his best stories were quoted, in particular the one about the man who visited the World's Fair and said that the one thing lacking, the one important thing, was a screamatorium, a place where everyone who wished might go to scream because of the quality of life in this period.

Leon was walking crosstown and losing his feeling of pleasure that he was going to the party. He stopped to have a drink, but this did not help him very much. Resentment mounted in him and he wondered if they were laughing at him because he had asked to come to the party. He decided that this was an untrue view inspired by his sense of persecution, but he was none too sure.

As these thoughts went through Leon like swords, Delia Jones at the party was going from one man to another, making amorous proposals which were regarded for the most part as efforts at wit.

'Who are you?' Delia cooed at the strange men, staring deeply into their eyes. Shenandoah, regarding this action from a distance, saw that Nicholas would be the next candidate, and then, fearing perhaps wrongly, that Nicholas might welcome the overture far too well, moved forward to prevent his friend. He tugged his sleeve and said as softly as possible:

'Don't be foolish, she's very drunk.'

Since there was no immediate justification for the fear that Nicholas might welcome Delia, Nicholas turned on Shenandoah in silent fury.

Shenandoah's move was observed by Oliver and he was upset by it. He decided that something must be done. But he was afraid that an open scandal might occur.

'Who are you?' said Delia to Leon as the door opened on his face.

For a split second, Leon thought that he had rung the wrong bell. Then he saw Arthur, who had just opened the door and was standing at an angle to it. Leon was grossly taken aback. He had not counted on much of a reception, but he was so uncertain as to being welcome that this seemed to be a direct attack.

But all the wit and fury in him rose in inspiration.

'Who are *you?*' he cried back at Delia.

Her face fell. All looked, for Leon had spoken loudly. Two laughed. No one knew if Delia's consternation was the consequence of Leon's triumphant and leering face, or the result of her actually being unable to think of who she was.

Oliver saw the relaxation and defeat in her. He decided that this was the best moment to correct her or to send her home without an outbreak of recrimination. He drew her into one of the bedrooms and asked her to behave herself. Unfortunately he was unable to keep the irony in his mind from entering his voice, though he had tried to be gentle and reasonable in tone.

'Everyone feels as you do,' he said foolishly, 'there is no need for this self-indulgence.'

Her hysteria became positive again.

'I am not self-indulgent, you are!' said Delia in overflowing hatred.

'All right, you are not, *I* am,' said Oliver, 'but please try in any case to behave yourself.'

'Why?' screamed Delia in fury, 'Why? Why should I behave myself? *What does it ever get me? Everyone is against me, anyway. No one cares for me and no one ever will.*'

Oliver agreed with her, but was unable to endure the shame of her screaming, audible all over.

'Why?' she continued to scream without adding any explanation.

'Behave yourself because I brought you here,' said Oliver curtly.

'Why?' she screamed more loudly than ever.

'This is what I get for bringing you here, out of a misplaced sense of pity,' said Oliver.

She slapped him in the face and said that she was going to kill herself. He held her arms and she struggled against him. Arthur entered.

'Come now,' he said in a friendly way which Delia misunderstood, 'everything will be all right.'

'Who asked you to come in here?' she said screaming again.

'After all, I live here,' said Arthur, astounded by her attack. Delia broke loose from Oliver's hold and slapped Arthur, who now regretted profoundly his entrance, as well as what he had just said.

And then Frances came into the room with a cold compress for Delia. Frances had been kind to Delia, and Delia felt that at last she had an ally.

'Go away,' said Frances to Oliver, and Arthur.

'You are my friend,' said Delia to Frances, weeping and once more limp. And thus, after a time, Frances succeeded in quieting Delia, who became very ashamed, although Frances sought to assure her that no one regarded her behavior as anything but an attack of illness.

Meanwhile the unseen scene was discussed in the living room. And then Wilhelmina noticed that they had not marked the moment of the New Year, when the party horns are blown, whistles peal, everyone kisses, and sings 'Auld Lang Syne.' The radio was playing that they might know the exact moment of passage and unbearable beauty. But Delia's screaming had made them unaware of everything else.

They all went to the window to make sure that it was already the New Year; and they saw that the rain had turned into snow, the most beautiful of all the illusions of the natural world. Yes, it was 1938. How strange that it should be 1938, how strange seemed the word and the fact.

No one knew that this was to be the infamous year of the Munich Pact, but everyone knew that soon there would be a new world war because only a few unimportant or powerless people believed in God or in the necessity of a just society sufficiently to be willing to give anything dear for it.

As Shenandoah, Nicholas, and Wilhelmina parted in emptiness and depression, Shenandoah was already locked in what was soon to be a post-Munich sensibility: complete hopelessness of perception and feeling.

'Some other world,' he said to himself, 'some world of goodness; some other life; some life where the nobility we admire is lived; some life in which those who have dedicated their being to the examination of consciousness live by the laws they face at every turn.'

'What are you babbling about?' said Wilhelmina.

'I am sorry for the whole world, said Sadie Thompson,' was Shenandoah's reply. But he knew well enough that he was chiefly sorry for himself. But he shrewdly decided not to admit this to Nicholas and Wilhelmina.

'I wish I had not come,' said Wilhelmina, 'I will never have any children.'

'I won't marry you, unless we are going to have children,' said Shenandoah stupidly.

'I don't want to marry you,' said Wilhelmina.

'I wish everyone would drop dead,' said Nicholas as they descended into the subway.

'*Why?*' asked Shenandoah.

'Who are *you?*' replied Nicholas, deciding to have nothing further to do with Shenandoah and going home by himself.

VLADIMIR NABOKOV

PNIN GIVES A PARTY

(1955)

THE 1954 FALL TERM had begun. Again the marble neck of a homely Venus in the vestibule of Humanities Hall, Waindell College, received the vermilion imprint, in applied lipstick, of a mimicked kiss. Again the Waindell Recorder discussed the parking problem. Again in the margins of library books earnest freshmen inscribed such helpful glosses as 'Description of nature,' 'Irony,' and 'How true!' Again autumn gales plastered dead leaves against one side of the latticed gallery leading from Humanities to Frieze Hall. Again, on serene afternoons, huge amber-brown monarch butterflies flapped over asphalt and lawn as they lazily drifted south, their incompletely retracted black legs hanging rather low beneath their polka-dotted bodies.

And still the college creaked on. Hard-working graduates, with pregnant wives, still wrote dissertations on Dostoevski and Simone de Beauvoir. Literary departments still labored under the impression that Stendhal, Galsworthy, Dreiser, and Mann were great writers. Word plastics like 'conflict' and 'pattern' were still in vogue. As usual, sterile instructors successfully endeavored to 'produce' by reviewing the books of more fertile colleagues, and, as usual, a crop of lucky faculty members were enjoying or about to enjoy various awards received earlier in the year. Thus an amusing little grant was affording the versatile Starr couple – baby-faced Christopher Starr and his child-wife Louise – of the Fine Arts Department, the unique opportunity of recording postwar folk songs in East Germany, into which these amazing young people had somehow obtained permission to penetrate. Tristram W. Thomas ('Tom' to his friends), Professor of Anthropology, had obtained ten thousand dollars from the Mandeville Foundation for a study of the eating habits of Cuban fishermen and palm climbers. And another charitable institution had come to the assistance of Dr Bodo von Falternfels, to enable him to complete 'a bibliography concerned with such published and manuscript material as has been devoted in recent years to a critical appraisal of the influence of Nietzsche's disciples on Modern Thought.'

The fall term had begun, and Dr Hagen, Chairman of the German Department, was faced with a complicated situation. During the summer, he had been informally approached by an old friend about whether he might consider accepting next year a delightfully lucrative professorship at Seaboard University, a far more important seat of learning than Waindell. This part of the problem was comparatively easy to solve – he would accept. On the other hand, there remained the chilling fact that the department he had so lovingly built would be relinquished into the claws of the treacherous Falternfels, whom he, Hagen, had obtained from Austria, and who had turned against him – had actually managed to appropriate by underhand methods the direction of *Europa Nova*, an influential quarterly Hagen had founded in 1945. Hagen's proposed departure, of which, as yet, he had divulged nothing to his colleagues, would have a still more heart-rending consequence: Assistant Professor Timofey Pnin must be left in the lurch. There had never been any regular Russian Department at Waindell, and my poor friend Pnin's academic existence had always depended on his being employed by the eclectic German Department in a kind of Comparative Literature extension of one of its branches. Out of pure spite, Bodo von Falternfels, who had grudgingly shared an office with Pnin, was sure to lop off that limb, and Pnin, who was only an Assistant Professor and had no life tenure at Waindell, would be forced to leave – unless some other literature-and-language department agreed to adopt him. The only department that was flexible enough to do so was that of English. But Jack Cockerell, Chairman of the English Department, disapproved of everything Hagen did, and considered Pnin a joke.

For Pnin, who was totally unaware of his protector's woes, the new term had begun particularly well; he had never had so few students to bother about, or so much time for his own research. This research had long entered the charmed stage when the quest overrides the goal. Index cards were gradually loading a shoe box with their compact weight. The collation of two legends, a precious detail of manners or dress, a reference checked and found to be falsified by incompetence or fraud, the spine thrill of a felicitous guess, and all the other innumerable triumphs of bezkorïstnïy (disinterested, devoted) scholarship had corrupted Pnin and made of him a happy, footnote-drugged maniac.

On another, more human plane, there was the little brick house that he had rented on Todd Road, at the corner of Cliff Avenue. The sense of living in a discrete building all by himself was to Pnin something singularly delightful, and amazingly satisfying to a weary old want of his innermost self, battered and stunned by thirty-five years of homelessness. One of the sweetest things about the place was the silence – angelic, rural, and perfectly secure, and thus in blissful contrast to the persistent cacophonies that had surrounded him from six sides in the rented room of his former habitations. And the tiny house was so spacious! (With grateful surprise,

Pnin thought that had there been no Russian Revolution, no exodus, no expatriation in France, no naturalization in America, everything – at the best, at the best, Timofey – would have been much the same: a professorship, perhaps, in Kharkov or Kazan, a suburban house such as this, old books within, late blooms without.) It was – to be more precise – a two-story house of cherry-red brick, with white shutters and a shingle roof. The green plat on which it stood had a frontage of about fifty arshins and was limited at the back by a vertical stretch of mossy cliff with tawny shrubs on its crest. A rudimentary driveway along the south side of the house led to a small whitewashed garage for the poor man's car Pnin owned. A curious basketlike net, somewhat like a glorified billiard pocket – lacking, however, a bottom – was suspended for some reason above the garage door, upon the white of which it cast a shadow as distinct as its own weave but larger and in a bluer tone. Lilacs – those Russian garden graces, to whose springtime splendor, all honey and hum, my poor Pnin greatly looked forward – crowded in sapless ranks along one wall of the house. And a tall deciduous tree, which Pnin, a birch-lime-willow-aspen-poplar-oak man, was unable to identify, cast its large, heart-shaped, rust-colored leaves and Indian-summer shadows upon the wooden steps of the open porch.

A cranky-looking oil furnace in the basement did its best to send up its weak, warm breath through registers in the floors. The living room was scantily and dingily furnished, but had a rather attractive bay at one end, harboring a huge old globe, on which Russia was painted a pale blue. In a very small dining room, a pair of crystal candlesticks, with pendants, was responsible in the early mornings for iridescent reflections, which glowed charmingly on the sideboard, reminding my sentimental friend of the stained glass that colored the sunlight orange and green and violet on the verandas of Russian country houses. A china closet, every time he passed by it, went into a rumbling act that also was somehow familiar from dim back rooms of the past. The second floor consisted of two bedrooms, both of which had been the abode of many small children, with incidental adults. The floors had been chafed by tin toys. From the wall of the chamber Pnin had decided to sleep in he had untacked a pennant-shaped piece of red cardboard with the enigmatic word 'Cardinals' daubed on it in white, but a tiny rocker for a three-year-old Pnin, painted pink, was allowed to remain in its corner. A disabled sewing machine occupied a passageway leading to the bathroom, where the usual short tub, made for dwarfs by a nation of giants, took as long to fill as the tanks and basins of the arithmetic in Russian schoolbooks.

Timofey was now ready to give a housewarming party. The living room had a sofa that could seat three, and there were a wingback chair, an overstuffed easy chair, two chairs with rush seats, one hassock, and two footstools. He had planned a buffet supper, which he would serve in the dining room. All of a sudden, he experienced an odd feeling of dissatisfaction as he checked, mentally, the little list of his guests – the Clementses, the Hagens, the Thayers, and Betty Bliss. It had body but it lacked bouquet. Of course, he was tremendously fond of the Clementses (real people – not like most of the campus dummies), with whom he had had such exhilarating talks in the days when he was their roomer; of course, he felt very grateful to Herman Hagen for many a good turn, such as that raise Hagen had recently arranged; of course, Mrs Hagen was, in Waindell parlance, 'a lovely person'; of course, Mrs Thayer was always so helpful at the library, and her husband, of the English Department, had such a soothing capacity for showing how silent a man could be if he strictly avoided comments on the weather. While visiting a famous grocery between Waindellville and Isola, he had run into Betty Bliss, a former student of his, and had asked her to the party, and she had said she still remembered Turgenev's prose poem about roses, with its refrain 'Kak horoshi, kak svezhi' ('How fair, how fresh'), and would certainly be delighted to come.

But there was nothing extraordinary, nothing original, about this combination of people, and old Pnin recalled those birthday parties in his boyhood – the half-dozen children invited who were somehow always the same, and the pinching shoes, and the aching temples, and the kind of heavy, unhappy, constraining dullness that would settle on him after all the games had been played and a rowdy cousin had started putting nice new toys to vulgar and stupid uses. And he also recalled the time when, in the course of a protracted hide-and-seek routine, after an hour of uncomfortable concealment he had emerged from a dark and stuffy wardrobe in the maid's chamber only to find that all his playmates had gone home.

Pnin, returning to his unsatisfactory list of guests, decided to invite the celebrated mathematician, Professor Idelson, and his wife, the sculptress. He called them up and they said they would come with joy but later telephoned to say they were tremendously sorry – they had overlooked a previous engagement. He next asked Miller, a young instructor in the German Department, and Charlotte, his pretty, freckled wife, but it turned out she was on the point of having a baby. The party was to be the next day and he was about to ask the Cockerells when a perfectly new and really admirable idea occurred to him.

Pnin and I had long accepted the disturbing but seldom

discussed fact that on any given college staff one was likely to find at least one person who was the twin, so far as looks went, of another man within the same professional group. I know, indeed, of a case of triplets at a comparatively small college, and I remember that among the fifty or so faculty members of a wartime 'intensive language school' there were as many as six Pnins, besides the genuine and, to me, unique article. It should not be deemed surprising, therefore, that even Pnin, not a very observant man in everyday life, could not help becoming aware (some time during his ninth year at Waindell) that a lanky, bespectacled old fellow with scholarly strands of steel-gray hair falling over the right side of his small but corrugated brow, and with a deep furrow descending from his sharp nose to each corner of his long upperlip – a person whom Pnin knew as Professor Thomas Wynn, head of the Ornithology Department, having once talked to him at a garden party about golden orioles and other Russian countryside birds – was not always Professor Wynn. At times he graded, as it were, into somebody else, whom Pnin did not know by name but whom he classified, with a bright foreigner's fondness for puns, as 'Twynn' or, in Pninian, 'Tvin.' My friend and compatriot soon realized that he could never be sure whether the owlish, rapidly stalking gentleman whose path he would cross every other day at different points of progress between office and classroom was really his chance acquaintance, the ornithologist, whom he felt bound to greet in passing, or the Wynnlike stranger who acknowledged Pnin's sombre salute with exactly the same degree of automatic politeness that any chance acquaintance would. The moment of meeting would be very brief since both Pnin and Wynn (or Twynn) walked fast; and sometimes Pnin, in order to avoid the exchange of urbane barks, would feign reading a letter on the run, or would manage to dodge his rapidly advancing colleague and tormentor by swerving into a stairway and then continuing along a lower-floor corridor; but no sooner had he begun to rejoice in the smartness of the device than upon using it one day he almost collided with Tvin (or Vin) pounding along the subjacent passage.

By great good luck, on the day of the party, as Pnin was finishing a late lunch in Frieze Hall, Wynn, or his double, neither of whom had ever appeared there before, suddenly sat down beside him and said, 'I have long wanted to ask you something – you teach Russian, don't you? Last summer I was reading a magazine article on birds. ['Vin! This is Vin!' said Pnin to himself, and forthwith perceived a decisive course of action.] Well, the author of that article – I don't recall his name; I think it was a Russian one – mentioned that in the Skoff region (I hope I pronounce it right?) a local cake is baked in the form of a bird. Basically, of course, the symbol is phallic, but I was wondering if you knew of such a custom.'

'Sir, I am at your service,' Pnin said, a note of exultation quivering in his throat, for he now saw his way not only to carry out his brilliant idea but also to pin down definitely the personality of at least the initial Wynn, who liked birds. 'Yes, sir, I know all about those zhavoronkí, those alouettes, those— We must consult a dictionary for the English name. So I take the opportunity to extend a cordial invitation to you to visit me this evening. Half past eight, post meridiem. A little house-heating soirée, nothing more. Bring also your spouse – or perhaps you are a Bachelor of Hearts?' (Oh, punster Pnin!)

His interlocutor said he was not married and he would sure love to come. What was the address?

'It is 999 Todd Rodd – very simple! At the very, very end

of the rodd, where it unites with Cliff Ahvnue. A little brick house with a big black cliff behind.'

That afternoon, Pnin could hardly wait to start culinary operations. He began them soon after five and only interrupted them to don, for the reception of his guests, a sybaritic smoking jacket of blue silk, with tasselled belt and satin lapels, won at an émigré charity bazaar in Paris twenty years ago. (How time flies!) This jacket he wore with a pair of old tuxedo trousers, likewise of European origin. Peering at himself in the cracked mirror of the medicine chest, he put on his heavy tortoise-shell reading glasses, from under the saddle of which his Russian potato nose smoothly bulged. He bared his synthetic teeth. He inspected his cheeks and chin to see if his morning shave still held. It did. With finger and thumb he grasped a long nostril hair, plucked it out after a second hard tug, and sneezed lustily, an 'Ah!' of well-being rounding out the explosion.

At half past seven, Betty Bliss arrived to help with the final arrangements. Betty now taught English and History at Isola High School. She had not changed since the days when she was a buxom graduate student. Her pink-rimmed, myopic gray eyes peered at you with the same ingenuous sympathy. She wore the same Gretchenlike coil of thick hair around her head. There was the same scar on her soft throat. But an engagement ring with a diminutive diamond had appeared on her plump hand, and this she displayed with coy pride to Pnin, who vaguely experienced a twinge of sadness. He reflected that there was a time he might have courted her – would have done so, in fact, had she not had a servant maid's mind, which he soon found had remained unaltered, too. She could still relate a long story on a 'she said-I said-she said' basis, and nothing on earth could make her disbelieve in the wisdom and wit of her favorite women's magazine. She still had the curious trick – shared by two or three other small-town young women within Pnin's limited ken – of giving you a delayed little tap on the sleeve in acknowledgment of, rather than in retaliation for, any remark reminding her of some minor lapse. You would say, 'Betty, you forgot to return that book,' or 'I thought, Betty, you said you would never marry,' and before she actually answered, there it would come – that demure gesture, retracted at the very moment her stubby fingers came into contact with your wrist.

'He is a biochemist, and is now in Pittsburgh,' said Betty as she helped Pnin to arrange buttered slices of French bread around a pot of glossy-gray fresh caviar. There was also a large plate of cold cuts, real German pumpernickel, a dish of very special vinaigrette where shrimps hobnobbed with pickles and peas, some miniature sausages in tomato sauce, hot pirozhki (mushroom tarts, meat tarts, cabbage tarts), various interesting Oriental sweets, and a bowl of fruit and nuts. Drinks were to be represented by whiskey (Betty's contribution), ryabinovka (a rowanberry liqueur), brandy-and-grenadine cocktails, and, of course, Pnin's Punch, a heady mixture of chilled Château Yquem, grapefruit juice, and maraschino, which the solemn host had already started to stir in a large bowl of brilliant aquamarine glass with a decorative design of swirled ribbing and lily pads.

'My, what a lovely thing!' cried Betty.

Pnin eyed the bowl with pleased surprise, as if seeing it for the first time, and explained that it was a recent present from young Victor, his former wife's son by a second marriage. Victor was at St Bartholomew's, a boarding school at Cranton, near Boston, and Timofey had never met the boy until last spring, when his mother, who lived in California, had arranged to have Victor spend his Easter vacation with

Pnin at Waindell. The visit had proved a success and was followed by the arrival of this bowl, enclosed in a box within another box inside a third one, and wrapped up in an extravagant mass of excelsior and paper that had spread all over the kitchen like a carnival storm. The bowl that emerged was one of those gifts whose first impact produces in the recipient's mind a colored image, a blazoned blur, reflecting with such emblematic force the sweet nature of the donor that the tangible attributes of the thing are dissolved, as it were, in this pure inner blaze, but suddenly and forever leap into brilliant being when praised by an outsider to whom the true glory of the object is unknown. Timofey was using the precious bowl for the first time tonight, he told Betty.

A musical tinkle reverberated through the small house and the Clementses entered with a bottle of French champagne and a cluster of dahlias.

Dark-eyed, long-limbed, bob-haired Joan Clements wore an old black silk dress that was smarter than anything other faculty wives could devise, and it was always a pleasure to watch good old bald Tim Pnin bend slightly to touch with his lips the light hand that Joan, alone of all the Waindell ladies, knew how to raise to exactly the right level for a Russian gentleman to kiss. Her husband, Laurence, a nice fat Professor of Philosophy in a nice gray flannel suit, sank into the easiest chair and immediately grabbed the first book at hand, which happened to be an English-Russian and Russian-English pocket dictionary. Holding his glasses, he looked away, trying to recall something he had always wished to look up, and his attitude accentuated his striking resemblance, somewhat en jeune, to Jan van Eyck's ample-jowled, fluff-haloed Canon van der Paele, seized by a fit of abstraction in the presence of the puzzled Virgin to whom a super, rigged up as St George, is directing the good Canon's attention. Everything was there – the knotty temple, the sad, musing gaze, the folds and furrows of facial flesh, the thin lips, and even the wart on the left cheek.

Hardly had the Clementses settled down when Betty let in the man interested in bird-shaped cakes. Pnin was about to say 'Professor Vin' but Joan – rather unfortunately, perhaps – interrupted the introduction with 'Oh, we know Thomas! Who doesn't know Tom?' Pnin returned to the kitchen, and Betty handed around some Bulgarian cigarettes.

'I thought, Thomas,' remarked Clements, crossing his fat legs, 'you were out in Havana interviewing palm-climbing fishermen?'

'Well, I'll be on my way after mid-years,' said Professor Thomas. 'Of course, most of the actual field work has been done already by others.'

'Still, it was nice to get that grant, wasn't it?'

'In our branch,' replied Thomas with perfect composure, 'we have to undertake many difficult journeys. In fact, I may push on to the Windward Islands. If,' he added, with a hollow laugh, 'Senator McCarthy does not crack down on foreign travel.'

'Tom received a grant of ten thousand dollars,' said Joan to Betty, whose face dropped a curtsy as she made that special grimace consisting of a slow half bow and a tensing of chin and lower lip that automatically conveys, on the part of Bettys, a respectful, congratulatory, and slightly awed recognition of such grand things as dining with one's boss, being in Who's Who, or meeting a duchess.

The last to arrive were the Thayers, who came in a new station wagon and presented their host with an elegant box of mints, and Dr Hagen, who came on foot, and now triumphantly held aloft a bottle of vodka.

'Good evening, good evening,' said the hearty Hagen.

'Dr Hagen,' said Thomas as he shook hands with him. 'I hope the Senator did not see you walking about with that stuff.'

The good Doctor, a square-shouldered, aging man, explained that Mrs Hagen had been prevented from coming, alas, at the very last moment, by a dreadful migraine.

Pnin served the cocktails. 'Or better to say flamingo tails – specially for ornithologists,' he slyly quipped, looking, as he supposed, at his friend Vin.

'Thank you!' chanted Mrs Thayer as she received her glass, raising her eyebrows on that bright note of genteel inquiry that is meant to combine the notions of surprise, unworthiness, and pleasure. An attractive, prim, pink-faced lady of forty or so, with pearly dentures and wavy goldenized hair, she was the provincial cousin of the smart, relaxed Joan Clements, who had been all over the world and was married to the most original and least liked scholar on the Waindell campus. A good word should be also put in at this point for Margaret Thayer's husband, Roy, a mournful and mute member of the Department of English, which, except for its ebullient chairman, Cockerell, was an aerie of hypochondriacs. Outwardly, Roy was an obvious figure. If you drew a pair of old brown loafers, two beige elbow patches, a black pipe, and two baggy eyes under hoary eyebrows, the rest was easy to fill out. Somewhere in the middle distance hung an obscure liver ailment, and somewhere in the background there was 'Eighteenth Century Poetry,' Roy's particular field, an overgrazed pasture, with the trickle of a brook and a clump of initialled trees; a barbed-wire arrangement on either side of this field separated it from Professor Stowe's domain, the preceding century, where the lambs were whiter, the turf softer, the rills purlier, and from Dr Shapiro's early nineteenth century, with its glen mists, sea fogs, and imported grapes. Roy Thayer always avoided talking of his subject, and kept a detailed diary, in cryptogrammed verse, which he hoped posterity would someday decipher and, in sober backcast, proclaim the greatest literary achievement of our time.

When everybody was comfortably lapping and lauding the cocktails, Professor Pnin sat down on the wheezy hassock near his newest friend and said, 'I have to report, sir, on the skylark – "zhavoronok," in Russian – about which you made me the honor to interrogate me. Take this with you to your home. I have here tapped on the typewriting machine a condensed account with bibliography. . . . I think we will now transport ourselves to the other room, where a supper à la fourchette is, I think, awaiting us.'

Presently, guests with full plates drifted back into the parlor. The punch was brought in.

'Gracious, Timofey, where on earth did you get that perfectly divine bowl!' exclaimed Joan.

'Victor presented it to me.'

'But where did he get it?'

'Antiquaire store in Cranton, I think.'

'Gosh, it must have cost a fortune!'

'One dollar? Ten dollars? Less, maybe?'

'Ten dollars – nonsense! Two hundred, I should say. Look at it! Look at this writhing pattern. You know, you should show it to the Cockerells. They know everything about old glass. In fact, they have a Lake Dunmore pitcher that looks like a poor relation of this.'

Margaret Thayer admired the bowl in her turn, and said that when she was a child, she imagined Cinderella's glass shoes to be exactly of that greenish-blue tint, whereupon Professor Pnin remarked that, primo, he would like everybody to say whether contents was as good as container, and, secundo, Cendrillon's shoes were not made of glass but of Russian squirrel fur – vair, in French. It was, he said, an obvious case of the survival of the fittest among words, 'verre' being more evocative than 'vair,' which, he submitted, came not from 'varius,' variegated, but from 'veveritsa,' Slavic for a certain beautiful, pale winter squirrel fur, having a bluish, or better say sizïy – columbine – shade. 'So you see, Mrs Fire,' he concluded, 'you were, in general, correct.'

'The contents are fine,' said Laurence Clements.

'This beverage is certainly delicious,' said Margaret Thayer.

By ten o'clock, Pnin's Punch and Betty's Scotch were causing some of the guests to talk louder than they thought they did. A carmine flush had spread over one side of Mrs Thayer's neck, under the little blue star of her left earring, and, sitting very straight, she regaled her host with an account of the feud between two of her co-workers at the library. It was a simple office story, but her changes of tone from Miss Shrill to Mr Basso, and the consciousness of the soiree's going so nicely, made Pnin bend his head and guffaw ecstatically behind his hand. Mrs Thayer's husband was weakly twinkling to himself as he looked into his punch, down his gray, porous nose, and politely listened to Joan Clements, who, when she was a little high, as she was now, had a fetching way of rapidly blinking or even completely closing her black-eyelashed blue eyes. Betty remained her controlled little self, and expertly looked after the refreshments. In the bay end of the room, Clements kept morosely revolving the slow globe as Hagen told him and the grinning Thomas a bit of campus gossip.

At a still later stage of the party, certain rearrangements had again taken place. In a corner of the davenport, Clements was now flipping through an album of 'Flemish Masterpieces,' which Victor had been given by his mother and had left with Pnin. Joan sat on a footstool at her husband's knee, a plate of grapes in the lap of her wide skirt. The others were listening to Hagen discussing modern education.

'You may laugh,' he said, casting a sharp glance at Clements, who shook his head, denying the charge, and then passed the album to his wife, pointing out something in it that had suddenly provoked his glee. 'You may laugh,' he continued to the others, 'but I affirm that the only way to escape from the morass – just a drop, Timofey; that will do – is to lock up the student in a soundproof cell and eliminate the lecture room.'

'Yes, that's it,' said Joan to her husband under her breath, handing the album back to him.

'I am glad you agree, Joan,' said Hagen, and went on, 'I have been called an enfant terrible for expounding this theory, and perhaps you will not go on agreeing quite as lightly when you hear me out. Phonograph records on every possible subject will be at the isolated student's disposal—'

'But the personality of the lecturer,' said Margaret Thayer. 'Surely that counts for something.'

'It does not!' shouted Hagen. 'That is the tragedy. Who, for example, wants him?' He pointed to the radiant Pnin. 'Who wants his personality? Nobody! They will reject Timofey's wonderful personality without a quaver. The world wants a machine, not a Timofey.'

'Why, Timofey is good enough to be televised,' said Clements.

'Oh, I'd love that,' said Joan, beaming at her host, and Betty nodded vigorously. Pnin bowed deeply to them with an 'I-am-disarmed' spreading of both hands.

'And what do you think of my controversial plan?' asked Hagen of Thomas.

'I can tell you what Tom thinks,' said Laurence, still contemplating the same picture in the book that lay open on his knees. 'Tom thinks that the best method of teaching anything is to take it easy and rely on discussion in class, which means letting twenty young blockheads and two cocky neurotics discuss for fifty minutes something that neither their teacher nor they know. Now, for the last three months,' he went on, without any logical transition, 'I have been looking for this picture, and here it is. The publisher of my new book on the Philosophy of Gesture wants a portrait of me, and Joan and I knew we had seen somewhere a stunning likeness by an Old Master but could not even recall his period. Well, here it is. The only retouching needed would be the addition of a sports shirt and the deletion of this warrior's hand.'

'I must really protest—' began Thomas.

Clements passed the open book to Margaret Thayer, and she burst out laughing.

'I must protest, Laurence,' said Tom. 'A relaxed discussion in an atmosphere of broad generalizations is a more realistic approach to education than the old-fashioned formal lecture.'

'Sure, sure,' said Clements.

At this point, Joan scrambled up to her feet and Mrs Thayer looked at her wristwatch, and then at her husband. Betty asked Thomas whether he knew a man called Fogelman, an expert on bats who lived in Santa Clara, Cuba. A soft yawn distended Laurence Clements' mouth. The party was drawing to a close.

The setting of the final scene was the hallway. Hagen could not find the cane he had come with; it had fallen behind the umbrella stand.

'And I think I left my purse where I was sitting,' said

Mrs Thayer, pushing her husband ever so slightly toward the living room.

Pnin and Clements, in last-minute discourse, stood on either side of the living-room doorway, like two well-fed caryatids, and drew in their abdomens to let the silent Thayer pass. In the middle of the room, Professor Thomas and Miss Bliss – he with his hands behind his back and rising up every now and then on his toes, she holding a tray – were standing and talking of Cuba, where a cousin of Betty's fiancé had lived for quite a while, Betty understood. Thayer blundered from chair to chair, and found himself with a white bag, not knowing really where he picked it up, his mind being occupied by the adumbrations of lines he was to write down in his diary later in the night:

We sat and drank, each with a separate past
locked up in him, and fate's alarm clocks set
at unrelated futures – when, at last,
a wrist was cocked, and eyes of consorts met. . . .

Meanwhile, Pnin asked Joan Clements and Margaret Thayer if they would care to see how he had embellished the upstairs rooms. They were enchanted by the idea, and he led the way upstairs. His so-called kabinet, or study, now looked very cozy, its scratched floor snugly covered with the more or less Turkish rug that Pnin had once acquired for his office in Humanities Hall and had recently removed in drastic silence from under the feet of the surprised Falternfels. A tartan lap robe, under which Pnin had crossed the ocean from Europe in 1940, and some endemic cushions had disguised the unremovable bed. The pink shelves, which he had found supporting several generations of children's books, were now loaded with three hundred and sixty-five items from the Waindell College Library.

'And to think I have stamped all these,' sighed Mrs Thayer, rolling up her eyes in mock dismay.

'Some stamped by Mrs Miller,' said Pnin, a stickler for historical truth.

What struck the visitors most in the bedroom was a large folding screen that cut off the fourposter bed from insidious drafts, and the view from the four small windows: a dark rock wall rising abruptly some fifty feet away, with a stretch of pale, starry sky above the black growth of its crest. On the back lawn, across a reflection of a window, Laurence strolled into the shadows.

'At last you are really comfortable,' said Joan.

'And you know what I will say to you,' replied Pnin in a confidential undertone vibrating with triumph. 'Tomorrow morning, under the curtain of mysteree, I will see a gentleman who is wanting to help me to buy this house!'

They came down again. Roy Thayer handed his wife Betty's bag. Herman Hagen found his cane. Laurence Clements reappeared.

'Goodbye, goodbye, Professor Vin!' sang out Pnin, his cheeks ruddy and round in the lamplight of the porch.

'Now, I wonder why he called me that,' said T. W. Thomas, Professor of Anthropology, to Laurence and Joan Clements as they walked through blue darkness toward four cars parked under the elms on the other side of the road.

'Our friend employs a nomenclature all his own,' answered Clements. 'His verbal vagaries add a new thrill to life. His mispronunciations are mythopoeic. His slips of the tongue are oracular. He calls my wife John.'

'Still, I find it a little disturbing,' said Thomas.

'He probably mistook you for somebody else,' said Clements. 'And for all I know you may be somebody else.'

Before they had crossed the street, they were overtaken by Dr Hagen. Professor Thomas, still looking puzzled, took his leave.

'Well,' said Hagen.

It was a fair fall night, velvet below, steel above.

Joan asked, 'You're sure you don't want us to give you a lift, Herman?'

'It's only a ten-minute walk,' he said. 'And a walk is a must on such a wonderful night.'

The three of them stood for a moment gazing at the stars. 'And all these are worlds,' said Hagen.

From the lighted porch came Pnin's rich laughter as he finished recounting to the Thayers and Betty Bliss how he, too, had once retrieved the wrong reticule.

'Come, Laurence, let's be moving,' said Joan. 'It was so nice to see you, Herman. Give my love to Irmgard. What a delightful party! I have never seen Timofey so happy.'

'Yes, thank you,' said Hagen absent-mindedly.

'You should have seen his face when he told us he was going to talk to a real-estate man tomorrow about buying that dream house,' said Joan.

'He did? You're sure he said that?' Hagen asked sharply.

'Quite sure,' said Joan. 'And if anybody needs a home, it is certainly Timofey.'

'Well, good night,' said Hagen. 'So glad you could come. Good night.'

He waited for them to reach their car, hesitated, and then marched back to the lighted porch, where, standing as on a stage, Pnin was shaking hands a second or third time with the Thayers and Betty.

'I shall not forgive you for not letting me do the dishes,' said Betty to her merry host.

'I'll help him,' said Hagen, ascending the porch steps and

thumping upon them with his cane. 'You, children, run along now.'

There was a final round of handshakes, and the Thayers and Betty left.

'First,' said Hagen as he and Pnin re-entered the living room, 'I guess I'll have a last cup of wine with you.'

'Perfect, perfect!' cried Pnin. 'Let us finish my cruchon.'

They made themselves comfortable and Dr Hagen said, 'You are a wonderful host, Timofey. This is a very delightful moment. My grandfather used to say that a glass of good wine should be always sipped and savored as if it were the last one before the execution. I wonder what you put into this punch. I also wonder if, as our charming Joan affirms, you are really contemplating buying this house.'

'Not contemplating – peeping a little at possibilities,' replied Pnin with a gurgling laugh.

'I question the wisdom of it,' continued Hagen, nursing his goblet.

'Naturally, I am expecting that I will get tenure at last,' said Pnin rather slyly. 'I am now Assistant Professor nine years. Years run. Soon I will be Assistant Emeritus. Why, Hagen, are you silent?'

'You place me in a very embarrassing position, Timofey. I hoped you would not raise this particular question.'

'I do not raise the question. I say that I only expect – oh, not next year, but, example given, at hundredth anniversary of Liberation of Serfs – that Waindell will make me Associate.'

'Well, you see, my dear friend, I must tell you a sad secret. It is not official yet, and you must promise not to mention it to anyone.'

'I swear,' said Pnin, raising his hand.

'You cannot but know with what loving care I have built

up our great department,' continued Hagen. 'I, too, am no longer young. You say, Timofey, you have been here for nine years. But I have been giving my all for twenty-nine years to this university! And what happens now? I have nursed this Falternfels, this poltergeist, in my bosom, and he has now worked himself into a key position. I spare you the details of the intrigue.'

'Yes,' said Pnin with a sigh, 'intrigue is horrible, horrible. But, on the other side, honest work will always prove its advantage. You and I will give next year some splendid new courses which I have planned long ago. On Tyranny. On the Boot. On Nicholas the First. On all the precursors of modern atrocity. Hagen, when we speak of injustice, we forget Armenian massacres, tortures which Tibet invented, colonists in Africa. The history of man is the history of pain!'

'You are a wonderful romantic, Timofey, and under happier circumstances . . . However, I can tell you that in the spring term we are going to do something unusual. We're going to stage a dramatic program – scenes from Kotzebue to Hauptmann. I see it as a sort of apotheosis— But let us not anticipate. I, too, am a romantic, Timofey, and therefore cannot work with people like Bodo von Falternfels, as our trustees wish me to do. Kraft is retiring at Seaboard, and it has been offered me that I replace him there, beginning next fall.'

'I congratulate you,' said Pnin warmly.

'Thanks, my friend. It is certainly a very fine and very prominent position. I shall apply to a wider field of scholarship and administration the rich experience I have gained here. Of course, my first move was to suggest that you come with me, but they tell me at Seaboard that they have enough Slavists without you. It is hardly necessary to tell you that Bodo won't continue you in the German Department. This is unfortunate, because Waindell feels that it would be too much of a financial burden to establish a special Russian Department and pay you for two or three Russian courses that have ceased to attract students. Political trends in America, as we all know, discourage interest in things Russian.'

Pnin cleared his throat and asked, 'It signifies that they are firing me?'

'Now, don't take it too hard, Timofey. We shall just go on teaching, you and I, as if nothing had happened, nicht wahr? We must be brave, Timofey!'

'So they have fired me,' said Pnin, clasping his hands and nodding his head.

'Yes, we are in the same boat,' said the jovial Hagen, and he stood up. It was getting very late.

'I go now,' said Hagen, who, though a lesser addict of the present tense than Pnin, also held it in favor. 'It has been a wonderful party, and I would never have allowed myself to spoil the merriment if our mutual friend had not informed me of your optimistic intentions. Good night. Oh, by the way, I hope you will participate vitally in the dramatic program in New Hall this spring. I think you should actually play in it. It would distract you from sad thoughts. Now go to bed at once, and put yourself to sleep with a good mystery story.'

On the porch, he pumped Pnin's unresponsive hand with enough vigor for two. Then he flourished his cane and marched down the wooden steps.

The screen door banged behind him.

'Der arme Kerl,' muttered kindhearted Hagen to himself as he walked homeward. 'At least, I have sweetened the pill.'

From the sideboard and dining-room table Pnin removed to the kitchen sink the used china and silverware. He put away what food remained into the bright arctic light of the refrigerator. The ham and tongue had all gone, and so had the little pink sausages, but the vinaigrette had not been a success, and enough caviar and meat tarts were left over for a meal or two tomorrow. 'Boom-boom-boom,' said the china closet as he passed by. He surveyed the living room and started to tidy it up. A last drop of Pnin's Punch glistened in its beautiful bowl. Joan had crooked a lipstick-stained cigarette butt in her saucer; Betty had left no trace and had taken all the glasses back to the kitchen. Mrs Thayer had forgotten a booklet of pretty multicolored matches on her plate; it lay next to a bit of nougat. Mr Thayer had crumpled into all kinds of weird shapes half a dozen paper napkins. Hagen had quenched a messy cigar in an uneaten bunchlet of grapes.

In the kitchen, Pnin prepared to wash up the dishes. He removed his silk coat, his tie, and his dentures. To protect his shirt front and tuxedo trousers, he donned a soubrette's dappled apron. He scraped various tidbits off the plates into a brown-paper bag, to be given eventually to a mangy little white dog, with pink patches on its back, that visited him sometimes in the afternoon – there was no reason a human's misfortune should interfere with a canine's pleasure.

He prepared a bubble bath in the sink for the crockery, glass, and silverware, and with infinite care lowered the aquamarine bowl into the tepid foam. Its resonant flint glass emitted a sound full of muffled mellowness as it settled down to soak. He rinsed the amber goblets and the silverware under the tap and submerged them in the same foam. Then he fished out the knives, forks, and spoons, rinsed them, and began to wipe them. He worked very slowly, with a certain vagueness of manner, which might have been taken, in a less methodical man, for a mist of abstraction. He gathered the wiped spoons into a posy, placed them in a pitcher, which he had washed but not dried, and then took them out one by one and wiped them all over again. He groped under the bubbles, around the goblets and under the melodious bowl, for any piece of forgotten silver, and retrieved a nutcracker. Fastidious Pnin rinsed it, and was wiping it, when the leggy thing somehow slipped out of the towel and fell like a man from a roof. He almost caught it – his fingertips actually came into contact with it in midair, but this only helped to propel it into the treasure-concealing foam of the sink, where an excruciating crack of broken glass followed upon the plunge.

Pnin hurled the towel into a corner and, turning away, stood for a moment staring at the blackness beyond the threshold of the open back door. A quiet, lacy-winged little green insect circled in the glare of a naked lamp above Pnin's glossy bald head. He looked very old, with his toothless mouth half open and a film of tears dimming his blank, unblinking eyes. Then, with a moan of anguished anticipation, he went back to the sink and, bracing himself, dipped his hand deep into the foam. A jagger of glass stung him. Gently he removed a broken goblet. Victor's beautiful bowl was intact. Pnin rubbed it dry with a fresh towel, working the cloth very tenderly over the recurrent design of the docile glass. Then, with both hands, in a statuesque gesture, he raised the bowl and placed it on a high, safe shelf. The sense of its security there communicated itself to his own state of mind, and he felt that 'losing one's job' dwindled to a meaningless echo in the rich, round inner world where none could really hurt him.

PARTYING TO EXCESS

F. SCOTT FITZGERALD

JAY GATSBY'S PARTY IN WEST EGG

From *The Great Gatsby*

(1925)

CHAPTER III

THERE WAS MUSIC from my neighbor's house through the summer nights. In his blue gardens men and girls came and went like moths among the whisperings and the champagne and the stars. At high tide in the afternoon I watched his guests diving from the tower of his raft, or taking the sun on the hot sand of his beach while his two motor-boats slit the waters of the Sound, drawing aquaplanes over cataracts of foam. On week-ends his Rolls-Royce became an omnibus, bearing parties to and from the city between nine in the morning and long past midnight, while his station wagon scampered like a brisk yellow bug to meet all trains. And on Mondays eight servants, including an extra gardener, toiled all day with mops and scrubbing-brushes and hammers and garden-shears, repairing the ravages of the night before.

Every Friday five crates of oranges and lemons arrived from a fruiterer in New York – every Monday these same oranges and lemons left his back door in a pyramid of pulpless halves. There was a machine in the kitchen which could extract the juice of two hundred oranges in half an hour if a little button was pressed two hundred times by a butler's thumb.

At least once a fortnight a corps of caterers came down with several hundred feet of canvas and enough colored lights to make a Christmas tree of Gatsby's enormous garden. On buffet tables, garnished with glistening hors d'œuvre, spiced baked hams crowded against salads of harlequin designs and pastry pigs and turkeys bewitched to a dark gold. In the main hall a bar with a real brass rail was set up, and stocked with gins and liquors and with cordials so long forgotten that most of his female guests were too young to know one from another.

By seven o'clock the orchestra has arrived, no thin five-piece affair, but a whole pitful of oboes and trombones and saxophones and viols and cornets and piccolos, and low and high drums. The last swimmers have come in from the beach now and are dressing upstairs; the cars from New York are parked five deep in the drive, and already the halls and salons and verandas are gaudy with primary colors, and hair bobbed in strange new ways, and shawls beyond the dreams of Castile. The bar is in full swing, and floating rounds of cocktails permeate the garden outside, until the air is alive with chatter and laughter, and casual innuendo and introductions forgotten on the spot, and enthusiastic meetings between women who never knew each other's names.

The lights grow brighter as the earth lurches away from the sun, and now the orchestra is playing yellow cocktail music, and the opera of voices pitches a key higher. Laughter is easier minute by minute, spilled with prodigality, tipped out at a cheerful word. The groups change more swiftly, swell with new arrivals, dissolve and form in the same breath; already there are wanderers, confident girls who weave here and there among the stouter and more stable, become for a sharp, joyous moment the center of a group, and then, excited with triumph, glide on through the sea-change of faces and voices and color under the constantly changing light.

Suddenly one of these gypsies, in trembling opal, seizes a cocktail out of the air, dumps it down for courage and, moving her hands like Frisco, dances out alone on the canvas platform. A momentary hush; the orchestra leader varies his rhythm obligingly for her, and there is a burst of chatter as the erroneous news goes around that she is Gilda Gray's understudy from the *Follies*. The party has begun.

I believe that on the first night I went to Gatsby's house I was one of the few guests who had actually been invited. People were not invited – they went there. They got into automobiles which bore them out to Long Island, and somehow they ended up at Gatsby's door. Once there they were introduced by somebody who knew Gatsby, and after that they conducted themselves according to the rules of behavior associated with an amusement park. Sometimes they came and went without having met Gatsby at all, came for the party with a simplicity of heart that was its own ticket of admission.

I had been actually invited. A chauffeur in a uniform of robin's-egg blue crossed my lawn early that Saturday morning with a surprisingly formal note from his employer: the honor would be entirely Gatsby's, it said, if I would attend his 'little party' that night. He had seen me several times, and had intended to call on me long before, but a peculiar combination of circumstances had prevented it – signed Jay Gatsby, in a majestic hand.

Dressed up in white flannels I went over to his lawn a little while after seven, and wandered around rather ill at ease among swirls and eddies of people I didn't know – though here and there was a face I had noticed on the commuting train. I was immediately struck by the number of young Englishmen dotted about; all well dressed, all looking a little hungry, and all talking in low, earnest voices to solid and prosperous Americans. I was sure that they were selling something: bonds or insurance or automobiles. They were at least agonizingly aware of the easy money in the vicinity and convinced that it was theirs for a few words in the right key.

As soon as I arrived I made an attempt to find my host, but the two or three people of whom I asked his whereabouts stared at me in such an amazed way, and denied so vehemently any knowledge of his movements, that I slunk off in the direction of the cocktail table – the only place in the garden where a single man could linger without looking purposeless and alone.

I was on my way to get roaring drunk from sheer embarrassment when Jordan Baker came out of the house and stood at the head of the marble steps, leaning a little backward and looking with contemptuous interest down into the garden.

Welcome or not, I found it necessary to attach myself to someone before I should begin to address cordial remarks to the passers-by.

'Hello!' I roared, advancing toward her. My voice seemed unnaturally loud across the garden.

'I thought you might be here,' she responded absently as I came up. 'I remembered you lived next door to—'

She held my hand impersonally, as a promise that she'd take care of me in a minute, and gave ear to two girls in twin yellow dresses, who stopped at the foot of the steps.

'Hello!' they cried together. 'Sorry you didn't win.'

That was for the golf tournament. She had lost in the finals the week before.

'You don't know who we are,' said one of the girls in yellow, 'but we met you here about a month ago.'

'You've dyed your hair since then,' remarked Jordan, and I started, but the girls had moved casually on and her remark was addressed to the premature moon, produced like the supper, no doubt, out of a caterer's basket. With Jordan's slender golden arm resting in mine, we descended the steps and sauntered about the garden. A tray of cocktails floated at us through the twilight, and we sat down at a table with the two girls in yellow and three men, each one introduced to us as Mr Mumble.

'Do you come to these parties often?' inquired Jordan of the girl beside her.

'The last one was the one I met you at,' answered the girl, in an alert confident voice. She turned to her companion: 'Wasn't it for you, Lucille?'

It was for Lucille, too.

'I like to come,' Lucille said. 'I never care what I do, so I always have a good time. When I was here last I tore my gown on a chair, and he asked me my name and address – inside of a week I got a package from Croirier's with a new evening gown in it.'

'Did you keep it?' asked Jordan.

'Sure I did, I was going to wear it to-night, but it was too big in the bust and had to be altered. It was gas blue and lavender beads. Two hundred and sixty-five dollars.'

'There's something funny about a fellow that'll do a thing like that,' said the other girl eagerly. 'He doesn't want any trouble with *any*body.'

'Who doesn't?' I inquired.

'Gatsby. Somebody told me—'

The two girls and Jordan leaned together confidentially.

'Somebody told me they thought he killed a man once.'

A thrill passed over all of us. The three Mr Mumbles bent forward and listened eagerly.

'I don't think it's so much *that*,' argued Lucille skeptically; 'it's more that he was a German spy during the war.'

One of the men nodded in confirmation.

'I heard that from a man who knew all about him, grew up with him in Germany,' he assured us positively.

'Oh, no,' said the first girl, 'it couldn't be that, because he was in the American army during the war.' As our credulity switched back to her she leaned forward with enthusiasm. 'You look at him sometimes when he thinks nobody's looking at him. I'll bet he killed a man.'

She narrowed her eyes and shivered. Lucille shivered. We all turned and looked around for Gatsby. It was testimony to the romantic speculation he inspired that there were whispers about him from those who had found little that it was necessary to whisper about in this world.

The first supper – there would be another one after midnight – was now being served, and Jordan invited me to join her own party, who were spread around a table on the other side of the garden. There were three married couples and Jordan's escort, a persistent undergraduate given to violent innuendo, and obviously under the impression that sooner or later Jordan was going to yield him up her person to a greater or lesser degree. Instead of rambling, this party had preserved a dignified homogeneity, and assumed to itself the function of representing the staid nobility of the countryside – East Egg condescending to West Egg, and carefully on guard against its spectroscopic gaiety.

'Let's get out,' whispered Jordan, after a somehow wasteful and inappropriate half-hour; 'this is much too polite for me.'

We got up, and she explained that we were going to find the host: I had never met him, she said, and it was making me uneasy. The undergraduate nodded in a cynical, melancholy way.

The bar, where we glanced first, was crowded, but Gatsby was not there. She couldn't find him from the top of the steps, and he wasn't on the veranda. On a chance we tried an important-looking door, and walked into a high Gothic library, panelled with carved English oak, and probably transported complete from some ruin overseas.

A stout, middle-aged man, with enormous owl-eyed spectacles, was sitting somewhat drunk on the edge of a great table, staring with unsteady concentration at the shelves of books. As we entered he wheeled excitedly around and examined Jordan from head to foot.

'What do you think?' he demanded impetuously.

'About what?'

He waved his hand toward the book-shelves.

'About that. As a matter of fact you needn't bother to ascertain. I ascertained. They're real.'

'The books?'

He nodded.

'Absolutely real – have pages and everything. I thought they'd be a nice durable cardboard. Matter of fact, they're absolutely real. Pages and— Here! Lemme show you.'

Taking our skepticism for granted, he rushed to the bookcases and returned with Volume One of the 'Stoddard Lectures.'

'See!' he cried triumphantly. 'It's a bona-fide piece of printed matter. It fooled me. This fella's a regular Belasco. It's a triumph. What thoroughness! What realism! Knew when to stop, too – didn't cut the pages. But what do you want? What do you expect?'

He snatched the book from me and replaced it hastily on its shelf, muttering that if one brick was removed the whole library was liable to collapse.

'Who brought you?' he demanded. 'Or did you just come? I was brought. Most people were brought.'

Jordan looked at him alertly, cheerfully, without answering.

'I was brought by a woman named Roosevelt,' he

continued. 'Mrs Claude Roosevelt. Do you know her? I met her somewhere last night. I've been drunk for about a week now, and I thought it might sober me up to sit in a library.'

'Has it?'

'A little bit, I think. I can't tell yet. I've only been here an hour. Did I tell you about the books? They're real. They're—'

'You told us.'

We shook hands with him gravely and went back outdoors.

There was dancing now on the canvas in the garden; old men pushing young girls backward in eternal graceless circles, superior couples holding each other tortuously, fashionably, and keeping in the corners – and a great number of single girls dancing individualistically or relieving the orchestra for a moment of the burden of the banjo or the traps. By midnight the hilarity had increased. A celebrated tenor had sung in Italian, and a notorious contralto had sung in jazz, and between the numbers people were doing 'stunts' all over the garden, while happy, vacuous bursts of laughter rose toward the summer sky. A pair of stage twins, who turned out to be the girls in yellow, did a baby act in costume, and champagne was served in glasses bigger than finger-bowls. The moon had risen higher, and floating in the Sound was a triangle of silver scales, trembling a little to the stiff, tinny drip of the banjoes on the lawn.

I was still with Jordan Baker. We were sitting at a table with a man of about my age and a rowdy little girl, who gave way upon the slightest provocation to uncontrollable laughter. I was enjoying myself now. I had taken two finger-bowls of champagne, and the scene had changed before my eyes into something significant, elemental, and profound.

At a lull in the entertainment the man looked at me and smiled.

'Your face is familiar,' he said, politely. 'Weren't you in the First Division during the war?'

'Why, yes. I was in the Twenty-eighth Infantry.'

'I was in the Sixteenth until June nineteen-eighteen. I knew I'd seen you somewhere before.'

We talked for a moment about some wet, gray little villages in France. Evidently he lived in this vicinity, for he told me that he had just bought a hydroplane, and was going to try it out in the morning.

'Want to go with me, old sport? Just near the shore along the Sound.'

'What time?'

'Any time that suits you best.'

It was on the tip of my tongue to ask his name when Jordan looked around and smiled.

'Having a gay time now?' she inquired.

'Much better.' I turned again to my new acquaintance. 'This is an unusual party for me. I haven't even see the host. I live over there—' I waved my hand at the invisible hedge in the distance, 'and this man Gatsby sent over his chauffeur with an invitation.'

For a moment he looked at me as if he failed to understand.

'I'm Gatsby,' he said suddenly.

'What!' I exclaimed. 'Oh, I beg your pardon.'

'I thought you knew, old sport. I'm afraid I'm not a very good host.'

He smiled understandingly – much more than understandingly. It was one of those rare smiles with a quality of eternal reassurance in it, that you may come across four or five times in life. It faced – or seemed to face – the whole eternal world for an instant, and then concentrated on *you* with an irresistible prejudice in your favor. It understood you just as far as you wanted to be understood, believed in you as you would like to believe in yourself, and assured you that it had precisely the impression of you that, at your best, you hoped to convey. Precisely at that point it vanished – and I was looking at an elegant young roughneck, a year or two over thirty, whose elaborate formality of speech just missed being absurd. Some time before he introduced himself I'd got a strong impression that he was picking his words with care.

Almost at the moment when Mr Gatsby identified himself, a butler hurried toward him with the information that Chicago was calling him on the wire. He excused himself with a small bow that included each of us in turn.

'If you want anything just ask for it, old sport,' he urged me. 'Excuse me. I will rejoin you later.'

When he was gone I turned immediately to Jordan – constrained to assure her of my surprise. I had expected that Mr Gatsby would be a florid and corpulent person in his middle years.

'Who is he?' I demanded. 'Do you know?'

'He's just a man named Gatsby.'

'Where is he from, I mean? And what does he do?'

'Now *you're* started on the subject,' she answered with a wan smile. 'Well, he told me once he was an Oxford man.'

A dim background started to take shape behind him, but at her next remark it faded away.

'However, I don't believe it.'

'Why not?'

'I don't know,' she insisted, 'I just don't think he went there.'

Something in her tone reminded me of the other girl's 'I think he killed a man,' and had the effect of stimulating my curiosity. I would have accepted without question the information that Gatsby sprang from the swamps of Louisiana or from the lower East Side of New York. That was comprehensible. But young men didn't – at least in my provincial inexperience I believed they didn't – drift coolly out of nowhere and buy a palace on Long Island Sound.

'Anyhow, he gives large parties,' said Jordan, changing the subject with an urban taste for the concrete. 'And I like large parties. They're so intimate. At small parties there isn't any privacy.'

There was the boom of a brass drum, and the voice of the orchestra leader rang out suddenly above the echolalia of the garden.

'Ladies and gentlemen,' he cried. 'At the request of Mr Gatsby we are going to play for you Mr Vladimir Tostoff's latest work, which attracted so much attention at Carnegie Hall last May. If you read the papers, you know there was a big sensation.' He smiled with jovial condescension, and added: 'Some sensation!' Whereupon everybody laughed.

'The piece is known,' he concluded lustily, 'as Vladimir Tostoff's *Jazz History of the World*.'

The nature of Mr Tostoff's composition eluded me, because just as it began my eyes fell on Gatsby, standing alone on the marble steps and looking from one group to another with approving eyes. His tanned skin was drawn attractively tight on his face and his short hair looked as though it were trimmed every day. I could see nothing sinister about him. I wondered if the fact that he was not drinking helped to set him off from his guests, for it seemed to me that he grew more correct as the fraternal hilarity increased. When the *Jazz History of the World* was over, girls were putting their heads on men's shoulders in a puppyish, convivial way, girls were swooning backward playfully into men's arms, even into groups, knowing that someone would arrest their falls

– but no one swooned backward on Gatsby, and no French bob touched Gatsby's shoulder, and no singing quartets were formed with Gatsby's head for one link.

'I beg your pardon.'

Gatsby's butler was suddenly standing beside us.

'Miss Baker?' he inquired. 'I beg your pardon, but Mr Gatsby would like to speak to you alone.'

'With me?' she exclaimed in surprise.

'Yes, madame.'

She got up slowly, raising her eyebrows at me in astonishment, and followed the butler toward the house. I noticed that she wore her evening-dress, all her dresses, like sports clothes – there was a jauntiness about her movements as if she had first learned to walk upon golf courses on clean, crisp mornings.

I was alone and it was almost two. For some time confused and intriguing sounds had issued from a long, many-windowed room which overhung the terrace. Eluding Jordan's undergraduate, who was now engaged in an obstetrical conversation with two chorus girls, and who implored me to join him, I went inside.

The large room was full of people. One of the girls in yellow was playing the piano, and beside her stood a tall, red-haired young lady from a famous chorus, engaged in song. She had drunk a quantity of champagne, and during the course of her song she had decided, ineptly, that everything was very, very sad – she was not only singing, she was weeping too. Whenever there was a pause in the song she filled it with gasping, broken sobs, and then took up the lyric again in a quavering soprano. The tears coursed down her cheeks – not freely, however, for when they came into contact with her heavily beaded eyelashes they assumed an inky colour, and pursued the rest of their way in slow black rivulets. A humorous suggestion was made that she sing the notes on her face, whereupon she threw up her hands, sank into a chair, and went off into a deep vinous sleep.

'She had a fight with a man who says he's her husband,' explained a girl at my elbow.

I looked around. Most of the remaining women were now having fights with men said to be their husbands. Even Jordan's party, the quartet from East Egg, were rent asunder by dissension. One of the men was talking with curious intensity to a young actress, and his wife, after attempting to laugh at the situation in a dignified and indifferent way, broke down entirely and resorted to flank attacks – at intervals she appeared suddenly at his side like an angry diamond, and hissed: 'You promised!' into his ear.

The reluctance to go home was not confined to wayward men. The hall was at present occupied by two deplorably sober men and their highly indignant wives. The wives were sympathizing with each other in slightly raised voices.

'Whenever he sees I'm having a good time he wants to go home.'

'Never heard anything so selfish in my life.'

'We're always the first ones to leave.'

'So are we.'

'Well, we're almost the last to-night,' said one of the men sheepishly. 'The orchestra left half an hour ago.'

In spite of the wives' agreement that such malevolence was beyond credibility, the dispute ended in a short struggle, and both wives were lifted, kicking, into the night.

As I waited for my hat in the hall the door of the library opened and Jordan Baker and Gatsby came out together. He was saying some last word to her, but the eagerness in his manner tightened abruptly into formality as several people approached him to say good-bye.

Jordan's party were calling impatiently to her from the porch, but she lingered for a moment to shake hands.

'I've just heard the most amazing thing,' she whispered. 'How long were we in there?'

'Why, about an hour.'

'It was . . . simply amazing,' she repeated abstractedly. 'But I swore I wouldn't tell it and here I am tantalizing you.' She yawned gracefully in my face. 'Please come and see me. . . . Phone book. . . . Under the name of Mrs Sigourney Howard. . . . My aunt. . . .' She was hurrying off as she talked – her brown hand waved a jaunty salute as she melted into her party at the door.

Rather ashamed that on my first appearance I had stayed so late, I joined the last of Gatsby's guests, who were clustered around him. I wanted to explain that I'd hunted for him early in the evening and to apologize for not having known him in the garden.

'Don't mention it,' he enjoined me eagerly. 'Don't give it another thought, old sport.' The familiar expression held no more familiarity than the hand which reassuringly brushed my shoulder. 'And don't forget we're going up in the hydroplane to-morrow morning, at nine o'clock.'

Then the butler, behind his shoulder:

'Philadelphia wants you on the 'phone, sir.'

'All right, in a minute. Tell them I'll be right there. . . . Good night.'

'Good night.'

'Good night.' He smiled – and suddenly there seemed to be a pleasant significance in having been among the last to go, as if he had desired it all the time. 'Good night, old sport. . . . Good night.'

But as I walked down the steps I saw that the evening was not quite over. Fifty feet from the door a dozen headlights illuminated a bizarre and tumultuous scene. In the ditch beside the road, right side up, but violently shorn of one wheel, rested a new coupé which had left Gatsby's drive not two minutes before. The sharp jut of a wall accounted for the detachment of the wheel, which was now getting considerable attention from half a dozen curious chauffeurs. However, as they had left their cars blocking the road, a harsh, discordant din from those in the rear had been audible for some time, and added to the already violent confusion of the scene.

A man in a long duster had dismounted from the wreck and now stood in the middle of the road, looking from the car to the tire and from the tire to the observers in a pleasant, puzzled way.

'See!' he explained. 'It went in the ditch.'

The fact was infinitely astonishing to him, and I recognized first the unusual quality of wonder, and then the man – it was the late patron of Gatsby's library.

'How'd it happen?'

He shrugged his shoulders.

'I know nothing whatever about mechanics,' he said decisively.

'But how did it happen? Did you run into the wall?'

'Don't ask me,' said Owl Eyes, washing his hands of the whole matter. 'I know very little about driving – next to nothing. It happened, and that's all I know.'

'Well, if you're a poor driver you oughtn't to try driving at night.'

'But I wasn't even trying,' he explained indignantly, 'I wasn't even trying.'

An awed hush fell upon the bystanders.

'Do you want to commit suicide?'

'You're lucky it was just a wheel! A bad driver and not even *try*ing!'

'You don't understand,' explained the criminal. 'I wasn't driving. There's another man in the car.'

The shock that followed this declaration found voice in a sustained 'Ah-h-h!' as the door of the coupé swung slowly open. The crowd – it was now a crowd – stepped back involuntarily, and when the door had opened wide there was a ghostly pause. Then, very gradually, part by part, a pale, dangling individual stepped out of the wreck, pawing tentatively at the ground with a large uncertain dancing shoe.

Blinded by the glare of the headlights and confused by the incessant groaning of the horns, the apparition stood swaying for a moment before he perceived the man in the duster.

'Wha's matter?' he inquired calmly. 'Did we run outa gas?'

'Look!'

Half a dozen fingers pointed at the amputated wheel – he stared at it for a moment, and then looked upward as though he suspected that it had dropped from the sky.

'It came off,' someone explained.

He nodded.

'At first I din' notice we'd stopped.'

A pause. Then, taking a long breath and straightening his shoulders, he remarked in a determined voice:

'Wonder'ff tell me where there's a gas'line station?'

At least a dozen men, some of them a little better off than he was, explained to him that wheel and car were no longer joined by any physical bond.

'Back out,' he suggested after a moment. 'Put her in reverse.'

'But the *wheel's* off!'

He hesitated.

'No harm in trying,' he said.

The caterwauling horns had reached a crescendo and

I turned away and cut across the lawn toward home. I glanced back once. A wafer of a moon was shining over Gatsby's house, making the night fine as before, and surviving the laughter and the sound of his still glowing garden. A sudden emptiness seemed to flow now from the windows and the great doors, endowing with complete isolation the figure of the host, who stood on the porch, his hand up in a formal gesture of farewell.

ERNEST HEMINGWAY

THE FESTIVAL OF SAN FERMIN

From *The Sun Also Rises*

(1926)

CHAPTER XV

AT NOON OF Sunday, the 6th of July, the fiesta exploded. There is no other way to describe it. People had been coming in all day from the country, but they were assimilated in the town and you did not notice them. The square was as quiet in the hot sun as on any other day. The peasants were in the outlying wine-shops. There they were drinking, getting ready for the fiesta. They had come in so recently from the plains and the hills that it was necessary that they make their shifting in values gradually. They could not start in paying café prices. They got their money's worth in the wine-shops. Money still had a definite value in hours worked and bushels of grain sold. Late in the fiesta it would not matter what they paid, nor where they bought.

Now on the day of the starting of the fiesta of San Fermin they had been in the wine-shops of the narrow streets of the town since early morning. Going down the streets in the morning on the way to mass in the cathedral, I heard them singing through the open doors of the shops. They were warming up. There were many people at the eleven o'clock mass. San Fermin is also a religious festival.

I walked down the hill from the cathedral and up the street to the café on the square. It was a little before noon. Robert Cohn and Bill were sitting at one of the tables. The marble-topped tables and the white wicker chairs were gone. They were replaced by cast-iron tables and severe folding chairs. The café was like a battleship stripped for action.

To-day the waiters did not leave you alone all morning to read without asking if you wanted to order something. A waiter came up as soon as I sat down.

'What are you drinking?' I asked Bill and Robert.

'Sherry,' Cohn said.

'Jerez,' I said to the waiter.

Before the waiter brought the sherry the rocket that announced the fiesta went up in the square. It burst and there was a gray ball of smoke high up above the Theatre Gayarre, across on the other side of the plaza. The ball of smoke hung in the sky like a shrapnel burst, and as I watched, another rocket came up to it, trickling smoke in the bright sunlight. I saw the bright flash as it burst and another little cloud of smoke appeared. By the time the second rocket had burst there were so many people in the arcade, that had been empty a minute before, that the waiter, holding the bottle high up over his head, could hardly get through the crowd to our table. People were coming into the square from all sides, and down the street we heard the pipes and the fifes and the drums coming. They were playing the *riau-riau* music, the pipes shrill and the drums pounding, and behind them came the men and boys dancing. When the fifers stopped they all crouched down in the street, and when the reed-pipes and the fifes shrilled, and the flat, dry, hollow drums tapped it out again, they all went up in the air dancing. In the crowd you saw only the heads and shoulders of the dancers going up and down.

In the square a man, bent over, was playing on a reed-pipe, and a crowd of children were following him shouting, and pulling at his clothes. He came out of the square, the children following him, and piped them past the café and down a side street. We saw his blank pockmarked face as he went by, piping, the children close behind him shouting and pulling at him.

'He must be the village idiot,' Bill said. 'My God! look at that!'

Down the street came dancers. The street was solid with dancers, all men. They were all dancing in time behind their own fifers and drummers. They were a club of some sort, and all wore workmen's blue smocks, and red handkerchiefs around their necks, and carried a great banner on two poles. The banner danced up and down with them as they came down surrounded by the crowd.

'Hurray for Wine! Hurray for the Foreigners!' was painted on the banner.

'Where are the foreigners?' Robert Cohn asked.

'We're the foreigners,' Bill said.

All the time rockets were going up. The café tables were all full now. The square was emptying of people and the crowd was filling the cafés.

'Where's Brett and Mike?' Bill asked.

'I'll go and get them,' Cohn said.

'Bring them here.'

The fiesta was really started. It kept up day and night for seven days. The dancing kept up, the drinking kept up, the noise went on. The things that happened could only have happened during a fiesta. Everything became quite unreal finally and it seemed as though nothing could have any consequences. It seemed out of place to think of consequences during the fiesta. All during the fiesta you had the feeling, even when it was quiet, that you had to shout any remark to make it heard. It was the same feeling about any action. It was a fiesta and it went on for seven days.

That afternoon was the big religious procession. San Fermin was translated from one church to another. In the procession were all the dignitaries, civil and religious. We could not see them because the crowd was too great. Ahead of the formal procession and behind it danced the *riau-riau* dancers. There was one mass of yellow shirts dancing up and down in the crowd. All we could see of the procession through the closely pressed people that crowded all the side streets and curbs were the great giants, cigar-store Indians, thirty feet high, Moors, a King and Queen, whirling and waltzing solemnly to the *riau-riau*.

They were all standing outside the chapel where San Fermin and the dignitaries had passed in, leaving a guard of soldiers, the giants, with the men who danced in them standing beside their resting frames, and the dwarfs moving with their whacking bladders through the crowd. We started inside and there was a smell of incense and people filing back into the church, but Brett was stopped just inside the door because she had no hat, so we went out again and along the street that ran back from the chapel into town. The street was lined on both sides with people keeping their place at the curb for the return of the procession. Some dancers formed a circle around Brett and started to dance. They wore big wreaths of white garlics around their necks. They took Bill and me by the arms and put us in the circle. Bill started to dance, too. They were all chanting. Brett wanted to dance but they did not want her to. They wanted her as an image to dance around. When the song ended with the sharp *riau-riau!* they rushed us into a wine-shop.

We stood at the counter. They had Brett seated on a wine-cask. It was dark in the wine-shop and full of men singing, hard-voiced singing. Back of the counter they drew the wine from casks. I put down money for the wine, but one of the men picked it up and put it back in my pocket.

'I want a leather wine-bottle,' Bill said.

'There's a place down the street,' I said. 'I'll go get a couple.'

The dancers did not want me to go out. Three of them were sitting on the high wine-cask beside Brett, teaching her to drink out of the wine-skins. They had hung a wreath of garlics around her neck. Some one insisted on giving her a glass. Somebody was teaching Bill a song. Singing it into his ear. Beating time on Bill's back.

I explained to them that I would be back. Outside in the street I went down the street looking for the shop that made leather wine-bottles. The crowd was packed on the sidewalks and many of the shops were shuttered, and I could not find it. I walked as far as the church, looking on both sides of the street. Then I asked a man and he took me by the arm and led me to it. The shutters were up but the door was open.

Inside it smelled of fresh tanned leather and hot tar. A man was stencilling completed wine-skins. They hung from the roof in bunches. He took one down, blew it up, screwed the nozzle tight, and then jumped on it.

'See! It doesn't leak.'

'I want another one, too. A big one.'

He took down a big one that would hold a gallon or more, from the roof. He blew it up, his cheeks puffing ahead of the wine-skin, and stood on the bota holding on to a chair.

'What are you going to do? Sell them in Bayonne?'

'No. Drink out of them.'

He slapped me on the back.

'Good man. Eight pesetas for the two. The lowest price.'

The man who was stencilling the new ones and tossing them into a pile stopped.

'It's true,' he said. 'Eight pesetas is cheap.'

I paid and went out and along the street back to the wine-shop. It was darker than ever inside and very crowded. I did not see Brett and Bill, and some one said they were in the back room. At the counter the girl filled the two wine-skins for me. One held two litres. The other held five litres. Filling them both cost three pesetas sixty centimos. Some one at the counter, that I had never seen before, tried to pay for the wine, but I finally paid for it myself. The man who had wanted to pay then bought me a drink. He would not let me buy one in return, but said he would take a rinse of the mouth from the new wine-bag. He tipped the big five-litre bag up and squeezed it so the wine hissed against the back of his throat.

'All right,' he said, and handed back the bag.

In the back room Brett and Bill were sitting on barrels surrounded by the dancers. Everybody had his arms on everybody else's shoulders, and they were all singing. Mike was sitting at a table with several men in their shirt-sleeves, eating from a bowl of tuna fish, chopped onions and vinegar. They were all drinking wine and mopping up the oil and vinegar with pieces of bread.

'Hello, Jake. Hello!' Mike called. 'Come here. I want you to meet my friends. We're all having an hors d'œuvre.'

I was introduced to the people at the table. They supplied their names to Mike and sent for a fork for me.

'Stop eating their dinner, Michael,' Brett shouted from the wine-barrels.

'I don't want to eat up your meal,' I said when some one handed me a fork.

'Eat,' he said. 'What do you think it's here for?'

I unscrewed the nozzle of the big wine-bottle and handed it around. Every one took a drink, tipping the wine-skin at arm's length.

Outside, above the singing, we could hear the music of the procession going by.

'Isn't that the procession?' Mike asked.

'Nada,' some one said. 'It's nothing. Drink up. Lift the bottle.'

'Where did they find you?' I asked Mike.

'Some one brought me here,' Mike said. 'They said you were here.'

'Where's Cohn?'

'He's passed out,' Brett called. 'They've put him away somewhere.'

'Where is he?'

'I don't know.'

'How should we know,' Bill said. 'I think he's dead.'

'He's not dead,' Mike said. 'I know he's not dead. He's just passed out on Anis del Mono.'

As he said Anis del Mono one of the men at the table looked up, brought out a bottle from inside his smock, and handed it to me.

'No,' I said. 'No, thanks!'

'Yes. Yes. Arriba! Up with the bottle!'

I took a drink. It tasted of licorice and warmed all the way. I could feel it warming in my stomach.

'Where the hell is Cohn?'

'I don't know,' Mike said. 'I'll ask. Where is the drunken comrade?' he asked in Spanish.

'You want to see him?'

'Yes,' I said.

'Not me,' said Mike. 'This gent.'

The Anis del Mono man wiped his mouth and stood up.

'Come on.'

In a back room Robert Cohn was sleeping quietly on some wine-casks. It was almost too dark to see his face. They had covered him with a coat and another coat was folded under his head. Around his neck and on his chest was a big wreath of twisted garlics.

'Let him sleep,' the man whispered. 'He's all right.'

Two hours later Cohn appeared. He came into the front room still with the wreath of garlics around his neck. The Spaniards shouted when he came in. Cohn wiped his eyes and grinned.

'I must have been sleeping,' he said.

'Oh, not at all,' Brett said.

'You were only dead,' Bill said.

'Aren't we going to go and have some supper?' Cohn asked.

'Do you want to eat?'

'Yes. Why not? I'm hungry.'

'Eat those garlics, Robert,' Mike said. 'I say. Do eat those garlics.'

Cohn stood there. His sleep had made him quite all right.

'Do let's go and eat,' Brett said. 'I must get a bath.'

'Come on,' Bill said. 'Let's translate Brett to the hotel.'

We said goodbye to many people and shook hands with many people and went out. Outside it was dark.

'What time is it do you suppose?' Cohn asked.

'It's to-morrow,' Mike said. 'You've been asleep two days.'

'No,' said Cohn, 'what time is it?'

'It's ten o'clock.'

'What a lot we've drunk.'

'You mean what a lot *we've* drunk. You went to sleep.'

Going down the dark streets to the hotel we saw the sky-rockets going up in the square. Down the side streets that led to the square we saw the square solid with people, those in the centre all dancing.

It was a big meal at the hotel. It was the first meal of the prices being doubled for the fiesta, and there were several new courses. After the dinner we were out in the town. I remember resolving that I would stay up all night to watch the bulls go through the streets at six o'clock in the morning, and being so sleepy that I went to bed around four o'clock. The others stayed up.

My own room was locked and I could not find the key, so I went upstairs and slept on one of the beds in Cohn's room. The fiesta was going on outside in the night, but I was too sleepy for it to keep me awake. When I woke it was the sound of the rocket exploding that announced the release of the bulls from the corrals at the edge of town. They would race through the streets and out to the bull-ring. I had been sleeping heavily and I woke feeling I was too late. I put on a coat of Cohn's and went out on the balcony. Down below the narrow street was empty. All the balconies were crowded with people. Suddenly a crowd came down the street. They were all running, packed close together. They passed along and up the street toward the bull-ring and behind them came more men running faster, and then some stragglers who were really running. Behind them was a little bare space, and then the bulls galloping, tossing their heads up and down. It all went out of sight around the corner. One man fell, rolled to the gutter, and lay quiet. But the bulls went right on and did not notice him. They were all running together.

After they went out of sight a great roar came from the bull-ring. It kept on. Then finally the pop of the rocket that meant the bulls had gotten through the people in the ring and into the corrals. I went back in the room and got into bed. I had been standing on the stone balcony in bare feet. I knew our crowd must have all been out at the bull-ring. Back in bed, I went to sleep.

Cohn woke me when he came in. He started to undress

and went over and closed the window because the people on the balcony of the house just across the street were looking in.

'Did you see the show?' I asked.

'Yes. We were all there.'

'Anybody get hurt?'

'One of the bulls got into the crowd in the ring and tossed six or eight people.'

'How did Brett like it?'

'It was all so sudden there wasn't any time for it to bother anybody.'

'I wish I'd been up.'

'We didn't know where you were. We went to your room but it was locked.'

'Where did you stay up?'

'We danced at some club.'

'I got sleepy,' I said.

'My gosh! I'm sleepy now,' Cohn said. 'Doesn't this thing ever stop?'

'Not for a week.'

Bill opened the door and put his head in.

'Where were you, Jake?'

'I saw them go through from the balcony. How was it?'

'Grand.'

'Where you going?'

'To sleep.'

No one was up before noon. We ate at tables set out under the arcade. The town was full of people. We had to wait for a table. After lunch we went over to the Iruña. It had filled up, and as the time for the bull-fight came it got fuller, and the tables were crowded closer. There was a close, crowded hum that came every day before the bull-fight. The café did not make this same noise at any other time, no matter how crowded it was. This hum went on, and we were in it and a part of it.

I had taken six seats for all the fights. Three of them were barreras, the first row at the ring-side, and three were sobrepuertos, seats with wooden backs, half-way up the amphitheatre. Mike thought Brett had best sit high up for her first time, and Cohn wanted to sit with them. Bill and I were going to sit in the barreras, and I gave the extra ticket to a waiter to sell. Bill said something to Cohn about what to do and how to look so he would not mind the horses. Bill had seen one season of bull-fights.

'I'm not worried about how I'll stand it. I'm only afraid I may be bored,' Cohn said.

'You think so?'

'Don't look at the horses, after the bull hits them,' I said to Brett. 'Watch the charge and see the picador try and keep the bull off, but then don't look again until the horse is dead if it's been hit.'

'I'm a little nervy about it,' Brett said. 'I'm worried whether I'll be able to go through with it all right.'

'You'll be all right. There's nothing but that horse part that will bother you, and they're only in for a few minutes with each bull. Just don't watch when it's bad.'

'She'll be all right,' Mike said. 'I'll look after her.'

'I don't think you'll be bored,' Bill said.

'I'm going over to the hotel to get the glasses and the wine-skin,' I said. 'See you back here. Don't get cock-eyed.'

'I'll come along,' Bill said. Brett smiled at us.

We walked around through the arcade to avoid the heat of the square.

'That Cohn gets me,' Bill said. 'He's got this Jewish superiority so strong that he thinks the only emotion he'll get out of the fight will be being bored.'

'We'll watch him with the glasses,' I said.

'Oh, to hell with him!'

'He spends a lot of time there.'

'I want him to stay there.'

In the hotel on the stairs we met Montoya.

'Come on,' said Montoya. 'Do you want to meet Pedro Romero?'

'Fine,' said Bill. 'Let's go see him.'

We followed Montoya up a flight and down the corridor.

'He's in room number eight,' Montoya explained. 'He's getting dressed for the bull-fight.'

Montoya knocked on the door and opened it. It was a gloomy room with a little light coming in from the window on the narrow street. There were two beds separated by a monastic partition. The electric light was on. The boy stood very straight and unsmiling in his bull-fighting clothes. His jacket hung over the back of a chair. They were just finishing winding his sash. His black hair shone under the electric light. He wore a white linen shirt and the sword-handler finished his sash and stood up and stepped back. Pedro Romero nodded, seeming very far away and dignified when we shook hands. Montoya said something about what great aficionados we were, and that we wanted to wish him luck. Romero listened very seriously. Then he turned to me. He was the best-looking boy I have ever seen.

'You go to the bull-fight,' he said in English.

'You know English,' I said, feeling like an idiot.

'No,' he answered, and smiled.

One of three men who had been sitting on the beds came up and asked us if we spoke French. 'Would you like me to interpret for you? Is there anything you would like to ask Pedro Romero?'

We thanked him. What was there that you would like to ask? The boy was nineteen years old, alone except for his sword-handler, and the three hangers-on, and the bull-fight was to commence in twenty minutes. We wished him 'Mucha suerte,' shook hands, and went out. He was standing, straight and handsome and altogether by himself, alone in the room with the hangers-on as we shut the door.

'He's a fine boy, don't you think so?' Montoya asked.

'He's a good-looking kid,' I said.

'He looks like a torero,' Montoya said. 'He has the type.'

'He's a fine boy.'

'We'll see how he is in the ring,' Montoya said.

We found the big leather wine-bottle leaning against the wall in my room, took it and the field-glasses, locked the door, and went downstairs.

It was a good bull-fight. Bill and I were very excited about Pedro Romero. Montoya was sitting about ten places away. After Romero had killed his first bull Montoya caught my eye and nodded his head. This was a real one. There had not been a real one for a long time. Of the other two matadors, one was very fair and the other was passable. But there was no comparison with Romero, although neither of his bulls was much.

Several times during the bull-fight I looked up at Mike and Brett and Cohn, with the glasses. They seemed to be all right. Brett did not look upset. All three were leaning forward on the concrete railing in front of them.

'Let me take the glasses,' Bill said.

'Does Cohn look bored?' I asked.

'That kike!'

Outside the ring, after the bull-fight was over, you could not move in the crowd. We could not make our way through but had to be moved with the whole thing, slowly, as a glacier, back to town. We had that disturbed emotional feeling that always comes after a bull-fight, and the feeling of elation that comes after a good bull-fight. The fiesta was going on. The drums pounded and the pipe music was shrill, and everywhere the flow of the crowd was broken by patches of dancers. The dancers were in a crowd, so you did not see the intricate play of the feet. All you saw was the heads and shoulders going up and down, up and down. Finally, we got out of the crowd and made for the café. The waiter saved chairs for the others, and we each ordered an absinthe and watched the crowd in the square and the dancers.

'What do you suppose that dance is?' Bill asked.

'It's a sort of jota.'

'They're not all the same,' Bill said. 'They dance differently to all the different tunes.'

'It's swell dancing.'

In front of us on a clear part of the street a company of boys were dancing. The steps were very intricate and their faces were intent and concentrated. They all looked down while they danced. Their rope-soled shoes tapped and spatted on the pavement. The toes touched. The heels touched. The balls of the feet touched. Then the music broke wildly and the step was finished and they were all dancing on up the street.

'Here come the gentry,' Bill said.

They were crossing the street.

'Hello, men,' I said.

'Hello, gents!' said Brett. 'You saved us seats? How nice.'

'I say,' Mike said, 'that Romero what'shisname is somebody. Am I wrong?'

'Oh, isn't he lovely,' Brett said. 'And those green trousers.'

'Brett never took her eyes off them.'

'I say, I must borrow your glasses to-morrow.'

'How did it go?'

'Wonderfully! Simply perfect. I say, it is a spectacle!'

'How about the horses?'

'I couldn't help looking at them.'

'She couldn't take her eyes off them,' Mike said. 'She's an extraordinary wench.'

'They do have some rather awful things happen to them,' Brett said. 'I couldn't look away, though.'

'Did you feel all right?'

'I didn't feel badly at all.'

'Robert Cohn did,' Mike put in. 'You were quite green, Robert.'

'The first horse did bother me,' Cohn said.

'You weren't bored, were you?' asked Bill.

Cohn laughed.

'No. I wasn't bored. I wish you'd forgive me that.'

'It's all right,' Bill said, 'so long as you weren't bored.'

'He didn't look bored,' Mike said. 'I thought he was going to be sick.'

'I never felt that bad. It was just for a minute.'

'*I* thought he was going to be sick. You weren't bored, were you, Robert?'

'Let up on that, Mike. I said I was sorry I said it.'

'He was, you know. He was positively green.'

'Oh, shove it along, Michael.'

'You mustn't ever get bored at your first bull-fight, Robert,' Mike said. 'It might make such a mess.'

'Oh, shove it along, Michael,' Brett said.

'He said Brett was a sadist,' Mike said. 'Brett's not a sadist. She's just a lovely, healthy wench.'

'Are you a sadist, Brett?' I asked.

'Hope not.'

'He said Brett was a sadist just because she has a good, healthy stomach.'

'Won't be healthy long.'

Bill got Mike started on something else than Cohn. The waiter brought the absinthe glasses.

'Did you really like it?' Bill asked Cohn.

'No, I can't say I liked it. I think it's a wonderful show.'

'Gad, yes! What a spectacle!' Brett said.

'I wish they didn't have the horse part,' Cohn said.

'They're not important,' Bill said. 'After a while you never notice anything disgusting.'

'It is a bit strong just at the start,' Brett said. 'There's a dreadful moment for me just when the bull starts for the horse.'

'The bulls were fine,' Cohn said.

'They were very good,' Mike said.

'I want to sit down below, next time.' Brett drank from her glass of absinthe.

'She wants to see the bull-fighters close by,' Mike said.

'They are something,' Brett said. 'That Romero lad is just a child.'

'He's a damned good-looking boy,' I said. 'When we were up in his room I never saw a better-looking kid.'

'How old do you suppose he is?'

'Nineteen or twenty.'

'Just imagine it.'

The bull-fight on the second day was much better than on the first. Brett sat between Mike and me at the barrera, and Bill and Cohn went up above. Romero was the whole show. I do not think Brett saw any other bull-fighter. No one else did either, except the hard-shelled technicians. It was all Romero. There were two other matadors, but they did not count. I sat beside Brett and explained to Brett what it was all about. I told her about watching the bull, not the horse, when the bulls charged the picadors, and got her to watching the picador place the point of his pic so that she saw what it was all about, so that it became more something that was going on with a definite end, and less of a spectacle with unexplained horrors. I had her watch how Romero took the bull away from a fallen horse with his cape, and how he held him with the cape and turned him, smoothly and suavely, never wasting the bull. She saw how Romero avoided every brusque movement and saved his bulls for the last when he wanted them, not winded and discomposed but smoothly worn down. She saw how close Romero always worked to the bull, and I pointed out to her the tricks the other bull-fighters used to make it look as though they were working closely. She saw why she liked Romero's cape-work and why she did not like the others.

Romero never made any contortions, always it was straight and pure and natural in line. The others twisted themselves like cork-screws, their elbows raised, and leaned against the flanks of the bull after his horns had passed, to give a faked look of danger. Afterward, all that was faked turned bad and gave an unpleasant feeling. Romero's bull-fighting gave real emotion, because he kept the absolute purity of line in his movements and always quietly and calmly let the horns pass him close each time. He did not have to emphasize their closeness. Brett saw how something that was beautiful done close to the bull was ridiculous if it were done a little way off. I told her how since the death of Joselito all the bull-fighters had been developing a technic that simulated this appearance of danger in order to give a fake emotional feeling, while the bull-fighter was really safe. Romero had the old thing, the holding of his purity of line through the maximum of exposure, while he dominated the bull by making him realize he was unattainable, while he prepared him for the killing.

'I've never seen him do an awkward thing,' Brett said.

'You won't until he gets frightened,' I said.

'He'll never be frightened,' Mike said. 'He knows too damned much.'

'He knew everything when he started. The others can't ever learn what he was born with.'

'And God, what looks,' Brett said.

'I believe, you know, that she's falling in love with this bull-fighter chap,' Mike said.

'I wouldn't be surprised.'

'Be a good chap, Jake. Don't tell her anything more about him. Tell her how they beat their old mothers.'

'Tell me what drunks they are.'

'Oh, frightful,' Mike said. 'Drunk all day and spend all their time beating their poor old mothers.'

'He looks that way,' Brett said.

'Doesn't he?' I said.

They had hitched the mules to the dead bull and then the whips cracked, the men ran, and the mules, straining forward, their legs pushing, broke into a gallop, and the bull, one horn up, his head on its side, swept a swath smoothly across the sand and out the red gate.

'This next is the last one.'

'Not really,' Brett said. She leaned forward on the barrera. Romero waved his picadors to their places, then stood, his cape against his chest, looking across the ring to where the bull would come out.

After it was over we went out and were pressed tight in the crowd.

'These bull-fights are hell on one,' Brett said. 'I'm limp as a rag.'

'Oh, you'll get a drink,' Mike said.

The next day Pedro Romero did not fight. It was Miura bulls, and a very bad bull-fight. The next day there was no bull-fight scheduled. But all day and all night the fiesta kept on.

TOM WOLFE

THE MASQUE OF THE RED DEATH

From *The Bonfire of the Vanities*

(1987)

CHAPTER 15

SHERMAN AND JUDY arrived at the Bavardages' building on Fifth Avenue in a black Buick sedan, with a white-haired driver hired for the evening from Mayfair Town Car, Inc. They lived only six blocks from the Bavardages, but walking was out of the question. For a start, there was Judy's dress. It was bare-shouldered but had short puffed sleeves the size of Chinese lampshades covering the upper arms. It had a fitted waist but was puffed up in the skirt to a shape that reminded Sherman of an aerial balloon. The invitation to dinner at the Bavardages' prescribed 'informal' dress. But this season, as *tout le monde* knew, women dressed far more extravagantly for informal dinners in fashionable apartments than for formal dances in grand ballrooms. In any event, it was impossible for Judy to walk down the street in this dress. A five-mile-an-hour head wind would have stopped her cold.

But there was a yet more compelling reason for the hired car and driver. It would be perfectly *okay* for the two of them to arrive for dinner at a Good Building (the going term) on Fifth Avenue by taxi, and it would cost less than three dollars. But what would they do *after* the party? How could they walk *out* of the Bavardages' building and have all the world, *tout le monde*, see them standing out in the street, the McCoys, that game couple, their hands up in the air, bravely, desperately, pathetically trying to hail a taxi? The doormen would be no help, because they would be tied up ushering *tout le monde* to their limousines. So he had hired this car and this driver, this white-haired driver, who would drive them six blocks, wait three and a half or four hours, then drive them six blocks and depart. Including a 15 percent tip and the sales tax, the cost would be $197.20 or $246.50, depending on whether they were charged for four or five hours in all.

Hemorrhaging money! Did he even have a job left! Churning fear . . . Lopwitz . . . Surely, Lopwitz wouldn't *sack* him . . . because of three miserable days . . . *and $6 million, you ninny!* . . . Must start cutting back . . . tomorrow . . . Tonight, of course, it was imperative to have a car and driver.

To make matters worse, the driver couldn't pull up to the sidewalk near the entrance, because so many limousines were in the way. He had to double-park. Sherman and Judy had to thread their way between the limousines . . . Envy . . . envy . . . From the license plates Sherman could tell that these limousines were not hired. They were *owned* by those whose sleek hides were hauled here in them. A chauffeur, a good one willing to work long hours and late hours, cost $36,000 a year, minimum; garage space, maintenance, insurance, would cost another $14,000 at least; a total of $50,000, none of it deductible. *I make a million dollars a year – and yet I can't afford that!*

He reached the sidewalk. *Whuh?* Just to the left, in the gloaming, a figure – *a photographer* – right over there—

Sheer terror!

My picture in the paper!

The other boy, the big one, the brute, sees him and goes to the police!

The police! The two detectives! The fat one! The one with the lopsided face! McCoy – goes to parties at the Bavardages', does he! Now they truly smell blood!

Horrified, he stares at the photographer—

—and discovers that it's only a young man walking a dog. He has stopped near the canopy that leads up to the entrance . . . Not even looking at Sherman . . . staring at a couple who are nearing the door . . . an old man in a dark suit and a young woman, blonde, in a short dress.

Calm down, for God's sake! Don't be crazy! Don't be paranoid!

But a smirking, insulting voice says: *You got something you wanna get off your chest?*

Now Sherman and Judy were under the canopy, only three or four steps behind the old man and the blonde heading for the entrance. A doorman in a starched white dickie pushed it open. He wore white cotton gloves. The blonde entered first. The old man, who was not much taller than she was, looked sleepy and somber. His thinning gray hair was combed straight back. He had a big nose and heavy eyelids, like a movie Indian. *Wait a minute – I know him . . .* No, he had *seen* him somewhere . . . But where? . . . *Bango!* . . . In a picture, of course . . . It was Baron Hochswald, the German financier.

This was all Sherman needed, on this night of all nights . . . After the catastrophes of the past three days, in this perilous low point of his career on Wall Street, to run into this man, whose success was so complete, so permanent, whose wealth was so vast and unassailable – to have to set eyes upon this immovably secure and ancient German—

Perhaps the baron merely *lived* in this building . . . Please, God, don't let him be going to the same dinner party—

In that very moment he heard the baron say to the doorman in a heavy European accent: 'Bavardage.' The doorman's white glove gestured toward the rear of the lobby.

Sherman despaired. He despaired of this evening and of this life. Why hadn't he gone to Knoxville six months ago? A little Georgian house, a leaf-blowing machine, a badminton net in the back yard for Campbell . . . But no! He had to tag along behind this walnut-eyed German, heading for the home of some overbearingly vulgar people named Bavardage, a glorified traveling salesman and his wife.

Sherman said to the doorman, 'The Bavar*dages*', please.' He hit the accented syllable hard, so that no one would think he had paid the slightest attention to the fact that the noble one, Baron Hochswald, had said the same thing. The baron, the blonde, Judy, and Sherman headed for the elevator. The elevator was paneled in old mahogany. It glowed. The grain was showy but rich and mellow. As he entered, Sherman overheard Baron Hochswald saying the name *Bavardage* to the operator. So Sherman repeated it, as before, "The Bavar*dages*" – lest the baron himself get the impression that he, Sherman, was cognizant of his existence.

Now all four of them knew they were going to the same dinner party, and they had to make a decision. Did you do the decent, congenial, neighborly, and quite American thing – the sort of thing that would have been done without hesitation on an elevator in a similar building on Beacon Hill or Rittenhouse Square – or in a building in New York, for that matter, if the party were being given by someone of good blood and good bone, such as Rawlie or Pollard (in the present company, Pollard suddenly seemed quite okay, quite a commendable old Knickerbocker) – did you do the good-spirited thing and smile and introduce yourselves to one another . . . or did you do the vulgar snobbish thing and stand there and pretend you were unaware of your common destination and stare stiffly at the back of the elevator operator's neck while this mahogany cab rose up its shaft?

Sherman cut an exploratory glance at Hochswald and the blonde. Her dress was a black sheath that ended several inches above her knees and hugged her luscious thighs and the lubricious declivity of her lower abdomen and rose up to a ruff at the top that resembled flower petals. Christ, she was sexy! Her creamy white shoulders and the tops of her breasts swelled up as if she was dying to shed the sheath and run naked through the begonias . . . Her blond hair was swept back to reveal a pair of enormous ruby earrings . . . No more than twenty-five years old . . . A tasty morsel! A panting animal! . . . The old bastard had taken what he wanted, hadn't he! . . . Hochswald wore a black serge suit, a white shirt with a spread collar, and a black silk necktie with a large, almost rakish knot . . . all of it fashioned *just so* . . . Sherman was glad Judy had pressured him into wearing the navy suit and navy tie . . . Nevertheless, the baron's ensemble seemed terribly smart by comparison.

Now he caught the old German flicking his eyes up and down Judy and himself. Their glances engaged for the briefest of instants. Then both stared once more at the piping on the back of the collar of the elevator operator.

So they ascended, an elevator operator and four social mutes, toward some upper floor. The answer was: You did the vulgar snobbish thing.

The elevator stopped, and the four mutes walked out into the Bavardages' elevator vestibule. It was lit by clusters of tiny silk lampshades on either side of a mirror with a gilded frame. There was an open doorway . . . a rich and rosy glow . . . the sound of a hive of excited voices . . .

They went through the doorway, into the apartment's entry gallery. Such voices! Such delight! Such laughter! Sherman faced catastrophe in his career, catastrophe in his marriage – and the police were circling – and yet the hive – the hive – the hive! – the sonic waves of the hive made his very innards vibrate. Faces full of grinning, glistening, boiling teeth! How fabulous and fortunate we are, we few, to be in these upper rooms together with our radiant and incarnadine glows!

The entry gallery was smaller than Sherman's, but whereas his (decorated by his wife, the interior designer) was grand and solemn, this one was dazzling, effervescent. The walls were covered in a brilliant Chinese-red silk, and the silk was framed by narrow gilded moldings, and the moldings were framed by a broad burnt-umber upholsterer's webbing, and the webbing was framed by more gilded moldings, and the light of a row of brass sconces made the gilt gleam, and the glow of the gilt and the Chinese-red silk made all the grinning faces and lustrous gowns yet more glorious.

He surveyed the crowd and immediately sensed a pattern . . . *presque vu! presque vu!* almost seen! . . . and yet he couldn't have put it into words. That would have been beyond him. All the men and women in this hall were arranged in clusters, conversational bouquets, so to speak. There were no solitary figures, no strays. All faces were white. (Black faces might show up, occasionally, at fashionable charity dinners but not in fashionable private homes.) There were no men under thirty-five and precious few under forty. The women came in two varieties. First, there were women in their late thirties and in their forties and older (women 'of a certain age'), all of them skin and bones (starved to near perfection). To compensate for the concupiscence missing from their juiceless ribs and atrophied backsides, they turned to the dress designers. This season no puffs, flounces, pleats, ruffles, bibs, bows, battings, scallops, laces, darts, or shirs on the bias were too extreme. They were the social X rays, to use the phrase that had bubbled up into Sherman's own brain. Second, there were the so-called Lemon Tarts. These were women in their twenties or early thirties, mostly blondes (the Lemon in the Tarts), who were the second, third, fourth wives or live-in girlfriends of men over forty or fifty or sixty (or seventy), the sort of women men refer to, quite without thinking, as *girls*. This season the Tart was able to flaunt the natural advantages of youth by showing her legs from well above the knee and emphasizing her round bottom (something no X ray had). What was entirely missing from *chez* Bavardage was that manner of woman who is neither very young nor very old, who has laid in a lining of subcutaneous fat, who glows with plumpness and a rosy face that speaks, without a word, of home and hearth and hot food ready at six and stories read aloud at night and conversations while seated on the edge of the bed, just before the Sandman comes. In short, no one ever invited . . . Mother.

Sherman's attention was drawn to a bouquet of ecstatic boiling faces in the immediate foreground. Two men and an impeccably emaciated woman were grinning upon a huge young man with pale blond hair and a cowlick at the top of his forehead . . . *Met him somewhere . . . but who is he?* . . . *Bango!* . . . Another face from the press . . . The Golden Hillbilly, the Towheaded Tenor . . . That was what they called him . . . His name was Bobby Shaflett. He was the new featured tenor of the Metropolitan Opera, a grossly fat creature who had somehow emerged from the upland hollows of the Appalachians. You could hardly read a magazine or a newspaper without seeing his picture. As Sherman watched, the young man's mouth opened wide. *Haw haw haw haw haw haw haw haw haw*, he broke out into a huge barnyard laugh, and the grinning faces around him became even more radiant, more transported, than before.

Sherman lifted his Yale chin, squared his shoulders, straightened his back, raised himself to his full height, and assumed the Presence, the presence of an older, finer New

York, the New York of his father, the Lion of Dunning Sponget.

A butler materialized and asked Judy and Sherman what they wanted to drink. Judy asked for 'sparkling water.' (To say 'Perrier' or any other brand name had become too trite.) Sherman had intended to drink nothing. He had intended to be aloof from everything about these people, these Bavardages, starting with their liquor. But the hive had closed in, and the cowlicked towhead of the Golden Hillbilly boomed away.

'A gin-and-tonic,' said Sherman McCoy from the eminence of his chin.

A blazing bony little woman popped out from amid all the clusters in the entry gallery and came toward them. She was an X ray with a teased blond pageboy bob and many tiny grinning teeth. Her emaciated body was inserted into a black-and-red dress with ferocious puffed shoulders, a very narrow waist, and a long skirt. Her face was wide and round – but without an ounce of flesh on it. Her neck was much more drawn than Judy's. Her clavicle stuck out so far Sherman had the feeling he could reach out and pick up the two big bones. He could see lamplight through her rib cage.

'Dear Judy!'

'Inez!' said Judy, and the two of them kissed or, rather, swung their cheeks past one another, first on this side then on that side, in a European fashion that Sherman, now the son of that staunch Knickerbocker, that Old Family patriarch, that Low Church Episcopal scourge of the fleshpots, John Campbell McCoy, found pretentious and vulgar.

'Inez! I don't think you've met Sherman!' She forced her voice into an exclamation, in order to be heard above the hive. 'Sherman, this is Inez Bavardage!'

'Howja do,' said the Lion's scion.

'I certainly *feel* like I know you!' said the woman, looking him squarely in the eye and flashing her tiny teeth and thrusting her hand toward him. Overwhelmed, he took it. 'You should hear Gene Lopwitz go on about you!' Lopwitz! When? Sherman found himself clutching at this rope of hope. (Perhaps he had built up so many points in the past, the Giscard debacle would not finish him!) 'And I know your father, too. Scared to death of him!' With this the woman gripped Sherman's forearm and fastened her eyes onto his and broke into an extraordinary laugh, a hacking laugh, not *hah hah hah* but *hack hack hack hack hack hack hack hack hack*, a laugh of such heartiness and paroxysmal rapture that Sherman found himself grinning foolishly and saying:

'You don't say!'

'Yes!' *Hack hack hack hack hack hack hack*. 'I never told you this, Judy!' She reached out and hooked one arm inside Judy's and the other inside Sherman's and pulled the two of them toward her, as if they were the two dearest chums she had ever had. 'There was this dreadful man named Derderian who was suing Leon. Kept trying to attach things. Pure harassment. So one weekend we were out on Santa Catalina Island at Angie Civelli's.' She dropped the name of the famous comedian without so much as a syncopation. 'And we're having dinner, and Leon starts talking about all the trouble he's having with this man Derderian, and Angie says – believe me, he was absolutely serious – he says, "You want me to take care of it?"' With this, Inez Bavardage pushed her nose to one side with her forefinger to indicate the Bent-Nose Crowd. 'Well, I mean I'd *heard* about Angie and The Boys, but I didn't believe it – but he was *serious*!' *Hack hack hack hack hack hack hack hack*. She pulled Sherman yet closer and put her eyes right in his face. 'When Leon got back to New York, he went to see your father, and he told him what Angie had said, and then he said to your father, "Maybe that's the simplest way to take care of it." I'll never forget what your father said. He said, "No, Mr Bavardage, you let *me* take care of it. It won't be simple, it won't be fast, and it'll cost you a *lot* of money. But my bill you can pay. The other – no one is rich enough to pay them. They'll keep collecting until the day you die." '

Inez Bavardage remained close to Sherman's face and gave him a look of bottomless profundity. He felt obliged to say something.

'Well . . . which did your husband do?'

'What your father said, of course. When he spoke – people jumped!' A *hack-hack-hack-hacking* peeeeallll of laughter.

'And what about the bill?' asked Judy, as if delighted to be in on this story about Sherman's incomparable father.

'It was sensational! It was astonishing, that bill!' *Hack hack hack hack hack*. Vesuvius, Krakatoa, and Mauna Loa erupted with laughter, and Sherman felt himself swept up in the explosion, in spite of himself. It was irresistible – Gene Lopwitz loves you! – your incomparable father! – your aristocratic lineage! – what euphoria you arouse in my bony breast!

He knew it was irrational, but he felt warm, aglow, high, in Seventh Heaven. He eased the revolver of his Resentment back into his waistband and told his Snobbery to go lie down by the hearth. Really a very charming woman! Who would have thought it, after all the things one hears about the Bavardages! A social X ray, to be sure, but one can't very well hold that against her! Really very warm – and quite amusing!

Like most men, Sherman was innocent of the routine salutatory techniques of the fashionable hostesses. For at least forty-five seconds every guest was the closest, dearest, jolliest, most wittily conspiratorial friend a girl ever had.

Every male guest she touched on the arm (any other part of the body presented problems) and applied a little heartfelt pressure. Every guest, male or female, she looked at with a radar lock upon the eyes, as if captivated (by the brilliance, the wit, the beauty, and the incomparable memories).

The butler returned with the drinks for Judy and Sherman,

Sherman took a long deep draught of the gin-and-tonic, and the gin hit bottom, and the sweet juniper rose, and he relaxed and let the happy buzz of the hive surge into his head.

Hack hack hack hack hack hack hack went Inez Bavardage.

Haw haw haw haw haw haw haw haw went Bobby Shaflett.

Hah hah hah hah hah hah hah hah went Judy.

Heh heh heh heh heh heh heh heh went Sherman.

The hive buzzed and buzzed.

In no time Inez Bavardage had steered him and Judy over to the bouquet where the Golden Hillbilly held forth. Nods, hellos, handshakes, under the aegis of Sherman's new best friend, Inez. Before he quite realized what had happened, Inez had steered Judy out of the entry gallery, into some inner salon, and Sherman was left with the celebrated Appalachian fat boy, two men, and an X ray. He looked at each of them, starting with Shaflett. None returned his gaze. The two men and the woman stared, rapt, at the huge pale head of the tenor as he recounted a story of something that had happened on an airplane:

'—so I'm settin'up'eh waitin' fuh Barb'ra – she's supposed to be ridin' back to New York with me?' He had a way of ending a declarative sentence with a question that reminded Sherman of Maria . . . Maria . . . and the huge Hasidic Jew! The great blond ball of fat before him was like that huge sow from the real-estate company – if that was where he was from.

A cold tremor . . . They were out there circling, circling . . . 'And I'm in my seat – I got the one by the window? And from back'eh, here come 'is *un*believable, *out*rageous black man.' The way he hit the *un* and the *out* and fluttered his hands in the air made Sherman wonder if this hillbilly giant was, in fact, a homosexual. 'He's wearin' this'eh ermine overcoat? – down to here? – and 'is'eh matchin' ermine fedora? – and he's got more rings'n Barb'ra's got and he's got three re*tain*ers with 'im? – right outta *Shaft*?'

The giant bubbled on, and the two men and the woman kept their eyes on his huge round face and their grins fixed; and the giant, for his part, looked only at them, never at Sherman. As the seconds rolled by, he grew increasingly aware that all four of them were acting as if he didn't exist. A giant fairy with a hillbilly accent, thought Sherman, and they were hanging on his every word. Sherman took three deep gulps of his gin-and-tonic.

The story seemed to revolve about the fact that the regal black man, who had sat down next to Shaflett on the airplane, was the cruiser-weight champion of the world, Sam (Assassin Sam) Assinore. Shaflett found the term 'cruiser weight' vastly amusing – *haw haw haw haw haw haw haw* – and the two men went into excited screams of laughter. Sherman labeled them homosexual, too. Assassin Sam hadn't known who Shaflett was, and Shaflett hadn't known who Assassin Sam was. The point of the entire story seemed to be that the only two people in the first-class section of the airliner who hadn't known who both these celebrities were . . . were Shaflett and Assinore themselves! *Haw haw haw haw haw haw haw haw – hee hee hee hee hee hee hee* – and – *aha!* – a conversational nugget about Assassin Sam Assinore popped into Sherman's brain. Oscar Suder – *Oscar Suder!* – he winced at the memory but pressed on – Oscar Suder was part of a syndicate of Midwestern investors who backed Assinore and controlled his finances. A nugget! A conversational nugget! A means of entry into this party cluster!

As soon as the laughter had receded, Sherman said to Bobby Shaflett, 'Did you know that Assinore's contract, and his ermine coat, for all I know, is owned by a syndicate of businessmen in Ohio, mostly from Cleveland and Columbus?'

The Golden Hillbilly looked at him as if he were a panhandler. 'Hmmmmmmmm,' he said. It was the *hmmmmmmmm* that says, 'I understand, but I couldn't care less,' whereupon he turned back to the other three and said, 'So I asked him if he'd sign my menu. You know, they give you this menu? – and—'

That was all for Sherman McCoy. He pulled the revolver of Resentment back out of his waistband. He wheeled away from the cluster and turned his back on them. Not one of them noticed. The hive raged in his head.

Now what would he do? All at once he was alone in this noisy hive with no place to roost. Alone! He became acutely aware that the entire party was now composed of these bouquets and that not to be in one of them was to be an abject, incompetent social failure. He looked this way and that. Who was that, right there? A tall, handsome, smug-looking man . . . admiring faces looking up at his . . . Ah! . . . It registered . . . an author . . . His name was Nunnally Voyd . . . a novelist . . . he'd seen him on a television talk show . . . snide, acerbic . . . Look at the way those fools doted on him . . . Didn't dare try that bouquet . . . Would be a repeat of the Golden Hillbilly, no doubt . . . Over there, someone he knew . . . No! Another famous face . . . the ballet dancer . . . Boris Korolev . . . Another circle of adoring faces . . . glistening with rapture . . . The idiots! Human specks! What is this business of groveling before dancers, novelists, and gigantic fairy opera singers? They're nothing but court jesters, nothing but light entertainment for . . . the Masters of the Universe, those who push the levers that move the world . . . and yet these idiots worship them as if they were pipelines to the godhead . . . They didn't even want to know who he was . . . and wouldn't even be capable of understanding, even if they had . . .

He found himself standing by another cluster . . . Well, at least no one famous in this one, no smirking court jester . . . A fat, reddish man was talking, in a heavy English accent: 'He was lying in the road, you see, with a broken leg . . .' *The delicate skinny boy! Henry Lamb! He was talking about the story in the newspaper! But wait a minute – a broken leg –* '. . . and he kept saying, "How very boring, how very boring." ' No, he was talking about some Englishman. *Nothing to do with me* . . . The others in the cluster were laughing . . . a woman, about fifty, with pink powder all over her face . . . How grotesque . . . Wait! . . . He knew that face. The sculptor's daughter, now a stage designer. He couldn't remember her name . . . But then he did . . . Barbara Cornagglia . . . He moved on . . . Alone! . . . Despite all, despite the fact that *they* were circling – the police! – he felt the pressure of social failure . . . What could he do to make it appear as if he *meant* to be by himself, as if he were moving through the hive alone by choice? The hive buzzed and buzzed.

Near the doorway through which Judy and Inez Bavardage had disappeared was an antique console bearing a pair of miniature Chinese easels. Upon each easel was a burgundy velvet disk the size of a pie, and in slits in the velvet, little pockets, were stuck name cards. They were models of the seating arrangement for dinner, so that each guest would know who his dinner partners were going to be. It struck Sherman, the leonine Yale man, as another piece of vulgarity. Nevertheless, he looked. It was a way of appearing occupied, as if he were alone for no other reason than to study the seating arrangement.

There were evidently two tables. Presently he saw a card with *Mr McCoy* on it. He would be sitting next to, let's see, a Mrs Rawthrote, whoever she might be, and a Mrs Ruskin. *Ruskin!* His heart bolted. It couldn't be – not Maria!

But of course it could be. This was precisely the sort of event to which she and her rich but somewhat shadowy husband would be invited. He downed the rest of his gin-and-tonic and hurried through the doorway into the other room. Maria! Had to talk to her! – but also had to keep Judy away from her! *Don't need that on top of everything else!*

He was now in the apartment's living room, or salon, since it was obviously meant for entertaining. It was enormous, but it appeared to be . . . stuffed . . . with sofas, cushions, fat chairs, and hassocks, all of them braided, tasseled, banded, bordered and . . . *stuffed* . . . Even the walls; the walls were covered in some sort of padded fabric with stripes of red, purple, and rose. The windows overlooking Fifth Avenue were curtained in deep folds of the same material, which was pulled back to reveal its rose lining and a trim of striped rope braid. There was not so much as a hint of the twentieth century in the decor, not even in the lighting. A few table lamps with rosy shades provided all the light, so that the terrain of this gloriously stuffed little planet was thrown into deep shadows and mellow highlights.

The hive buzzed with the sheer ecstasy of being in this mellow rosy stuffed orbit. *Hack hack hack hack hack hack*, the horse laugh of Inez Bavardage rose somewhere. So many bouquets of people . . . grinning faces . . . boiling teeth . . .

A butler appeared and asked him if he wanted a drink. He ordered another gin-and-tonic. He stood there. His eyes jumped around the deep stuffed shadows.

Maria.

She was standing by one of the two corner windows. Bare shoulders . . . a red sheath . . . She caught his eye and smiled. Just that, a smile. He answered with the smallest smile imaginable. Where was Judy?

In Maria's cluster was a woman he didn't recognize, a man he didn't recognize, and a bald-headed man he knew from somewhere, another of the . . . *famous faces* this zoo specialized in . . . a writer of some sort, a Brit . . . He couldn't think of his name. Com*plete*ly bald; not a hair on his long thin head; gaunt; a skull.

Sherman panned the room, desperately searching for Judy. Well, what difference would it make if Judy did meet someone in this room named Maria? It wasn't that unusual a name. But would Maria be discreet? She was no genius, and she had a mischievous streak – and he was supposed to sit next to her!

He could feel his heart kicking up in his chest. Christ! Was it possible that Inez Bavardage knew about the two of them and put them together on purpose? *Wait a minute! That's very paranoid!* She'd never risk having an ugly scene. Still—

Judy.

There she was, standing over near the fireplace, laughing so hard – *her new party laugh – wants to be an Inez Bavardage* – laughing so hard her hair was bouncing. She was making a new sound, *hock hock hock hock hock hock hock*. Not yet Inez Bavardage's *hack hack hack hack*, just an intermediary *hock hock hock hock*. She was listening to a barrel-chested old man with receding gray hair and no neck. The third member of the bouquet, a woman, elegant, slim, and fortyish, was not nearly so amused. She stood like a marble angel. Sherman made his way through the hive, past the knees of some people sitting down on a huge round Oriental hassock, toward the fireplace. He had to push his way through a dense flotilla of puffed gowns and boiling faces . . .

Judy's face was a mask of mirth. She was so enthralled by the conversation of the barrel-chested man she didn't notice Sherman at first. *Then* she saw him. Startled! But of course! – it was a sign of social failure for one spouse to be reduced to joining another in a conversational cluster. *But so what! Keep her away from Maria!* That was the main thing. Judy didn't look at him. Once again she beamed her grinning rapture at the old man.

'—so last week,' he was saying, 'my wife comes back from Italy and informs me we have a summer place on "Como." "Como," she says. It's this Lake Como. So all right! We'll have a summer place on "Como." It's better than Hammamet. That was two summers ago.' He had a rough voice, a brushed-up New York street voice. He was holding a glass of soda water and looking back and forth, from Judy to the marble angel, as he told his story, getting vast effusions of approval from Judy and the occasional wriggle of the upper lip when he looked directly into the angel's face. A wriggle; it could have been the beginning of a polite smile. 'At least I know where "Como" is. I never hearda Hammamet. My wife's gone gaga about Italy. Italian paintings, Italian clothes, and now "Como."'

Judy went off into another automatic-weapon burst of laughter, *Hock hock hock hock hock hock*, as if the way the old man pronounced 'Como,' in mockery of his wife's love of things Italian, was the funniest thing in the world – *Maria*. It came over him, *just like that*. It was Maria he was talking about. This old man was her husband, Arthur Ruskin. Had he mentioned her by name yet, or had he been talking only about 'my wife'?

The other woman, marble angel, just stood there. The old man suddenly reached toward her left ear and took her earring between his thumb and forefinger. Appalled, the woman stiffened. She would have jerked her head away, but her ear was now between the thumb and forefinger of this ancient and appalling ursine creature.

'Very nice,' said Arthur Ruskin, still holding on to the earring. 'Nadina D., right?' Nadina Dulocci was a highly mentionable jewelry designer.

'I believe so!' said the woman in a timorous, European voice. Hurriedly she brought her hands to her ears and unfastened both earrings and handed them to him, most emphatically, as if to say, 'There, take them. But be so kind as not to rip my ears off my head.'

Unconcerned, Ruskin took them in his hairy paws and inspected them further. 'Nadina D., all right. Very nice. Where'd you get 'em?'

'They were a gift.' Cold as marble. He returned them to her, and she quickly put them in her purse.

'Very nice, very nice. My wife—'

Suppose he said 'Maria'! Sherman broke in. 'Judy!' To the others: 'Excuse me.' To Judy: 'I was wondering—'

Judy instantly transformed her startled expression into one of radiance. No wife in all of history had ever been more charmed to see her husband arrive at a conversational bouquet.

'Sherman! Have you met Madame Prudhomme?'

Sherman extended his Yale chin and put on an expression of the most proper Knickerbocker charm to greet the shaken Frenchwoman. 'Howja do?'

'And Arthur Ruskin,' said Judy. Sherman shook the hairy mitt firmly.

Arthur Ruskin was not a young seventy-one. He had big ears with thick rinds and wire hairs sprouting out. There were curdled wattles under his big jaws. He stood erectly, rocking back on his heels, which brought out his chest and his ponderous gut. His heft was properly swathed in a navy suit, white shirt, and navy tie.

'Forgive me,' said Sherman. To Judy with a charming smile: 'Come over here a moment.' To Ruskin and the Frenchwoman he flashed a smile of apology and moved off a few feet, Judy in tow. Madame Prudhomme's face fell. She had looked to his arrival in the bouquet as a salvation from Ruskin.

Judy, with a fireproof smile still on her face: 'What is it?'

Sherman, a smiling mask of Yale Chin charm: 'I want you to . . . uh . . . to come meet Baron Hochswald.'

'Who?'

'Baron Hochswald. You know, the German – one of the Hochswalds.'

Judy, the smile still locked on: 'But why?'

'We rode up in the elevator with him.'

This obviously made no sense to Judy at all. Urgently: 'Well, where is he?' Urgently, because it was bad enough to be caught in a large conversational cluster with your husband. To form a minimal cluster with him, just the two of you—

Sherman, looking around: 'Well, he was here just a minute ago.'

Judy, the smile gone: 'Sherman, what on earth are you doing? What are you talking about, "Baron Hochswald"?'

Just then the butler arrived with Sherman's gin-and-tonic. He took a big swallow and looked around some more. He felt dizzy. Everywhere . . . social X rays in puffed dresses shimmering in the burnt-apricot glow of the little table lamps . . .

'Well – you two! What are *you* trying to cook up!' *Hack hack hack hack hack hack hack.* Inez Bavardage took them both by their arms. For a moment, before she could get her fireproof grin back onto her face, Judy looked stricken. Not only had she ended up in a minimal cluster with her husband, but New York's reigning hostess, this month's ringmistress of the century, had spotted them and felt compelled to make this ambulance run to save them from social ignominy.

'Sherman was—'

'I was looking for you! I want you to meet Ronald Vine. He's doing over the Vice President's house, in Washington.'

Inez Bavardage towed them through the hive of grins and gowns and inserted them in a bouquet dominated by a tall, slender, handsome, youngish man, the aforesaid Ronald Vine. Mr Vine was saying '. . . jabots, jabots, jabots. I'm afraid the Vice President's wife has discovered jabots.' A weary roll of the eyes. The others in the bouquet, two women and a bald man, laughed and laughed. Judy could barely summon up even a smile . . . Crushed . . . Had to be rescued from social death by the hostess . . .

Such sad irony! Sherman hated himself. He hated himself for all the catastrophes she didn't yet know about.

The Bavardages' dining-room walls had been painted with so many coats of burnt-apricot lacquer, fourteen in all, they had the glassy brilliance of a pond reflecting a campfire at night. The room was a triumph of nocturnal reflections, one of many such victories by Ronald Vine, whose forte was the creation of glitter without the use of mirrors. Mirror Indigestion was now regarded as one of the gross sins of the 1970s. So in the early 1980s, from Park Avenue to Fifth, from Sixty-second Street to Ninety-sixth, there had arisen the hideous cracking sound of acres of hellishly expensive plate-glass mirror being pried off the walls of the great apartments. No, in the Bavardages' dining room one's eyes fluttered in a cosmos of glints, twinkles, sparkles, highlights, sheens, shimmering pools, and fiery glows that had been achieved in subtler ways, by using lacquer, glazed tiles in a narrow band just under the ceiling cornices, gilded English Regency furniture, silver candelabra, crystal bowls, School of Tiffany vases, and sculpted silverware that was so heavy the knives weighed on your fingers like saber handles.

The two dozen diners were seated at a pair of round Regency tables. The banquet table, the sort of Sheraton landing field that could seat twenty-four if you inserted all the leaves, had disappeared from the smarter dining rooms. One shouldn't be so formal, so grand. Two small tables were much better. So what if these two small tables were surrounded and bedecked by a buildup of *objets*, fabrics, and *bibelots* so lush it would have made the Sun King blink? Hostesses such as Inez Bavardage prided themselves on their gift for the informal and the intimate.

To underscore the informality of the occasion there had been placed, in the middle of each table, deep within the forest crystal and silver a basket woven from hardened vines in a highly rustic Appalachian Handicrafts manner. Wrapped around the vines, on the outside of the basket, was a profusion of wildflowers. In the center of the basket were massed three or four dozen poppies. This *faux-naïf* centerpiece was the trademark of Huck Thigg, the young florist, who would present the Bavardages with a bill for $3,300 for this one dinner party.

Sherman stared at the plaited vines. They looked like

something dropped by Gretel or little Heidi of Switzerland at a feast of Lucullus. He sighed. All . . . too much. Maria was sitting next to him, on his right, chattering away at the cadaverous Englishman, whatever his name was, who was on her right. Judy was at the other table – but had a clear view of him and Maria. He had to talk to Maria about the interrogation by the two detectives – but how could he do it with Judy looking right at them? He'd do it with an innocuous party grin on his face. That was it! He'd grin through the whole discussion! She'd never know the difference . . . Or would she? . . . Arthur Ruskin was at Judy's table . . . But thank God, he was four seats away from her . . . wouldn't be chatting with her . . . Judy was sitting between Baron Hochswald and some rather pompous-looking youngish man . . . Inez Bavardage was two seats away from Judy, and Bobby Shaflett was on Inez's right. Judy was grinning an enormous social grin at the pompous man . . . *Hock hock hock hock hock hock hock hock hock!* Clear above the buzz of the hive he could hear her laughing her new laugh . . . Inez was talking to Bobby Shaflett but also to the grinning social X ray seated to the Golden Hillbilly's right and to Nunnally Voyd, who was to the right of the X ray. *Haw haw haw haw haw haw haw*, sang the Towheaded Tenor . . . *Hack hack hack hack hack hack*, sang Inez Bavardage . . . *Hock hock hock hock hock hock hock hock hock*, bawled his own wife . . .

Leon Bavardage sat four chairs to Sherman's right, beyond Maria, the cadaverous Englishman, and the woman with the pink powder on her face, Barbara Cornagglia. In contrast to Inez Bavardage, Leon had all the animation of a raindrop. He had a placid, passive, lineless face, wavy blondish hair, which was receding, a long delicate nose, and very pale, almost livid skin. Instead of a 300-watt social grin, he had a shy, demure smile, which he was just now bestowing upon Miss Cornagglia.

Belatedly it occurred to Sherman that he should be talking to the woman on his left. Rawthrote, Mrs Rawthrote; who in the name of God was she? What could he say to her? He turned to his left – *and she was waiting*. She was staring straight at him, her laser eyes no more than eighteen inches from his face. A real X ray with a huge mane of blond hair and a look of such intensity he thought at first that she must *know* something . . . He opened his mouth . . . he smiled . . . he ransacked his brain for something to say . . . he did the best he could . . . He said to her, 'Would you do me a great favor? What is the name of the gentleman to my right, the *thin* gentleman? His face is so familiar but I can't think of his name for the life of me.'

Mrs Rawthrote leaned still closer, until their faces were barely eight inches apart. She was so close she seemed to have three eyes. 'Aubrey Buffing,' she said. Her eyes kept burning into his.

'Aubrey Buffing,' said Sherman lamely. It was really a question.

'The poet,' said Mrs Rawthrote. 'He's on the short list for the Nobel Prize. His father was the Duke of Bray.' Her tone said, 'How on earth could you not know that?'

'Of course,' said Sherman, feeling that in addition to his other sins he was also a philistine. 'The poet.'

'How do you think he looks?' She had eyes like a cobra's. Her face remained right in his. He wanted to pull back but couldn't. He felt paralyzed.

'Looks?' he asked.

'Lord Buffing,' she said. 'The state of his health.'

'I – can't really say. I don't know him.'

'He's being treated at Vanderbilt Hospital. He has AIDS.'

She pulled back a few inches, the better to see how this zinger hit Sherman.

'That's terrible!' said Sherman. 'How do you know that?'

'I know his best boyfriend.' She closed her eyes and then opened them, as if to say: 'I know such things, but don't ask too many questions.' Then she said, 'This is *entre nous.*' *But I've never met you before!* 'Don't tell Leon or Inez,' she continued. 'He's their house guest – has been for the past two and a half weeks. Never invite an Englishman for a weekend. You can't get them out.' She said this without smiling, as if it was the most serious advice she had ever offered free of charge. She continued her myopic study of Sherman's face.

In order to break eye contact, Sherman took a quick glance at the gaunt Englishman, Lord Buffing the Short-List Poet.

'Don't worry,' said Mrs Rawthrote. 'You can't get it at the table. If you could, we'd all have it by now. Half the waiters in New York are gay. You show me a happy homosexual, I'll show you a gay corpse.' She repeated this *mot farouche* in the same rat-tat-tat voice as everything else, without a trace of a smile.

Just then a good-looking young waiter, Latin in appearance, began serving the first course, which looked like an Easter egg under a heavy white sauce on a plateau of red caviar resting on a bed of Bibb lettuce.

'Not these,' said Mrs Rawthrote, right in front of the young man. 'They work full-time for Inez and Leon. Mexicans from New Orleans. They live in their place in the country and drive in to serve dinner parties.' Then, without any preamble, she said, 'What do you do, Mr McCoy?'

Sherman was taken aback. He was speechless. He was as flabbergasted as he had been when Campbell asked the same question. A nonentity, a thirty-five-year-old X ray, and yet . . . *I want to impress her!* The possible answers came thundering through his mind . . . *I'm a senior member of the bond division at Pierce & Pierce* . . . No . . . makes it sound as if he's a replaceable part in a bureaucracy and proud to be one . . . *I'm the number one producer* . . . No . . . sounds like something a vacuum-cleaner salesman would say . . . *There's a group of us who make the major decisions* . . . No . . . not accurate and an utterly gauche observation . . . *I made $980,000 selling bonds last year* . . . That was the true heart of the matter, but there was no way to impart such information without appearing foolish . . . *I'm – a Master of the Universe!* . . . Dream on! – and besides, there's no way to utter it! . . . So he said, 'Oh, I try to sell a few bonds for Pierce & Pierce.' He smiled ever so slightly, hoping the modesty of the statement would be taken as a sign of confidence to burn, thanks to tremendous and spectacular achievements on Wall Street.

Mrs Rawthrote lasered in on him again. From six inches away: 'Gene Lopwitz is one of our clients.'

'Your client?'

'At Benning and Sturtevant.'

Where? He stared at her.

'You do know Gene,' she said.

'Well, yes, I work with him.'

Evidently the woman did not find that convincing. To Sherman's astonishment, she turned ninety degrees, without another word, to her left, where a jolly, florid, red-faced man was talking to the Lemon Tart who had arrived with Baron Hochswald. Sherman now realized who he was . . . a television executive named Rale Brigham. Sherman stared at Mrs Rawthrote's bony vertebrae, where they popped up from out of her gown . . . Perhaps she had turned away for only a moment and would turn back to resume their conversation

. . . But no . . . she had barged in on the conversation of Brigham and the Tart . . . He could hear her rat-tat-tat voice . . . She was leaning in on Brigham . . . lasering in . . . She had devoted all the time she cared to devote . . . to a mere bond salesman!

He was stranded again. To his right, Maria was still deep in conversation with Lord Buffing. He was facing social death once more. He was a man sitting utterly solo at a dinner table. The hive buzzed all around him. Everyone else was in a state of social bliss. Only he was stranded. Only he was a wallflower with no conversational mate, a social light of no wattage whatsoever in the Bavardage Celebrity Zoo . . . *My life is coming apart!* – and yet through everything else in his overloaded central nervous system burned the shame – the shame! – of social incompetence.

He stared at Huck Thigg's hardened vines in the center of the table, as if a student of floral arrangements. Then he put a smirk on his face, as if confidently amused. He took a deep gulp of wine and looked across to the other table, as if he had caught the eye of someone there . . . He smiled . . . He murmured soundlessly toward vacant spots on the wall. He drank some more wine and studied the hardened vines some more. He counted the vertebrae in Mrs Rawthrote's backbone. He was happy when one of the waiters, one of the *varones* from the country, materialized and refilled his glass of wine.

The main course consisted of slices of pink roast beef brought in on huge china platters, with ruffs of stewed onions, carrots, and potatoes. It was a simple, hearty American main course. Simple Hearty American main courses, insinuated between exotically contrived prologues and epilogues, were *comme il faut*, currently, in keeping with the informal mode. When the Mexican waiter began hoisting the huge platters over the shoulders of the diners, so that they could take what they wanted, that served as the signal to change conversational partners. Lord Buffing, the stricken English poet, *entre nous*, turned toward the powdered Madame Cornagglia. Maria turned toward Sherman. She smiled and looked deeply into his eyes. Too deeply! Suppose Judy should look at them right now! He put on a frozen social grin.

'Whew!' said Maria. She rolled her eyes in the direction of Lord Buffing. Sherman didn't want to talk about Lord Buffing. He wanted to talk about the visit from the two detectives. *But best start off slowly, in case Judy is looking.*

'Ah, that's right!' he said. A great social grin. 'I forgot. You don't care for Brits.'

'Oh, it's not that,' said Maria. 'He seems like a nice man. I could hardly understand what he was saying. You never heard such an accent.'

Social grin: 'What did he talk about?'

'The purpose of life. I'm not kidding.'

Social grin: 'Did he happen to mention what it is?'

'As a matter of fact, he did. Reproduction.'

Social grin: 'Reproduction?'

'Yes. He said id'd taken him seventy years to realize that's the sole purpose of life: reproduction. Said, "Nature is concerned with but one thing: reproduction for the sake of reproduction." '

Social grin: 'That's very interesting, coming from him. You know he's homosexual, don't you?'

'Aw, come on. Who told you that?'

'This one.' He gestured toward the back of Mrs Rawthrote. 'Who is she, anyhow? Do you know her?'

'Yeah. Sally Rawthrote. She's a real-estate broker.'

Social grin: 'A real-estate broker!' Dear God. Who on earth would invite a *real-estate broker* to dinner!

As if reading his mind, Maria said, 'You're behind the times, Sherman. Real-estate brokers are very chic now. She goes everywhere with that old red-faced tub over there, Lord Gutt.' She nodded toward the other table.

'The fat man with the British accent?'

'Yes.'

'Who is he?'

'Some banker or other.'

Social grin: 'I've got something to tell you, Maria, but – I don't want you to get excited. My wife is at the next table and she's facing us. So please be cool.'

'Well, well, well. Why, Mr McCoy, honey.'

Keeping the social grin clamped on his mug the whole time, Sherman gave her a quick account of his confrontation with the two policemen.

Just as he feared, Maria's composure broke. She shook her head and scowled. 'Well, why didn't you let 'em see the goddamned car, Sherman! You said it's clean!'

Social grin: 'Hey! Calm down! My wife may be looking. I wasn't worried about the car. I just didn't want them to talk to the attendant. It may be the same one who was there that night, when I brought the car back.'

'Jesus Christ, Sherman. You talk to me about being cool, and you're so uncool. You sure you didn't tell 'em anything?'

Social grin: 'Yes, I'm sure.'

'For Christ's sake, get that stupid smile off your face. You're allowed to have a serious conversation with a girl at the dinner table, even if your wife is looking. I don't know why you agreed to talk to the goddamned police in the first place.'

'It seemed like the right thing to do at the time.'

'I *told* you you weren't cut out for this.'

Clamping the social grin back on, Sherman glanced at Judy. She was busy grinning toward the Indian face of Baron Hochswald. He turned back to Maria, still grinning.

'Oh, for God's sake,' said Maria.

He turned off the grin. 'When can I talk to you? When can I see you?'

'Call me tomorrow night.'

'Okay. Tomorrow night. Let me ask you something. Have you heard anybody talking about the story in *The City Light*? Anybody here, tonight?'

Maria started laughing. Sherman was glad. If Judy was watching, it would appear they were having an amusing conversation. 'Are you serious?' said Maria. 'The only thing these people read in *The City Light* is *her* column.' She motioned toward a large woman across the table, a woman of a certain age with an outrageous mop of blond hair and false eyelashes so long and thick she could barely lift her upper lids.

Social grin: 'Who's that?'

'That's "The Shadow." '

Sherman's heart kicked up. 'You're joking! They invite a newspaper columnist to dinner?'

'Sure. Don't worry. She id'n interested in you. And she id'n interested in automobile accidents in the Bronx, either. If I shot Arthur, she'd be interested in that. And I'd be glad to oblige her.'

Maria launched into a denunciation of her husband. He was consumed with jealousies and resentments. He was making her life hell. He kept calling her a whore. Her face was becoming more and more contorted. Sherman was alarmed – Judy might be looking! He wanted to put his social grin back on, but how could he, in the face of this lamentation? 'I mean, he goes around the apartment calling me a *whore*. "You whore! You whore!" – right in front of the servants! How do you think that feels? If he calls me that one more time, I'm gonna hit him over the head with something, I swear to God!'

Out of the corner of his eye, Sherman could see Judy's face turned toward the two of them. Oh Christ! – and him without his grin on! Quickly he retrieved it and clamped it on his face and said to Maria, 'That's terrible! It sounds like he's senile.'

Maria stared at his pleasant social visage for a moment, then shook her head. 'Go to hell, Sherman. You're as bad as he is.'

Startled, Sherman kept the grin on and let the sound of the hive engulf him. Such ecstasy on all sides! Such radiant eyes and fireproof grins! So many boiling teeth! *Hack hack hack hack hack hack hack*, Inez Bavardage's laugh rose in social triumph. *Haw haw haw haw haw haw haw haw haw*, the Golden Hillbilly's barnyard bray rose in response. Sherman gulped down another glass of wine.

The dessert was apricot soufflé, prepared individually, for each diner, in a stout little crock of the Normandy sort, with borders *au rustaud* painted by hand near the rim. Rich desserts were back in fashion this season. The sort of dessert that showed you were conscious of calories and cholesterol, all the berries and melon balls with dollops of sherbet, had become just a bit Middle America. On top of that, to be able to serve twenty-four individual soufflés was a *tour de force*. It required quite a kitchen and a staff and a half.

Once the *tour de force* had run its course, Leon Bavardage rose to his feet and tapped on his wineglass – a glass of sauterne of a deep rosy golden hue – heavy dessert wines were also *comme il faut* this season – and was answered by the happy drunken percussion of people at both tables tapping their wineglasses in a risory fashion. *Haw haw haw haw*, Bobby Shaflett's laugh rang out. He was banging his glass for all he was worth. Leon Bavardage's red lips spread across his face, and his eyes crinkled, as if the crystal percussion was a great tribute to the joy the assembled celebrities found in his home.

'You are all such dear and special friends of Inez's and mine that we don't need a *spec*ial occasion to want to have you all around us in our home,' he said in a bland, slightly feminine, Gulf Coast drawl. Then he turned toward the other table, where Bobby Shaflett sat. 'I mean, sometimes we ask Bobby to come over just so we can listen to his *laugh*. Bobby's laugh is music, far as I'm concerned – besides, we never can get him to sing for us, even when Inez plays the piano!'

Hack hack hack hack hack hack hack hack went Inez Bavardage. *Haw haw haw haw haw haw haw*, the Golden Hillbilly drowned her out with a laugh of his own. It was an amazing laugh, this one. *Haw haw haww hawww hawwww hawwwww hawwwwww*, it rose and rose and rose, and then it began to fall in a curious, highly stylized way, and then it broke into a sob. The room froze – dead silence – for that instant it took the diners, or most of them, to realize they had just heard the famous laughing sob of the 'Vesti la giubba' aria from *Pagliacci*.

Tremendous applause from both tables, beaming grins, laughter, and cries of 'More! More! More!'

'Aw, naw!' said the great blond giant. 'I only sing for my supper, an'at's enough for supper right'eh! My sou*fflé* wud'n big enough, Leon!'

Storms of laughter, more applause. Leon Bavardage motioned languidly toward one of the Mexican waiters.

'More soufflé for Mr Shaflett!' he said. 'Make it in the bathtub!' The waiter stared back with a face of stone.

Grinning, eyes glistening, swept up by this duet of the great wits, Rale Brigham yelled out, 'Bootleg soufflé!' This was so lame, Sherman was pleased to note, that everyone ignored it, even the ray-eyed Mrs Rawthrote.

'But this *is* a special occasion, all the same,' said Leon Bavardage, 'because we have a very special friend as our guest during his visit to the United States, Aubrey Buffing.' He beamed toward the great man, who turned his gaunt face toward Leon Bavardage with a small tight wary smile. 'Now, last year our friend Jacques Prudhomme' – he beamed toward the French Minister of Culture, who was to his right – 'told Inez and me he had it on good authority – I hope I'm not speaking out of turn, Jacques—'

'I hope so, too,' said the Minister of Culture in his grave voice, shrugging in an exaggerated fashion for humorous effect. Appreciative laughter.

'Well, you *did tell* Inez and me you had it on good authority that Aubrey had won the Nobel Prize. I'm sorry, Jacques, but your intelligence operations are not so hot in Stockholm!'

Another grand shrug, more of the elegant sepulchral voice: 'Fortunately, we do not contemplate hostilities with Sweden, Leon.' Great laughter.

'But Aubrey was *that close*, anyway,' said Leon, putting his forefinger and thumb close together, 'and next year may be his year.' The old Englishman's small tight smile didn't budge. 'But of course, it really doesn't matter, because what Aubrey means to our . . . our *cul*ture . . . goes way beyond prizes, and I know that what Aubrey means to Inez and me as a *friend* . . . well, it goes beyond prizes and culture . . . and—' He was stumped for a way to finish off his tricolon, and so he said: '—and everything else. Anyway, I want to propose a toast to Aubrey, with best wishes for his visit to America—'

'He just bought himself another month of house guest,' Mrs Rawthrote said to Rale Brigham in a stage whisper.

Leon lifted his glass of sauterne: 'Lord Buffing!'

Raised glasses, applause, British-style *hear-hears*.

The Englishman rose slowly to his feet. He was terribly haggard. His nose seemed a mile long. He was not tall, and yet somehow his great hairless skull made him seem imposing.

'You're much too kind, Leon,' he said, looking at Leon and then casting his eyes down modestly. 'As you may know . . . anyone who entertains the notion of the Nobel Prize is advised to act as if he is oblivious of its very existence, and in any case, I'm far too old to worry about it . . . And so I'm sure I don't know what you're talking about.' Light puzzled laughter. 'But one can scarcely help being aware of the marvelous friendship and hospitality of you and Inez, and thank goodness I don't have to pretend for a moment to be otherwise.' The litotes had now trebled so rapidly, the company was baffled. But they murmured their encouragement. 'So much so,' he went on, 'that I, for one, should be happy to sing for my supper—'

'I should think so,' whispered Mrs Rawthrote.

'—but I don't see how anyone would dare do so after Mr Shaflett's remarkable allusion to Canio's grief in *Pagliacci*.'

As only the English can do it, he pronounced 'Mr Shaflett' very archly, to bring out the ludicrous aspect of giving the dignified title 'Mister' to this rustic clown.

Suddenly he stopped and lifted his head and gazed straight ahead, as if looking through the walls of the building and out upon the metropolis beyond. He laughed dryly.

'Forgive me. All at once I was hearing the sound of my own voice, and it occurred to me that I now have the sort of British voice which, had I heard it half a century ago, when I was a young man – a delightfully hotheaded young man, as I recall – would have caused me to leave the room.'

People cut glances at one another.

'But I know you won't leave,' Buffing continued. 'It has always been wonderful to be an Englishman in the United States. Lord *Gutt* may disagree with me' – he pronounced *Gutt* with such a guttural bark, it was as if he were saying *Lord Shithead* – 'but I doubt that he will. When I first came to the United States, as a young man, before the Second Great War, and people heard my voice, they would say, "Oh, you're English!" and I always got my way, because they were so impressed. Nowadays, when I come to the United States and people hear my voice, they say, "Oh, you're English – you poor thing!" – and I still get my way, because your countrymen never fail to take pity on us.'

Much appreciative laughter and relief. The old man was mining the lighter vein. He paused again, as if trying to decide whether he should go on or not. His conclusion, evidently, was yes.

'Why I've never written a poem about the States I really don't know. Well, I take that back. I *do* know, of course. I have lived in a century in which poets are not supposed to write poems *about* anything, at least not anything you can put a geographical name to. But the United States deserve an epic poem. At various times in my career I considered writing an epic, but I didn't do that, either. Poets are also not supposed to write epics any longer, despite the fact that the only poets who have endured and will endure are poets who have written epics. Homer, Virgil, Dante, Shakespeare, Milton, Spenser – where will Mr Eliot or Mr Rimbaud' – pronounced like

Mr Shaflett – 'be in their light, even twenty-five years from now? In the shadows, I'm afraid, in the footnotes, deep in the *ibid.* thickets . . . along with Aubrey Buffing and a lot of other poets I have thought very highly of from time to time. No, we poets no longer even have the vitality to write epics. We don't even have the courage to make rhymes, and the American epic should have rhymes, rhyme on top of rhyme in a shameless cascade, rhymes of the sort that Edgar Allan Poe gave us . . . Yes . . . Poe, who lived his last years just north of here, I believe, in a part of New York called the Bronx . . . in a little cottage with lilacs and a cherry tree . . . and a wife dying of tuberculosis. A drunk he was, of course, perhaps a psychotic – but with the madness of prophetic vision. He wrote a story that tells all we need to know about the moment we live in now . . . "The Masque of the Red Death" . . . A mysterious plague, the Red Death, is ravaging the land. Prince Prospero – Prince *Pros*pero – even the name is perfect – Prince Prospero assembles all the best people in his castle and lays in two years' provision of food and drink, and shuts the gates against the outside world, against the virulence of all lesser souls, and commences a masked ball that is to last until the plague has burnt itself out beyond the walls. The party is endless and seamless, and it takes place in seven grand salons, and in each the revel becomes more intense than in the one before, and the revelers are drawn on, on, on toward the seventh room, which is appointed entirely in black. One night, in this last room, appears a guest shrouded in the most clever and most hideously beautiful costume this company of luminous masqueraders has ever seen. This guest is dressed as Death, but so convincingly that Prospero is offended and orders him ejected. But none dares touch him, so that the task is left to the Prince himself, and the moment he touches the ghastly shroud, he falls down dead for the Red Death has entered the house of Prospero . . . *Pros*pero, my friends . . . Now, the exquisite part of the story is that somehow the guests have known all along what awaits them in this room, and yet they are drawn irresistibly toward it, because the excitement is so intense and the pleasure is so unbridled and the gowns and the food and the drink and the flesh are so sumptuous – and that is all they have. Families, homes, children, the great chain of being, the eternal tide of chromosomes mean nothing to them any longer. They are bound together, and they whirl about one another, endlessly, particles in a doomed atom – and what else could the Red Death be but some sort of final stimulation, the *ne plus ultra*? So Poe was kind enough to write the ending for us more than a hundred years ago. Knowing that, who can possibly write all the sunnier passages that should come before? Not I, not I. The sickness – the nausea – the pitiless pain – have ceased with the fever that maddened my brain – with the fever called "Living" that burned in my brain. The fever called "Living" – those were among the last words he wrote . . . No . . . I cannot be the epic poet you deserve. I am too old and far too tired, too weary of the fever called "Living," and I value your company too much, your company and the whirl, the whirl, the whirl. Thank you, Leon. Thank you, Inez.'

And with that the spectral Englishman slowly took his seat.

The intruder the Bavardages dreaded most, silence, now commanded the room. The diners looked at one another in embarrassment, three kinds of it. They were embarrassed for this old man, who had committed the gaffe of injecting a somber note into an evening at the Bavardages'. They were embarrassed because they felt the need to express their cynical superiority to his solemnity, but they didn't know how to go about it. Dared they snigger? After all, he was Lord Buffing of the Nobel Short List and their hosts' house guest. And they were embarrassed because there was always the possibility that the old man had said something profound and they had failed to get it. Sally Rawthrote rolled her eyes and pulled a mock long face and looked about to see if anyone was following her lead. Lord Gutt put a downcast smile on his great fat face and glanced at Bobby Shaflett, who was himself looking at Inez Bavardage for a clue. She offered none. She stared, dumbstruck. Judy was smiling an entirely foolish smile, it seemed to Sherman, as if she thought something very pleasant had just been expressed by the distinguished gentleman from Great Britain.

Inez Bavardage rose up and said, 'We'll have coffee in the other room.'

Gradually, without conviction, the hive began to buzz again.

On the ride back home, the six-block ride, costing $123.25, which is to say, one half of $246.50, with Mayfair Town Car Inc.'s white-haired driver at the wheel, Judy chattered away. She was bubbling over. Sherman hadn't seen her this animated for more than two weeks, since the night she caught him in *flagrante telephone* with Maria. Tonight, obviously, she had not detected a thing concerning Maria, didn't even know the pretty girl sitting next to her husband at dinner had been *named* Maria. No, she was in great spirits. She was intoxicated, not by alcohol – alcohol was fattening – but by Society.

With a pretense of amused detachment she burbled about the shrewdness with which Inez had chosen her celebrity all-stars: three titles (Baron Hochswald, Lord Gutt, and Lord Buffing), one ranking politician with a cosmopolitan cachet

(Jacques Prudhomme), four giants of arts and letters (Bobby Shaflett, Nunnally Voyd, Boris Korolev, and Lord Buffing), two designers (Ronald Vine and Barbara Cornagglia), three V.I.F.'s – 'V.I.F.'s?' asked Sherman – 'Very Important Fags,' said Judy, 'that's what everybody calls them' (the only name Sherman caught was that of the Englishman who had sat to her right, St John Thomas), and three business titans (Hochswald, Rale Brigham, and Arthur Ruskin). Then she went on about Ruskin. The woman on his left, Madame Prudhomme, wouldn't talk to him, and the woman on his right, Rale Brigham's wife, wasn't interested, and so Ruskin had leaned over and started telling Baron Hochswald about his air charter service in the Middle East. 'Sherman, have you any idea how that man makes his money? He takes Arabs to Mecca on airplanes – 747s! – by the tens of thousands! – and he's Jewish!'

It was the first time she had passed on a piece of chitchat to him, in the sunny vein of yore, since he couldn't remember when. But he was past caring about the life and times of Arthur Ruskin. He could think only of the gaunt and haunted Englishman, Aubrey Buffing.

And then Judy said, 'What on earth do you suppose got into Lord Buffing? The whole thing was so . . . so mortifying.'

Mortifying, indeed, thought Sherman. He started to tell her that Buffing was dying of AIDS, but he was long past the joys of gossip also.

'I have no idea,' he said.

But of course he did. He knew precisely. That mannered, ghostly English voice had been the voice of an oracle. Aubrey Buffing had been speaking straight to him, as if he were a medium dispatched by God Himself. Edgar Allan Poe! – *Poe!* – the ruin of the dissolute! – in the Bronx – *the Bronx!* The meaningless whirl, the unbridled flesh, the obliteration of home and hearth! – and, waiting in the last room, the Red Death.

Eddie had the door open for them by the time they walked from the Mayfair Town Car sedan to the entrance. Judy sang out, 'Hello, Eddie!' Sherman barely looked at him and said nothing – at all. He felt dizzy. In addition to being consumed by fear, he was drunk. His eyes darted about the lobby . . . The Street of Dreams . . . He half expected to see the shroud.

DON DELILLO

THE BLACK AND WHITE BALL

(1996)

THE FIRST MAN stood by the window of his stately suite at the Waldorf. He watched the yellow cabs sink into soulful dusk, that particular spendthrift light that falls dyingly on Park Avenue in the hour before people take leave of the office and become husbands and wives again, or whatever people become in whatever murmurous words when evenings grow swift and whispered.

The second man sat on the sofa, legs crossed, looking at Bureau reports.

Edgar said, 'Of course you packed the mask.'

The second man nodded, a gesture that went unseen.

'Junior, the masks.'

'We have them, yes. I'm looking at a security memo that's a little, actually, rankling.'

'I don't want to hear it. File it somewhere. I feel too good.'

'Protest. Outside the Plaza tonight.'

'What is it the bastards are protesting? Pray tell,' Edgar said in a tone he'd perfected through the years, a tight amusement etched in eleven kinds of irony.

'The war, it seems.'

'The war.'

'Yes, that,' the second man said.

They were staying at the Waldorf Towers, which was J. Edgar Hoover's hotel of choice during his sojourns in New York, but the party was taking place – the ball, the fête, the social event of the season, the decade, the half century no doubt – in the ballroom at the Plaza.

Edgar gazed far up Park, where the earth curved toward Canada, haven for draft dodgers and other misfits. He heard the muted clamor of taxi horns below, a cheerful sound at this protected distance, little toots and beeps that carried a carefree pitch.

'Let's talk about the war tomorrow.'

'A protest by a group we don't know much about.'

'Don't ruin my evening, Junior.'

Clyde Tolson, known as Junior, was Edgar's staunchest aide in the Bureau, his dearest friend and inseparable companion.

They were getting on, of course. Clyde was five years younger than Edgar but not so sharp as he used to be, his flash-card memory a little less prodigious now. But where Edgar was pug-nosed and compact, with brows like bat wings, Clyde was long-jawed and tallish, sort of semi-debonair, a fairly gentle fellow who liked conversation – again, unlike his boss, who thought you gave yourself away, word by word, every time you opened your trap to speak.

Edgar held a tumbler of Scotch. He checked the glass for smudges, then sniffed and sipped, feeling the charred fumes prickle his tongue. The handsome suite, the soothing booze, the presence of Junior on the scene, the party that everybody'd been talking about for months, famous long before it happened, the uninvited lapsing into states of acute confusion, insomniac, unable to function – yes, Edgar was feeling pretty good tonight.

Talkative or not, he loved a first-rate party. He loved celebrities in particular, and there would be an abundance of mammal glamour at the Plaza tonight. Personage and flair and wicked wit. A frail and lonely lad still crouched inside the Director's pudgy corpus, and this crypto-schoolboy came to robust life in the presence of show people and other living icons – child stars, ballplayers, prizefighters, even Hollywood horses and dogs.

Celebrated people were master spirits, men and women who spiked the temper of the age. Whatever Edgar's own claim to rank and notoriety, he found himself subject to anal flutters when chatting with a genuine celeb.

Clyde said, 'And this, of course, as well.'

Edgar did not turn to see what the second man was reading. He studied the carpet instead. The carpets at the Waldorf were thick and lush, nesting grounds for bacteria of every sort.

Clyde said, 'I knew it was a mistake to publicize our methods of ransacking the garbage of organized-crime figures.'

'Makes good copy.'

'And creates a copycat mentality. Now we have a situation that's a public-relations nightmare. To wit, so-called garbage guerrillas are targeting guess whose garbage, Boss?'

'Please. I'm enjoying my drink. A man enjoys a drink when the day winds down.'

'Yours,' Clyde said.

Edgar could not believe he'd heard the fellow correctly.

'This is what our confidential source tells us.' And Clyde rattled the page he was reading for maximum nuisance effect. 'Team of urban guerrillas planning a garbage raid at 4936 Thirtieth Place Northwest, Washington, D.C.'

It was the end of the world, in triplicate.

'When is this supposed to happen?'

'More or less momentarily.'

'You've posted guards?'

'In unmarked cars. But whether we arrest them or not, they will find a way to make public theatre of your garbage.'

'I won't put the garbage out.'

'You have to put it out eventually.'

'I'll put it out and lock it up.'

'How will the garbage collectors collect it?'

Edgar walked over to another window. He needed a change, as they say, of scene.

'Confidential source says they intend to take your garbage on tour. Rent halls in major cities. Get lefty sociologists to analyze the stuff item by item. Get hippies to rub it on their naked bodies. More or less have sex with it. Get poets to write poems about it. In the last city on the tour, they plan to eat it.'

Edgar could see part of the east façade of the Plaza, about a dozen blocks away.

'And expel it,' Clyde said. 'Publicly.'

The great slate roof, the gables and dormers and copper cresting. How odd it seemed that such a taken-for-granted thing, putting out the garbage, could suddenly be a source of the gravest anxiety.

'Do we have a dossier on these guerrillas?'

'Yes.'

'Is it massive?' Edgar said.

In the endless estuarial mingling of paranoia and control, the dossier was an essential device. Edgar had many enemies-for-life, and the way to deal with such people was to compile massive dossiers. Photographs, surveillance reports, detailed allegations, linked names, transcribed tapes – wiretaps, bugs, break-ins. The dossier was a deeper form of truth, transcending facts and actuality. The second you placed an item in the file, a fuzzy photograph, an unfounded rumor, it became promiscuously true. It was a truth without authority and therefore incontestable. Factoids seeped out of the file and crept across the horizon, consuming bodies and minds. The file was everything, the life nothing. And this was the essence of Edgar's revenge. He rearranged the lives of his enemies, their conversations, their relationships, their very memories, and he made these people answerable to the details of his creation.

'We'll arrest them and charge them,' Clyde said. 'That's all we can do.'

Edgar turned from the window, smiling.

'Maybe I can sympathize with the Mafia over this.'

Clyde smiled.

'You were always half a gangster,' he said.

They laughed.

'Remember the tommy guns we carried?' Edgar said.

'When photographers were around.'

They laughed again.

'You were right there alongside me, posed heroically.'

'Edgar and Clyde,' said Clyde.

'Clyde and Edgar,' said Edgar.

Where the current of his need for control met the tide of his paranoia, this was where the dossier was reciprocally satisfying. He fed both forces in a single stroke.

'I liked the thirties,' Edgar said. 'I don't like the sixties. No, not at all.'

The desk at the end of the room was out of the thirties, in a way, equipped with items fashioned to Edgar's specifications. Two nibbed black pens. Two bottles of Skrip Permanent Royal Blue ink, No. 52. Six sharpened Eberhard Faber pencils, No. 2. A pair of five-by-eight linen-finish writing pads, white. A new sixty-watt bulb in the standing lamp. The Director did not want to breathe the dust of old bulbs used to illuminate the reading matter of total strangers. Newspapers, guidebooks, Gideon Bibles, erotic literature, subversive literature, underground literature,

literature – whatever people read in hotels, alone, thumbing and breathing.

Clyde checked his watch. Dinner first, the two of them, alone, a practice spanning the decades – then the short ride to the Plaza.

It was called the Black-and-White Ball. A godlike gathering of five hundred, a masked affair, invitation only, dinner jacket and black mask for men, evening gown and white mask for women.

The party was being given by a writer, Truman Capote, for a publisher, Katharine Graham, and the factoidal data generated by the guests would surely bridge the narrowing gap between journalism and fiction.

Edgar had not been invited, initially. But arranging an invitation was not difficult. A word from Edgar to Clyde. A word from Clyde to someone close to Capote. They were in the files, of course, a number of those involved in planning the event – all catalogued and dossiered up to their eyeballs, and none of them eager to offend the Director.

Clyde took a call from the desk. The mask lady was coming up for a fitting.

Edgar noticed that Clyde was wearing a necktie with a driblet design. The little figures made him think of paramecia, sinister organisms with gullets and feeding grooves. At home Edgar sat on a toilet that was raised on a platform to isolate him from floorbound forms of life. And he'd ordered his lab people to build a clean room at the Bureau with unprecedented standards of hygiene. A white room manned by white-clad technicians, preferably white themselves, who would work in an environment completely free of contaminants, dust, bacteria, and so on, with big white lights shining down, where Edgar himself might like to spend time when he was feeling vulnerable to the forces around him.

She walked in the door, Tanya Berenger, in a maxidress and thrift-shop boots, once a well-known costume designer, now ancient and frowzy, living in a room in a sad hotel off Times Square, a place where the desk clerk sits behind a grille eating a tongue sandwich. People tracked her down, three or four times a year, to do masks for special occasions, and she found fairly steady work doing sadomasochistic accessories for a private club in the Village.

The two men, as always with a female in the room, someone they didn't know, and without others present, and lacking an atmosphere of sociable cheer – well, they tended to become stiff and defensive, as though surprised by an armed intruder.

Clyde did not stray from Edgar's side, sensing a potential for wayward behavior on the woman's part. She wore heavy makeup that she might have poured from a paint can and cooked. Clyde noted how one pocket on her dress drooped just a bit, becoming unseamed.

She spoke to Edgar with a sort of rueful affection.

'You know I can't let you wear one of my masks, dear man, without a consultation. I must put my hands on the living head. Bad enough I had to create my objet from a set of written specifications, like I'm a plumber installing a sink already.'

She had a European accent slashed and burned by long-term residence in New York. And her hair had the retouched gloss of a dead crow mounted on a stick.

Of course Clyde had been briefed on Tanya Berenger. She was in the files in a fairly big way. She'd been accused at various times of being a lesbian, a Socialist, a Communist, a dope addict, a divorcée, a Jew, a Catholic, a Negro, an immigrant, and an unwed mother.

Just about everything Edgar distrusted and feared. But

she did exquisite masks, and Clyde had been quick to commission her for the job.

He hurried into Edgar's bedroom and fetched the mask.

When she held it in her hands, she looked at Edgar and looked at the mask, weighing the equation, and the Director experienced a queer tension in his chest, wondering whether he was worthy.

She held the object at eye level, six inches from her face, and looked through the eyeholes at Edgar.

And Edgar, in turn, looked at the mask as if it had a life, an identity of its own that he might feel ballsy enough to borrow for a single midnight on the town.

It was a sleek black leather mask with handlebar extensions at the temples and a scatter of shiny sequins around the eyes.

Tanya said, 'You want to put it on or have a conversation with it?'

But he wasn't quite ready.

'Do I want to put it on, Junior?'

'Be brave.'

Tanya said, 'Leather. It's so real, you know? Like wearing someone else's face.'

She fitted the mask over Edgar's head, the padded band not too tight and the leather alive on his skin.

Then she took him by the shoulders and turned him slowly toward the mirror over the desk.

Clyde took the whiskey glass from Edgar's hand.

The mask transformed him. For the first time in some years, he did not see himself as a tenant in an old short popover body with an immense and lumpish head.

'I can call you Edgar – this is O.K.? I can tell you how I see you? I see you as a mature and careful man who has a sexy motorcycle thug writhing to get out. Which the spangles give a crazy twist, you know?'

He felt creamy, dreamy, and drugged.

She made a slight adjustment in the fit, and even as he cringed at her touch Edgar felt himself tingle thrillingly. She was insidious and corrupt, and it was like hearing your grandmother talk dirty in your ear.

'You are a butch biker to me, you know, riding into town to take over leadership of the sadists and necrophiles.'

Clyde watched in civilized alarm as a cockroach crawled out of Tanya's pocket and moved slowly down her flank. It was Spanish Harlem-sized, with antennae that could pick up the BBC.

'It's a lovely fit, darling. You have savage cheekbones for a full-figured man. I would love to do the total face, you know? Highlights and shadows.'

Clyde took her gently by the arm, concealing her roach side from Edgar's view.

'In fact, shall I tell you something? The ball tonight is a perfect setting for you. Because you are very black-and-white to me. So you'll be totally in character, yes?'

When she was gone, the men busied themselves with practical preparations. Clyde made dinner reservations and set out their evening clothes. Edgar placed the mask on a tabletop and took a bath.

When he was finished, he put on his fluffy white robe and stood by the window, sipping the rest of the drink. He heard a sound above the beeping traffic, something strident rising in the night.

'Junior, that noise. Can you hear it?'

Clyde walked into the room in his shirtsleeves, a shoe-brush in hand.

'Yes, barely.'

'Is it possible?'

'Yes, it could be the protesters at the Plaza.'

'The wind.'

'Yes, the wind is carrying the sound this way.'

They heard the hard rhythmic salvo of voices chanting angry slogans, again, louder, fading when the wind shifted, then audible once more.

'You know what they want, don't you?' Edgar said.

He thought the old alarums might be sounding once again, figures coming out of the shadows, anarchists, terrorists, revolutionaries, wild-eyed men and women, scruffy and free-fucking, who moved toward armed and organized resistance, trying to break the state and bring about the end of the existing order.

'They want the power to shake the world,' he said. 'It's the old Bolshevik dream, and it's happening here. And you know where it begins, don't you?'

'These are kids, mostly, who lie down in the street and wave flowers at the police,' Clyde said. 'Vietnam is the war, the reality. This is the movie, where the scripts are written and the actors perform. American kids don't want to seize control. They want movies, music.'

Let Junior devise his measured perceptions. He didn't understand that once you patronize the enemy, you begin the process of your own undoing.

'It begins in the inmost person,' Edgar said. 'Once you yield to random sexual urges, you want to see everything come loose. You mistake your own looseness for some political concept, whereas in truth . . .'

He didn't finish the thought. Some thoughts had to remain unspoken, even unfinished in one's own mind. This was the point of his relationship with Clyde. To keep the subject unspoken. To keep the feelings unfelt, the momentary urges unacted-upon. How strange and foolish this would seem to the young people running in the streets, or living six to a room, or three to a bed, and to many other people, for that matter – how sad and rare.

Clyde went back to his duties, leaving the Boss by the window.

Edgar thought there was something noble in a constant companionship that does not fall to baser claims. He assumed Clyde believed likewise. But then Clyde was the second man, wasn't he, and perhaps he only followed Edgar's line of march wherever it led, or didn't.

He heard the chanting intermittently on the wind. Clyde was in the shower now. Edgar turned to see where he'd left the mask and saw himself unexpectedly in a full-length mirror, across the room, in his white robe and soft slippers, and he was startled by the image.

Of course it was him, but him in the guise of a macrocephalic baby, sexless and so just born as to be, in essence, unearthly.

Mother Hoover's cuddled runt.

He crossed the room and picked up the mask. He noted how the stylized handlebars were simple swirls of cut leather designed to fit snugly over the temples.

He heard Clyde come out of the shower.

When they were younger and on vacation together, or away on business, sharing a suite or taking adjoining rooms and keeping the connecting door open so they could talk from their respective beds well into the night, Edgar sometimes managed to angle the mirrors in such a way that he could catch a glimpse – by taking the freestanding antique in an old inn, the cheval glass, for example, and simply moving it to another part of the floor, or opening the medicine cabinet to a certain position when he shaved and letting the mirror absorb the light from the bed in the next room, or leaving a hand mirror propped on a desk – a glimpse, a passing glance, a spy-hole peek at Junior as he busied himself dressing or undressing or taking a bath, the arrangement being such that the moment would seem wholly accidental should the subject realize he was being watched, and an accident not just from his perspective but to Edgar's own mind as well, Junior's likeness being a thing that might simply float across his ken in the normal course of events, away on urgent Bureau business, his companion's body lean and virile, or at a golf resort, or following the ponies west to Del Mar, when they were both a great deal younger.

Junior was going bald now, and bulb-nosed, and he walked with a stoop. But then Junior had always walked with a stoop, in an effort to appear no taller than the Boss.

Edgar was in the bedroom with the door closed. He stood at the mirror, a seventy-one-year-old man wearing nothing but his sequinned biker's mask and his wool-lined slippers, listening to the voices in the street.

The second man made the decision to show up late. It was the kind of firm determination that Clyde Tolson liked to make.

It proved his mettle. And when you're a man who is variously described as dutiful, deferential, obsequious, slavish, and brownnosingly corrupt, in descending order of distinction, you need to make a show of character now and then.

But first Clyde had to convince the Boss that missing an hour or two of party time was not going to haunt the twilight years of his directorate.

An F.B.I. security detail at the Plaza had reported that the protest was growing loud and that the party guests, as they entered, were being cursed in rhyming couplets, exposed to obscene signs and gestures, spat upon at close range, and forced to duck an occasional flying object.

It did not make sense to Clyde to allow the Director to enter a situation – and Edgar finally agreed – in which the dignity of the Bureau might be compromised.

So it was midnight when the two men rolled through the deserted midtown streets in their bulletproof black Cadillac. They'd had a leisurely dinner, bantering with the wine steward and then enjoying a brandy at the bar with old acquaintances because there were old acquaintances wherever J. Edgar Hoover went, some who were loyal supporters, others residing in the files, a few who were enemies-for-life but didn't know it, and Edgar and Clyde were in a mellow enough mood, despite reports from the site, seated in the plush rear seat, in black tie, of course, and wearing their masks, like a suave and jaunty crime fighter out of the Sunday comics – a master bureaucrat by day who becomes dashing Maskman at night – cruising the streets in formal dress with his trusted right-hand man.

The driver activated the intercom to report that a car was tailing them.

Clyde turned to look while the Director slumped in his seat, getting his head below the window line.

'Little Volkswagen bug,' Clyde said. 'Painted top to bottom in very bright colors. Psychedelic. Big bright swirls and streaks. Can't make out the driver's face.'

The Cadillac coasted slowly past the Plaza. The klieg lights were gone, the media pack was gone, there was no trace of the crush of curious onlookers drawn by news of the event. There were still a few demonstrators – not enough to cause concern, but a few – a scatter of young people in their grimy tie-dyes, and city cops, of course, idler still, showing the eternal laden strain of a big meal hustled down the gullet, where it sits for hours earning overtime.

The car circled the block, purring with bated power, and Clyde checked the other entrances.

The north steps were empty and he tapped on the glass, and the driver pulled up and the two men exited, and suddenly there was the VW, cutting in front, and people came scrambling out, three, four, six, what, seven people – it's circus car debouching clowns – about nine people tumbling onto the sidewalk and hurrying up the steps to flank the doorway.

All wore masks, the faces of Asian kids, some blood-spattered, others with eyes seamed shut, and they commenced their shouting as Hoover and Tolson moved up the stairs.

The first man was clumsy and slow and the second took his arm to assist, and they made their plodding way toward the entrance.

They heard, 'Society scum!'

They heard, 'A dead Asian baby for every Gucci loafer!'

Clyde wasn't sure the protesters knew who they were. Was Edgar's mask sufficient cover for his gnarled old media mug?

They heard mottoes, slurs, and technical terms.

'Vietnam! Love it or leave it!'

'White killers in black tie!'

A young woman stood at the entrance wearing the mask of a child's shattered face, and she said somewhat softly to Edgar, blocking his way and speaking evenly, whispering, in fact, 'We'll never disappear, old man, until you're in a landfill with your trash.'

Clyde said, 'Coming through' like a waiter with a bulky tray, and a couple of minutes later, after a stop in the men's room to collect themselves, the Director and his aide were ready to party.

But first Edgar said, 'Who were those jaspers?'

'Hecklers, that's all. It's public theatre. We'll find out more and place an informant.'

'Did you hear what she said about trash? I think they're connected to the garbage guerrillas.'

'Straighten your mask,' Clyde said.

'I'd like to see them maimed in the slowest possible manner. Over weeks and months, with voice tapes made.'

They walked down the hall to the grand ballroom. They'd walked down five hundred halls on their way to some ceremonial event, some testimonial dinner, one or another ritual salute to Edgar's decades in the Bureau, but they'd never heard a sound as inviting as this.

A subdued roar, a sort of rumblebuzz, with a chandelier jingle in the mix and the dreamy sway of dance music and an element of self-delight – the lure, the enticement of a life defined by its remoteness from the daily drudge of world complaint.

'Tapes of cries and moans,' Edgar said, 'which I would play to help me sleep.'

They moved through the ballroom, they circulated, seeing prominent people everywhere. The room was high and white and primrose gold, flanked by Greek columns that caught the lickety amber light of a thousand candles.

Swan-necked women in textured satin gowns. Masks by Halston, Adolfo, and Saint Laurent. The mother and the sister of one American President and the daughter of another. Crisp little men aswagger with assets. Titled jet-setters, a maharaja and maharani, a Baroness Somebody in a beaded mask. Famous and raging alcoholic poets. Tough smart stylish women who ran fashion books and designed clothes. Hair by Kenneth – teased, swirled, back-combed, and ringleted.

'Did you see?'

'Yes, I did,' Edgar said.

'In the dime-store mask.'

'Yes, decorated with pearls.'

They shook hands here and there, daintily, and dropped a flattering remark to this or that person, and Clyde knew how the Director felt, mixing with people of the rarest social levels, the anointed and predestined, aura'd like Inca kings, but also the talented and the original and the self-made and the born beautiful and the ego-driven and the hard-bargaining, all bearing signs of astral radiance, and the ruthless and brutish as well.

Yes, Edgar was excited.

He stopped to chat with Frank Sinatra and his young actress wife, a nymph in a boy's haircut and a butterfly mask.

'Jedgar, you old warhorse. How long has it been?'

'Far too long, my friend.'

'Tempus fugits, don't it, pal?'

'Introduce me to your lovely bride.'

Sinatra was in the files. Many people in the room were in the files. Not a single one of them, Clyde imagined, more accomplished in his occupational strokes than Edgar himself. But Edgar did not carry the glow. Edgar worked in the semidark, manipulating and bringing ruin. He carried the small wan grudging glory of the civil servant. Not the open and confident show, the wide-striding boom of some of these cosmic bravos.

On the stage, under the furled curtain, two bands took turns. A white society band and a black soul group. All musicians masked.

People admired Edgar's leather mask. They told him so. A woman in ostrich feathers ran her tongue over the handlebars. Another woman called him Biker Boy. A gay playwright rolled his eyes.

They found their table and settled in for a spell, sipping champagne and nibbling on buffet tidbits. Clyde uttered the names of people dancing past and Edgar commented on their lives and careers and personal predilections. Whatever anecdotal lore he failed to recall, Clyde was quick to provide.

Andy Warhol walked by wearing a mask that was a photograph of his own face.

A woman asked Edgar to dance, and he flushed and lit a cigarette.

Lord and Lady Somebody held their masks on sticks.

A woman wore a sexy nun's wimple.

A man wore an executioner's hood.

Edgar spoke rapidly in his old staccato voice, like a radio reporter doing a series of punchy news items. It made Clyde feel good to see the Boss show such animation. They spotted a number of people they knew professionally, Administration faces, past and present, men who held sensitive and critical positions, and Clyde noted how the ballroom seemed to throb with crosscurrent interests and appetites. Political power mingling lubriciously with art and literature. Domed historians clubbing with the beautiful people of society and fashion. There were diplomats dancing with movie stars, and Nobel laureates telling chummy stories to shipping tycoons, and the demimonde of Broadway and the gossip industry hobnobbing with foreign correspondents.

There was a self-conscious sense of some profound moment in the making. A dreadful prospect, Clyde thought, because it suggested a continuation of the Kennedy years. In which well-founded categories began to seem irrelevant. In which a certain fluid movement became possible. In which sex, drugs, and dirty words began to unstratify the culture.

'I think you ought to dance,' Edgar said.

Clyde looked at him.

'It's a party. Why not? Find a suitable lady and spin her around the floor.'

'I do believe the man is serious.'

'Then come back and tell me what you talked about.'

'Do I remember a single step?'

'You were quite a good dancer, Junior. Go ahead. Do your stuff. It's a party.'

On the floor the guests were doing the twist with all the articulated pantomime of the unfrozen dead come back for a day. Soon the white band reemerged and the music turned to foxtrots and waltzes. Clyde watched the slowly shuffling mass of careful dancers, barely touching, heedful of hairdos and jewelry and gowns and masks and always on the alert for other fabulous people – heads turning, eyes bright in the great black-and-white gyre.

'Yes, show your true colors,' Edgar said with a twisted grin.

So that was it. Tipsy and bitter. All right, thought Clyde. If this was to be a night in which old restrictions were eased, why not a turn around the floor?

He approached a woman not only masked but wholly medieval, it seemed, a cloth wound about the head and a long plain cloak sashed at the waist and a tight bodice girdled high under her breasts.

She smiled at him, and Clyde said, 'Shall we?'

She was tall and fair and wore no makeup and spoke without awe of the evening and its trappings. A levelheaded and well-brought-up young lady of the sort that Edgar admired and therefore Clyde as well.

She wore a raven's mask.

Clyde's own mask, an unadorned domino, was in his pocket now.

'Are we using names,' he said, 'or shall we abide by strict rules of anonymity?'

'Are there rules in effect? I wasn't aware.'

'We'll make our own,' he said, surprised by the slightly sexy banter he was generating.

He led her in and out of pairs of bodies ghost-floating to the tune of an old ballad from his youth.

Clyde used to have women friends. But when the Boss started to court other possible protégés, strong-bodied young agents who would serve a social function more than a Bureau function, Clyde knew it was time to submit to Edgar's need for a steadfast and unquestioning friend, a mate of soul and word and unvarying routine. This was a choice that answered Clyde's own deep need for protection, a place on the safe side of the fortified wall.

Power made his suits fit better.

He saw Edgar being photographed with a group at the far end of the ballroom. Clyde recognized most of the people and noticed how eager Edgar seemed to nestle among them.

Edgar's own power had always been double-skinned. He had the power of his office, of course. And also the power that his self-repression gave him. His stern measures as director were given an odd legitimacy by his personal life, the rigor of his insistent celibacy. Clyde believed this, that Edgar had earned his monocratic power through the days and nights of his self-denial, the rejection of unacceptable impulses. The man was consistent. Every official secret in the Bureau had its blood birth in Edgar's own soul.

This was what made him a great man.

Conflict. The nature of his desire and the unremitting attempts he made to expose homosexuals in the government. The secret of his desire and the refusal to yield. Great in his conviction. Great in his harsh judgment and traditional background and early-American righteousness and great in his quibbling fear and dark shame and great and sad and miserable in his dread of physical contact and in a thousand other torments too deep to name.

Clyde would have done whatever the Boss required.

Knelt down.

Bent over.

Spread out.

Reached around.

But the Boss wanted only his company and his loyalty down to the last sentient instant of his dying breath.

Clyde saw another man, and another, in executioner's hoods. And a figure in a white winding-sheet.

'And that man over there. Having his picture snapped,' the young woman said. 'That's the person you were sitting with.'

'Mr Hoover.'

'Mr Hoover, yes.'

'And with him, let me see. The wife of a famous poet. The husband of a famous actress. Two unattached composers. A billionaire with a double chin.' Clyde realized he was showing off.

'And you are Mr Tolson,' said the woman.

And how clever, thought Clyde, who was rarely recognized in public, and felt a bit flattered, and somewhat unsettled as well.

They were dancing cheek to cheek.

He saw another woman in modified medieval dress, and then a man in a skeleton mask and a woman with a monk's cowl standing on the fringes of the dance floor.

'You know my name,' Clyde said, 'but I'm at a loss, I'm afraid.'

'Which doesn't happen very often, does it? But I thought our rules tended to favor nondisclosure.'

They were dancing to show tunes from the forties. She pressed slightly closer and seemed to breathe rhythmically in his ear.

'Have you ever seen so many men gathered in one place,' she whispered, 'in order to be rich, powerful, and disgusting together? We can look around us, Clyde, and see the business executives, the government officials, the industrialists, the writers, the bankers, the academics, the pig-faced aristocrats in exile, and we can know the soul of one by the bitter wrinkled body of the other and then know all by the soul of the one. Because they're all part of the same motherfucking thing,' she whispered. 'Don't you think?'

Well, she just about took his breath away, whoever she was.

'The same thing. What thing?' he said.

Lynda Bird Johnson danced past with a Secret Service agent.

'The state, the nation, the corporation, the power structure, the system, the establishment.'

So young and lithe and trite. He felt the electric tension of her thighs and breasts passing through his suit.

'If you kiss me,' she said, 'I'll stick my tongue so far down your throat.'

'Yes?'

'It will pierce your heart.'

Then everything happened at once. Figures in raven faces and skull masks. Figures in white winding-sheets. Monks, nuns, executioners. And he understood of course that the woman in his arms was one of them.

They formed a death rank on the dance floor, halting the music and sending the guests to the fringes. They commanded the room, a masque of silent figures, a plague, a spray of pathogens, and Clyde looked around for Edgar.

The woman slipped away. Then the figures trooped across the floor, draped, masked, sheeted, and cowled. How had they assembled so deftly? How had they entered the ballroom in the first place?

He looked for Edgar.

An executioner and a nun did a pas de deux, a round of simple circling steps, and then the others gradually joined, the skeleton men and raven women, and in the end it was a graceful pavane they did, courtly and deadly and slow, with gestures so deliberate they seemed acted as well as danced, and Clyde saw his young partner move silkenly in their midst.

I will stick my tongue so far down your throat.

The guests watched in a trance – five hundred and forty men and women by actual count, and musicians and waiters and other personnel, all part of the audience for an entertainment other than themselves – hushed and half stunned.

It will pierce your heart.

When they were finished, the troupe stood in a line and removed their headpieces and masks. Then they opened their mouths, saying nothing, and directed hollow stares at the guests. An extended moment, a long gaping silence in the columned hall.

They departed single file.

A couple of minutes later, Clyde found the Boss and they went to the men's room to collect themselves.

'Enjoy your dance, Junior?'

'Turn around.'

'It's all connected. I'm convinced of this. It's all linked in one massive network. The war, the garbage, the promiscuity, the music, the drugs, the hair.'

'There's some dandruff on your jacket,' Clyde said.

Men entered and left, carrying a post-performance buzz into the tiled room. They unzipped and peed. They urinated into mounds of crushed ice garnished with lemon wedges. They unzipped and zipped. They peed, they waggled, and they zipped.

Clyde blew scaly flakes from the Boss's suit and shirt collar.

Back in the ballroom, half the guests were gone. The rest measured out the time so their departure would not seem influenced by the spectacle, the protest, whatever it was – the mockery of their sleek and precious evening.

The society band played some danceable numbers but nobody wanted to dance. Edgar sat, drank, and hated. He had the sheen of Last Things in his eye. Clyde knew this look. It meant the Boss was meditating on his coffin. It gave him dark solace, planning the details of his interment. A lead-lined coffin of a thousand pounds plus. To protect his body from worms, germs, moles, voles, and vandals. They were planning to steal his garbage, so why not his corpse? Lead-lined, yes, to keep him safe from nuclear war, from the blast wave, the shock wave, the fallout.

It was after four in the morning when Clyde led the way down the steps to the Cadillac as the spent trash of a day and a night in a great coastal city went wind-skidding through the streets.

Edgar dead, pray God, not for ten, fifteen, twenty years yet.

Maybe the sixties would be over by then.

The armored limousine moved slowly back to the Waldorf. Clyde had let that young woman charm and tempt him, and he'd liked it, and he'd been disappointed when she slipped away before the kiss, and he'd been played for a fool in the oldest, weariest way – that radical calculating heartless self-possessed melon-breasted bitch.

Clyde spotted the bug.

He glanced at Edgar, who sat mute and brooding in his sequinned mask. He'd worn the mask steadily since dinner. A hard man, they said. Cold and laconic. And they made smutty swishy jokes about Edgar and Clyde. But these were not a couple of old queens doddering on. They were men of sovereign authority. And Edgar did not intend to yield control anytime on this earth. This is why he wore the mask – to ease, if only briefly, the burden of control, and maybe to mock, at some level, the painful artifice beneath the shiny leather.

And when Clyde spotted the bug, the poky little Volkswagen with its incandescent doodles and whorls, he decided to say nothing to Edgar. The car was a hundred feet behind them, like a Day-Clo roach, slow and sleepless and clinging.

He said nothing to Edgar because the night had been filled with shock and distress and it was time, finally, for Junior, the life companion and loyal second man, to keep a secret from the Boss.

DISHONOURED GUESTS

JANE AUSTEN

THE MERYTON BALL

From *Pride and Prejudice*

(1813)

CHAPTER III

NOT ALL THAT Mrs Bennet, however, with the assistance of her five daughters, could ask on the subject, was sufficient to draw from her husband any satisfactory description of Mr Bingley. They attacked him in various ways; with barefaced questions, ingenious suppositions, and distant surmises; but he eluded the skill of them all; and they were at last obliged to accept the second-hand intelligence of their neighbour, Lady Lucas. Her report was highly favourable. Sir William had been delighted with him. He was quite young, wonderfully handsome, extremely agreeable, and to crown the whole, he meant to be at the next assembly with a large party. Nothing could be more delightful! To be fond of dancing was a certain step towards falling in love; and very lively hopes of Mr Bingley's heart were entertained.

'If I can but see one of my daughters happily settled at Netherfield,' said Mrs Bennet to her husband, 'and all the others equally well married, I shall have nothing to wish for.'

In a few days Mr Bingley returned Mr Bennet's visit, and sat about ten minutes with him in his library. He had entertained hopes of being admitted to a sight of the young ladies, of whose beauty he had heard much; but he saw only the father. The ladies were somewhat more fortunate, for they had the advantage of ascertaining from an upper window, that he wore a blue coat and rode a black horse.

An invitation to dinner was soon afterwards dispatched; and already had Mrs Bennet planned the courses that were to do credit to her housekeeping, when an answer arrived which deferred it all. Mr Bingley was obliged to be in town the following day, and consequently unable to accept the honour of their invitation, &c. Mrs Bennet was quite disconcerted. She could not imagine what business he could have in town so soon after his arrival in Hertfordshire; and she began to fear that he might be always flying about from one place to another, and never settled at Netherfield as he ought to be. Lady Lucas quieted her fears a little by starting the idea of his being gone to London only to get a large party for the ball; and a report soon followed that Mr Bingley was to bring twelve ladies and seven gentlemen with him to the assembly. The girls grieved over such a number of ladies; but were comforted the day before the ball by hearing, that instead of twelve, he had brought only six with him from London, his five sisters and a cousin. And when the party entered the assembly-room, it consisted of only five altogether; Mr Bingley, his two sisters, the husband of the eldest, and another young man.

Mr Bingley was good looking and gentlemanlike; he had a pleasant countenance, and easy, unaffected manners. His sisters were fine women, with an air of decided fashion. His brother-in-law, Mr Hurst, merely looked the gentleman; but his friend Mr Darcy soon drew the attention of the room by his fine, tall person, handsome features, noble mien; and the report which was in general circulation within five minutes after his entrance, of his having ten thousand a-year. The gentlemen pronounced him to be a fine figure of a man, the ladies declared he was much handsomer than Mr Bingley, and he was looked at with great admiration for about half the evening, till his manners gave a disgust which turned the tide of his popularity; for he was discovered to be proud, to be above his company, and above being pleased;

and not all his large estate in Derbyshire could then save him from having a most forbidding, disagreeable countenance, and being unworthy to be compared with his friend.

Mr Bingley had soon made himself acquainted with all the principal people in the room; he was lively and unreserved, danced every dance, was angry that the ball closed so early, and talked of giving one himself at Netherfield. Such amiable qualities must speak for themselves. What a contrast between him and his friend! Mr Darcy danced only once with Mrs Hurst and once with Miss Bingley, declined being introduced to any other lady, and spent the rest of the evening in walking about the room, speaking occasionally to one of his own party. His character was decided. He was the proudest, most disagreeable man in the world, and every body hoped that he would never come there again. Amongst the most violent against him was Mrs Bennet, whose dislike of his general behaviour was sharpened into particular resentment by his having slighted one of her daughters.

Elizabeth Bennet had been obliged, by the scarcity of gentlemen, to sit down for two dances; and during part of that time, Mr Darcy had been standing near enough for her to overhear a conversation between him and Mr Bingley, who came from the dance for a few minutes, to press his friend to join it.

'Come, Darcy,' said he, 'I must have you dance. I hate to see you standing about by yourself in this stupid manner. You had much better dance.'

'I certainly shall not. You know how I detest it, unless I am particularly acquainted with my partner. At such an assembly as this, it would be insupportable. Your sisters are engaged, and there is not another woman in the room, whom it would not be a punishment to me to stand up with.'

'I would not be so fastidious as you are,' cried Bingley,

'for a kingdom! Upon my honour, I never met with so many pleasant girls in my life, as I have this evening; and there are several of them you see uncommonly pretty.'

'*You* are dancing with the only handsome girl in the room,' said Mr Darcy, looking at the eldest Miss Bennet.

'Oh! she is the most beautiful creature I ever beheld! But there is one of her sisters sitting down just behind you, who is very pretty, and I dare say very agreeable. Do let me ask my partner to introduce you.'

'Which do you mean?' and turning round, he looked for a moment at Elizabeth, till catching her eye, he withdrew his own and coldly said, 'She is tolerable, but not handsome enough to tempt *me*; and I am in no humour at present to give consequence to young ladies who are slighted by other men. You had better return to your partner and enjoy her smiles, for you are wasting your time with me.'

Mr Bingley followed his advice. Mr Darcy walked off; and Elizabeth remained with no very cordial feelings towards him. She told the story however with great spirit among her friends; for she had a lively, playful disposition, which delighted in any thing ridiculous.

The evening altogether passed off pleasantly to the whole family. Mrs Bennet had seen her eldest daughter much admired by the Netherfield party. Mr Bingley had danced with her twice, and she had been distinguished by his sisters. Jane was as much gratified by this as her mother could be, though in a quieter way. Elizabeth felt Jane's pleasure. Mary had heard herself mentioned to Miss Bingley as the most accomplished girl in the neighbourhood; and Catherine and Lydia had been fortunate enough to be never without partners, which was all that they had yet learnt to care for at a ball. They returned therefore in good spirits to Longbourn, the village where they lived, and of which they were the principal inhabitants. They found Mr Bennet still up. With a book he was regardless of time; and on the present occasion he had a good deal of curiosity as to the event of an evening which had raised such splendid expectations. He had rather hoped that all his wife's views on the stranger would be disappointed; but he soon found that he had a very different story to hear.

'Oh! my dear Mr Bennet,' as she entered the room, 'we have had a most delightful evening, a most excellent ball. I wish you had been there. Jane was so admired, nothing could be like it. Every body said how well she looked; and Mr Bingley thought her quite beautiful, and danced with her twice! Only think of *that*, my dear; he actually danced with her twice! and she was the only creature in the room that he asked a second time. First of all, he asked Miss Lucas. I was so vexed to see him stand up with her; but, however, he did not admire her at all; indeed, nobody can, you know; and he seemed quite struck with Jane as she was going down the dance. So he inquired who she was, and got introduced, and asked her for the two next. Then the two third he danced with Miss King, and the two fourth with Maria Lucas, and the two fifth with Jane again, and the two sixth with Lizzy, and the Boulanger—'

'If he had had any compassion for *me,*' cried her husband impatiently, 'he would not have danced half so much! For God's sake, say no more of his partners. Oh! that he had sprained his ankle in the first dance!'

'Oh! my dear,' continued Mrs Bennet, 'I am quite delighted with him. He is so excessively handsome! and his sisters are charming women. I never in my life saw any thing more elegant than their dresses. I dare say the lace upon Mrs Hurst's gown—'

Here she was interrupted again. Mr Bennet protested

against any description of finery. She was therefore obliged to seek another branch of the subject, and related, with much bitterness of spirit and some exaggeration, the shocking rudeness of Mr Darcy.

'But I can assure you,' she added, 'that Lizzy does not lose much by not suiting *his* fancy; for he is a most disagreeable, horrid man, not at all worth pleasing. So high and so conceited that there was no enduring him! He walked here, and he walked there, fancying himself so very great! Not handsome enough to dance with! I wish you had been there, my dear, to have given him one of your set downs. I quite detest the man.'

SAKI

THE BOAR-PIG

(1914)

'THERE IS A back way on to the lawn,' said Mrs Philidore Stossen to her daughter, 'through a small grass paddock and then through a walled fruit garden full of gooseberry bushes. I went all over the place last year when the family were away. There is a door that opens from the fruit garden into a shrubbery, and once we emerge from there we can mingle with the guests as if we had come in by the ordinary way. It's much safer than going in by the front entrance and running the risk of coming bang up against the hostess; that would be so awkward when she doesn't happen to have invited us.'

'Isn't it a lot of trouble to take for getting admittance to a garden party?'

'To a garden party, yes; to *the* garden party of the season, certainly not. Every one of any consequence in the county, with the exception of ourselves, has been asked to meet the Princess, and it would be far more troublesome to invent explanations as to why we weren't there than to get in by a roundabout way. I stopped Mrs Cuvering in the road yesterday and talked very pointedly about the Princess. If she didn't choose to take the hint and send me an invitation it's not my fault, is it? Here we are: we just cut across the grass and through that little gate into the garden.'

Mrs Stossen and her daughter, suitably arrayed for a county garden party function with an infusion of Almanack de Gotha, sailed through the narrow grass paddock and the ensuing gooseberry garden with the air of state barges making an unofficial progress along a rural trout stream. There was a certain amount of furtive haste mingled with the stateliness of their advance as though hostile searchlights might be turned on them at any moment; and, as a matter of fact, they were not unobserved. Matilda Cuvering, with the alert eyes of thirteen years and the added advantage of an exalted position in the branches of a medlar tree, had enjoyed a good view of the Stossen flanking movement and had foreseen exactly where it would break down in execution.

'They'll find the door locked, and they'll jolly well have to go back the way they came,' she remarked to herself. 'Serves them right for not coming in by the proper entrance. What a pity Tarquin Superbus isn't loose in the paddock. After all, as every one else is enjoying themselves, I don't see why Tarquin shouldn't have an afternoon out.'

Matilda was of an age when thought is action; she slid down from the branches of the medlar tree, and when she clambered back again, Tarquin the huge white Yorkshire boar-pig, had exchanged the narrow limits of his sty for the wider range of the grass paddock. The discomfited Stossen expedition, returning in recriminatory but otherwise orderly retreat from the unyielding obstacle of the locked door, came to a sudden halt at the gate dividing the paddock from the gooseberry garden.

'What a villainous-looking animal,' exclaimed Mrs Stossen; 'it wasn't there when we came in.'

'It's there now, anyhow,' said her daughter. 'What on earth are we to do? I wish we had never come.'

The boar-pig had drawn nearer to the gate for a closer inspection of the human intruders, and stood champing his jaws and blinking his small red eyes in a manner that was doubtless intended to be disconcerting, and, as far as the Stossens were concerned, thoroughly achieved that result.

'Shoo!! Hish! Hish! Shoo!' cried the ladies in chorus.

'If they think they're going to drive him away by reciting lists of the kings of Israel and Judah they're laying themselves out for disappointment,' observed Matilda from her seat in the medlar tree. As she made the observation aloud Mrs Stossen became for the first time aware of her presence. A moment or two earlier she would have been anything but pleased at the discovery that the garden was not as deserted as it looked, but now she hailed the fact of the child's presence on the scene with absolute relief. 'Little girl, can you find some one to drive away—' she began hopefully.

'*Comment? Comprends pas*,' was the response.

'Oh, are you French? *Êtes vous française?*'

'*Pas de tout. 'Suis anglaise.*'

'Then why not talk English? I want to know if—'

'*Permettez-moi expliquer*. You see, I'm rather under a cloud,' said Matilda. 'I'm staying with my aunt, and I was told I must behave particularly well today, as lots of people were coming for a garden party, and I was told to imitate Claude, that's my young cousin, who never does anything wrong except by accident, and then is always apologetic about it. It seems they thought I ate too much raspberry trifle at lunch, and they said Claude never eats too much raspberry trifle. Well, Claude always goes to sleep for half an hour after lunch, because he's told to, and I waited till he was asleep, and tied his hands and started forcible feeding with a whole bucketful of raspberry trifle that they were keeping for the garden party. Lots of it went on to his sailor-suit and some of it on to the bed, but a good deal went down Claude's throat, and they can't say again that he has never been known to eat too much raspberry trifle. That is why I am not allowed to go to the party, and as an additional punishment I must speak French all the afternoon. I've had to tell you all this in English, as there were words like "forcible feeding" that I didn't know the French for; of course I wouldn't have had the least idea what I was talking about. *Mais maintenant, nous parlons français.*'

'Oh, very well, *très bien*,' said Mrs Stossen reluctantly; in moments of flurry such French as she knew was not under very good control. '*Là, à l'autre côté de la porte, est un cochon—*'

'*Un cochon? Ah, le petit charmant!*' exclaimed Matilda with enthusiasm.

'*Mais non, pas du tout petit, et pas du tout charmant; un bête féroce—*'

'*Une bête*,' corrected Matilda, 'a pig is masculine as long as you call it a pig, but if you lose your temper with it and call it a ferocious beast it becomes one of us at once. French is a dreadfully unsexing language.'

'For goodness' sake let us talk English then,' said Mrs Stossen. 'Is there any way out of this garden except through the paddock where the pig is?'

'I always go over the wall, by way of the plum tree,' said Matilda.

'Dressed as we are we could hardly do that,' said Mrs Stossen; it was difficult to imagine her doing it in any costume.

'Do you think you could go and get some one who would drive the pig away?' asked Miss Stossen.

'I promised my aunt I would stay here till five o'clock; it's not four yet.'

'I am sure, under the circumstances, your aunt would permit—'

'My conscience would not permit,' said Matilda with cold dignity.

'We can't stay here till five o'clock,' exclaimed Mrs Stossen with growing exasperation.

'Shall I recite to you to make the time pass quicker?' asked Matilda obligingly. '"Belinda, the little Breadwinner", is considered my best piece, or, perhaps, it ought to be something in French. Henri Quatre's address to his soldiers is the only thing I really know in that language.'

'If you will go and fetch some one to drive that animal away I will give you something to buy yourself a nice present,' said Mrs Stossen.

Matilda came several inches lower down the medlar tree.

'That is the most practical suggestion you have made yet for getting out of the garden,' she remarked cheerfully; 'Claude and I are collecting money for the Children's Fresh Air Fund, and we are seeing which of us can collect the biggest sum.'

'I shall be very glad to contribute half a crown, very glad indeed,' said Mrs Stossen, digging that coin out of the depths of a receptacle which formed a detached outwork of her toilet.

'Claude is a long way ahead of me at present,' continued Matilda, taking no notice of the suggested offering; 'you see, he's only eleven, and has golden hair, and those are enormous advantages when you're on the collecting job. Only the other day a Russian lady gave him ten shillings. Russians understand the art of giving far better than we do. I expect Claude will net quite twenty-five shillings this afternoon; he'll have the field to himself, and he'll be able to do the pale, fragile, not-long-for-this-world business to perfection after his raspberry trifle experience. Yes, he'll be quite two pounds ahead of me by now.'

With much probing and plucking and many regretful murmurs the beleaguered ladies managed to produce seven-and-sixpence between them.

'I am afraid this is all we've got,' said Mrs Stossen.

Matilda showed no sign of coming down either to the earth or to their figure.

'I could not do violence to my conscience for anything less than ten shillings,' she announced stiffly.

Mother and daughter muttered certain remarks under their breath, in which the word 'beast' was prominent, and probably had no reference to Tarquin.

'I find I *have* got another half-crown,' said Mrs Stossen in a shaking voice; 'here you are. Now please fetch some one quickly.'

Matilda slipped down from the tree, took possession of the donation, and proceeded to pick up a handful of over-ripe medlars from the grass at her feet. Then she climbed over the gate and addressed herself affectionately to the boar-pig.

'Come, Tarquin, dear old boy; you know you can't resist medlars when they're rotten and squashy.'

Tarquin couldn't. By dint of throwing the fruit in front of him at judicious intervals Matilda decoyed him back to his sty, while the delivered captives hurried across the paddock.

'Well, I never! The little minx!' exclaimed Mrs Stossen when she was safely on the high road. 'The animal wasn't savage at all, and as for the ten shillings, I don't believe the Fresh Air Fund will see a penny of it!'

There she was unwarrantably harsh in her judgement. If you examine the books of the fund you will find the acknowledgement: 'Collected by Miss Matilda Cuvering, 2s. 6d.'

DAPHNE DU MAURIER

THE MANDERLEY FANCY DRESS BALL

From *Rebecca*

(1938)

EVERYBODY LOOKED AT me and smiled. I felt pleased and flushed and rather happy. People were being nice. They were all so friendly. It was suddenly fun, the thought of the dance, and that I was to be the hostess.

The dance was being given for me, in my honour, because I was the bride. I sat on the table in the library, swinging my legs, while the rest of them stood round, and I had a longing to go upstairs and put on my dress, try the wig in front of the looking-glass, turn this way and that before the long mirror on the wall. It was new this sudden unexpected sensation of being important, of having Giles, and Beatrice, and Frank and Maxim all looking at me and talking about my dress. All wondering what I was going to wear. I thought of the soft white dress in its folds of tissue paper, and how it would hide my flat dull figure, my rather sloping shoulders. I thought of my own lank hair covered by the sleek and gleaming curls.

'What's the time?' I said carelessly, yawning a little, pretending I did not care. 'I wonder if we ought to think about going upstairs . . .?'

As we crossed the great hall on the way to our rooms I realized for the first time how the house lent itself to the occasion, and how beautiful the rooms were looking. Even the drawing-room, formal and cold to my consideration when we were alone, was a blaze of colour now, flowers in every corner, red roses in silver bowls on the white cloth of the supper table, the long windows open to the terrace, where, as soon as it was dusk, the fairy lights would shine. The band had stacked their instruments ready in the minstrels' gallery above the hall, and the hall itself wore a strange, waiting air; there was a warmth about it I had never known before, due to the night itself, so still and clear, to the flowers beneath the pictures, to our own laughter as we hovered on the wide stone stairs.

The old austerity had gone. Manderley had come alive in a fashion I would not have believed possible. It was not the still quiet Manderley I knew. There was a certain significance about it now that had not been before. A reckless air, rather triumphant, rather pleasing. It was as if the house remembered other days, long, long ago, when the hall was a banqueting hall indeed, with weapons and tapestry hanging upon the walls, and men sat at a long narrow table in the centre laughing louder than we laughed now, calling for wine, for song, throwing great pieces of meat upon the flags to the slumbering dogs. Later, in other years, it would still be gay, but with a certain grace and dignity, and Caroline de Winter, whom I should present tonight, would walk down the wide stone stairs in her white dress to dance the minuet. I wished we could sweep away the years and see her. I wished we did not have to degrade the house with our modern jig-tunes, so out-of-place and unromantic. They would not suit Manderley. I found myself in sudden agreement with Mrs Danvers. We should have made it a period ball, not the hotchpotch of humanity it was bound to be, with Giles, poor fellow, well-meaning and hearty in his guise of Arabian sheik. I found Clarice waiting for me in my bedroom, her round face scarlet with excitement. We giggled at one another like schoolgirls, and I bade her lock my door. There was much sound of tissue paper, rustling and mysterious.

We spoke to one another softly like conspirators, we walked on tiptoe. I felt like a child again on the eve of Christmas. This padding to and fro in my room with bare feet, the little furtive bursts of laughter, the stifled exclamations, reminded me of hanging up my stocking long ago. Maxim was safe in his dressing-room, and the way through was barred against him. Clarice alone was my ally and favoured friend. The dress fitted perfectly. I stood still, hardly able to restrain my impatience while Clarice hooked me up with fumbling fingers.

'It's handsome, Madam,' she kept saying, leaning back on her heels to look at me. 'It's a dress fit for the Queen of England.'

'What about under the left shoulder there,' I said, anxiously. 'That strap of mine, is it going to show?'

'No, Madam, nothing shows.'

'How is it? How do I look?' I did not wait for her answer, I twisted and turned in front of the mirror, I frowned, I smiled. I felt different already, no longer hampered by my appearance. My own dull personality was submerged at last. 'Give me the wig,' I said excitedly, 'careful, don't crush it, the curls mustn't be flat. They are supposed to stand out from the face.' Clarice stood behind my shoulder, I saw her round face beyond mine in the reflection of the looking-glass, her eyes shining, her mouth a little open. I brushed my own hair sleek behind my ears. I took hold of the soft gleaming curls with trembling fingers, laughing under my breath, looking up at Clarice.

'Oh, Clarice,' I said, 'what will Mr de Winter say?'

I covered my own mousy hair with the curled wig, trying to hide my triumph, trying to hide my smile. Somebody came and hammered on the door.

'Who's there?' I called in panic. 'You can't come in.'

'It's me, my dear, don't alarm yourself,' said Beatrice, 'how far have you got? I want to look at you.'

'No, no,' I said, 'you can't come in, I'm not ready.'

The flustered Clarice stood beside me, her hand full of hairpins, while I took them from her one by one, controlling the curls that had become fluffed in the box.

'I'll come down when I am ready,' I called. 'Go on down, all of you. Don't wait for me. Tell Maxim he can't come in.'

'Maxim's down,' she said. 'He came along to us. He said he hammered on your bathroom door and you never answered. Don't be too long, my dear, we are all so intrigued. Are you sure you don't want any help?'

'No,' I shouted impatiently, losing my head, 'go away, go on down.'

Why did she have to come and bother just at this moment? It fussed me, I did not know what I was doing. I jabbed with a hairpin, flattening it against a curl. I heard no more from Beatrice, she must have gone along the passage. I wondered if she was happy in her Eastern robes and if Giles had succeeded in painting his face. How absurd it was, the whole thing. Why did we do it, I wonder, why were we such children?

I did not recognize the face that stared at me in the glass. The eyes were larger surely, the mouth narrower, the skin white and clear? The curls stood away from the head in a little cloud. I watched this self that was not me at all and then smiled; a new, slow smile.

'Oh, Clarice!' I said. 'Oh, Clarice!' I took the skirt of my dress in my hands and curtseyed to her, the flounces sweeping the ground. She giggled excitedly, rather embarrassed, flushed though, very pleased. I paraded up and down in front of my glass watching my reflection.

'Unlock the door,' I said. 'I'm going down. Run ahead

and see if they are there.' She obeyed me, still giggling, and I lifted my skirts off the ground and followed her along the corridor.

She looked back at me and beckoned. 'They've gone down,' she whispered, 'Mr de Winter, and Major and Mrs Lacy. Mr Crawley has just come. They are all standing in the hall.' I peered through the archway at the head of the big staircase, and looked down on the hall below.

Yes, there they were. Giles, in his white Arab dress, laughing loudly, showing the knife at his side; Beatrice swathed in an extraordinary green garment and hung about the neck with trailing beads; poor Frank self-conscious and slightly foolish in his striped jersey and sea-boots; Maxim, the only normal one of the party, in his evening clothes.

'I don't know what she's doing,' he said, 'she's been up in her bedroom for hours. What's the time, Frank? The dinner crowd will be upon us before we know where we are.'

The band were changed, and in the gallery already. One of the men was tuning his fiddle. He played a scale softly, and then plucked at a string. The light shone on the picture of Caroline de Winter.

Yes, the dress had been copied exactly from my sketch of the portrait. The puffed sleeve, the sash and the ribbon, the wide floppy hat I held in my hand. And my curls were her curls, they stood out from my face as hers did in the picture. I don't think I have ever felt so excited before, so happy and so proud. I waved my hand at the man with the fiddle, and then put my finger to my lips for silence. He smiled and bowed. He came across the gallery to the archway where I stood.

'Make the drummer announce me,' I whispered, 'make him beat the drum, you know how they do, and then call out Miss Caroline de Winter. I want to surprise them below.' He nodded his head, he understood. My heart fluttered absurdly, and my cheeks were burning. What fun it was, what mad ridiculous childish fun! I smiled at Clarice still crouching on the corridor. I picked up my skirt in my hands. Then the sound of the drum echoed in the great hall, startling me for a moment, who had waited for it, who knew that it would come. I saw them look up surprised and bewildered from the hall below.

'Miss Caroline de Winter,' shouted the drummer.

I came forward to the head of the stairs and stood there, smiling, my hat in my hand, like the girl in the picture. I waited for the clapping and laughter that would follow as I walked slowly down the stairs. Nobody clapped, nobody moved.

They all stared at me like dumb things. Beatrice uttered a little cry and put her hand to her mouth. I went on smiling, I put one hand on the banister.

'How do you do, Mr de Winter,' I said.

Maxim had not moved. He stared up at me, his glass in his hand. There was no colour in his face. It was ashen white. I saw Frank go to him as though he would speak, but Maxim shook him off. I hesitated, one foot already on the stairs. Something was wrong, they had not understood. Why was Maxim looking like that? Why did they all stand like dummies, like people in a trance?

Then Maxim moved forward to the stairs, his eyes never leaving my face.

'What the hell do you think you are doing?' he asked. His eyes blazed in anger. His face was still ashen white.

I could not move, I went on standing there, my hand on the banister.

'It's the picture,' I said, terrified at his eyes, at his voice. 'It's the picture, the one in the gallery.'

There was a long silence. We went on staring at each other. Nobody moved in the hall. I swallowed, my hand moved to my throat. 'What is it?' I said. 'What have I done?'

If only they would not stare at me like that with dull blank faces. If only somebody would say something. When Maxim spoke again I did not recognize his voice. It was still and quiet, icy cold, not a voice I knew.

'Go and change,' he said, 'it does not matter what you put on. Find an ordinary evening frock, anything will do. Go now, before anybody comes.'

I could not speak, I went on staring at him. His eyes were the only living things in the white mask of his face.

'What are you standing there for?' he said, his voice harsh and queer. 'Didn't you hear what I said?'

I turned and ran blindly through the archway to the corridors beyond. I caught a glimpse of the astonished face of the drummer who had announced me. I brushed past him, stumbling, not looking where I went. Tears blinded my eyes. I did not know what was happening. Clarice had gone. The corridor was deserted. I looked about me stunned and stupid like a haunted thing. Then I saw that the door leading to the west wing was open wide, and that someone was standing there.

It was Mrs Danvers. I shall never forget the expression on her face, loathsome, triumphant. The face of an exulting devil. She stood there, smiling at me.

And then I ran from her, down the long narrow passage to my own room, tripping, stumbling over the flounces of my dress.

DOROTHY PARKER

ARRANGEMENT IN BLACK AND WHITE

(1944)

THE WOMAN WITH the pink velvet poppies twined round the assisted gold of her hair traversed the crowded room at an interesting gait combining a skip with a sidle, and clutched the lean arm of her host.

'Now I got you!' she said. 'Now you can't get away!'

'Why, hello,' said her host. 'Well. How are you?'

'Oh, I'm finely,' she said. 'Just simply finely. Listen. I want you to do me the most terrible favor. Will you? Will you please? Pretty please?'

'What is it? said her host.

'Listen,' she said. 'I want to meet Walter Williams. Honestly, I'm just simply crazy about that man. Oh, when he sings! When he sings those spirituals! Well, I said to Burton, "It's a good thing for you Walter Williams is colored," I said, "or you'd have lots of reason to be jealous." I'd really love to meet him. I'd like to tell him I've heard him sing. Will you be an angel and introduce me to him?'

'Why, certainly,' said her host. 'I thought you'd met him. The party's for him. Where is he, anyway?'

'He's over there by the bookcase,' she said. 'Let's wait till those people get through talking to him. Well, I think you're simply marvelous, giving this perfectly marvelous party for him, and having him meet all these white people, and all. Isn't he terribly grateful?'

'I hope not,' said her host.

'I think it's really terribly nice,' she said. 'I do. I don't see why on earth it isn't perfectly all right to meet colored people. I haven't any feeling at all about it – not one single bit. Burton – oh, he's just the other way. Well, you know, he comes from Virginia, and you know how they are.'

'Did he come tonight?' said her host.

'No, he couldn't,' she said. 'I'm a regular grass widow tonight. I told him when I left, "There's no telling what I'll do," I said. He was just so tired out, he couldn't move. Isn't it a shame?'

'Ah,' said her host.

'Wait till I tell him I met Walter Williams!' she said. 'He'll just about die. Oh, we have more arguments about colored people. I talk to him like I don't know what, I get so excited. "Oh, don't be so silly," I say. But I must say for Burton, he's heaps broader-minded than lots of these Southerners. He's really awfully fond of colored people. Well, he says himself, he wouldn't have white servants. And you know, he had this old colored nurse, this regular old nigger mammy, and he just simply loves her. Why, every time he goes home, he goes out in the kitchen to see her. He does, really, to this day. All he says is, he says he hasn't got a word to say against colored people as long as they keep their place. He's always doing things for them – giving them clothes and I don't know what all. The only things he says, he says he wouldn't sit down at the table with one for a million dollars. "Oh," I say to him, "you make me sick, talking like that." I'm just terrible to him. Aren't I terrible?'

'Oh, no, no, no,' said her host. 'No, no.'

'I am,' she said. 'I know I am. Poor Burton! Now, me, I don't feel that way at all. I haven't the slightest feeling about colored people. Why, I'm just crazy about some of them. They're just like children – just as easygoing, and always singing and laughing and everything. Aren't they the happiest things you ever saw in your life? Honestly, it makes me laugh just to hear them. Oh, I like them. I really do. Well, now, listen, I have this colored laundress, I've had her for years, and I'm devoted to her. She's a real character. And I want to tell you. I think of her as my friend. That's the way I think of her. As I say to Burton, "Well, for heaven's sakes, we're all human beings!" Aren't we?'

'Yes,' said her host. 'Yes, indeed.'

'Now this Walter Williams,' she said. 'I think a man like that's a real artist. I do. I think he deserves an awful lot of credit. Goodness, I'm so crazy about music or anything, I don't care *what* color he is. I honestly think if a person's an artist, nobody ought to have any feeling at all about meeting them. That's absolutely what I say to Burton. Don't you think I'm right?'

'Yes,' said her host. 'Oh, yes.'

'That's the way I feel,' she said. 'I just can't understand people being narrow-minded. Why, I absolutely think it's a privilege to meet a man like Walter Williams. Yes, I do. I haven't any feeling at all. Well, my goodness, the good Lord made him, just the same as He did any of us. Didn't He?'

'Surely,' said her host. 'Yes, indeed.'

'That's what I say,' she said. 'Oh, I get so furious when people are narrow-minded about colored people. It's just all I can do not to say something. Of course, I do admit when you get a bad colored man, they're simply terrible. But as I say to Burton, there are some bad white people, too, in this world. Aren't there?'

'I guess there are,' said her host.

'Why, I'd really be glad to have a man like Walter Williams come to my house and sing for us, some time,' she said. 'Of course, I couldn't ask him on account of Burton, but I wouldn't have any feeling about it at all. Oh, can't he sing!

Isn't it marvelous, the way they all have music in them? It just seems to be right *in* them. Come on, let's us go on over and talk to him. Listen, what shall I do when I'm introduced? Ought I to shake hands? Or what?'

'Why, do whatever you want,' said her host.

'I guess maybe I'd better,' she said. 'I wouldn't for the world have him think I had any feeling. I think I'd better shake hands, just the way I would with anybody else. That's just exactly what I'll do.'

They reached the tall young Negro, standing by the bookcase. The host performed introductions; the Negro bowed.

'How do you do?' he said.

The woman with the pink velvet poppies extended her hand at the length of her arm and held it so for all the world to see, until the Negro took it, shook it, and gave it back to her.

'Oh, how do you do, Mr Williams,' she said. 'Well, how do you do. I've just been saying, I've enjoyed your singing so awfully much. I've been to your concerts, and we have you on the phonograph and everything. Oh, I just enjoy it!'

She spoke with great distinctness, moving her lips meticulously, as if in parlance with the deaf.

'I'm so glad,' he said.

'I'm just simply crazy about that "Water Boy" thing you sing,' she said. 'Honestly, I can't get it out of my head. I have my husband nearly crazy, the way I go around humming it all the time. Oh, he looks just as black as the ace of— Well. Tell me, where on earth do you ever get all those songs of yours? How do you ever get hold of them?'

'Why,' he said, 'there are so many different—'

'I should think you'd love singing them,' she said. 'It must be more fun. All those darling old spirituals – oh, I just love them! Well, what are you doing, now? Are you still keeping up your singing? Why don't you have another concert, some time?'

'I'm having one the sixteenth of this month,' he said.

'Well, I'll be there,' she said. 'I'll be there, if I possibly can. You can count on me. Goodness, here comes a whole raft of people to talk to you. You're just a regular guest of honor! Oh, who's that girl in white? I've seen her some place.'

'That's Katherine Burke,' said her host.

'Good Heavens,' she said, 'is that Katherine Burke? Why she looks entirely different off the stage. I thought she was much better-looking. I had no idea she was so terribly dark. Why, she looks almost like— Oh, I think she's a wonderful actress! Don't you think she's a wonderful actress, Mr Williams? Oh, I think she's marvelous. Don't you?'

'Yes, I do,' he said.

'Oh, I do, too,' she said. 'Just wonderful. Well, goodness, we must give someone else a chance to talk to the guest of honor. Now, don't forget, Mr Williams, I'm going to be at that concert if I possibly can. I'll be there applauding like everything. And if I can't come, I'm going to tell everybody I know to go, anyway. Don't you forget!'

'I won't,' he said. 'Thank you so much.'

The host took her arm and piloted her into the next room.

'Oh, my dear,' she said. 'I nearly died! Honestly, I give you my word, I nearly passed away. Did you hear that terrible break I made? I was just going to say Katherine Burke looked almost like a nigger. I just caught myself in time. Oh, do you think he noticed?'

'I don't believe so,' said her host.

'Well, thank goodness,' she said, 'because I wouldn't have embarrassed him for anything. Why, he's awfully nice. Just as nice as he can be. Nice manners, and everything. You know, so many colored people, you give them an inch, and they walk all over you. But he doesn't try any of that. Well, he's got more sense, I suppose. He's really nice. Don't you think so?'

'Yes,' said her host.

'I liked him,' she said. 'I haven't any feeling at all because he's a colored man. I felt just as natural as I would with anybody. Talked to him just as naturally, and everything. But honestly, I could hardly keep a straight face. I kept thinking of Burton. Oh, wait till I tell Burton I called him "Mister"!'

OLD FRIENDS AND REMEMBRANCES

JAMES JOYCE

THE DEAD

(1914)

LILY, THE CARETAKER'S daughter, was literally run off her feet. Hardly had she brought one gentleman into the little pantry behind the office on the ground floor and helped him off with his overcoat than the wheezy hall-door bell clanged again and she had to scamper along the bare hallway to let in another guest. It was well for her she had not to attend to the ladies also. But Miss Kate and Miss Julia had thought of that and had converted the bathroom upstairs into a ladies' dressing-room. Miss Kate and Miss Julia were there, gossiping and laughing, and fussing, walking after each other to the head of the stairs, peering down over the banisters and calling down to Lily to ask her who had come.

It was always a great affair, the Misses Morkan's annual dance. Everybody who knew them came to it, members of the family, old friends of the family, the members of Julia's choir, any of Kate's pupils that were grown up enough and even some of Mary Jane's pupils too. Never once had it fallen flat. For years and years it had gone off in splendid style as long as anyone could remember; ever since Kate and Julia, after the death of their brother Pat, had left the house in Stoney Batter and taken Mary Jane, their only niece, to live with them in the dark gaunt house on Usher's Island, the upper part of which they had rented from Mr Fulham, the corn-factor on the ground floor. That was a good thirty years ago if it was a day. Mary Jane, who was then a little girl in short clothes, was now the main prop of the household for she had the organ in Haddington Road. She had been through the Academy and gave a pupils' concert every year in the upper room of the Antient Concert Rooms. Many of her pupils belonged to the better-class families on the Kingstown and Dalkey line. Old as they were, her aunts also did their share. Julia, though she was quite grey, was still the leading soprano in Adam and Eve's, and Kate, being too feeble to go about much, gave music lessons to beginners on the old square piano in the back room. Lily, the caretaker's daughter, did housemaid's work for them. Though their life was modest they believed in eating well; the best of everything: diamond-bone sirloins, three-shilling tea and the best bottled stout. But Lily seldom made a mistake in the orders so that she got on well with her three mistresses. They were fussy, that was all. But the only thing they would not stand was back answers.

Of course they had good reason to be fussy on such a night. And then it was long after ten o'clock and yet there was no sign of Gabriel and his wife. Besides they were dreadfully afraid that Freddy Malins might turn up screwed. They would not wish for worlds that any of Mary Jane's pupils should see him under the influence; and when he was like that it was sometimes very hard to manage him. Freddy Malins always came late but they wondered what could be keeping Gabriel: and that was what brought them every two minutes to the banisters to ask Lily had Gabriel or Freddy come.

—O, Mr Conroy, said Lily to Gabriel when she opened the door for him, Miss Kate and Miss Julia thought you were never coming. Good-night, Mrs Conroy.

—I'll engage they did, said Gabriel, but they forget that my wife here takes three mortal hours to dress herself.

He stood on the mat, scraping the snow from his goloshes,

while Lily led his wife to the foot of the stairs and called out:

—Miss Kate, here's Mrs Conroy.

Kate and Julia came toddling down the dark stairs at once. Both of them kissed Gabriel's wife, said she must be perished alive and asked was Gabriel with her.

—Here I am as right as the mail, Aunt Kate! Go on up, I'll follow, called out Gabriel from the dark.

He continued scraping his feet vigorously while the three women went upstairs, laughing, to the ladies' dressing-room. A light fringe of snow lay like a cape on the shoulders of his overcoat and like toecaps on the toes of his goloshes; and, as the buttons of his overcoat slipped with a squeaking noise through the snow-stiffened frieze, a cold fragrant air from out-of-doors escaped from crevices and folds.

—Is it snowing again, Mr Conroy? asked Lily.

She had preceded him into the pantry to help him off with his overcoat. Gabriel smiled at the three syllables she had given his surname and glanced at her. She was a slim, growing girl, pale in complexion and with hay-coloured hair. The gas in the pantry made her look still paler. Gabriel had known her when she was a child and used to sit on the lowest step nursing a rag doll.

—Yes, Lily, he answered, and I think we're in for a night of it.

He looked up at the pantry ceiling, which was shaking with the stamping and shuffling of feet on the floor above, listened for a moment to the piano and then glanced at the girl, who was folding his overcoat carefully at the end of a shelf.

—Tell me, Lily, he said in a friendly tone, do you still go to school?

—O no, sir, she answered. I'm done schooling this year and more.

—O, then, said Gabriel gaily, I suppose we'll be going to your wedding one of these fine days with your young man, eh?

The girl glanced back at him over her shoulder and said with great bitterness:

—The men that is now is only all palaver and what they can get out of you.

Gabriel coloured as if he felt he had made a mistake and, without looking at her, kicked off his goloshes and flicked actively with his muffler at his patent-leather shoes.

He was a stout tallish young man. The high colour of his cheeks pushed upwards even to his forehead where it scattered itself in a few formless patches of pale red; and on his hairless face there scintillated restlessly the polished lenses and the bright gilt rims of the glasses which screened his delicate and restless eyes. His glossy black hair was parted in the middle and brushed in a long curve behind his ears where it curled slightly beneath the groove left by his hat.

When he had flicked lustre into his shoes he stood up and pulled his waistcoat down more tightly on his plump body. Then he took a coin rapidly from his pocket.

—O Lily, he said, thrusting it into her hands, it's Christmas-time, isn't it? Just . . . here's a little. . . .

He walked rapidly towards the door.

—O no, sir! cried the girl, following him. Really, sir, I wouldn't take it.

—Christmas-time! Christmas-time! said Gabriel, almost trotting to the stairs and waving his hand to her in deprecation.

The girl, seeing that he had gained the stairs, called out after him:

—Well, thank you, sir.

He waited outside the drawing-room door until the waltz

should finish, listening to the skirts that swept against it and to the shuffling of feet. He was still discomposed by the girl's bitter and sudden retort. It had cast a gloom over him which he tried to dispel by arranging his cuffs and the bows of his tie. He then took from his waistcoat pocket a little paper and glanced at the headings he had made for his speech. He was undecided about the lines from Robert Browning for he feared they would be above the heads of his hearers. Some quotation that they would recognize from Shakespeare or from the Melodies would be better. The indelicate clacking of the men's heels and the shuffling of their soles reminded him that their grade of culture differed from his. He would only make himself ridiculous by quoting poetry to them which they could not understand. They would think that he was airing his superior education. He would fail with them just as he had failed with the girl in the pantry. He had taken up a wrong tone. His whole speech was a mistake from first to last, an utter failure.

Just then his aunts and his wife came out of the ladies' dressing-room. His aunts were two small plainly dressed old women. Aunt Julia was an inch or so the taller. Her hair, drawn low over the tops of her ears, was grey; and grey also, with darker shadows, was her large flaccid face. Though she was stout in build and stood erect her slow eyes and parted lips gave her the appearance of a woman who did not know where she was or where she was going. Aunt Kate was more vivacious. Her face, healthier than her sister's, was all puckers and creases, like a shrivelled red apple, and her hair, braided in the same old-fashioned way, had not lost its ripe nut colour.

They both kissed Gabriel frankly. He was their favourite nephew, the son of their dead elder sister, Ellen, who had married T. J. Conroy of the Port and Docks.

—Gretta tells me you're not going to take a cab back to Monkstown to-night, Gabriel, said Aunt Kate.

—No, said Gabriel, turning to his wife, we had quite enough of that last year, hadn't we? Don't you remember, Aunt Kate, what a cold Gretta got out of it? Cab windows rattling all the way, and the east wind blowing in after we passed Merrion. Very jolly it was. Gretta caught a dreadful cold.

Aunt Kate frowned severely and nodded her head at every word.

—Quite right, Gabriel, quite right, she said. You can't be too careful.

—But as for Gretta there, said Gabriel, she'd walk home in the snow if she were let.

Mrs Conroy laughed.

—Don't mind him, Aunt Kate, she said. He's really an awful bother, what with green shades for Tom's eyes at night and making him do the dumb-bells, and forcing Eva to eat the stirabout. The poor child! And she simply hates the sight of it! . . . O, but you'll never guess what he makes me wear now!

She broke out into a peal of laughter and glanced at her husband, whose admiring and happy eyes had been wandering from her dress to her face and hair. The two aunts laughed heartily too, for Gabriel's solicitude was a standing joke with them.

—Goloshes! said Mrs Conroy. That's the latest. Whenever it's wet underfoot I must put on my goloshes. To-night even he wanted me to put them on, but I wouldn't. The next thing he'll buy me will be a diving suit.

Gabriel laughed nervously and patted his tie reassuringly while Aunt Kate nearly doubled herself, so heartily did she enjoy the joke. The smile soon faded from Aunt Julia's face and her mirthless eyes were directed towards her nephew's face. After a pause she asked:

—And what are goloshes, Gabriel?

—Goloshes, Julia! exclaimed her sister. Goodness me, don't you know what goloshes are? You wear them over your . . . over your boots, Gretta, isn't it?

—Yes, said Mrs Conroy. Guttapercha things. We both have a pair now. Gabriel says everyone wears them on the continent.

—O, on the continent, murmured Aunt Julia, nodding her head slowly.

Gabriel knitted his brows and said, as if he were slightly angered:

—It's nothing very wonderful but Gretta thinks it very funny because she says the word reminds her of Christy Minstrels.

—But tell me, Gabriel, said Aunt Kate, with brisk tact. Of course, you've seen about the room. Gretta was saying . . .

—O, the room is all right, replied Gabriel. I've taken one in the Gresham.

—To be sure, said Aunt Kate, by far the best thing to do. And the children, Gretta, you're not anxious about them?

—O, for one night, said Mrs Conroy. Besides, Bessie will look after them.

—To be sure, said Aunt Kate again. What a comfort it is to have a girl like that, one you can depend on! There's that Lily, I'm sure I don't know what has come over her lately. She's not the girl she was at all.

Gabriel was about to ask his aunt some questions on this point but she broke off suddenly to gaze after her sister who had wandered down the stairs and was craning her neck over the banisters.

—Now, I ask you, she said, almost testily, where is Julia going? Julia! Julia! Where are you going?

Julia, who had gone halfway down one flight, came back and announced blandly:

—Here's Freddy.

At the same moment a clapping of hands and a final flourish of the pianist told that the waltz had ended. The drawing-room door was opened from within and some couples came out. Aunt Kate drew Gabriel aside hurriedly and whispered into his ear:

—Slip down, Gabriel, like a good fellow and see if he's all right, and don't let him up if he's screwed. I'm sure he's screwed. I'm sure he is.

Gabriel went to the stairs and listened over the banisters. He could hear two persons talking in the pantry. Then he recognized Freddy Malins' laugh. He went down the stairs noisily.

—It's such a relief, said Aunt Kate to Mrs Conroy, that Gabriel is here. I always feel easier in my mind when he's here. . . . Julia, there's Miss Daly and Miss Power will take some refreshment. Thanks for your beautiful waltz, Miss Daly. It made lovely time.

A tall wizen-faced man, with a stiff grizzled moustache and swarthy skin, who was passing out with his partner said:

—And may we have some refreshment, too, Miss Morkan?

—Julia, said Aunt Kate summarily, and here's Mr Browne and Miss Furlong. Take them in, Julia, with Miss Daly and Miss Power.

—I'm the man for the ladies, said Mr Browne, pursing his lips until his moustache bristled and smiling in all his wrinkles. You know, Miss Morkan, the reason they are so fond of me is—

He did not finish his sentence, but, seeing that Aunt Kate was out of earshot, at once led the three young ladies into the back room. The middle of the room was occupied by two square tables placed end to end, and on these Aunt Julia and the caretaker were straightening and smoothing a large cloth. On the sideboard were arrayed dishes and plates, and glasses and bundles of knives and forks and spoons. The top of the closed square piano served also as a sideboard for viands and sweets. At a smaller sideboard in one corner two young men were standing, drinking hop-bitters.

Mr Browne led his charges thither and invited them all, in jest, to some ladies' punch, hot, strong and sweet. As they said they never took anything strong he opened three bottles of lemonade for them. Then he asked one of the young men to move aside, and, taking hold of the decanter, filled out for himself a goodly measure of whisky. The young men eyed him respectfully while he took a trial sip.

—God help me, he said, smiling, it's the doctor's orders.

His wizened face broke into a broader smile, and the three young ladies laughed in musical echo to his pleasantry, swaying their bodies to and fro, with nervous jerks of their shoulders. The boldest said:

—O, now, Mr Browne, I'm sure the doctor never ordered anything of the kind.

Mr Browne took another sip of his whisky and said, with sidling mimicry:

—Well, you see, I'm like the famous Mrs Cassidy, who is reported to have said: *Now, Mary Grimes, if I don't take it, make me take it, for I feel I want it.*

His hot face had leaned forward a little too confidentially and he had assumed a very low Dublin accent so that the young ladies, with one instinct, received his speech in silence. Miss Furlong, who was one of Mary Jane's pupils, asked Miss Daly what was the name of the pretty waltz she had played; and Mr Browne, seeing that he was ignored, turned promptly to the two young men who were more appreciative.

A red-faced young woman, dressed in pansy, came into the room, excitedly clapping her hands and crying:

—Quadrilles! Quadrilles!

Close on her heels came Aunt Kate, crying:

—Two gentlemen and three ladies, Mary Jane!

—O, here's Mr Bergin and Mr Kerrigan, said Mary Jane. Mr Kerrigan, will you take Miss Power? Miss Furlong, may I get you a partner, Mr Bergin. O, that'll just do now.

—Three ladies, Mary Jane, said Aunt Kate.

The two young gentlemen asked the ladies if they might have the pleasure, and Mary Jane turned to Miss Daly.

—O, Miss Daly, you're really awfully good, after playing for the last two dances, but really we're so short of ladies to-night.

—I don't mind in the least, Miss Morkan.

—But I've a nice partner for you, Mr Bartell D'Arcy, the tenor, I'll get him to sing later on. All Dublin is raving about him.

—Lovely voice, lovely voice! said Aunt Kate.

As the piano had twice begun the prelude to the first figure Mary Jane led her recruits quickly from the room. They had hardly gone when Aunt Julia wandered slowly into the room, looking behind her at something.

—What is the matter, Julia? asked Aunt Kate anxiously. Who is it?

Julia, who was carrying in a column of table-napkins, turned to her sister and said, simply, as if the question had surprised her:

—It's only Freddy, Kate, and Gabriel with him.

In fact right behind her Gabriel could be seen piloting Freddy Malins across the landing. The latter, a young man of about forty, was of Gabriel's size and build, with very round shoulders. His face was fleshy and pallid, touched with colour only at the thick hanging lobes of his ears and at the wide wings of his nose. He had coarse features, a blunt nose, a convex and receding brow, tumid and protruded lips. His heavy-lidded eyes and the disorder of his scanty hair made him look sleepy. He was laughing heartily in a high key at a story which he had been telling Gabriel on the stairs and at the same time rubbing the knuckles of his left fist backwards and forwards into his left eye.

—Good evening, Freddy, said Aunt Julia.

Freddy Malins bade the Misses Morkan good-evening in what seemed an offhand fashion by reason of the habitual catch in his voice and then, seeing that Mr Browne was grinning at him from the sideboard, crossed the room on rather shaky legs and began to repeat in an undertone the story he had just told to Gabriel.

—He's not so bad, is he? said Aunt Kate to Gabriel.

Gabriel's brows were dark but he raised them quickly and answered:

—O no, hardly noticeable.

—Now, isn't he a terrible fellow! she said. And his poor mother made him take the pledge on New Year's Eve. But come on, Gabriel, into the drawing-room.

Before leaving the room with Gabriel she signalled to Mr Browne by frowning and shaking her forefinger in warning to and fro. Mr Browne nodded in answer and, when she had gone, said to Freddy Malins:

—Now, then, Teddy, I'm going to fill you out a good glass of lemonade just to buck you up.

Freddy Malins, who was nearing the climax of his story,

waved the offer aside impatiently but Mr Browne, having first called Freddy Malins' attention to a disarray in his dress, filled out and handed him a full glass of lemonade. Freddy Malins' left hand accepted the glass mechanically, his right hand being engaged in the mechanical readjustment of his dress. Mr Browne, whose face was once more wrinkling with mirth, poured out for himself a glass of whisky while Freddy Malins exploded, before he had well reached the climax of his story, in a kink of high-pitched bronchitic laughter and, setting down his untasted and overflowing glass, began to rub the knuckles of his left fist backwards and forwards into his left eye, repeating words of his last phrase as well as his fit of laughter would allow him.

Gabriel could not listen while Mary Jane was playing her Academy piece, full of runs and difficult passages, to the hushed drawing-room. He liked music but the piece she was playing had no melody for him and he doubted whether it had any melody for the other listeners, though they had begged Mary Jane to play something. Four young men, who had come from the refreshment-room to stand in the doorway at the sound of the piano, had gone away quietly in couples after a few minutes. The only persons who seemed to follow the music were Mary Jane herself, her hands racing along the key-board or lifted from it at the pauses like those of a priestess in momentary imprecation, and Aunt Kate standing at her elbow to turn the page.

Gabriel's eyes, irritated by the floor, which glittered with beeswax under the heavy chandelier, wandered to the wall above the piano. A picture of the balcony scene in *Romeo and Juliet* hung there and beside it was a picture of the two murdered princes in the Tower which Aunt Julia had worked in red, blue and brown wools when she was a girl. Probably in the school they had gone to as girls that kind of work had been taught for one year his mother had worked for him as a birthday present a waistcoat of purple tabinet, with little foxes' heads upon it, lined with brown satin and having round mulberry buttons. It was strange that his mother had had no musical talent though Aunt Kate used to call her the brains carrier of the Morkan family. Both she and Julia had always seemed a little proud of their serious and matronly sister. Her photograph stood before the pierglass. She had an open book on her knees and was pointing out something in it to Constantine who, dressed in a man-o'-war suit, lay at her feet. It was she who had chosen the names for her sons for she was very sensible of the dignity of family life. Thanks to her, Constantine was now senior curate in Balbriggan and, thanks to her, Gabriel himself had taken his degree in the Royal University. A shadow passed over his face as he remembered her sullen opposition to his marriage. Some slighting phrases she had used still rankled in his memory; she had once spoken of Gretta as being country cute and that was not true of Gretta at all. It was Gretta who had nursed her during all her last long illness in their house at Monkstown.

He knew that Mary Jane must be near the end of her piece for she was playing again the opening melody with runs of scales after every bar and while he waited for the end the resentment died down in his heart. The piece ended with a trill of octaves in the treble and a final deep octave in the bass. Great applause greeted Mary Jane as, blushing and rolling up her music nervously, she escaped from the room. The most vigorous clapping came from the four young men in the doorway who had gone away to the refreshment-room at the beginning of the piece but had come back when the piano had stopped.

Lancers were arranged. Gabriel found himself partnered with Miss Ivors. She was a frank-mannered talkative young lady, with a freckled face and prominent brown eyes. She did not wear a low-cut bodice and the large brooch which was fixed in the front of her collar bore on it an Irish device.

When they had taken their places she said abruptly:

—I have a crow to pluck with you.

—With me? said Gabriel.

She nodded her head gravely.

—What is it? asked Gabriel, smiling at her solemn manner.

—Who is G. C.? answered Miss Ivors, turning her eyes upon him.

Gabriel coloured and was about to knit his brows, as if he did not understand, when she said bluntly:

—O, innocent Amy! I have found out that you write for *The Daily Express*. Now, aren't you ashamed of yourself?

—Why should I be ashamed of myself? asked Gabriel, blinking his eyes and trying to smile.

—Well, I'm ashamed of you, said Miss Ivors frankly. To say you'd write for a rag like that. I didn't think you were a West Briton.

A look of perplexity appeared on Gabriel's face. It was true that he wrote a literary column every Wednesday in *The Daily Express*, for which he was paid fifteen shillings. But that did not make him a West Briton surely. The books he received for review were almost more welcome than the paltry cheque. He loved to feel the covers and turn over the pages of newly printed books. Nearly every day when his teaching in the college was ended he used to wander down the quays to the second-hand booksellers, to Hickey's on Bachelor's Walk, to Webb's or Massey's on Aston's Quay, or to O'Clohissey's in the by-street. He did not know how to meet her charge. He wanted to say that literature was above politics. But they were friends of many years' standing and their careers had been parallel, first at the University and then as teachers: he could not risk a grandiose phrase with her. He continued blinking his eyes and trying to smile and murmured lamely that he saw nothing political in writing reviews of books.

When their turn to cross had come he was still perplexed and inattentive. Miss Ivors promptly took his hand in a warm grasp and said in a soft friendly tone:

—Of course, I was only joking. Come, we cross now.

When they were together again she spoke of the University question and Gabriel felt more at ease. A friend of hers had shown her his review of Browning's poems. That was how she had found out the secret: but she liked the review immensely. Then she said suddenly:

—O, Mr Conroy, will you come for an excursion to the Aran Isles this summer? We're going to stay there a whole month. It will be splendid out in the Atlantic. You ought to come. Mr Clancy is coming, and Mr Kilkelly and Kathleen Kearney. It would be splendid for Gretta too if she'd come. She's from Connacht, isn't she?

—Her people are, said Gabriel shortly.

—But you will come, won't you? said Miss Ivors, laying her warm hand eagerly on his arm.

—The fact is, said Gabriel, I have already arranged to go—

—Go where? asked Miss Ivors.

—Well, you know, every year I go for a cycling tour with some fellows and so—

—But where? asked Miss Ivors.

—Well, we usually go to France or Belgium or perhaps Germany, said Gabriel awkwardly.

—And why do you go to France and Belgium, said Miss Ivors, instead of visiting your own land?

—Well, said Gabriel, it's partly to keep in touch with the languages and partly for a change.

—And haven't you your own language to keep in touch with – Irish? asked Miss Ivors.

—Well, said Gabriel, if it comes to that, you know, Irish is not my language.

Their neighbours had turned to listen to the cross-examination. Gabriel glanced right and left nervously and tried to keep his good humour under the ordeal which was making a blush invade his forehead.

—And haven't you your own land to visit, continued Miss Ivors, that you know nothing of, your own people, and your own country?

—O, to tell you the truth, retorted Gabriel suddenly, I'm sick of my own country, sick of it!

—Why? asked Miss Ivors.

Gabriel did not answer for his retort had heated him.

—Why? repeated Miss Ivors.

They had to go visiting together and, as he had not answered her, Miss Ivors said warmly:

—Of course, you've no answer.

Gabriel tried to cover his agitation by taking part in the dance with great energy. He avoided her eyes for he had seen a sour expression on her face. But when they met in the long chain he was surprised to feel his hand firmly pressed. She looked at him from under her brows for a moment quizzically until he smiled. Then, just as the chain was about to start again, she stood on tiptoe and whispered into his ear:

—West Briton!

When the lancers were over Gabriel went away to a remote corner of the room where Freddy Malins' mother was sitting. She was a stout feeble old woman with white hair. Her voice had a catch in it like her son's and she stuttered slightly. She had been told that Freddy had come and that he was nearly all right. Gabriel asked her whether she had had a good crossing. She lived with her married daughter in Glasgow and came to Dublin on a visit once a year. She answered placidly that she had had a beautiful crossing and that the captain had been most attentive to her. She spoke also of the beautiful house her daughter kept in Glasgow, and of all the nice friends they had there. While her tongue rambled on Gabriel tried to banish from his mind all memory of the unpleasant incident with Miss Ivors. Of course the girl or woman, or whatever she was, was an enthusiast but there was a time for all things. Perhaps he ought not to have answered her like that. But she had no right to call him a West Briton before people, even in joke. She had tried to make him ridiculous before people, heckling him and staring at him with her rabbit's eyes.

He saw his wife making her way towards him through the waltzing couples. When she reached him she said into his ear:

—Gabriel, Aunt Kate wants to know won't you carve the goose as usual. Miss Daly will carve the ham and I'll do the pudding.

—All right, said Gabriel.

—She's sending in the younger ones first as soon as this waltz is over so that we'll have the table to ourselves.

—Were you dancing? asked Gabriel.

—Of course I was. Didn't you see me? What words had you with Molly Ivors?

—No words. Why? Did she say so?

—Something like that. I'm trying to get that Mr D'Arcy to sing. He's full of conceit, I think.

—There were no words, said Gabriel moodily, only she wanted me to go for a trip to the west of Ireland and I said I wouldn't.

His wife clasped her hands excitedly and gave a little jump.

—O, do go, Gabriel, she cried. I'd love to see Galway again.

—You can go if you like, said Gabriel coldly.

She looked at him for a moment, then turned to Mrs Malins and said:

—There's a nice husband for you, Mrs Malins.

While she was threading her way back across the room Mrs Malins, without adverting to the interruption, went on to tell Gabriel what beautiful places there were in Scotland and beautiful scenery. Her son-in-law brought them every year to the lakes and they used to go fishing. Her son-in-law was a splendid fisher. One day he caught a fish, a beautiful big big fish, and the man in the hotel boiled it for their dinner.

Gabriel hardly heard what she said. Now that supper was coming near he began to think again about his speech and about the quotation. When he saw Freddy Malins coming across the room to visit his mother Gabriel left the chair free for him and retired into the embrasure of the window. The room had already cleared and from the back room came the clatter of plates and knives. Those who still remained in the drawing-room seemed tired of dancing and were conversing quietly in little groups. Gabriel's warm trembling fingers tapped the cold pane of the window. How cool it must be outside! How pleasant it would be to walk out alone, first along by the river and then through the park! The snow would be lying on the branches of the trees and forming a bright cap on the top of the Wellington Monument.

How much more pleasant it would be there than at the supper-table!

He ran over the headings of his speech: Irish hospitality, sad memories, the Three Graces, Paris, the quotation from Browning. He repeated to himself a phrase he had written in his review: *One feels that one is listening to a thought-tormented music.* Miss Ivors had praised the review. Was she sincere? Had she really any life of her own behind all her propagandism? There had never been any ill-feeling between them until that night. It unnerved him to think that she would be at the supper-table, looking up at him while he spoke with her critical quizzing eyes. Perhaps she would not be sorry to see him fail in his speech. An idea came into his mind and gave him courage. He would say, alluding to Aunt Kate and Aunt Julia: *Ladies and Gentlemen, the generation which is now on the wane among us may have had its faults but for my part I think it had certain qualities of hospitality, of humour, of humanity, which the new and very serious and hypereducated generation that is growing up around us seems to me to lack.* Very good: that was one for Miss Ivors. What did he care that his aunts were only two ignorant old women?

A murmur in the room attracted his attention. Mr Browne was advancing from the door, gallantly escorting Aunt Julia, who leaned upon his arm, smiling and hanging her head. An irregular musketry of applause escorted her also as far as the piano and then, as Mary Jane seated herself on the stool, and Aunt Julia, no longer smiling, half turned so as to pitch her voice fairly into the room, gradually ceased. Gabriel recognized the prelude. It was that of an old song of Aunt Julia's – *Arrayed for the Bridal.* Her voice, strong and clear in tone, attacked with great spirit the runs which embellish the air and though she sang very rapidly she did not miss even the smallest of the grace notes. To follow the voice, without looking at the singer's face, was to feel and share the excitement of swift and secure flight. Gabriel applauded loudly with all the others at the close of the song and loud applause was borne in from the invisible supper-table. It sounded so genuine that a little colour struggled into Aunt Julia's face as she bent to replace in the music-stand the old leather-bound song-book that had her initials on the cover. Freddy Malins, who had listened with his head perched sideways to hear her better, was still applauding when every one else had ceased and talking animatedly to his mother who nodded her head gravely and slowly in acquiescence. At last, when he could clap no more, he stood up suddenly and hurried across the room to Aunt Julia whose hand he seized and held in both his hands, shaking it when words failed him or the catch in his voice proved too much for him.

—I was just telling my mother, he said, I never heard you sing so well, never. No, I never heard your voice so good as it is to-night. Now! Would you believe that now? That's the truth. Upon my word and honour that's the truth. I never heard your voice sound so fresh and so . . . so clear and fresh, never.

Aunt Julia smiled broadly and murmured something about compliments as she released her hand from his grasp. Mr Browne extended his open hand towards her and said to those who were near him in the manner of a showman introducing a prodigy to an audience:

—Miss Julia Morkan, my latest discovery!

He was laughing very heartily at this himself when Freddy Malins turned to him and said:

—Well, Browne, if you're serious you might make a worse discovery. All I can say is I never heard her sing half so well as long as I am coming here. And that's the honest truth.

—Neither did I, said Mr Browne. I think her voice has greatly improved.

Aunt Julia shrugged her shoulders and said with meek pride:

—Thirty years ago I hadn't a bad voice as voices go.

—I often told Julia, said Aunt Kate emphatically, that she was simply thrown away in that choir. But she never would be said by me.

She turned as if to appeal to the good sense of the others against a refractory child while Aunt Julia gazed in front of her, a vague smile of reminiscence playing on her face.

—No, continued Aunt Kate, she wouldn't be said or led by anyone, slaving there in that choir night and day, night and day. Six o'clock on Christmas morning! And all for what?

—Well, isn't it for the honour of God, Aunt Kate? asked Mary Jane, twisting round on the piano-stool and smiling.

Aunt Kate turned fiercely on her niece and said:

—I know all about the honour of God, Mary Jane, but I think it's not at all honourable for the pope to turn out the women out of the choirs that have slaved there all their lives and put little whipper-snappers of boys over their heads. I suppose it is for the good of the Church if the pope does it. But it's not just, Mary Jane, and it's not right.

She had worked herself into a passion and would have continued in defence of her sister for it was a sore subject with her but Mary Jane, seeing that all the dancers had come back, intervened pacifically:

—Now, Aunt Kate, you're giving scandal to Mr Browne who is of the other persuasion.

Aunt Kate turned to Mr Browne, who was grinning at this allusion to his religion, and said hastily:

—O, I don't question the pope's being right. I'm only

a stupid old woman and I wouldn't presume to do such a thing. But there's such a thing as common everyday politeness and gratitude. And if I were in Julia's place I'd tell that Father Healey straight up to his face . . .

—And besides, Aunt Kate, said Mary Jane, we really are all hungry and when we are hungry we are all very quarrelsome.

—And when we are thirsty we are also quarrelsome, added Mr Browne.

—So that we had better go to supper, said Mary Jane, and finish the discussion afterwards.

On the landing outside the drawing-room Gabriel found his wife and Mary Jane trying to persuade Miss Ivors to stay for supper. But Miss Ivors, who had put on her hat and was buttoning her cloak, would not stay. She did not feel in the least hungry and she had already overstayed her time.

—But only for ten minutes, Molly, said Mrs Conroy. That won't delay you.

—To take a pick itself, said Mary Jane, after all your dancing.

—I really couldn't, said Miss Ivors.

—I am afraid you didn't enjoy yourself at all, said Mary Jane hopelessly.

—Ever so much, I assure you, said Miss Ivors, but you really must let me run off now.

—But how can you get home? asked Mrs Conroy.

—O, it's only two steps up the quay.

Gabriel hesitated a moment and said:

—If you will allow me, Miss Ivors, I'll see you home if you really are obliged to go.

But Miss Ivors broke away from them.

—I won't hear of it, she cried. For goodness sake go in to your suppers and don't mind me. I'm quite well able to take care of myself.

—Well, you're the comical girl, Molly, said Mrs Conroy frankly.

—*Beannacht libh*, cried Miss Ivors, with a laugh, as she ran down the staircase.

Mary Jane gazed after her, a moody puzzled expression on her face, while Mrs Conroy leaned over the banisters to listen for the hall-door. Gabriel asked himself was he the cause of her abrupt departure. But she did not seem to be in ill humour: she had gone away laughing. He stared blankly down the staircase.

At that moment Aunt Kate came toddling out of the supper-room, almost wringing her hands in despair.

—Where is Gabriel? she cried. Where on earth is Gabriel? There's everyone waiting in there, stage to let, and nobody to carve the goose!

—Here I am, Aunt Kate! cried Gabriel, with sudden animation, ready to carve a flock of geese, if necessary.

A fat brown goose lay at one end of the table and at the other end, on a bed of creased paper strewn with sprigs of parsley, lay a great ham, stripped of its outer skin and peppered over with crust crumbs, a neat paper frill round its shin and beside this was a round of spiced beef. Between these rival ends ran parallel lines of side-dishes: two little minsters of jelly, red and yellow; a shallow dish full of blocks of blancmange and red jam, a large green leaf-shaped dish with a stalk-shaped handle, on which lay bunches of purple raisins and peeled almonds, a companion dish on which lay a solid rectangle of Smyrna figs, a dish of custard topped with grated nutmeg, a small bowl full of chocolates and sweets wrapped in gold and silver papers and a glass vase in which stood some tall celery stalks. In the centre of the table there stood, as sentries to a fruit-stand which upheld a pyramid of oranges and American apples, two squat old-fashioned decanters of cut glass, one containing port and the other dark sherry. On the closed square piano a pudding in a huge yellow dish lay in waiting and behind it were three squads of bottles of stout and ale and minerals, drawn up according to the colours of their uniforms, the first two black, with brown and red labels, the third and smallest squad white, with transverse green sashes.

Gabriel took his seat boldly at the head of the table and, having looked to the edge of the carver, plunged his fork firmly into the goose. He felt quite at ease now for he was an expert carver and liked nothing better than to find himself at the head of a well-laden table.

—Miss Furlong, what shall I send you? he asked. A wing or a slice of the breast?

—Just a small slice of the breast.

—Miss Higgins, what for you?

—O, anything at all, Mr Conroy.

While Gabriel and Miss Daly exchanged plates of goose and plates of ham and spiced beef Lily went from guest to guest with a dish of hot floury potatoes wrapped in a white napkin. This was Mary Jane's idea and she had also suggested apple sauce for the goose but Aunt Kate had said that plain roast goose without apple sauce had always been good enough for her and she hoped she might never eat worse. Mary Jane waited on her pupils and saw that they got the best slices and Aunt Kate and Aunt Julia opened and carried across from the piano bottles of stout and ale for the gentlemen and bottles of minerals for the ladies. There was a great deal of confusion and laughter and noise, the noise of orders and counter-orders, of knives and forks, of corks and glass-stoppers. Gabriel began to carve second helpings as soon as he had finished the first round without serving himself. Every one protested loudly so that he compromised by taking a long draught of stout for he had found the carving hot work. Mary Jane settled down quietly to her supper but Aunt Kate and Aunt Julia were still toddling round the table, walking on each other's heels, getting in each other's way and giving each other unheeded orders. Mr Browne begged of them to sit down and eat their suppers and so did Gabriel but they said there was time enough so that, at last Freddy Malins stood up and, capturing Aunt Kate, plumped her down on her chair amid general laughter.

When everyone had been well served Gabriel said, smiling:

—Now, if anyone wants a little more of what vulgar people call stuffing let him or her speak.

A chorus of voices invited him to begin his own supper and Lily came forward with three potatoes which she had reserved for him.

—Very well, said Gabriel amiably, as he took another preparatory draught, kindly forget my existence, ladies and gentlemen, for a few minutes.

He set to his supper and took no part in the conversation with which the table covered Lily's removal of the plates. The subject of talk was the opera company which was then at the Theatre Royal. Mr Bartell D'Arcy, the tenor, a dark-complexioned young man with a smart moustache, praised very highly the leading contralto of the company but Miss Furlong thought she had a rather vulgar style of production. Freddy Malins said there was a negro chieftain singing in the second part of the Gaiety pantomime who had one of the finest tenor voices he had ever heard.

—Have you heard him? he asked Mr Bartell D'Arcy across the table.

—No, answered Mr Bartell D'Arcy carelessly.

—Because, Freddy Malins explained, now I'd be curious

to hear your opinion of him. I think he has a grand voice.

—It takes Teddy to find out the really good things, said Mr Browne familiarly to the table.

—And why couldn't he have a voice too? asked Freddy Malins sharply. Is it because he's only a black?

Nobody answered this question and Mary Jane led the table back to the legitimate opera. One of her pupils had given her a pass for *Mignon*. Of course it was very fine, she said, but it made her think of poor Georgina Burns. Mr Browne could go back farther still, to the old Italian companies that used to come to Dublin – Tietjens, Ilma de Murzka, Campanini, the great Trebilli, Giuglini, Ravelli, Aramburo. Those were the days, he said, when there was something like singing to be heard in Dublin. He told too of how the top gallery of the old Royal used to be packed night after night, of how one night an Italian tenor had sung five encores to *Let me Like a Soldier Fall*, introducing a high C every time, and of how the gallery boys would sometimes in their enthusiasm unyoke the horses from the carriage of some great *prima donna* and pull her themselves through the streets to her hotel. Why did they never play the grand old operas now, he asked, *Dinorah*, *Lucrezia Borgia*? Because they could not get the voices to sing them: that was why.

—O, well, said Mr Bartell D'Arcy, I presume there are as good singers to-day as there were then.

—Where are they? asked Mr Browne defiantly.

—In London, Paris, Milan, said Mr Bartell D'Arcy warmly. I suppose Caruso, for example, is quite as good, if not better than any of the men you have mentioned.

—Maybe so, said Mr Browne. But I may tell you I doubt it strongly.

—O, I'd give anything to hear Caruso sing, said Mary Jane.

—For me, said Aunt Kate, who had been picking a bone, there was only one tenor. To please me, I mean. But I suppose none of you ever heard of him.

—Who was he, Miss Morkan? asked Mr Bartell D'Arcy politely.

—His name, said Aunt Kate, was Parkinson. I heard him when he was in his prime and I think he had then the purest tenor voice that was ever put into a man's throat.

—Strange, said Mr Bartell D'Arcy. I never even heard of him.

—Yes, yes, Miss Morkan is right, said Mr Browne. I remember hearing of old Parkinson, but he's too far back for me.

—A beautiful pure sweet mellow English tenor, said Aunt Kate with enthusiasm.

Gabriel having finished, the huge pudding was transferred to the table. The clatter of forks and spoons began again. Gabriel's wife served out spoonfuls of the pudding and passed the plates down the table. Midway down they were held up by Mary Jane, who replenished them with raspberry or orange jelly or with blancmange and jam. The pudding was of Aunt Julia's making and she received praises for it from all quarters. She herself said that it was not quite brown enough.

—Well, I hope, Miss Morkan, said Mr Browne, that I'm brown enough for you because, you know, I'm all brown.

All the gentlemen, except Gabriel, ate some of the pudding out of compliment to Aunt Julia. As Gabriel never ate sweets the celery had been left for him. Freddy Malins also took a stalk of celery and ate it with his pudding. He had been told that celery was a capital thing for the blood and he was just then under doctor's care. Mrs Malins, who had been silent all through the supper, said that her son was going down to Mount Melleray in a week or so. The table then spoke of Mount Melleray, how bracing the air was down there, how hospitable the monks were and how they never asked for a penny-piece from their guests.

—And do you mean to say, asked Mr Browne incredulously, that a chap can go down there and put up there as if it were a hotel and live on the fat of the land and then come away without paying a farthing?

—O, most people give some donation to the monastery when they leave, said Mary Jane.

—I wish we had an institution like that in our Church, said Mr Browne candidly.

He was astonished to hear that the monks never spoke, got up at two in the morning and slept in their coffins. He asked what they did it for.

—That's the rule of the order, said Aunt Kate firmly.

—Yes, but why? asked Mr Browne.

Aunt Kate repeated that it was the rule, that was all. Mr Browne still seemed not to understand. Freddy Malins explained to him, as best he could, that the monks were trying to make up for the sins committed by all the sinners in the outside world. The explanation was not very clear for Mr Browne grinned and said:

—I like that idea very much but wouldn't a comfortable spring bed do them as well as a coffin?

—The coffin, said Mary Jane, is to remind them of their last end.

As the subject had grown lugubrious it was buried in a silence of the table during which Mrs Malins could be heard saying to her neighbour in an indistinct undertone:

—They are very good men, the monks, very pious men.

The raisins and almonds and figs and apples and oranges and chocolates and sweets were now passed about the table and Aunt Julia invited all the guests to have either port or sherry. At first Mr Bartell D'Arcy refused to take either but one of his neighbours nudged him and whispered something to him upon which he allowed his glass to be filled. Gradually as the last glasses were being filled the conversation ceased. A pause followed, broken only by the noise of the wine and by unsettlings of chairs. The Misses Morkan, all three, looked down at the tablecloth. Some one coughed once or twice and then a few gentlemen patted the table gently as a signal for silence. The silence came and Gabriel pushed back his chair and stood up.

The patting at once grew louder in encouragement and then ceased altogether. Gabriel leaned his ten trembling fingers on the tablecloth and smiled nervously at the company. Meeting a row of upturned faces he raised his eyes to the chandelier. The piano was playing a waltz tune and he could hear the skirts sweeping against the drawing-room door. People, perhaps, were standing in the snow on the quay outside, gazing up at the lighted windows and listening to the waltz music. The air was pure there. In the distance lay the park where the trees were weighted with snow. The Wellington Monument wore a gleaming cap of snow that flashed westward over the white field of Fifteen Acres.

He began:

—Ladies and Gentlemen.

—It has fallen to my lot this evening, as in years past, to perform a very pleasing task but a task for which I am afraid my poor powers as a speaker are all too inadequate.

—No, no! said Mr Browne.

—But, however that may be, I can only ask you to-night to take the will for the deed and to lend me your attention for a few moments while I endeavour to express to you in words what my feelings are on this occasion.

—Ladies and Gentlemen. It is not the first time that we have gathered together under this hospitable roof, around this hospitable board. It is not the first time that we have been the recipients – or perhaps, I had better say, the victims – of the hospitality of certain good ladies.

He made a circle in the air with his arm and paused. Every one laughed or smiled at Aunt Kate and Aunt Julia and Mary Jane who all turned crimson with pleasure. Gabriel went on more boldly:

—I feel more strongly with every recurring year that our country has no tradition which does it so much honour and which it should guard so jealously as that of its hospitality. It is a tradition that is unique as far as my experience goes (and I have visited not a few places abroad) among the modern nations. Some would say, perhaps, that with us it is rather a failing than anything to be boasted of. But granted even that, it is, to my mind, a princely failing, and one that I trust will long be cultivated among us. Of one thing, at least, I am sure. As long as this one roof shelters the good ladies aforesaid – and I wish from my heart it may do so for many and many a long year to come – the tradition of genuine warm-hearted courteous Irish hospitality, which our forefathers have handed down to us and which we in turn must hand down to our descendants, is still alive among us.

A hearty murmur of assent ran round the table. It shot through Gabriel's mind that Miss Ivors was not there and that she had gone away discourteously: and he said with confidence in himself:

—Ladies and Gentlemen.

—A new generation is growing up in our midst, a generation actuated by new ideas and new principles. It is serious and enthusiastic for these new ideas and its enthusiasm, even when it is misdirected, is, I believe, in the main sincere. But we are living in a sceptical and, if I may use the phrase, a thought-tormented age: and sometimes I fear that this new generation, educated or hypereducated as it is, will lack those qualities of humanity, of hospitality, of kindly humour which belonged to an older day. Listening to-night to the names of all those great singers of the past it seemed to me, I must confess, that we were living in a less spacious age. Those days might, without exaggeration, be called spacious days: and if they are gone beyond recall let us hope, at least, that in gatherings such as this we shall still speak of them with pride and affection, still cherish in our hearts the memory of those dead and gone great ones whose fame the world will not willingly let die.

—Hear, hear! said Mr Browne loudly.

—But yet, continued Gabriel, his voice falling into a softer inflection, there are always in gatherings such as this sadder thoughts that will recur to our minds: thoughts of the past, of youth, of changes, of absent faces that we miss here tonight. Our path through life is strewn with many such sad memories and were we to brood upon them always we could not find the heart to go on bravely with our work among the living. We have all of us living duties and living affections which claim, and rightly claim, our strenuous endeavours.

—Therefore, I will not linger on the past. I will not let any gloomy moralizing intrude upon us here to-night. Here we are gathered together for a brief moment from the bustle and rush of our everyday routine. We are met here as friends, in the spirit of good-fellowship, as colleagues, also to a certain extent, in the true spirit of *camaraderie*, and as the guest of – what shall I call them? – the Three Graces of the Dublin musical world.

The table burst into applause and laughter at this sally.

Aunt Julia vainly asked each of her neighbours in turn to tell her what Gabriel had said.

—He says we are the Three Graces, Aunt Julia, said Mary Jane.

Aunt Julia did not understand but she looked up, smiling, at Gabriel, who continued in the same vein:

—Ladies and Gentlemen.

—I will not attempt to play to-night the part that Paris played on another occasion. I will not attempt to choose between them. The task would be an invidious one and one beyond my poor powers. For when I view them in turn, whether it be our chief hostess herself, whose good heart, whose too good heart, has become a byword with all who know her, or her sister, who seems to be gifted with perennial youth and whose singing must have been a surprise and a revelation to us all to-night, or, last but not least, when I consider our youngest hostess, talented, cheerful, hard-working and the best of nieces, I confess, Ladies and Gentlemen, that I do not know to which of them I should award the prize.

Gabriel glanced down at his aunts and, seeing the large smile on Aunt Julia's face and the tears which had risen to Aunt Kate's eyes, hastened to his close. He raised his glass of port gallantly, while every member of the company fingered a glass expectantly, and said loudly:

—Let us toast them all three together. Let us drink to their health, wealth, long life, happiness and prosperity and may they long continue to hold the proud and self-won position which they hold in their profession and the position of honour and affection which they hold in our hearts.

All the guests stood up, glass in hand, and, turning towards the three seated ladies, sang in unison, with Mr Browne as leader:

For they are jolly gay fellows,
For they are jolly gay fellows,
For they are jolly gay fellows,
Which nobody can deny.

Aunt Kate was making frank use of her handkerchief and even Aunt Julia seemed moved. Freddy Malins beat time with his pudding-fork and the singers turned towards one another, as if in melodious conference, while they sang with emphasis:

Unless he tells a lie,
Unless he tells a lie,

Then, turning once more towards their hostesses, they sang:

For they are jolly gay fellows,
For they are jolly gay fellows,
For they are jolly gay fellows,
Which nobody can deny.

The acclamation which followed was taken up beyond the door of the supper-room by many of the other guests and renewed time after time, Freddy Malins acting as officer with his fork on high.

The piercing morning air came into the hall where they were standing so that Aunt Kate said:

—Close the door, somebody. Mrs Malins will get her death of cold.

—Browne is out there, Aunt Kate, said Mary Jane.

—Browne is everywhere, said Aunt Kate, lowering her voice.

Mary Jane laughed at her tone.

—Really, she said archly, he is very attentive.

—He has been laid on here like the gas, said Aunt Kate in the same tone, all during the Christmas.

She laughed herself this time good-humouredly and then added quickly:

—But tell him to come in, Mary Jane, and close the door. I hope to goodness he didn't hear me.

At that moment the hall-door was opened and Mr Browne came in from the doorstep, laughing as if his heart would break. He was dressed in a long green overcoat with mock astrakhan cuffs and collar and wore on his head an oval fur cap. He pointed down the snow-covered quay from where the sound of shrill prolonged whistling was borne in.

—Teddy will have all the cabs in Dublin out, he said.

Gabriel advanced from the little pantry behind the office, struggling into his overcoat and, looking round the hall, said:

—Gretta not down yet?

—She's getting on her things, Gabriel, said Aunt Kate.

—Who's playing up there? asked Gabriel.

—Nobody. They're all gone.

—O no, Aunt Kate, said Mary Jane. Bartell D'Arcy and Miss O'Callaghan aren't gone yet.

—Someone is strumming at the piano, anyhow, said Gabriel.

Mary Jane glanced at Gabriel and Mr Browne and said with a shiver:

—It makes me feel cold to look at you two gentlemen muffled up like that. I wouldn't like to face your journey home at this hour.

—I'd like nothing better this minute, said Mr Browne stoutly, than a rattling fine walk in the country or a fast drive with a good spanking goer between the shafts.

—We used to have a very good horse and trap at home, said Aunt Julia sadly.

—The never-to-be-forgotten Johnny, said Mary Jane, laughing.

Aunt Kate and Gabriel laughed too.

—Why, what was wonderful about Johnny? asked Mr Browne.

—The late lamented Patrick Morkan, our grandfather, that is, explained Gabriel, commonly known in his later years as the old gentleman, was a glue-boiler.

—O, now, Gabriel, said Aunt Kate, laughing, he had a starch mill.

—Well, glue or starch, said Gabriel, the old gentleman had a horse by the name of Johnny. And Johnny used to work in the old gentleman's mill, walking round and round in order to drive the mill. That was all very well; but now comes the tragic part about Johnny. One fine day the old gentleman thought he'd like to drive out with the quality to a military review in the park.

—The Lord have mercy on his soul, said Aunt Kate compassionately.

—Amen, said Gabriel. So the old gentleman, as I said, harnessed Johnny and put on his very best tall hat and his very best stock collar and drove out in grand style from his ancestral mansion somewhere near Back Lane, I think.

Every one laughed, even Mrs Malins, at Gabriel's manner and Aunt Kate said:

—O now, Gabriel, he didn't live in Back Lane, really. Only the mill was there.

—Out from the mansion of his forefathers, continued Gabriel, he drove with Johnny. And everything went on beautifully until Johnny came in sight of King Billy's statue: and whether he fell in love with the horse King Billy sits on or whether he thought he was back again in the mill, anyhow he began to walk round the statue.

Gabriel paced in a circle round the hall in his goloshes amid the laughter of the others.

—Round and round he went, said Gabriel, and the old gentleman, who was a very pompous old gentleman, was highly indignant. *Go on, sir! What do you mean, sir? Johnny! Johnny! Most extraordinary conduct! Can't understand the horse!*

The peals of laughter which followed Gabriel's imitation of the incident were interrupted by a resounding knock at the hall-door. Mary Jane ran to open it and let in Freddy Malins. Freddy Malins, with his hat well back on his head and his shoulders humped with cold, was puffing and steaming after his exertions.

—I could only get one cab, he said.

—O, we'll find another along the quay, said Gabriel.

—Yes, said Aunt Kate. Better not keep Mrs Malins standing in the draught.

Mrs Malins was helped down the front steps by her son and Mr Browne and, after many manœuvres, hoisted into the cab. Freddy Malins clambered in after her and spent a long time settling her on the seat, Mr Browne helping him with advice. At last she was settled comfortably and Freddy Malins invited Mr Browne into the cab. There was a good deal of confused talk, and then Mr Browne got into the cab. The cabman settled his rug over his knees, and bent down for the address. The confusion grew greater and the cabman was directed differently by Freddy Malins and Mr Browne, each of whom had his head out through a window of the cab. The difficulty was to know where to drop Mr Browne along the route and Aunt Kate, Aunt Julia and Mary Jane helped the discussion from the doorstep with cross-directions and contradictions and abundance of laughter. As for Freddy Malins he was speechless with laughter. He popped his head in and out of the window every moment, to the great danger of his hat, and told his mother how the discussion was progressing, till at last Mr Browne shouted to the bewildered cabman above the din of everybody's laughter:

—Do you know Trinity College?

—Yes, sir, said the cabman.

—Well, drive bang up against Trinity College gates, said Mr Browne, and then we'll tell you where to go. You understand now?

—Yes, sir, said the cabman.

—Make like a bird for Trinity College.

—Right, sir, cried the cabman.

The horse was whipped up and the cab rattled off along the quay amid a chorus of laughter and adieus.

Gabriel had not gone to the door with the others. He was in a dark part of the hall gazing up the staircase. A woman was standing near the top of the first flight, in the shadow also. He could not see her face but he could see the terracotta and salmonpink panels of her skirt which the shadow made appear black and white. It was his wife. She was leaning on the banisters, listening to something. Gabriel was surprised at her stillness and strained his ear to listen also. But he could hear little save the noise of laughter and dispute on the front steps, a few chords struck on the piano and a few notes of a man's voice singing.

He stood still in the gloom of the hall, trying to catch the air that the voice was singing and gazing up at his wife. There was grace and mystery in her attitude as if she were a symbol of something. He asked himself what is a woman standing on the stairs in the shadow, listening to distant music, a symbol of. If he were a painter he would paint her in that attitude. Her blue felt hat would show off the bronze of her hair against the darkness and the dark panels of her skirt would show off the light ones. *Distant Music* he would call the picture if he were a painter.

The hall-door was closed; and Aunt Kate, Aunt Julia and Mary Jane came down the hall, still laughing.

—Well, isn't Freddy terrible? said Mary Jane. He's really terrible.

Gabriel said nothing but pointed up the stairs towards where his wife was standing. Now that the hall-door was closed the voice and the piano could be heard more clearly. Gabriel held up his hand for them to be silent. The song seemed to be in the old Irish tonality and the singer seemed uncertain both of his words and of his voice. The voice, made plaintive by distance and by the singer's hoarseness, faintly illuminated the cadence of the air with words expressing grief:

O, the rain falls on my heavy locks
And the dew wets my skin,
My babe lies cold . . .

—O, exclaimed Mary Jane. It's Bartell D'Arcy singing, and he wouldn't sing all the night. O, I'll get him to sing a song before he goes.

—O, do, Mary Jane, said Aunt Kate.

Mary Jane brushed past the others and ran to the staircase but before she reached it the singing stopped and the piano was closed abruptly.

—O, what a pity! she cried. Is he coming down, Gretta?

Gabriel heard his wife answer yes and saw her come down towards them. A few steps behind her were Mr Bartell D'Arcy and Miss O'Callaghan.

—O, Mr D'Arcy, cried Mary Jane, it's downright mean

of you to break off like that when we were all in raptures listening to you.

—I have been at him all the evening, said Miss O'Callaghan, and Mrs Conroy too and he told us he had a dreadful cold and couldn't sing.

—O, Mr D'Arcy, said Aunt Kate, now that was a great fib to tell.

—Can't you see that I'm as hoarse as a crow? said Mr D'Arcy roughly.

He went into the pantry hastily and put on his overcoat. The others, taken aback by his rude speech, could find nothing to say. Aunt Kate wrinkled her brows and made signs to the others to drop the subject. Mr D'Arcy stood swathing his neck carefully and frowning.

—It's the weather, said Aunt Julia, after a pause.

—Yes, everybody has colds, said Aunt Kate readily, everybody.

—They say, said Mary Jane, we haven't had snow like it for thirty years; and I read this morning in the newspapers that the snow is general all over Ireland.

—I love the look of snow, said Aunt Julia sadly.

—So do I, said Miss O'Callaghan. I think Christmas is never really Christmas unless we have the snow on the ground.

—But poor Mr D'Arcy doesn't like the snow, said Aunt Kate, smiling.

Mr D'Arcy came from the pantry, fully swathed and buttoned, and in a repentant tone told them the history of his cold. Every one gave him advice and said it was a great pity and urged him to be very careful of his throat in the night air. Gabriel watched his wife who did not join in the conversation. She was standing right under the dusty fan-light and the flame of the gas lit up the rich bronze of her hair which he had seen her drying at the fire a few days before. She was in the same attitude and seemed unaware of the talk about her. At last she turned towards them and Gabriel saw that there was colour on her cheeks and that her eyes were shining. A sudden tide of joy went leaping out of his heart.

—Mr D'Arcy, she said, what is the name of that song you were singing?

—It's called *The Lass of Aughrim*, said Mr D'Arcy, but I couldn't remember it properly. Why? Do you know it?

—*The Lass of Aughrim*, she repeated. I couldn't think of the name.

—It's a very nice air, said Mary Jane. I'm sorry you were not in voice to-night.

—Now, Mary Jane, said Aunt Kate, don't annoy Mr D'Arcy. I won't have him annoyed.

Seeing that all were ready to start she shepherded them to the door where good-night was said:

—Well, good-night, Aunt Kate, and thanks for the pleasant evening.

—Good-night, Gabriel. Good-night, Gretta!

—Good-night, Aunt Kate, and thanks ever so much. Good-night, Aunt Julia.

—O, good-night, Gretta, I didn't see you.

—Good-night, Mr D'Arcy. Good-night, Miss O'Callaghan.

—Good-night, Miss Morkan.

—Good-night, again.

—Good-night, all. Safe home.

—Good-night. Good-night.

The morning was still dark. A dull yellow light brooded over the houses and the river; and the sky seemed to be descending. It was slushy underfoot; and only streaks and patches of snow lay on the roofs, on the parapets of the quay and on the area railings. The lamps were still burning redly in the murky air and, across the river, the palace of the Four Courts stood out menacingly against the heavy sky.

She was walking on before him with Mr Bartell D'Arcy, her shoes in a brown parcel tucked under one arm and her hands holding her skirt up from the slush. She had no longer any grace of attitude but Gabriel's eyes were still bright with happiness. The blood went bounding along his veins; and the thoughts went rioting through his brain, proud, joyful, tender, valorous.

She was walking on before him so lightly and so erect that he longed to run after her noiselessly, catch her by the shoulders and say something foolish and affectionate into her ear. She seemed to him so frail that he longed to defend her against something and then to be alone with her. Moments of their secret life together burst like stars upon his memory. A heliotrope envelope was lying beside his breakfast-cup and he was caressing it with his hand. Birds were twittering in the ivy and the sunny web of the curtain was shimmering along the floor: he could not eat for happiness. They were standing on the crowded platform and he was placing a ticket inside the warm palm of her glove. He was standing with her in the cold, looking in through a grated window at a man making bottles in a roaring furnace. It was very cold. Her face, fragrant in the cold air, was quite close to his; and suddenly she called out to the man at the furnace:

—Is the fire hot, sir?

But the man could not hear her with the noise of the furnace. It was just as well. He might have answered rudely.

A wave of yet more tender joy escaped from his heart and went coursing in warm flood along his arteries. Like the tender fires of stars moments of their life together, that no one knew of or would ever know of, broke upon and illumined his memory. He longed to recall to her those moments, to make her forget the years of their dull existence together and remember only their moments of ecstasy. For the years, he felt, had not quenched his soul or hers. Their children, his writing, her household cares had not quenched all their souls' tender fire. In one letter that he had written to her then he had said: *Why is it that words like these seem to me so dull and cold? Is it because there is no word tender enough to be your name?*

Like distant music these words that he had written years before were borne towards him from the past. He longed to be alone with her. When the others had gone away, when he and she were in the room in the hotel, then they would be alone together. He would call her softly:

—Gretta!

Perhaps she would not hear at once: she would be undressing. Then something in his voice would strike her. She would turn and look at him. . . .

At the corner of Winetavern Street they met a cab. He was glad of its rattling noise as it saved him from conversation. She was looking out of the window and seemed tired. The others spoke only a few words, pointing out some building or street. The horse galloped along wearily under the murky morning sky, dragging his old rattling box after his heels, and Gabriel was again in a cab with her, galloping to catch the boat, galloping to their honeymoon.

As the cab drove across O'Connell Bridge Miss O'Callaghan said:

—They say you never cross O'Connell Bridge without seeing a white horse.

—I see a white man this time, said Gabriel.

—Where? asked Mr Bartell D'Arcy.

Gabriel pointed to the statue, on which lay patches of snow. Then he nodded familiarly to it and waved his hand.

—Good-night, Dan, he said gaily.

When the cab drew up before the hotel Gabriel jumped out and, in spite of Mr Bartell D'Arcy's protest, paid the driver. He gave the man a shilling over his fare. The man saluted and said:

—A prosperous New Year to you, sir.

—The same to you, said Gabriel cordially.

She leaned for a moment on his arm in getting out of the cab and while standing at the kerbstone, bidding the others good-night. She leaned lightly on his arm, as lightly as when she had danced with him a few hours before. He had felt proud and happy then, happy that she was his, proud of her grace and wifely carriage. But now, after the kindling again of so many memories, the first touch of her body, musical and strange and perfumed, sent through him a keen pang of lust. Under cover of her silence he pressed her arm closely to his side; and, as they stood at the hotel door, he felt that they had escaped from their lives and duties, escaped from home and friends and run away together with wild and radiant hearts to a new adventure.

An old man was dozing in a great hooded chair in the hall. He lit a candle in the office and went before them to the stairs. They followed him in silence, their feet falling in soft thuds on the thickly carpeted stairs. She mounted the stairs behind the porter, her head bowed in the ascent, her frail shoulders curved as with a burden, her skirt girt tightly about her. He could have flung his arms about her hips and held her still for his arms were trembling with desire to seize her and only the stress of his nails against the palms of his hands held the wild impulse of his body in check. The porter halted on the stairs to settle his guttering candle. They halted too on the steps below him. In the silence Gabriel could hear the falling of the molten wax into the tray and the thumping of his own heart against his ribs.

The porter led them along a corridor and opened a door. Then he set his unstable candle down on a toilet-table and asked at what hour they were to be called in the morning.

—Eight, said Gabriel.

The porter pointed to the tap of the electric-light and began a muttered apology but Gabriel cut him short.

—We don't want any light. We have light enough from the street. And I say, he added, pointing to the candle, you might remove that handsome article, like a good man.

The porter took up his candle again, but slowly for he was surprised by such a novel idea. Then he mumbled good-night and went out. Gabriel shot the lock to.

A ghostly light from the street lamp lay in a long shaft from one window to the door. Gabriel threw his overcoat and hat on a couch and crossed the room towards the window. He looked down into the street in order that his emotion might calm a little. Then he turned and leaned against a chest of drawers with his back to the light. She had taken off her hat and cloak and was standing before a large swinging mirror, unhooking her waist. Gabriel paused for a few moments, watching her, and then said:

—Gretta!

She turned away from the mirror slowly and walked along the shaft of light towards him. Her face looked so serious and weary that the words would not pass Gabriel's lips. No, it was not the moment yet.

—You looked tired, he said.

—I am a little, she answered.

—You don't feel ill or weak?

—No, tired: that's all.

She went on to the window and stood there, looking out. Gabriel waited again and then, fearing that diffidence was about to conquer him, he said abruptly:

—By the way, Gretta!

—What is it?

—You know that poor fellow Malins? he said quickly.

—Yes. What about him?

—Well, poor fellow, he's a decent sort of chap, after all, continued Gabriel in a false voice. He gave me back that sovereign I lent him and I didn't expect it really. It's a pity he wouldn't keep away from that Browne, because he's not a bad fellow at heart.

He was trembling now with annoyance. Why did she seem so abstracted? He did not know how he could begin. Was she annoyed, too, about something? If she would only turn to him or come to him of her own accord! To take her as she was would be brutal. No, he must see some ardour in her eyes first. He longed to be master of her strange mood.

—When did you lend him the pound? she asked, after a pause.

Gabriel strove to restrain himself from breaking out into brutal language about the sottish Malins and his pound. He longed to cry to her from his soul, to crush her body against his, to overmaster her. But he said:

—O, at Christmas, when he opened that little Christmas-card shop in Henry Street.

He was in such a fever of rage and desire that he did not hear her come from the window. She stood before him for an instant, looking at him strangely. Then, suddenly raising herself on tiptoe and resting her hands lightly on his shoulders, she kissed him.

—You are a very generous person, Gabriel, she said.

Gabriel, trembling with delight at her sudden kiss and at the quaintness of her phrase, put his hands on her hair and began smoothing it back, scarcely touching it with his fingers. The washing had made it fine and brilliant. His heart was brimming over with happiness. Just when he was wishing for it she had come to him of her own accord. Perhaps her thoughts had been running with his. Perhaps she had felt the impetuous desire that was in him and then the yielding mood had come upon her. Now that she had fallen to him so easily he wondered why he had been so diffident.

He stood, holding her head between his hands. Then, slipping one arm swiftly about her body and drawing her towards him, he said softly:

—Gretta dear, what are you thinking about?

She did not answer nor yield wholly to his arm. He said again, softly:

—Tell me what it is, Gretta. I think I know what is the matter. Do I know?

She did not answer at once. Then she said in an outburst of tears:

—O, I am thinking about that song, *The Lass of Aughrim*.

She broke loose from him and ran to the bed and, throwing her arms across the bed-rail, hid her face. Gabriel stood stock-still for a moment in astonishment and then followed her. As he passed in the way of the cheval-glass he caught sight of himself in full length, his broad, well-filled shirt-front, the face whose expression always puzzled him when he saw it in a mirror and his glimmering gilt-rimmed eye-glasses. He halted a few paces from her and said:

—What about the song? Why does that make you cry?

She raised her head from her arms and dried her eyes with the back of her hand like a child. A kinder note than he had intended went into his voice.

—Why, Gretta? he asked.

—I am thinking about a person long ago who used to sing that song.

—And who was the person long ago? asked Gabriel, smiling.

—It was a person I used to know in Galway when I was living with my grandmother, she said.

The smile passed away from Gabriel's face. A dull anger began to gather again at the back of his mind and the dull fires of his lust began to glow angrily in his veins.

—Someone you were in love with? he asked ironically.

—It was a young boy I used to know, she answered, named Michael Furey. He used to sing that song, *The Lass of Aughrim*. He was very delicate.

Gabriel was silent. He did not wish her to think that he was interested in this delicate boy.

—I can see him so plainly, she said after a moment. Such eyes as he had: big dark eyes! And such an expression in them – an expression!

—O then, you were in love with him? said Gabriel.

—I used to go out walking with him, she said, when I was in Galway.

A thought flew across Gabriel's mind.

—Perhaps that was why you wanted to go to Galway with that Ivors girl? he said coldly.

She looked at him and asked in surprise:

—What for?

Her eyes made Gabriel feel awkward. He shrugged his shoulders and said:

—How do I know? To see him perhaps.

She looked away from him along the shaft of light towards the window in silence.

—He is dead, she said at length. He died when he was

only seventeen. Isn't it a terrible thing to die so young as that?

—What was he? asked Gabriel, still ironically.

—He was in the gasworks, she said.

Gabriel felt humiliated by the failure of his irony and by the evocation of this figure from the dead, a boy in the gasworks. While he had been full of memories of their secret life together, full of tenderness and joy and desire, she had been comparing him in her mind with another. A shameful consciousness of his own person assailed him. He saw himself as a ludicrous figure, acting as a pennyboy for his aunts, a nervous well-meaning sentimentalist, orating to vulgarians and idealizing his own clownish lusts, the pitiable fatuous fellow he had caught a glimpse of in the mirror. Instinctively he turned his back more to the light lest she might see the shame that burned upon his forehead.

He tried to keep up his tone of cold interrogation but his voice when he spoke was humble and indifferent.

—I suppose you were in love with this Michael Furey, Gretta, he said.

—I was great with him at that time, she said.

Her voice was veiled and sad. Gabriel, feeling now how vain it would be to try to lead her whither he had purposed, caressed one of her hands and said, also sadly:

—And what did he die of so young, Gretta? Consumption, was it?

—I think he died for me, she answered.

A vague terror seized Gabriel at this answer as if, at that hour when he had hoped to triumph, some impalpable and vindictive being was coming against him, gathering forces against him in its vague world. But he shook himself free of it with an effort of reason and continued to caress her hand. He did not question her again for he felt that she would tell him of herself. Her hand was warm and moist: it did not respond to his touch but he continued to caress it just as he had caressed her first letter to him that spring morning.

—It was in the winter, she said, about the beginning of the winter when I was going to leave my grandmother's and come up here to the convent. And he was ill at the time in his lodgings in Galway and wouldn't be let out and his people in Oughterard were written to. He was in decline, they said, or something like that. I never knew rightly.

She paused for a moment and sighed.

—Poor fellow, she said. He was very fond of me and he was such a gentle boy. We used to go out together, walking, you know, Gabriel, like the way they do in the country. He was going to study singing only for his health. He had a very good voice, poor Michael Furey.

—Well; and then? asked Gabriel.

—And then when it came to the time for me to leave Galway and come up to the convent he was much worse and I wouldn't be let see him so I wrote a letter saying I was going up to Dublin and would be back in the summer and hoping he would be better then.

She paused for a moment to get her voice under control and then went on:

—Then the night before I left I was in my grandmother's house in Nuns' Island, packing up, and I heard gravel thrown up against the window. The window was so wet I couldn't see so I ran downstairs as I was and slipped out the back into the garden and there was the poor fellow at the end of the garden, shivering.

—And did you not tell him to go back? asked Gabriel.

—I implored of him to go home at once and told him he would get his death in the rain. But he said he did not want to live. I can see his eyes as well as well! He was standing at the end of the wall where there was a tree.

—And did he go home? asked Gabriel.

—Yes, he went home. And when I was only a week in the convent he died and he was buried in Oughterard where his people came from. O, the day I heard that, that he was dead!

She stopped, choking with sobs, and, overcome by emotion, flung herself face downward on the bed, sobbing in the quilt. Gabriel held her hand for a moment longer, irresolutely, and then, shy of intruding on her grief, let it fall gently and walked quietly to the window.

She was fast asleep.

Gabriel, leaning on his elbow, looked for a few moments unresentfully on her tangled hair and half-open mouth, listening to her deep-drawn breath. So she had had that romance in her life: a man had died for her sake. It hardly pained him now to think how poor a part he, her husband, had played in her life. He watched her while she slept as though he and she had never lived together as man and wife. His curious eyes rested long upon her face and on her hair: and, as he thought of what she must have been then, in that time of her first girlish beauty, a strange friendly pity for her entered his soul. He did not like to say even to himself that her face was no longer beautiful but he knew that it was no longer the face for which Michael Furey had braved death.

Perhaps she had not told him all the story. His eyes moved to the chair over which she had thrown some of her clothes. A petticoat string dangled to the floor. One boot stood upright, its limp upper fallen down: the fellow of it lay upon its side. He wondered at his riot of emotions of an hour before. From what had it proceeded? From his aunt's supper, from his own foolish speech, from the wine and dancing, the merry-making when saying good-night in the hall, the pleasure of the walk along the river in the snow. Poor Aunt

Julia! She, too, would soon be a shade with the shade of Patrick Morkan and his horse. He had caught that haggard look upon her face for a moment when she was singing *Arrayed for the Bridal.* Soon, perhaps, he would be sitting in that same drawing-room, dressed in black, his silk hat on his knees. The blinds would be drawn down and Aunt Kate would be sitting beside him, crying and blowing her nose and telling him how Julia had died. He would cast about in his mind for some words that might console her, and would find only lame and useless ones. Yes, yes: that would happen very soon.

The air of the room chilled his shoulders. He stretched himself cautiously along under the sheets and lay down beside his wife. One by one they were all becoming shades. Better pass boldly into that other world, in the full glory of some passion, than fade and wither dismally with age. He thought of how she who lay beside him had locked in her heart for so many years that image of her lover's eyes when he had told her that he did not wish to live.

Generous tears filled Gabriel's eyes. He had never felt like that himself towards any woman but he knew that such a feeling must be love. The tears gathered more thickly in his eyes and in the partial darkness he imagined he saw the form of a young man standing under a dripping tree. Other forms were near. His soul had approached that region where dwell the vast hosts of the dead. He was conscious of, but could not apprehend, their wayward and flickering existence. His own identity was fading out into a grey impalpable world: the solid world itself which these dead had one time reared and lived in was dissolving and dwindling.

A few light taps upon the pane made him turn to the window. It had begun to snow again. He watched sleepily the flakes, silver and dark, falling obliquely against the lamplight. The time had come for him to set out on his journey westward. Yes, the newspapers were right: snow was general all over Ireland. It was falling on every part of the dark central plain, on the treeless hills, falling softly upon the Bog of Allen and, farther westward, softly falling into the dark mutinous Shannon waves. It was falling, too, upon every part of the lonely churchyard on the hill where Michael Furey lay buried. It lay thickly drifted on the crooked crosses and headstones, on the spears of the little gate, on the barren thorns. His soul swooned slowly as he heard the snow falling faintly through the universe and faintly falling, like the descent of their last end, upon all the living and the dead.

VIRGINIA WOOLF

CLARISSA DALLOWAY'S PARTY

From *Mrs Dalloway*

(1925)

'HOW DELIGHTFUL TO see you!' said Clarissa. She said it to every one. How delightful to see you! She was at her worst – effusive, insincere. It was a great mistake to have come. He should have stayed at home and read his book, thought Peter Walsh; should have gone to a music hall; he should have stayed at home, for he knew no one.

Oh dear, it was going to be a failure; a complete failure, Clarissa felt it in her bones as dear old Lord Lexham stood there apologising for his wife who had caught cold at the Buckingham Palace garden party. She could see Peter out of the tail of her eye, criticising her, there, in that corner. Why, after all, did she do these things? Why seek pinnacles and stand drenched in fire? Might it consume her anyhow! Burn her to cinders! Better anything, better brandish one's torch and hurl it to earth than taper and dwindle away like some Ellie Henderson! It was extraordinary how Peter put her into these states just by coming and standing in a corner. He made her see herself; exaggerate. It was idiotic. But why did he come, then, merely to criticise? Why always take, never give? Why not risk one's one little point of view? There he was wandering off, and she must speak to him. But she would not get the chance. Life was that – humiliation, renunciation. What Lord Lexham was saying was that his wife would not wear her furs at the garden party because 'my dear, you ladies are all alike' – Lady Lexham being seventy-five at least! It was delicious, how they petted each other, that old couple.

She did like old Lord Lexham. She did think it mattered, her party, and it made her feel quite sick to know that it was all going wrong, all falling flat. Anything, any explosion, any horror was better than people wandering aimlessly, standing in a bunch at a corner like Ellie Henderson, not even caring to hold themselves upright.

Gently the yellow curtain with all the birds of Paradise blew out and it seemed as if there were a flight of wings into the room, right out, then sucked back. (For the windows were open.) Was it draughty, Ellie Henderson wondered? She was subject to chills. But it did not matter that she should come down sneezing to-morrow; it was the girls with their naked shoulders she thought of, being trained to think of others by an old father, an invalid, late vicar of Bourton, but he was dead now; and her chills never went to her chest, never. It was the girls she thought of, the young girls with their bare shoulders, she herself having always been a wisp of a creature, with her thin hair and meagre profile; though now, past fifty, there was beginning to shine through some mild beam, something purified into distinction by years of self-abnegation but obscured again, perpetually, by her distressing gentility, her panic fear, which arose from three hundred pounds income, and her weaponless state (she could not earn a penny) and it made her timid, and more and more disqualified year by year to meet well-dressed people who did this sort of thing every night of the season, merely telling their maids 'I'll wear so and so,' whereas Ellie Henderson ran out nervously and bought cheap pink flowers, half-a-dozen, and then threw a shawl over her old black dress. For her invitation to Clarissa's party had come at the last moment. She was not quite happy about it. She had a sort of feeling that Clarissa had not meant to ask her this year.

Why should she? There was no reason really, except

that they had always known each other. Indeed, they were cousins. But naturally they had rather drifted apart, Clarissa being so sought after. It was an event to her, going to a party. It was quite a treat just to see the lovely clothes. Wasn't that Elizabeth, grown up, with her hair done in the fashionable way, in the pink dress? Yet she could not be more than seventeen. She was very, very handsome. But girls when they first came out didn't seem to wear white as they used. (She must remember everything to tell Edith.) Girls wore straight frocks, perfectly tight, with skirts well above the ankles. It was not becoming, she thought.

So, with her weak eyesight, Ellie Henderson craned rather forward, and it wasn't so much she who minded not having any one to talk to (she hardly knew anybody there), for she felt that they were all such interesting people to watch; politicians presumably; Richard Dalloway's friends; but it was Richard himself who felt that he could not let the poor creature go on standing there all the evening by herself.

'Well, Ellie, and how's the world treating *you*?' he said in his genial way, and Ellie Henderson, getting nervous and flushing and feeling that it was extraordinarily nice of him to come and talk to her, said that many people really felt the heat more than the cold.

'Yes, they do,' said Richard Dalloway. 'Yes.'

But what more did one say?

'Hullo, Richard,' said somebody, taking him by the elbow, and, good Lord, there was old Peter, old Peter Walsh. He was delighted to see him – ever so pleased to see him! He hadn't changed a bit. And off they went together walking right across the room, giving each other little pats, as if they hadn't met for a long time, Ellie Henderson thought, watching them go, certain she knew that man's face. A tall man, middle aged, rather fine eyes, dark, wearing spectacles, with a look of John Burrows. Edith would be sure to know.

The curtain with its flight of birds of Paradise blew out again. And Clarissa saw – she saw Ralph Lyon beat it back, and go on talking. So it wasn't a failure after all! it was going to be all right now – her party. It had begun. It had started. But it was still touch and go. She must stand there for the present. People seemed to come in a rush.

'Colonel and Mrs Garrod . . . Mr Hugh Whitbread . . . Mr Bowley . . . Mrs Hilbery . . . Lady Mary Maddox . . . Mr Quin . . .' intoned Wilkins. She had six or seven words with each, and they went on, they went into the rooms; into something now, not nothing, since Ralph Lyon had beat back the curtain.

And yet for her own part, it was too much of an effort. She was not enjoying it. It was too much like being – just anybody, standing there; anybody could do it; yet this anybody she did a little admire, couldn't help feeling that she had, anyhow, made this happen, that it marked a stage, this post that she felt herself to have become, for oddly enough she had quite forgotten what she looked like, but felt herself a stake driven in at the top of her stairs. Every time she gave a party she had this feeling of being something not herself, and that every one was unreal in one way; much more real in another. It was, she thought, partly their clothes, partly being taken out of their ordinary ways, partly the background; it was possible to say things you couldn't say anyhow else, things that needed an effort; possible to go much deeper. But not for her; not yet anyhow.

'How delightful to see you!' she said. Dear old Sir Harry! He would know every one.

And what was so odd about it was the sense one had as they came up the stairs one after another, Mrs Mount and Celia, Herbert Ainsty, Mrs Dakers – oh, and Lady Bruton!

'How awfully good of you to come!' she said, and she meant it – it was odd how standing there one felt them going on, going on, some quite old, some . . .

What name? Lady Rosseter? But who on earth was Lady Rosseter?

'Clarissa!' That voice! It was Sally Seton! Sally Seton! after all these years! She loomed through a mist. For she hadn't looked like *that*, Sally Seton, when Clarissa grasped the hot-water can. To think of her under this roof, under this roof! Not like that!

All on top of each other, embarrassed, laughing, words tumbled out – passing through London; heard from Clara Haydon; what a chance of seeing you! So I thrust myself in – without an invitation . . .

One might put down the hot-water can quite composedly. The lustre had left her. Yet it was extraordinary to see her again, older, happier, less lovely. They kissed each other, first this cheek, then that, by the drawing-room door, and Clarissa turned, with Sally's hand in hers, and saw her rooms full, heard the roar of voices, saw the candlesticks, the blowing curtains, and the roses which Richard had given her.

'I have five enormous boys,' said Sally.

She had the simplest egotism, the most open desire to be thought first always, and Clarissa loved her for being still like that. 'I can't believe it!' she cried, kindling all over with pleasure at the thought of the past.

But alas, Wilkins; Wilkins wanted her; Wilkins was emitting in a voice of commanding authority, as if the whole company must be admonished and the hostess reclaimed from frivolity, one name:

'The Prime Minister,' said Peter Walsh.

The Prime Minister? Was it really? Ellie Henderson marvelled. What a thing to tell Edith!

One couldn't laugh at him. He looked so ordinary. You might have stood him behind a counter and bought biscuits – poor chap, all rigged up in gold lace. And to be fair, as he went his rounds, first with Clarissa, then with Richard escorting him, he did it very well. He tried to look somebody. It was amusing to watch. Nobody looked at him. They just went on talking, yet it was perfectly plain that they all knew, felt to the marrow of their bones, this majesty passing; this symbol of what they all stood for, English society. Old Lady Bruton, and she looked very fine too, very stalwart in her lace, swam up, and they withdrew into a little room which at once became spied upon, guarded, and a sort of stir and rustle rippled through every one openly: the Prime Minister!

Lord, lord, the snobbery of the English! thought Peter Walsh, standing in the corner. How they loved dressing up in gold lace and doing homage! There! That must be – by Jove it was – Hugh Whitbread, snuffing round the precincts of the great, grown rather fatter, rather whiter, the admirable Hugh!

He looked always as if he were on duty, thought Peter, a privileged but secretive being, hoarding secrets which he would die to defend, though it was only some little piece of tittle-tattle dropped by a court footman which would be in all the papers to-morrow. Such were his rattles, his baubles, in playing with which he had grown white, come to the verge of old age, enjoying the respect and affection of all who had the privilege of knowing this type of the English public school man. Inevitably one made up things like that about Hugh; that was his style; the style of those admirable letters which Peter had read thousands of miles across the sea in the *Times*, and had thanked God he was out of that pernicious hubble-bubble if it were only to hear baboons chatter and coolies beat their wives. An olive-skinned youth from one of the Universities stood obsequiously by. Him he would patronise, initiate, teach how to get on. For he liked nothing better than doing kindnesses, making the hearts of old ladies palpitate with the joy of being thought of in their age, their affliction, thinking themselves quite forgotten, yet here was dear Hugh driving up and spending an hour talking of the past, remembering trifles, praising the home-made cake, though Hugh might eat cake with a Duchess any day of his life, and, to look at him, probably did spend a good deal of time in that agreeable occupation. The All-judging, the All-merciful, might excuse. Peter Walsh had no mercy. Villains there must be, and, God knows, the rascals who get hanged for battering the brains of a girl out in a train do less harm on the whole than Hugh Whitbread and his kindness! Look at him now, on tiptoe, dancing forward, bowing and scraping, as the Prime Minister and Lady Bruton emerged, intimating for all the world to see that he was privileged to say something, something private, to Lady Bruton as she passed. She stopped. She wagged her fine old head. She was thanking him presumably for some piece of servility. She had her toadies, minor officials in Government offices who ran about putting through little jobs on her behalf, in return for which she gave them luncheon. But she derived from the eighteenth century. She was all right.

And now Clarissa escorted her Prime Minister down the room, prancing, sparkling, with the stateliness of her grey hair. She wore ear-rings, and a silver-green mermaid's dress. Lolloping on the waves and braiding her tresses she seemed, having that gift still; to be; to exist; to sum it all up in the moment as she passed; turned, caught her scarf in some other woman's dress, unhitched it, laughed, all with the most perfect ease and air of a creature floating in its element. But age had brushed her; even as a mermaid might behold in her glass the setting sun on some very clear evening over the waves. There was a breath of tenderness; her severity, her prudery, her woodenness were all warmed through now, and she had about her as she said goodbye to the thick gold-laced man who was doing his best, and good luck to him, to look important, an inexpressible dignity; an exquisite cordiality; as if she wished the whole world well, and must now, being on the very verge and rim of things, take her leave. So she made him think. (But he was not in love.)

Indeed, Clarissa felt, the Prime Minister had been good to come. And, walking down the room with him, with Sally there and Peter there and Richard very pleased, with all those people rather inclined, perhaps, to envy, she had felt that intoxication of the moment, that dilatation of the nerves of the heart itself till it seemed to quiver, steeped, upright; – yes, but after all it was what other people felt, that; for, though she loved it and felt it tingle and sting, still these semblances, these triumphs (dear old Peter, for example, thinking her so brilliant), had a hollowness; at arm's length they were, not in the heart; and it might be that she was growing old, but they satisfied her no longer as they used; and suddenly, as she saw the Prime Minister go down the stairs, the gilt rim of the Sir Joshua picture of the little girl with a muff brought back Kilman with a rush; Kilman her enemy. That was satisfying; that was real. Ah, how she hated her – hot, hypocritical, corrupt; with all that power; Elizabeth's seducer; the woman who had crept in to steal and defile (Richard would say, What nonsense!). She hated her: she loved her. It was enemies one wanted, not friends – not Mrs Durrant and Clara, Sir William and Lady Bradshaw, Miss Truelock and Eleanor Gibson (whom she saw coming upstairs). They must find her if they wanted her. She was for the party!

JHUMPA LAHIRI

P'S PARTIES

(2023)

THE ATMOSPHERE AT P's party was warm but impersonal, owing to the number of people invited, who knew one another either too well or not at all. You'd encounter two distinct groups, like two opposing currents that crisscross in the ocean, forming a perfectly symmetrical shape, only to cancel each other out a moment later. On one side, there were those like me and my wife, old friends of P and her husband who came every year, and on the other, our counterparts: foreigners who'd show up for a few years, or sometimes just once.

They came from different countries, for work or for love, for a change of scenery, or for some other mysterious reason. They were a nomadic population that piqued my interest – prototypes, perhaps, for one of my future stories, the kind of people I'd have the chance to meet and casually observe only at P's house. In no time at all they'd manage to visit nearly all parts of our country, tackling the smaller towns on the weekends, skiing our mountains in February, and swimming in our crystalline seas in July. They'd pick up a decent smattering of our language, adapt to the food, forgive the daily chaos. Overnight, they'd become minor experts in the historical events we'd memorized as kids and had all but forgotten – which emperor succeeded which, what they accomplished. They had a strategic relationship with this city without ever fully being a part of it, knowing that sooner or later their trip would end and one day they'd be gone.

They were so different from the group I belonged to: those of us born and raised in Rome, who bemoaned the city's alarming decline but could never leave it behind. The type of people for whom just moving to a new neighborhood in their thirties – going to a new pharmacy, buying the newspaper from a different newsstand, finding a table at a different coffee bar – was the equivalent of departure, displacement, complete rupture.

P was an old friend of my wife's. They'd known each other for many years before we started dating, having grown up on the same block lined with grand palazzi. As kids they played together until dark; they went to the same elementary school and then the same challenging high school; they wandered off to buy contraband cigarettes from a shady guy behind a piazza that was quiet in those days. They went to the same university and, after graduating, rented a fifth-floor apartment in the thick of the city center. In the summers they travelled together to other countries – experiences they still loved to talk about. Then matters of the heart intervened: my wife met me at a New Year's Eve party, while P married a staid but friendly lawyer, a man of average height, good-looking but slightly cross-eyed, and became a mother of four – three boys in quick succession, and then, like a simple but welcome dessert after a three-course meal, a girl.

Not long before the girl was born, P had a brush with death. A renowned doctor, always among those invited to the party, ended up saving her life with a tricky surgery. From then on, this yearly gathering became a constant: this sunny afternoon around her birthday, this merry, lavish lunch that brought together a wide range of people. P liked to fill the house and churn her friends together – relatives, neighbors, parents of her children's classmates. She liked to throw open the door at least fifty times, offering something to eat, playing host, exchanging a few words with everyone.

It was thanks to my wife, then, that I went to that house once a year, a somewhat secluded house on the city's outskirts. To get there, you took a curved, picturesque road, lined with cypresses and tumbling ivy. A road that swept you away, an urban road that ferried you toward the sea and put the frenzied city far behind. At a certain point there was a sharp right turn; you had to keep an eye out, it was easy to miss. After that it became a sort of residential labyrinth, with narrow, shaded, unpaved streets. You couldn't see the houses, just tall gates and the house numbers etched in stone.

P's house, where she lived with her children, her husband, and their two dogs, was at one end of this labyrinth. A spacious home, recently constructed, airy, with large, open rooms and plenty of space for a hundred-plus people to move about. At first glance – the house sat on a vast lawn, with no other structure in sight – it resembled a big, white, square-shaped rock jutting out of a green sea. In the distance you could glimpse the faint outline of the city where my wife and I and nearly all the other guests lived. It had a certain effect on me, coming to that house from our pleasant but compact apartment, where every book, every spoon, every shirt had its proper place, where I knew every shelf and hinge, and seating ten at the dinner table was a squeeze. An apartment whose windows looked out only onto other apartments, other windows, other lives like ours.

My memories of the past five or so parties had blurred together. Each year was different, and each year, for the most part, was the same. I made the same small talk I'd forget a minute later, I practiced my two rusty but still passable foreign languages, which I'd always brush up on a bit. I indulged, perhaps a little too much, in the same delicacies arrayed on the buffet table, circling back for more, with no regard for the extra kilos I'd put on and fret over after all those holiday meals. I said hello to friends and kissed the cheeks of women in their forties and fifties who staunchly refused to turn into signore. I absorbed the scent of their expensive perfumes, made brief contact with the warm skin of their shoulders, admired the elegant, form-fitting dresses they could still get away with at their age, at our age. At P's parties I felt embraced, cared for, and at the same time blissfully ignored, free. We were detached from our flawed, finely tuned lives, from our frustrations. I could sense time lengthening and the suspension, at least for a few hours, of all responsibility.

I wouldn't have been able to distinguish one party from the next, the incidents, the particulars, until one year when something out of the ordinary occurred, an ultimately banal disruption that remains a caesura in my life.

That year, I remember everything very precisely. I remember, for example, that there was more traffic than usual, which meant that we got there an hour late. It didn't matter; at P's it was always buffet style. I remember that my wife was telling me a story, talking ceaselessly as I drove, and that I was tuning her out. In fact, her slightly hoarse voice and her tendency to be long-winded were getting on my nerves. She managed an art gallery. I'd have preferred to drive that scenic stretch of road in silence, but she went on about clients and promising young painters. Before getting out of the car, she changed her shoes, trading her comfortable flats for a fancier pair with heels, partly to gain an extra inch or two and become just a touch taller than me.

Because P always invited all her children's friends, the first thing we saw, walking up to the house, was a swarm of younger and older kids playing out in the yard, in the sun. Their coats were strewn on the grass, like towels left on the beach while everyone goes for a swim. The grade schoolers and teen-agers ran around in good spirits, sweating, and P's pair of dogs were barking and chasing after them.

I thought of our own boy with a pang of nostalgia, the one child my wife and I had brought into this world. Just the other day he'd have come with us, and he, too, would have played in the yard without his coat. But now he was a grown man, a college graduate, a few months into his new life abroad, pursuing further studies at a foreign university.

My wife didn't mourn his absence – if anything, she was eager for him to become more and more independent. According to her, the fact that he was getting by on his own for the most part, and now had a woman in his life, and was far from us, was a much deserved and happy ending to our long and exhausting road as parents. It meant that we'd done a good job, and this was a milestone worth celebrating. I found her lack of worry astonishing: she who'd hovered over our son his whole life, who'd taken such exacting care of his every meal, every soccer game, every test, every report card. But then I realized that she was always looking ahead, very rarely behind, which was why she now had her sights on his career, his love life, his future children – in short, his complete separation from us. While, for me, not seeing him every day, not hearing his voice around the house, or even his mediocre violin playing, not knowing what he was up to, not adding his favorite juice to the grocery cart – it all came as a blow. I was proud of him, yes, I was excited about his prospects, but I still had a hole in my heart.

We rang the bell even though the door was ajar. We kissed cheeks with P and her husband, who were there to greet us at the entrance as always. P was in fine form, radiant, wearing a printed dress from the seventies that had belonged to her mother, with a leather belt to accentuate her waist.

We'd come bearing a few gifts: a scented candle, body cream, a new novel that everyone was talking about. After we chatted a minute, the doorbell rang again, and we were ushered down the hall. We took off our coats and threw them on the couch, atop an already precarious, promiscuous mound of fabric. It was warm in the house, but my wife, who is sensitive to cold and was wearing a sleeveless dress, decided to keep her pearl-gray wool shawl around her shoulders.

We found our way to the bar and picked up two glasses of prosecco. We made a toast, locking eyes for a moment. Then, with no hard feelings, for the rest of the afternoon my wife and I moved through the party in separate circles, paying each other no mind.

I began wandering about the house as if it were a favorite haunt, a place I knew fairly well but always partially, encountering one friend after another. It was only in this house, at this party, that we – mired in our responsibilities, in the personal and professional obligations that devour us, that define us – found the calm and the time to catch up. We ate, shared our news, chatted aimlessly.

All the while I was paying close attention to that other group: my potential fictional characters, the foreigners with whom I'd exchange just a few words, or more glances than words, really. I was intrigued by their point of view. They fascinated me precisely because, even though we were crammed into the same house, celebrating the same mutual friend, partaking in the same collective ritual, we remained two species, distinct and unmistakable. Eventually they'd drift off into their relaxed and secluded conversations, and we into ours. They seemed proud of their decision to uproot their lives, to acquire, in middle age, new points of reference. They evoked a world beyond my horizons, the risky steps

I'd never taken: a world that had perhaps snatched my son away for good.

After making the rounds inside, I went out onto the patio. I stole a cigarette, one of the few I allow myself on occasion when unwinding away from home, and I joined the others watching the mix of younger and older kids still playing soccer, making a racket in the yard. The trees scattered around the lawn were turning gold in the light. At first, we were all men. Then P joined our conversation for a minute, to make sure we had everything we needed, something to drink, something to eat. She treated each of us like a lifelong friend, even though she hardly knew most of her guests.

'You've got a fantastic lawn. It would be nice to put a pool back here,' one of the men said to her.

'It's not worth it. Every summer we spend two months at the sea,' P replied.

'Oh, where?'

'A tiny island, rather remote, still quite primitive. You have to take a boat to buy groceries.'

'You don't mind?'

'Not at all. It's the inconvenience I crave. I've been going there since I was a little girl.'

'How wonderful.'

'In August the entire island smells of rosemary. There's a small lighthouse, a pool in the middle, the sea all around, and that's about it,' P said.

I'd never been to that island, but I'd heard about it from my wife, who used to go there for a week or so every summer as a guest of P's family. Then one year – my wife told me – a man, a great swimmer who did twenty laps in the pool twice a day, died right there in the water, while racing a friend, struck by a heart attack in front of all those young kids and the teen-agers, including his own children. My wife, traumatized by the scene, never wanted to go back. And even though we did travel with P and her family from time to time, spending a weekend together in the countryside, we'd never gone to visit them on that island.

'And I don't really like swimming in pools,' P added, as if she'd been listening to my thoughts.

'Why not?'

'There's no life in that water.'

We talked about other seas, other islands, the pleasures of boating versus going to the beach: the frivolous patter of people with money. But as we spoke we became aware that a strange calm had descended over the yard. The children weren't yelling anymore. Something had happened.

We went down to see. A group of kids, a dozen or so, stood frozen in the distance. In the middle of their circle, someone was lying on the ground.

As we inched closer, we saw a handsome young boy, twelve or so, his hair dishevelled, legs splayed – it didn't look good. Had he fainted? Or had something worse happened? We had no information. Then the doctor arrived, the one who'd saved P's life years before. A tall, lanky man with black hair grazing his shoulders, a dangling mustache, a steady, good-natured demeanor.

Next to the boy was a pale-faced woman. The mother, I assumed. I hadn't noticed her before – we hadn't crossed paths, despite having just spent at least an hour in the same crowded house, in the same rooms, circling the same table, eating the same food.

She was a foreigner, you could tell right away by her facial features. She was wearing a summery dress unsuited to the season; a heavy and complicated necklace adorned a triangle of bare skin. She wore very little makeup – with the exception of wine-colored nail polish – and had a kind of prematurely weathered beauty. Her dark hair was tied up in a bun at her nape. She must have been around ten years younger than my wife, with a sharper gaze and, I felt, a more turbulent inner life.

'What happened?' the doctor asked her.

'I have no idea. I was inside while he was playing. Then one of his friends came and told me he wasn't feeling well. By the time I got here he was trembling – he seemed shaken and disoriented.'

The woman spoke in a strange mix of her language and ours, but it was easy enough to follow.

'And then?'

'He said his head was spinning, and that he couldn't hear anything for a few seconds, that everything went silent.'

'Give us a little space, please,' the doctor said.

The crowd backed off. Only the boy and his mother remained, with the doctor and P. I took a few steps back myself, but then I froze, paralyzed by the thought that the same thing could just as easily happen to my son – why not? – playing soccer in the park on a Sunday, with no parent at his side.

No one spoke for a minute or two. The doctor examined the boy, lifted his feet, felt his forehead, his wrist. After a little while, the boy sat up on his own and had a sip of water.

'It's not too serious, signora,' the doctor explained.

'But why? He's always been an active boy, nothing like this has ever happened.'

'Your son suffered a mild shock. Perhaps he didn't eat enough lunch. Kids are always running around non-stop without thinking. This kind of thing can happen sometimes when we get overexcited. Did your son have breakfast this morning?'

'Yes.'

'Is he an anxious boy?'

I got the impression that she didn't understand the question. In any case, she didn't respond. Her son was back on his feet now, a little embarrassed, insisting he was fine. His speech was normal. He had braces. He'd accepted a sandwich from someone and was eating.

'Can I keep playing?' he asked the doctor. Unlike his mother, he spoke our language perfectly well, and even had a touch of our city's accent.

'Of course you can. Just take it easy.'

And that was that. The party went on. We went back inside, they brought out the cake, we sang 'Happy Birthday,' raised our glasses to P. Her kids gave her a stiff gold bracelet. Then there was a real surprise: her husband stood on a chair and sang a short, sweet love song out of tune, while P, overwhelmed, in tears, burst out laughing, then gave her husband a long kiss, eyes closed, in front of everyone.

The crowd inside the house began to thin, guests were starting to leave. I rejoined my wife, who told me that she, too, was ready to head home. We said our goodbyes to P and her husband, thanked them for the pleasant afternoon, and returned to our car, where we waited for the long line ahead of us to budge.

'It's late. Did you have fun?' my wife asked me.

'I had a pretty good time. How about you?'

'Did you drink?'

'Not much.'

She looked me up and down.

'Let me drive.'

I was tired, and handed her the keys without protest. We switched places. She adjusted the seat, the mirror. She put on her seat belt, the comfortable shoes she liked to drive in. She was just about to start the car when she realized that she'd left her shawl in the house.

'I don't feel like getting out. Will you go?'

'Any idea where it is?'

'Check on the patio – I think I draped it over the back of a chair.'

The house was empty, silent, filled with abandoned glasses and soiled, crumpled paper napkins. P and her family must have retired to one room or another. My wife was right, the shawl was there, hanging limp as a fresh sheet of pasta over the back of a patio chair, not far from where I'd listened to P rave about her island, before the boy felt sick.

The boy's mother was standing in front of me – facing away, but I recognized her immediately, her hair in a bun, her taut neck. She was alone, staring at the yard, where a handful of kids, including her son, were still out playing. She was smoking a cigarette. When she turned to see who was there, she, too, seemed to recognize me right away. From the blanched look on her face, I could tell she was still distraught.

'What exactly does "a mild shock" even mean?' she asked me at once.

'A state of confusion, perhaps. A moment of psychosomatic distress.'

'I thought he was going to die. In the middle of a party, at this house filled with people I barely know.'

'Don't worry, it's over now, I heard what the doctor said.' I addressed her with the formal pronoun.

'I used to be such a centered person. I knew how to run my life. But these days, in this country, I can hardly manage a thing.'

'How did you end up here?'

'My husband is a journalist. He likes Rome. He says he loves this city more than he loves me.'

'And you, how do you like it?'

'I'm not happy and I'm not unhappy. Mind if we use the tu?'

'Of course.'

'Why did you stay with my son and me the whole time?'

'What do you mean?'

'On the grass. You didn't walk away with the others.'

'I was worried, like you. That's all.'

'Do you also have a son?'

'Yes. He lives abroad.'

'So you'll understand.'

'Understand what?'

'Today I brushed up against the worst thing that could possibly happen.'

For the next few days, I was left reeling from that abrupt exchange of words. Who was that woman? Why had she been so open with me, so unguarded, instantly bridging the solitary distance between two strangers? Why had she revealed to me, out of the blue, that she was in crisis? What was her name? When and how had she met P? Where was this husband she'd spoken of, who loved Rome more than he loved her?

One evening, after some hesitation, I asked my wife, 'Did you meet anyone interesting at P's this year?'

'Not really. Sometimes I have no patience for meeting new people.'

'There were so many foreigners, more every year.'

'They must be the parents of her kids' friends, who go to the same international school.'

'A good school?'

‘Expensive, and a little overrated if you ask me. I trust our school system.’

Then she told me about a friend of ours – he, too, a regular at P’s yearly party – who was thinking of quitting his job as the dean of a small suburban university to open a wine store in a foreign capital.

It would have been inappropriate to turn to P for any information. My wife was probably right, the woman who’d spoken to me was most likely the mother of one of P’s kids’ classmates. The more I thought about our conversation on the patio, the more I was struck by our strange synchronicity in that moment, as if she were expecting me, as if she knew, beforehand, that my wife would have forgotten her shawl, and that she’d send me back to the house to retrieve it. In the end, it was the only conversation of any real substance I’d had at the party. We’d looked each other in the eye, we’d been alone, our bodies close, but I’d never even introduced myself. I’d grabbed my wife’s shawl, mumbled something awkward, and then I’d slipped away.

Over time, the memory began to dim. I went on living with my wife, in the house where we’d raised our son. I made love to her still slender body, I invited the same friends over for dinner, cooked the same reliable recipes. While my wife went to the gallery or away on the occasional business trip, I worked at home, in the corner of our bedroom, making slow progress on my fifth novel, my articles, my tepid reviews. When she returned in the evenings, I’d pour us some wine and pretend to listen while she gave me the full rundown of her complicated days. On Saturdays, once a month, we’d go to hear classical music, then out to a restaurant, or else to the opening of a new art exhibit. I would go to the library, and we’d go on vacation: to the mountains every year, for her birthday, and to the sea, in the off-season, for mine.

At Christmas we travelled abroad to visit our son. He showed us his drab studio apartment, where he lived happily, and introduced us to his first girlfriend, an attractive young woman with parents from two different continents. He'd met her at the university. The two of them took us to a sprawling, noisy restaurant they loved. I noticed that my son, taller than I was now, was looking bulkier even though he'd become a vegetarian. He preferred beer over wine. The photo of a gawky boy which greeted me every time I picked up my cell phone, taken on a fishing boat the previous summer, looked nothing like him anymore.

Because of the girlfriend, we never spoke to each other in Italian. He gushed about the multiethnic neighborhood where they lived, where they'd go out every night of the week to eat food from seven different countries. His answers to my questions were polite but brief. We conversed in a language I struggled to keep up with, a sensation that I enjoyed at P's house but that here, with my own son, felt frustrating and artificial. For Easter, he told me, he planned to go hiking with his girlfriend among castles and sheep. In the course of a day or two I could sense his tacit rejection not only of Rome but of our way of life, of all the effort we'd put into raising him a certain way.

He was thriving in this new city – but, even so, I didn't like the thought of him in that drab apartment, at those loud restaurants, eating bizarre and expensive food, with his wisp of a girlfriend smiling beside him. I didn't like the thought of him in the crush of a subway car, or walking the streets alone and a little drunk at three in the morning, or going to the park on Sundays to play soccer with no breakfast in his stomach. I worried that he wasn't mature enough, that deep down he felt unhappy, that he'd end up in some kind of trouble. But that naïve and vulnerable boy was not my son: he was me. Or rather, he was the version of me I'd never allowed to form, that I'd neglected, blocked out – a version that, even without ever having existed, had defeated me. With this thought in my head, I strolled around my son's new city, patiently admiring bridges, gardens, and monuments, beneath a low and leaden sky.

On the plane, before taking off, watching my wife check her e-mail on her phone, I realized that it was just the two of us again, except this time with no desire to have a child, without that life project to tie us together, as it had until now. What was she reading? Who was writing to her? Hundreds of messages poured in every day from mysterious senders. A densely inhabited world, buzzing with activity, hers alone. But at a certain point she raised her head and reminded me of the date for P's next party.

Only once we were in the car, on the way to P's house, did I recall that distraught mother, that unexpected confession on the patio. It had been nearly a year since I'd thought of her. I'd left my curiosity back at P's, as if it were an umbrella, or the shawl my wife had asked me to retrieve: the kind of thing whose absence you feel for a little while and then easily let go of. But now that I was about to return to that house, again I sensed that she and I shared some secret link.

My foot was heavy on the gas, I was distracted. I missed the sharp right turn, took another road, had to put the car in reverse, as my wife's irritation grew. I was thinking: I should have chosen a different shirt, the one I'm wearing doesn't do much for me. The agitation I'd experienced after the abrupt exchange on the patio was back. I could picture it clearly now: the flattering but unseasonable dress, the complicated necklace, the color of her fingernail polish. As if the year gone by were nothing, nothing the passage of time. We hadn't even shaken hands, there was just that flash of understanding. So why was I feeling a little guilty?

An ancient, ridiculous memory came back to me then, from just before I met my wife. I was going to a gym with a pool at the time, and every week, by the pool's edge, the same girl would smile at me and say hello. She swam in the lane that I'd take over. For a few months my entire week revolved around that brief encounter by the pool, to the point where I'd even rush to the locker room to make sure I didn't miss her. We never talked about anything. She'd just say Have a good swim, or something like that. But every time she looked at me and spoke to me, it felt as if I were the center of her world. We ran into each other in this way for a few months, then she stopped showing up. A couple of months later I met my wife – but early on, in bed, I'd picture the swimmer's eyes, her smile. That's all.

Parking the car, I thought: Maybe the distraught woman won't even be here, maybe she wasn't invited this time around, or maybe she had another engagement. Her presence was hardly a given. But as soon as we entered, after P and her husband had welcomed us in, as my wife was already chatting without me in the adjoining room, I caught sight of her.

She was sitting in the dining room, beneath a window, in one of the chairs lined up against the wall so that guests could circulate. Next to her was her husband – a tall, handsome man with shiny white hair, a young-looking face, tan even in January. It had to be her husband because they were sharing a plate of food; that way, each could hold a glass of wine in the other hand. She wasn't talking to him. She was turned toward two other women seated to her right – but there was too much noise, I could barely even make out her voice.

She was utterly changed. She was laughing, telling a funny

anecdote about herself, while her husband listened and held the plate. He seemed like an attentive guy, amiable but a little bit tense. She was speaking with abandon, with irony. She didn't strike me at all as a woman in crisis.

She was dressed in black, like nearly all the other women at the party. No necklace, just that triangle of bare skin. She wore a pair of tight-fitting pants that matched the season, and hammered leather boots. Her hair, longer now, was streaked with gray, which she clearly didn't mind. She was thinner, even more beautiful – that weathered sort of beauty, which flattered her. Like my son, she had morphed over the past year into a sunnier, more confident version of herself. We lived in the same not particularly large city, and yet we'd never bumped into each other, not in a restaurant, not at a pharmacy, not on the street or at the gym. Our paths crossed only at this house, only at P's party.

'Hey, we're on the patio, it's nice out there,' an old friend said, running into me.

'Be there in a minute.'

I made a leisurely loop around the table, picking up some cheese, some crudités, some sliced salami. I was trying to make my presence felt. I couldn't hear her, all I could hear was my wife's gravelly voice, which worked its way under my skin even amid all those people.

When her husband stood to find a trash can where he could toss their plate, I looked at her, waiting for her to look back. Hoping for what, I don't know – a smile like the one the girl by the pool would give me? But she remained absorbed in her anecdote.

I continued staring, and she kept talking. Her husband was gone, my wife in the next room. The more I looked, the more she evaded me, unfazed. Until all of a sudden she lifted her gaze, for an instant, and revealed her eyes to me – filled

(I thought) with fury and exasperation, blinding eyes that were shining (I hoped) for me.

The idea appealed to me: a relationship punctuated with gaps; a fixed date, ours alone, in the middle of the party. It seemed like an acceptable form of infidelity, entirely forgivable, a bit like when I thought of the girl from the pool while I was already with my wife. In truth I wasn't looking for trouble. Just a few blazing hours spent together, checked by a year of separation.

I'd never betrayed my wife, in this city where everyone's always cheating on everyone. With the exception of my little crush on the girl from the pool, I'd always been a faithful man; I was used to being the one who got dumped or cheated on, even before I met my wife, and not the other way around. I didn't have infidelity in me, I suppose I lacked the impulse. I accepted my wife's activities, her obligations – the constant messages on her phone, her dinners without me, her work trips abroad, her quick jaunts to other cities – while also admitting the likely consequences: a quickly forgotten one-night stand with some guy, lunch and a stroll through the botanical garden with another. But since I wasn't jealous by nature, my conjectures never took hold of me. As with any couple, things left unsaid enter in to maintain your aging affection. Which was how we'd survived twenty-three years together with no major disruptions, no earthquakes.

I repeat, I'd have been fine dragging out that trifling dalliance. But just a few months later my wife informed me that P was having another party.

'So soon? What's that about?'

'She said she's been teaching her oldest son to dance, which got her thinking that she'd like to throw a different kind of party. At night this time. No kids.'

'Did we ever teach our son to dance?'

'Maybe?'

'Do you know who's coming?'

'The usual slew of people, I imagine.'

The weather was terrible that evening. I felt queasy the entire day. I couldn't eat, couldn't concentrate at my desk.

'It's been a long week, I can't shake this headache,' I said to my wife.

'And so . . .?'

'What do you say we stay in for the night?'

I already knew my suggestion was futile. She was taking her time getting ready, wearing a short dress she hadn't pulled out in years.

'Tonight we dance and let go. Time to perk up.'

In the dark, P's house seemed like a new destination – even more out of the way, more alien. The drive was stressful, the charming road slick with rain. And the spring air felt wrong to me. I couldn't get my bearings.

'Did you hear that their house was robbed recently?' my wife said as I was parking the car behind a long line of vehicles.

'Who?'

'P's family. They were gone for three days, all the jewelry was taken.'

'They didn't have it in a safe?'

'No, unfortunately, she's always been a bit disorganized.'

The house, too, was nearly dark, unfamiliar. They'd removed most of the furniture to make room. P's daughter greeted us at the door and whisked our coats off to who knows where. I stuck to my wife's side. We went to get our first glass of prosecco together, to fill our plastic plates with slices of bread, slivers of cheese, honey. We were attached at the hip as if we were a shy couple on an early date.

I saw all the known and unknown faces that were always

at P's. Apart from the new setup, the empty rooms, the scene was more or less identical, and yet I couldn't manage to wedge my way into conversations as I usually did; searching for that woman left me discombobulated. She was standing next to her husband, on the other side of the room. And this time she didn't avoid my gaze. She was looking straight at me through the crowd, registering my presence without smiling, without budging, without communicating anything.

After dinner, the dancing began. P's older son chose the music, a string of inane songs from our younger days. I danced with my wife, the woman with her husband. P's other kids danced between us, they danced with P and her husband. P danced with my wife, and then with me. She was a little drunk, barefoot, affectionate, shimmering, even without a bit of jewelry on. I really love you two, she said to me and my wife, as the three of us danced together.

The music felt liberating, at moments wrenching. It levitated us magically above the cramped and craggy present, it restored a glimmer of hope. We were, all of us, each on our own, replaying our previous lives: lives still in progress, foolish, makeshift, splendid lives. I glanced around at the women who refused to assume the role of signora, who'd kept up their looks. And yet we weren't getting any younger, we were accumulating wrinkles, health scares, disappointments. The songs took us back – to our first kiss, our first relationship, ancient emotions, our first heartbreak, minor grievances we'd buried, unresolved, but had never shaken off.

She and I danced, together, on our own. It was a torment, also a triumph. We would lock eyes for a moment, here and there I'd feel my body brushing hers, a shoulder, a hip. The two of us were still nailed to our respective lives, but underneath it all I sensed that we were being reckless, conspiratorial.

Outside it was still raining, but inside it was hot, oppressively hot. I was covered in sweat. I told my wife I could use a little water. I went to the bathroom, rinsed my face. Then I went to the kitchen to find a glass. There I noticed a complex surveillance system mounted on the wall, for monitoring the house's entry points. It had multiple tiny screens, each with a different view: the front gate, the yard, the patio. At night, in the heavy rain, every image looked to me like a kind of ominous ultrasound, ripe with meaning but completely indecipherable.

When I returned, I noticed that the lights were on. The barren room, only recently vacated, reminded me in some ways of my son's apartment. No one was dancing anymore, the music had stopped. In the old days we'd have merely taken a break, but we were already worn out.

My wife was over by the table. She was eating dessert. And she was talking to her. They didn't notice me. My wife said, 'I was just admiring your necklace while we were dancing, it's extraordinary. Can I ask where you bought it?'

'In a cute little shop, not far from where we live.'

'How long have you two lived in Rome?'

'Three years now.'

'Are you here for work?'

'My husband, yes. He'd like to live here forever.'

'What about you?'

She shrugged.' "Forever" is a big word.'

They went to grab their purses, they pulled out their phones. Right there on the spot they exchanged numbers, scheduled a date.

And this is where my story takes an unexpected turn. This stranger, with whom I'd had only one conversation, a fevered and fragmentary exchange, and with whom I'd felt an inexplicable bond from that moment on, despite never having learned her name, became my wife's friend. They met for lunch once a month, then went shopping for clothes and shoes together. She remained a secondary, casual friend for my wife. Not someone she'd invite over to the house, or fold into our everyday lives, but a person she'd spend time with on her own now and then, in her own way.

Through their friendship I learned a few things: her name – L – and the neighborhood where she lived (San Giovanni). One day she mentioned how often her husband had to travel, racing back and forth between cities. They had one son, the boy who'd felt sick in the yard. As my wife had intuited, he went to the same school as one of P's sons. L used to have a job herself, as a magazine editor, but here she spent her days diligently studying our language and belonged to a group of foreign women who relentlessly visited the city's infinite monuments, attractions, and ruins. Apart from these details, my wife never spoke of her new friendship.

I knew that it was normal, even healthy, to cultivate these kinds of friendships outside a marriage. It wasn't like there was anything sexual involved. And yet I agonized over it. My writing suffered, I began missing deadlines for my projects, I envied my wife.

I envied my wife and yet at the same time I was grateful. There was no way, when they went out together on their walks or to see an art exhibit, that L didn't think of me. No way my wife didn't speak of me, of our long marriage filled with the predictable ups and downs, of the flings she'd probably had with other men, of our strained relationship with our son. No way I didn't factor in to some extent. After more than twenty years of marriage, I knew what happened when women talked – all that archived information which loosens in the vapor of friendship, which floats to the surface while they're out buying shoes, eating salads, admiring paintings.

But what was I hoping for? An actual affair with L? A date, a few hours in a hotel, in bed together? I don't think so. Even after the dancing I never thought of her body, her hands. What I fixated on was our conversation on the patio, when she was distraught, sick with worry over her son, when she confided in me. That moment seemed more transgressive than any erotic act. What had we shared? An intimate exchange, inexplicably charged. And now, just as inexplicably, we shared my wife.

Soon enough the spring had gone by, an entire season. I remained passive, cagey, lying in wait for a new development: a dinner together, plans for a night at the theatre with L and her husband. But what I was really waiting for was winter, and P's next party, even if – and it was clear by now – those spirited occasions, those restorative afternoons I held so dear, were tainted.

But late that summer, once again, P suddenly changed the script. My wife and I were already back from vacation, had stashed away our bathing suits and beach towels and sandals. For my own part, I was looking forward to the firm and reassuring light of autumn, the plates of puntarelle at the trattorie, the starlings that dart in the sky, appearing and disappearing like tornadoes or ribbons or giant tadpoles made of ash, when P offered us a last-minute invitation to the island where she and her family spent two months each year. She had access to a spare bungalow with an ocean view – the usual tenants had cancelled – and she was certain that it would make an ideal spot for my writing, having heard from my wife that I'd been in a long slump.

'You know, I wouldn't mind going back there either, finally putting an end to my childhood fear,' my wife announced, referring to that poor man she'd seen die in the pool, decades earlier.

And given that it was a particularly stifling summer, and that my wife and I really had nothing to do but idle around the apartment, we packed our suitcases again, drove down to the harbor, and boarded a ferry. The island was a rock in the middle of nowhere, a bit like P's house.

For several days we did nothing but enjoy luxuriant, late-morning swims, light and refreshing lunches, and sunset strolls down to the lighthouse. The water was as clear as glass, filled with dark sea urchins. A beautiful path ran the length of the island, but in certain stretches you had to beware of clefts in the rock. Once, P told us, a woman had fallen to her death while taking a photo of her husband. We floated around the island on a rubber dinghy and ate baked fish on the terrace, with coils and citronella candles to repel the mosquitoes.

P and my wife took the boat every day, either before or after lunch, to pick up groceries. They wore flared linen dresses, and always came back with a little something extra: a clever bracelet made of cork, a perfume that smelled of salt, silicone kitchen utensils in various colors. They cooked together, reminiscing about the happy years when they'd shared an apartment, before they were married and had kids. P's husband came out on the weekend but left again for work. The kids played Ping-Pong all day or horsed around on the beach or tried out reckless dives at the pool or wandered off alone to some secret spot.

Our bungalow was very charming, picturesque, a bit dim inside but airy. It had belonged to one of P's uncles, he, too, a writer, and I discovered many old, well-loved books there, marked up in pencil. It was a cozy space, masculine in feeling, just one room, really, with no kitchen and one square window that looked out on the sea and opened like the door to a cupboard. The furniture had never been replaced – soft, faded armchairs, dark, glossy wood, a musty smell, all of it frozen in time.

As soon as I stepped inside I felt better; the space was invigorating, and had an effect on me similar to that of P's house, except here there was no party. This was a refuge where I could hole up and concentrate. Which got me thinking, a bit peeved: It would have been truly ideal to have had a place like this at our disposal, a place to write, if only my wife hadn't been avoiding this island, if only she'd brought me here before. Our son would have liked it, too, in the past, but now there was no room here for him and his girlfriend, there were just two couches, one across from the other, that became beds – two separate singles, one for me and one for my wife.

As soon as we were settled in, I hit a stride with my writing, hunched over a tiny desk against a wall, or else lying back on one of the sofa beds. I skipped lunch with P and my wife, instead grabbing a sandwich at the snack bar around three, my mind humming. I was pleased with this second summer of ours, with the inspiration I found on that island, in that cozy and comfortable bungalow.

The mistral arrived, as expected: three days of non-stop wind, of deafening gusts. On the storm's first day I started a new short story about L, set at P's house. In my invented version things took a more predictable course: she and I had a real affair. Staring out at the white shelf of sea lashing the shore, I thought back to our conversation on the patio – in the fake version we kissed immediately – looking for ways to stretch the details. I inserted the scene where we danced together, and also on our own – it felt like a critical juncture in the plot – and I left out L's friendship with my wife, which proved an unwieldy development. I molded and massaged the facts until it felt like a vaguely appealing story, the kind a literary magazine might take. All I needed was the ending, the grand finale.

One morning I decided to go for a swim, to clear out my head before sitting down to write. The mistral had just moved on, and the water was once again a sheet of glass. I climbed in from a small sheltered cove, first checking for jellyfish. My destination was a red buoy, which I swam toward through a beautiful patch of green sea, following a school of minnows. I was out in the middle of that patch when I saw a motorboat heading straight at me. I stopped and waved an arm, but the boat kept coming. I didn't shout, it would have been pointless. Out that far, all sounds are swallowed by the sea's silence. Feeling slow, weak, frightened, I somehow managed to move out of the way, and I made it to shore.

I walked back to the house, stricken, pale, still unnerved. But my wife wasn't there, and P's place was empty, too. On the little desk was a note: Out getting groceries, catch up with you later. My head was spinning. I felt like I needed a fresh glass of orange juice. At the snack bar I ran into one of P's boys, the thirteen-year-old.

'How's it going, all good?' he asked.

'A boat nearly ran me over.'

'Were you swimming alone?'

'I was.'

'Best to stay close to shore.'

'What about you guys? You having fun?'

'It gets a bit boring. I'd like to go somewhere else next year, but my mom always wants to come here.'

'Hang in there.'

'At least my friend's coming tonight.'

'Oh, who's that?'

'This foreign kid I go to school with. He's on a boat trip

with his parents, his dad's a really good navigator. They're stopping at the island and staying for dinner.'

At sunset we walked down to the harbor to greet them. It was a beautiful motorboat. They were dropping the fenders. Her husband was at the helm, her son hanging their wet things on a drying rack, L clambering around the boat. She was moving swiftly, asking her husband what to do before they docked. She was wearing a special pair of gloves for handling the anchor chain. I admired how deftly she tied and untied the mooring line. I noticed the ease and economy of communication between husband and wife.

With the task complete and the motor spent, they said their hellos. L had picked up a tan, her husband, too. Their son had outgrown both his parents. I glimpsed L's dark, muscular legs, a scar on her thigh. She was barefoot, sweaty, her hair a windblown mess. She quickly slipped into a sheer beach coverup, a pair of elegant but well-worn sandals.

I wanted to break up the scene right then and sneak down into the cabin, on that boat, with her. As if driven by the mistral, like the waves beating steadily in one direction, an impulse intensified by my own imagined version of our affair, I now yearned to kiss her mouth, to taste her salty skin, to solidify our connection at last without having to share it with anyone else. Instead, when she stepped off the boat, we greeted each other with a handshake, and all she said to me was 'Ciao.'

We took our seats out on P's terrace. There were five of us – P's husband would be back the next day, and L's son had rushed off to meet his friend in the small piazza. We spoke in Italian. By now, after all their meticulous studying, L and her husband could speak it more or less fluently. The windstorm had swept away the mosquitoes. The air felt crisp, refreshing. I was sitting next to L, at the head of the table, with P and my wife on one side and L and her husband across from them.

We drank heavily that night, though L a bit less than we did, since she was suffering from land sickness. Her husband weighed in on the recent elections, and told of their boating adventures, describing their favorite islands and inlets. At sea, he said, you live with less but have it all.

We ate a rice salad, followed by some fish and a few slices of melon. L passed me the fruit, the bottle of mirto. And while we ate and talked, while we looked at the stars and listened to the waves, while my eyes strayed now and then to that same triangle of bare skin, that extraordinary divot of flesh outlined by her collarbone and shoulders, I learned something new. In a month they'd be returning to their country; their time in Italy had come to an end. The reasons they gave were practical: her husband was tired of the constant travel, their son was about to start his first year of high school, and L, it turned out, was missing the working life that she'd sacrificed to be here. They were sad to go, already speaking with nostalgia about certain things, but you could see that the decision to reactivate their old life had restored the family balance, and that the cliff's edge they were once teetering on was no longer a threat.

'Maybe we'll come back around New Year's. It would be nice to get a little winter sun, have some panettone and pandoro, eat lunch outdoors in January.'

'Perfect. That means you'll be here for my party,' P said.

We accompanied them back to the harbor, said our goodbyes on the dock. 'Ciao,' L said to me again – nothing else – and in that moment of confusion I kissed her, at first on the cheek, but then my mouth drifted down toward the salty skin of her collarbone, planting itself in that sunken triangle. I latched on to her for a few seconds, then I lifted my head, mortified, and muttered, 'Forgive me.'

She immediately stepped back. And she may have glared at me then as she had once before, her eyes filled with fury and exasperation, but it was too dark to tell.

After she hugged and thanked everyone else, after she said her goodbyes to my wife and P, she left with her family to spend the night on their boat, by a secluded grotto, in a tiny cabin beside her husband. My wife, meanwhile, who'd glimpsed that errant kiss, started haranguing me as soon as we entered the bungalow and kept at it until dawn.

'Is there something going on with you two?'

'Nothing, I barely know her.'

'You imbecile, she was my friend.'

'And she still is.'

'I doubt it. The whole reason I came out here was to lay down an old burden, and now, thanks to you, I've picked up another.'

'I'm sorry.'

My wife refused to calm down. She went on attacking me, then burst into tears, transforming my creative sanctuary into a hell.

The next day, earlier than planned, we, too, left the island, in a rush. There was no need to explain our departure to P, given that I'd kissed L in front of her and her children, too. The whole lot of them were witnesses – and, worse, even with the whistling wind and the crashing waves, they'd probably heard us fighting until dawn. For days, back in the city, I cursed my own stupidity, steeped in embarrassment, but my wife never brought it up again, and soon the unpleasant feeling faded.

We fell back into our old routines, though for months I was adrift. I abandoned the short story – with those pages,

I realized, I'd been luring myself onto a precipice. What had happened between L and me made for a dull premise, it never would have worked. Yet for a moment, on that island, my embellished version of events had fused with reality: it had driven me to wound and demean my wife, in a way that she, with her discreet behavior, had never done to me in our long years of marriage.

I'd already decided, before Christmas, that I wouldn't be going to P's party that winter. On the off chance that L and her family were in town, I had my excuse prepared. But then, just before Christmas, P got sick again. Her decline was rapid, until the same good doctor who'd saved her life said there was nothing left to do.

Soon thereafter, I found myself at the funeral, and afterward at the house where we'd celebrated P so many times. Yet again on a bright and balmy winter day. A Saturday afternoon, a few weeks before her birthday, with all the guests from her previous parties, all of her closest friends.

My wife was devastated, she'd practically lost a sister. We clasped hands before entering the house. All the women, wearing black, were stone-faced. P's children, who'd been so drunk with joy on the island, who'd had so much fun that summer, were standing still in a row, in one of the rooms. The littlest one started weeping when my wife went to hug her.

'It was important to her, the party,' her husband said to me. 'She looked forward to it every year.'

'Me, too,' I replied.

We spoke about P. About how she was a singular person, a singular woman, radiant, the only one with the strength to bring us all together. To open the door a thousand times, to fill the house and churn the crowd.

Aside from the absence of P and her hospitality, things

were essentially the same. The funeral, too, was a kind of party. The kids, after a while, went out to play in the yard. Food covered the big oval table in the room with many windows, all the chairs lined up against the walls so that guests could circulate.

We ate, we conversed. But in the wake of a death even your own breath, your own shadow come as a shock. Everything feels inappropriate, indecent, for a while.

This would be the last time we ever set foot in that house. It was already up for sale. P's husband, her children, couldn't bear to live in it anymore.

L wasn't there. Which didn't surprise me. As a peripheral figure, an occasional guest, she wasn't invited to the funeral. I saw only a few members of her group, the people who spoke other languages, who passed in and out of our lives. Just like P, whatever had happened between us – that stalemate, that non-starter, brought to an end by my foolish gesture – was no longer.

I can't complain. Unlike me, P, to whom I owe these pages, didn't make it out of the story. She'll never visit her children in other countries, or cry about distances or the passing of days, that merciless, automatic plot device which propels us forward and brings us to our knees. Her parties, however, have stayed with me, and the thought of them still quickens the heart: the secluded house packed with people, the sunlit lawn, those hours of sublime detachment. A setting I cherished, a promising start I tried to finish, to put into words, in which I'd been, briefly, a wayward husband, an inspired author, a happy man.

ACKNOWLEDGMENTS

DON DELILLO: 'The Black and White Ball' from *Underworld* by Don DeLillo. Copyright © 1997 by Don DeLillo. Reprinted with the permission of Scribner, an imprint of Simon & Schuster LLC. All rights reserved.

TESSA HADLEY: 'Vincent's Party', first published in *The New Yorker*, 23rd June 2024. Copyright © Tessa Hadley, 2024. Reprinted with permission from United Agents.

ERNEST HEMINGWAY: 'The Festival of San Fermin' from *Fiesta* by Ernest Hemingway, published by Arrow. Copyright © Hemingway Foreign Rights Trust, 1927. Renewal of copyright Ernest Hemingway, 1954. Reprinted by permission of The Random House Group Limited.

ALAN HOLLINGHURST: 'Toby Fedden's 21st' excerpted from *The Line of Beauty*, © Alan Hollinghurst 2005, Bloomsbury Publishing, Inc. Reprinted with permission. Picador UK.

JHUMPA LAHIRI: 'P's Parties', first published in *The New Yorker*, 3rd July 2023. Copyright © 2023 by Jhumpa Lahiri. Reproduced by permission of WME Entertainment, LLC.

GUY DE MAUPASSANT: 'The Necklace', translated by Marjorie Laurie, from *Selected Stories*, Everyman's Library, 1934, 2021. Translation reprinted with the permission of the Estate of Marjorie Laurie.

DAPHNE DU MAURIER: 'The Manderley Fancy Dress Ball' from *Rebecca*. Reproduced with permission of Curtis Brown

Ltd, London, on behalf of The Chichester Partnership. Copyright © 1938 The Chichester Partnership.

VLADIMIR NABOKOV: 'Pnin Gives a Party' by Vladimir Nabokov. Copyright © 1955, Vladimir Nabokov, used by permission of The Wylie Agency (UK) Limited. 'Pnin Gives a Party', first published in *The New Yorker*, 4th November 1955. The Wylie Agency. Alfred A. Knopf, a division of Penguin Random House LLC.

EDNA O'BRIEN: 'Come into the Drawing Room, Doris' from *The Love Object* by Edna O'Brien reprinted by permission of Peters Fraser & Dunlop (www.petersfraserdunlop.com) on behalf of the Estate of Edna O'Brien.

DOROTHY PARKER: 'Arrangement in Black and White', copyright 1927, renewed © 1955 by Dorothy Parker; from *The Portable Dorothy Parker* by Dorothy Parker, edited by Marion Meade. Used by permission of Viking Books, an imprint of Penguin Publishing Group, a division of Penguin Random House LLC. All rights reserved.

DELMORE SCHWARTZ: 'New Year's Eve' by Delmore Schwartz, from *In Dreams Begin Responsibilities and Other Stories*, copyright © 1937 by New Directions Publishing Corp. Reprinted by permission of New Directions Publishing Corp. 'New Year's Eve' from *In Dreams Begin Responsibilities and Other Stories*, Profile Books. Reprinted with permission.

EVELYN WAUGH: 'Bella Fleace Gave a Party' from *The Complete Stories of Evelyn Waugh* by Evelyn Waugh. Copyright © 1998 by the Estate of Evelyn Waugh. Reprinted by permission of The Random House Group Limited. 'Bella Fleace Gave a Party' from *The Complete Stories of Evelyn Waugh* by Evelyn Waugh. Reprinted by permission of SLL/Sterling Lord Literistic, Inc. Copyright by Estate of Evelyn Waugh, 2000.

Titles in Everyman's Library Pocket Classics

African Stories
Selected by Ben Okri

Bedtime Stories
Selected by Diana Secker Tesdell

Berlin Stories
Selected by Philip Hensher

The Best Medicine: Stories of Healing
Selected by Theodore Dalrymple

Cat Stories
Selected by Diana Secker Tesdell

Christmas Stories
Selected by Diana Secker Tesdell

Detective Stories
Selected by Peter Washington

Dog Stories
Selected by Diana Secker Tesdell

Erotic Stories
Selected by Rowan Pelling

Fishing Stories
Selected by Henry Hughes

Florence Stories
Selected by Ella Carr

Garden Stories
Selected by Diana Secker Tesdell

Ghost Stories
Selected by Peter Washington

Golf Stories
Selected by Charles McGrath

Horse Stories
Selected by Diana Secker Tesdell

London Stories
Selected by Jerry White

Love Stories
Selected by Diana Secker Tesdell

Music Stories
Selected by Wesley Stace

New York Stories
Selected by Diana Secker Tesdell

Paris Stories
Selected by Shaun Whiteside

Party Stories
Selected by Ella Carr

Prague Stories
Selected by Richard Bassett

River Stories
Selected by Henry Hughes

Rome Stories
Selected by Jonathan Keates

Scottish Stories
Selected by Gerard Carruthers

Shaken and Stirred: Intoxicating Stories
Selected by Diana Secker Tesdell

Stories of Art and Artists
Selected by Diana Secker Tesdell

Stories of Books and Libraries
Selected by Jane Holloway

Stories of Fatherhood
Selected by Diana Secker Tesdell

Stories from the Kitchen
Selected by Diana Secker Tesdell

Stories of Motherhood
Selected by Diana Secker Tesdell

Stories of the Sea
Selected by Diana Secker Tesdell

Stories of Southern Italy
Selected by Ella Carr

Stories of Trees, Woods, and the Forest
Selected by Fiona Stafford

Venice Stories
Selected by Jonathan Keates

Wedding Stories
Selected by Diana Secker Tesdell

Saki: Stories
Selected by Diana Secker Tesdell

John Updike:
The Maples Stories
Olinger Stories